OR *THE SINNERS' GARDEN*

ᴗᴏᴍᴇ novels are about the head, some are about the heart. William Sirls' latest is decidedly the latter. A story of hope, humor, forgiveness, and deep restoration, it poignantly illustrates how all of us have the life-changing chance to enter *The Sinners' Garden*."

—JAMES L. RUBART, BEST-SELLING
AUTHOR OF *ROOMS* AND *SOUL'S GATE*

"Sirls writes a story of choice, change, and intrigue that is wrapped in supernatural fantasy, iPods, and a field of mysterious flowers. In *The Sinners' Garden*, he sets the narrative hook deep with multi-layered plots and heartwarming characterizations that reel readers in and refuse to let them go."

—GAIL WELBORN, *SEATTLE EXAMINER*

"Intriguing and inspirational . . . a story with exceptional details whose characters come to life and invite you along for the ride."

—KAY CAMPBELL, *HUNTSVILLE TIMES*

"Set in a fictionalized version of the Downriver suburbs of Detroit where I pastor, this engaging story presents a picture of God that is both personally and mysteriously involved in restoring lives that have been marred and scarred by mistakes of the past. Faith is the key that brings hope and healing . . . and this is portrayed beautifully in *The Sinners' Garden*."

—BRETT KAYS, LEAD MINISTER OF SOUTHPOINT
COMMUNITY CHRISTIAN CHURCH, TRENTON
AND ALLEN PARK, MICHIGAN

"William Sirls is a master at weaving God's transforming power into the lives of seemingly real people with real-life issues. His personal transformation makes his writing even more credible and faith strengthening."

—PASTOR PAT PITTSNOGLE, CHRIST EVANGELICAL
LUTHERAN CHURCH, MILTON, PENNSYLVANIA

"William Sirls has done it again! I was living inside the story, waiting on every word and turning each page with anticipation . . . and that was just the prologue! You will find yourself completely wrapped up in *The Sinners' Garden* . . . talking out loud, giving advice, and laughing with the characters. William gives you that rare chance to get lost in a story that you just can't wait to see how it ends. Grab this book now and thank me later!"

—CHRIS HARRELL, SPEAKER, AUTHOR, AND PASTOR
AT SOUTH HILLS CHURCH, CORONA, CALIFORNIA

"The problem I had with this book was that I couldn't put it down. I love fiction that touches both my soul and spirit, and once again, William Sirls did just that. *The Sinners' Garden* portrays heaven touching earth in a supernatural way that shows us how God uses everyday people . . . characters that seem so real that they become your friends, leaving you with a desire to see them in yet another book. "

—JOSEPH G. MILOSIC, ASSOCIATE PASTOR, MT. ZION CHURCH, CLARKSTON, MICHIGAN, AND AUTHOR OF *MY HOME THE FAMILY BUSINESS*

"Give yourself a gift and read *The Sinners' Garden*. I literally consumed it, every morsel of it. A great story that I couldn't put down. I found myself relating very easily to the characters. It is thought-provoking and encouraging with a hint of mystery for added flavor. Even in tragedy there was hope and comfort. It inspired me with renewed faith to change the things that I can and leave the rest to God. That is one peaceful place to be! And . . . I will never see a flower garden in quite the same way again."

—SUSAN M. TANT

"I am a fairly new Christian and consider William Sirls to be one of my favorite authors. *The Sinners' Garden* had me hooked at the prologue and I found it impossible to put down. Prepare yourself for all kinds of emotions while reading and keep the tissue box close by!"

—DONNA O'BRIEN

"As a resident of the web of small towns in Southeast Michigan known as Downriver, I appreciated the local references. Sirls played with landmarks in a fun way to create his small town setting that could easily be anywhere. Now, when I see kids like Andy riding their dirt bikes along fields and trails, grappling with their own demons, I will think of *The Sinners' Garden* . . . where Sirls opens the conversation about sin and redemption, but leaves it up to his readers to question and answer concepts for themselves. An excellent book club read."

—RHONDA RAFT

"*The Sinners' Garden* exposes the fact that God is alive and well and He's willing to go to great and unusual lengths to get people to listen to Him. This book reminds us that God has a plan, a purpose for each life, one that has healing and miracles and forgiveness. All He wants from us is to take that inexplicable thing called a 'leap of faith' and believe. As you will read, some people have to leap farther than others, but we can all be confident that when we land, we'll be surrounded by His goodness and grace."

—CINDY BENEDICT BARCLAY

THE
SINNERS' GARDEN

WILLIAM SIRLS

Northern Plains Public Library
Ault Colorado

THOMAS NELSON
Since 1798

NASHVILLE   DALLAS   MEXICO CITY   RIO DE JANEIRO

© 2013 by Canyon Insulation, Inc.

All rights reserved. No portion of this book may be reproduced, stored in a retrieval system, or transmitted in any form or by any means—electronic, mechanical, photocopy, recording, scanning, or other—except for brief quotations in critical reviews or articles, without the prior written permission of the publisher.

Published in Nashville, Tennessee, by Thomas Nelson. Thomas Nelson is a registered trademark of Thomas Nelson, Inc.

Thomas Nelson, Inc., titles may be purchased in bulk for educational, business, fund-raising, or sales promotional use. For information, please e-mail SpecialMarkets@ThomasNelson.com.

Scripture quotations are taken from the Holy Bible, New International Version®, NIV®. Copyright © 1973, 1978, 1984, 2011 by Biblica, Inc.™ Used by permission of Zondervan. All rights reserved worldwide. www.zondervan.com. *Holy Bible*, New Living Translation. © 1996, 2004, 2007 by Tyndale House Foundation. Used by permission of Tyndale House Publishers, Inc., Carol Stream, Illinois 60188. All rights reserved.

Publisher's Note: This novel is a work of fiction. Names, characters, places, and incidents are either products of the author's imagination or used fictitiously. All characters are fictional, and any similarity to people living or dead is purely coincidental.

Library of Congress Cataloging-in-Publication Data

Sirls, William, 1964-
 The sinners' garden / William Sirls.
   pages cm
 ISBN 978-1-4016-8738-0 (pbk.)
 1. Teenage boys--Fiction. 2. Uncles--Fiction. 3. Faith--Fiction. I. Title.
 PS3619.I753S56 2013
 813'.6--dc23
                         2013025301

Printed in the United States of America

13 14 15 16 17 18 RRD 6 5 4 3 2 1

for Kenneth

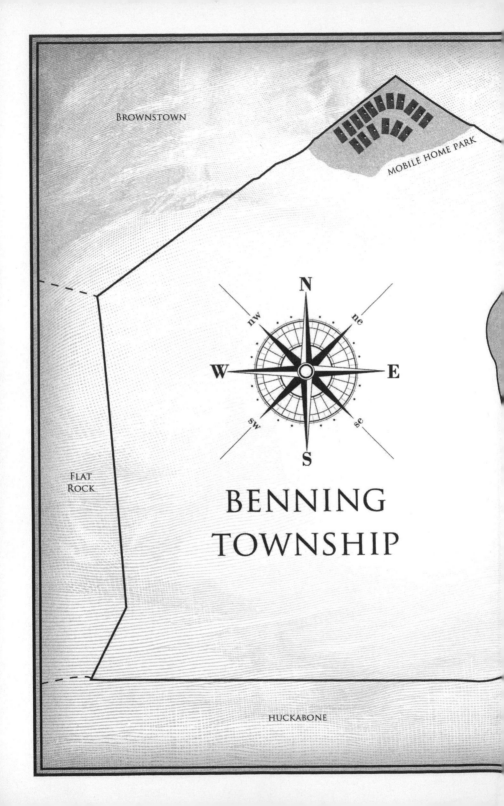

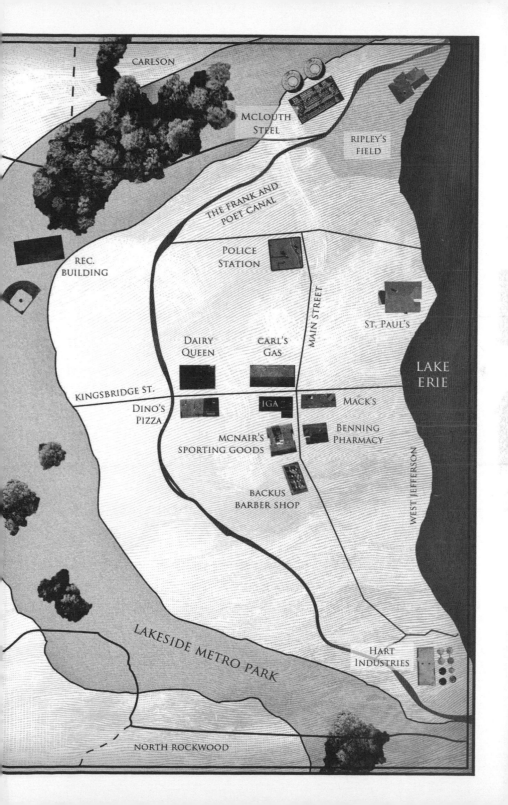

PROLOGUE

Judi walked to the kitchen window again and glanced out to the front yard, hoping to see Todd's headlights cutting through the darkness as he made his way up the winding gravel driveway toward their farmhouse. She swallowed a sip of cold coffee and shoved past a wave of disappointment, wondering why he was late *this* time. With a sigh, she opened the oven door, worried the food was getting dried out, three hours after she and Andy had eaten. The chicken and stuffing still looked okay, she decided, with some relief. And it definitely smelled good.

"Mumma?" a small voice called from the living room. It was Andy, her three-year-old son, who'd been sleeping on the living room couch for the better part of an hour. She knew she should've put him to bed long ago, but she kept hoping Todd would get home. That he'd want to tuck his son in this time.

"One second, baby," she said, walking over to the sink. She filled a pot halfway with water before taking it over to the stove. The *click-click-click* sound of the burner preceded a blue flame that quickly set to warming the bottom of the pot.

"Mumma?" Andy called again.

She walked across the kitchen and peeked into the living room. "What is it, Andy?"

He sat up, yawned, and rubbed his little blue eyes with his fists. He looked around the room, clearly half asleep and confused. "Where are you, Mumma?"

Judi laughed and came around the couch to kneel next to him. "I'm right here, silly."

He smiled in relief and held out his arms for a hug, which she gladly gave. Judi held him tight, feeling his little ribs while breathing in the smell of baby shampoo that still lingered in his thick brown hair.

"You gonna make the eggs, Mumma?" he asked. "So we can paint them?"

"I just put the water on," she said, running her hand across the side of his face. She had almost forgotten about boiling the eggs for Sunday's Easter egg hunt at church, which was only two days away. "They will be done tonight and then we will dye them tomorrow."

"Good," Andy said, smiling and clapping. His teeth looked like little white stones and the gap between his two front ones made her want to give him another hug, which she did.

"You go back to sleep and when you wake up you'll be upstairs in your big-boy bed."

"Okay," Andy said, his eyes widening. "Where did Uncle Rip go? Did he go home already?"

Judi laughed again. Rip sounded like "Whip." She walked over to the window and looked out past the garage toward the barn. Yellow light spilled out the barn door toward the lake and she could see her brother's broad shoulders as he leaned under the hood of the old Corvette he'd just bought. *Actually, it's not that old . . .* and though she suspected, Judi knew she didn't want to ask him where he got the money to buy it. Some things were best left alone.

"Uncle Rip is still here, baby," she said, shifting her eyes from the barn to Lake Erie. It looked like black glass, and a streak of moonlight shimmered toward her.

"Good night, Mumma," Andy said, lying back down. "I love you." There weren't three sweeter words in the world.

Judi made her way back to the couch, kissed Andy on the cheek, and then pressed her finger against his belly button, causing him to giggle. She kissed him again and then tucked the blanket tightly under his legs and feet. "I love you too, Andy."

He yawned and exhaled before giving her a smile that let her know he was counting on her. Counting on her to keep him safe.

She stood and looked back outside. Rip was now leaning against the barn door, smoking what she hoped was a regular cigarette. He pitched it to the ground, shuffled his foot over it, then walked back into the barn and closed the hood on the Corvette. He said he'd be gone by the time Todd got home. Judi wished he'd meant it. Did he suspect her secret? She shook her head. She'd been doing a good job hiding the bruises. He couldn't know. Could he? But then why was he hanging out, as if waiting?

If Todd was late, it was likely that he was in one of his moods. And if he was, the last person in the world Judi wanted around was her overprotective little brother—all six foot three of him. If Rip saw Todd in the act, she knew it wouldn't be good for Andy.

And it certainly wouldn't be good for Todd.

A narrow beam of light arced across the garage. Todd was home, and Judi quickly prayed that he would come far enough up the driveway to see Rip inside of the barn.

He didn't.

Please, Lord. Not tonight.

Judi glanced quickly back at the barn, causing her nightie to slide off her left shoulder. She pulled it back up and then went through the family room to meet Todd out on the front porch. He walked right by her, but at least he didn't have something nasty to say. Judi caught the odor of whiskey as he passed, but was thankful she couldn't smell some other girl's perfume. There'd been enough of that over the past year.

He went straight to the kitchen.

"Your supper is in the oven," she said, following him in. "Let me get it out for you."

He didn't say anything. He just walked to the cupboard where they used to store liquor, opened it, and then quickly closed it. Then he looked in the refrigerator and just stood with his back to her, slowly shaking his head. "No beer either?"

"I didn't get any, I thought that—"

"You just can't get anything right, can you?"

"I thought you weren't going to drink at home anymore."

"Looks like you thought wrong." He looked at her, hard and mean, and a shiver of fear ran down Judi's neck.

She wondered who he'd been out drinking with, but now wasn't the time to ask. Instead, she busied herself by going to the stove and turning off the boiling water. She put on an oven mitt with the word *Love* embroidered on it and then reached down and pulled open the oven door. She took out the hot plate, removed the aluminum foil, and when she turned around, he was standing right in front of her, startling her. She dropped the plate, and it crashed to the floor, breaking into three pieces while splashing the top of her bare foot with gravy.

Immediately, she bent to clean it up, but he took her by the shoulders, stopping her. He shrugged and let out a little laugh, then carefully put his hand on the side of her neck. Judi felt a whisper of

4

hope in his smile, in his surprisingly gentle touch. It reminded her of the old Todd. Her Todd.

His hand was soft and it felt good as he caressed her. She closed her eyes and smiled, slowly leaning her head into his hand. Her hope surged. Maybe they were finally going to have a *good* night, a night they could connect. A night they could remember all the things that were right between them. She put her hand on top of his, and Judi could feel his thumb slide across her chin to the other side of her neck. She lowered her hands to his waist. Todd's fingers moved slowly back and forth below her chin, and when she sighed, he stopped.

She glanced up at him and saw it in his eyes right away.

The look. Such a look of hate. Her heart seized painfully in her chest.

He squeezed, his fingers digging into her throat as he shoved her back, pinning her against the refrigerator.

"No," she choked out, clawing at his hand. The refrigerator felt cool through the paper-thin nightie, even as her body flushed with heat. "Andy . . . living room."

Todd abruptly let go, and Judi brought her hands to her throat, bending over and gasping. As soon as she could, she stumbled over to the opening that separated the living room from the kitchen and looked at Andy. *Thank God he's still asleep.* She couldn't bear it if he saw his father be mean to her. He wouldn't understand . . .

Judi turned around but kept her distance from her husband. He was standing by the stove, oddly still, his neck and shoulders stiff with frustration.

"There's more food in the fridge," she said nervously, rubbing her neck. "Let me clean the floor real quick and I'll make you another plate. It won't take long to heat up."

Todd turned around slowly, leaned back against the stove, and shook his head in what looked like pure disgust. "You'll probably screw that up too."

She stared at him. Maybe everything was her fault. Maybe she was responsible for what Todd had become. For what she had become. For what *they* had become.

"You're right," she said, anxious to say anything to appease him. "I'd probably mess up just putting food on a plate. But I can try. All I want is for you to give me another chance, Todd."

Todd crossed his arms. "Now you're getting smart with me?"

"I'm not getting smart with anyone."

Todd reached behind him and grabbed the handle on the pot of water.

"Oh, that's just for the Easter eggs," she said. "I was just going to—"

She belatedly saw his intent. She took a step backward into the living room, but Todd had already flung the scalding water at her. It arced in the air, catching the edge of her left leg and hip.

Judi shrieked, buckled over, and brought her hands to her hip, stunned at the pain, fighting to keep from blacking out. She stared at Todd in disbelief, and as he came in and out of focus, she thought she saw a rare look of remorse on his face.

But then she saw Rip coming through the door right behind him.

"I didn't know," Todd said. "I didn't know that Andy—"

Rip grabbed Todd by the back of his shirt collar and pulled his fist back to punch him. Judi turned away, pressing where it hurt most.

And discovered a little hand clinging to her thigh.

Andy.

In horror, she wrenched around and saw him then. He released his grip on her leg, and his little hands shook in front of his face. His beautiful blue eyes were wide and his mouth was open. The skin on the side of his face began to change. It was wet, red, and raw.

His whole body quivered, but he made no sound.

They must have awakened him and he'd come to her. He must have peeked out from behind her at the exact same time Todd threw the water.

When she picked him up, she forgot about her own pain.

That's when Andy's scream finally came.

It was unlike anything she'd ever heard.

ONE

ELEVEN YEARS LATER

Heather was parked on the far side of St. Paul's Church, half asleep, hoping a speeder wouldn't come by and trigger the radar gun. She'd been there for over an hour, resting her head against the bottom edge of the open driver's side window and staring dreamily at the full moon. Behind her, little puffs of wind came off of Lake Erie, gently blowing strands of brown hair across her cheek while cooling the sweat on the back of her neck.

She sat up and glanced at the clock on the dashboard. It was just past four in the morning, and her shift would be over in less than two hours. It had been another slow night, with only a few routine traffic stops, and one that was not so routine. She laughed out loud, thinking about it. She could still see the looks on the boys' faces—not one of them over seventeen—as she made them pour out the remaining nine beers on the side of the road. She had given the three a ride to their homes and then returned to drop a parking ticket under the driver's windshield wiper. It was part of the impromptu plea agreement that he'd graciously accepted. Such were the joys of being a small-town cop. Part peacekeeper. Part village mom.

Heather yawned and leaned forward to rest her chin on the steering wheel for another glance at that moon. Something seemed different about it tonight. It appeared to hover above the tree line that served as the southern border of Benning Township, a harbinger of a long, hot, sultry summer. Heather felt comforted by the peaceful glow it cast over the small town.

Her radio crackled to life, startling her. "Where are you, Heather?"

It was Natalie, from dispatch.

"Relaxing out near St. Paul's," Heather answered, gently tapping the radio against her cheek. "It's the only place in town that doesn't feel like a hundred degrees. Can you believe it's this hot in early June?"

A quick thread of static crackled over the radio and then Natalie's words came so clear it sounded like she was in the backseat.

"Get out to 1252 Old Parker Road, like ASAP!"

"Okay!" Heather said, fumbling to sit up straight and turn the key in the ignition. There were only five cops on the entire force and the department had never made a habit of using official radio jargon. "What's going on?"

"The woman who lives there called in to report an intruder. She and her kids are outside now."

"I'm on my way," Heather said, looking left and right.

"Heather." The tone in Natalie's voice had shifted from concerned to almost motherly.

"Yeah?"

"She says he may be armed. Be careful."

Heather felt a cool finger tap at the edge of her heart. She closed her eyes and tried to swallow. Her foot felt so heavy she couldn't let off the brake. Her mouth had gone dry and she glanced wildly out the window, finding it impossible not to think about her father.

Her eyes settled on the moon again. But it had changed.

Gone was the soothing glow, the promise of summer. Now it seemed more suited to black cats and trick-or-treaters than the beginning of summer in southeast Michigan. The glow now seemed more like a spooky yellow fog that outlined the tip of the church's steeple into something big enough to poke a hole in her tightly sealed box of bad memories.

She shook it off. *You have a job to do, woman. Do it!*

Heather slowly pulled onto West Jefferson Avenue, the two-lane highway that ran along the lake. She flipped on the roof lights, pressed on the accelerator, and when the speedometer passed a hundred, all she could hear was the wind and the continuous tapping of bugs dying on the cruiser's windshield.

With no other cars on the road, she made it out to Old Parker in less than five minutes and turned onto the heavily wooded road. The air now felt still and thick, even through her open window. She turned the roof lights off and tapped on the brakes, slowing the car down even more. The cruiser's tires chewed up gravel as she maneuvered around the potholes that littered Old Parker.

Natalie had given her the address, but only one house stood on this dead-end road.

As long as Heather could remember, the one-bedroom cottage had been a revolving door for welfare renters and a routine stop for domestic violence calls. Those visits had never bothered her, though. They normally just ended with someone spending the mandatory twenty hours in a cell to sleep something off before going back home for what would most likely be another round in the ring.

But this call was different. This was the type where a *really bad thing* could happen, because Natalie had used those four terrible words. Words she'd never heard before, in all her twelve years on the Benning Township police force.

He may be armed.

Heather thought about the new tenants and how she hadn't been to the house since they'd moved in. She had seen them a few times at church and heard they were the latest renters on Old Parker. The young mother kept her head bowed during most of the service, probably praying for a fresh start or enjoying the hour break from her three kids—the same munchkins who had quickly developed a reputation for tearing up the pre-K Sunday school room.

The woman was quiet and wore the same old beige dress every week. It needed a good cleaning and failed to cover the tattoos on her neck and arms that spoke of a past the woman herself seemed to want to forget. Once Heather gave her a smile as she walked into church, but the woman had instinctively covered her mouth to hide teeth rotting from years of drug use.

Most of the church knew the woman routinely collected whatever leftovers were on the punch table come Sunday noon. She waited for most of the congregation to leave before looking around the room to see who was watching. Then she'd stuff cookies, cheese, little sandwiches, or whatever else remained into oversized baggies and head home.

So who'd come after a woman like her? With nothing of note to steal? An ex-husband? An ex-accomplice?

Heather crouched forward, trying to spot the lone driveway that would soon be on her right. As she inched closer, the headlights slid off tree branches that hung over the road from both sides, giving her a tunneling effect that made her stomach turn.

She spotted the mailbox and put her foot on the brake. She paused and looked through the bug-smeared windshield, studying the road, waiting patiently to see if anything moved, then slowly pulled the car over to one side. She unsnapped her holster and ran her fingers across the top of the gun. Even touching it made her mouth dry.

She left the headlights on and stepped out of the car.

Despite the early hour, it was still ninety degrees, inviting what seemed like every insect in the world out for an early morning flight. All she could hear were crickets, and then a ship horn somewhere on the lake.

She took a few steps toward the mailbox and heard something. Whatever it was had run across some fallen branches and then stopped. She raised her pistol with both hands and took a few steps back. She waited and listened.

It moved again. It was closer this time, louder.

And then she saw them.

They looked like ghosts as they came out of the darkness into the tail end of the headlights' beams. They were coming right at her, directly down the center of the road. She lowered the gun. It was the woman from church, carrying a baby, and with her two other children clinging to her sides.

"Is anyone hurt?" Heather asked.

"No," the woman said, breathing hard. It was the first time Heather had heard her voice. It was a tiny voice, one that didn't belong to a rough crowd, but rather to a frightened little girl. It was also the first time Heather had seen the woman without makeup. Her cheeks were pockmarked and tear-soaked against the light, and Heather cringed, wondering again why an intruder would target the poorest woman in town.

"What's your name?" Heather asked.

"Becky," the woman said.

"Becky, I want you to get behind the car and stay put. I don't have backup."

"Okay," she said.

Heather reached through the driver's side window and turned off the headlights. She stepped back behind the car and glanced over her shoulder to the mailbox. She saw nothing. It was now completely black, but her eyes were quickly adjusting.

"Did he leave? Or is he still in the house?"

"I think he's still in there."

"Why?" Heather asked. "After all this time?"

"I don't know," she answered. "And he had something in his hand. I was worried it was a gun."

No, Heather thought. *Lord, no.*

The little boy on the woman's shoulder looked up at Heather. He was maybe a year old, and his big, round eyes blinked slowly, seemingly unconcerned. The other two kids continued to weep, still gripping at the lower half of their mother's pink pajama bottoms.

"There's a bad guy in our house," the oldest boy said. Heather guessed he was around five. He let go of his mother's leg and wiped tears with both hands. "I don't want him in my house."

"I want you to crouch down and stay put beside your mother," Heather said. "How many doors go in and out of the house?"

"Just two," the woman answered.

"Is there a basement?"

"No."

"Okay. Don't move."

The woman nodded obediently and lowered herself to sit down in the gravel. She shifted the baby to her other arm, and the other two kids knelt around her, their heads even with the back bumper.

"It's gonna be okay," Heather said, running her hand across the top of the woman's shoulder.

"I just cashed my check," Becky said. "It's in my purse. It's probably what he wants. What am I gonna do if he takes it?"

"That money is for our grocees," the little boy said. He looked at his sister, probably a year younger than him, and she nodded in agreement.

"Don't worry about that, honey," Heather said.

The little girl leaned against her mother's shoulder and looked at Heather. "Will you tell him to leave?"

Heather stood and turned back toward the mailbox again. She was no longer frightened. Something about the way the little boy said "groceries" had knocked her right off that tightrope of flight or fight.

She looked down at the woman and gritted her teeth, oddly welcoming the heat of rage that ran through her. This poor woman wasn't just some tattooed druggie trying to get her life together. She had been seeking God's help. And now this guy was threatening to send her into a tailspin of fear.

Heather put her pistol back in her holster and quickly opened the driver's side door of the cruiser. She leaned in and snatched the shotgun off its mount. She slammed the door shut and pulled the pump back on the gun. She glanced up at the sky, and that strange moon seemed to be staring right at her.

This is for you, Dad.

She checked the safety on the gun and then pushed the pump forward, sending the first shell into the barrel. She walked quickly, hugging the right side of the road until she passed the mailbox and stood at the foot of the driveway. She could see the house. It was nothing more than a shadow, a black square pressed back in the trees. Heather cut across the lawn toward the front door. She tip-toed behind a bed of shrubs near the front window and then slowly peeked in the house. It was too dark inside, and she glanced back down the driveway, then up at the sky. Her heart beat faster and the shot of adrenaline that went through her body let her know she was ready.

She ducked below the valance of the front window and stepped up on the porch. The main door was open, and the only thing that separated her from her first potential encounter of her career with an intruder—an *armed intruder*—was a screen door with a softball-size tear in the mesh.

She listened. She waited. She heard nothing.

Okay, buddy, she thought. *Game on.*

She pressed her thumb on the door handle and held her breath. Thankfully, it didn't make a sound and she slowly pulled the door open. She leaned against it and raised the gun, its long, dark barrel entering the house before she did. She paused again and then stepped inside, immediately greeted by the scents of mold and soiled diapers. She gently closed the screen door behind her and it clicked, sending what felt like an icy mallet against the side of her heart. She took a deep breath and waited.

It was time to be quiet. It was time to be still.

She couldn't hear anything. The stock of the shotgun was pressed firmly against her cheek, allowing the business end of the gun to follow her head and eyes. In the moonlight that came through the windows, she could see a playpen only a few feet away, directly in the center of the family room. Scattered on the thin carpeting around it were a collection of Barbie dolls, a blanket, and a sippy cup with a missing top. Beyond the playpen, a sofa was pulled a few feet away from the far wall. On second glance, the sofa was the *only* furniture in the room. There were no chairs, no tables, no decorations. All she could see on any of the walls were three head-high holes just beyond the couch that were about the size of fists.

She scanned the rest of the room and then turned to her right toward the adjoining small kitchen. No one was there. If he was still in the house, he would be down the narrow hallway that separated the family room and the kitchen. It split from the far side and led to what she assumed was the back of the house.

She stepped around the playpen and to the edge of the hallway. She lowered her gun, took another deep breath, and then slowly peeked around the corner.

Nothing.

She raised her gun again, took a step into the hallway, and the floor creaked. Anybody in the house would have heard it and she quickly crouched, waiting and listening.

Silence. Had he left?

She rose and took a few steps. About ten feet down to her right, she could see the outline of the back door. At the end of the hall was what looked like a bathroom, and just in front of it, to her left, was what had to be the only bedroom.

She passed the back door and came to the bedroom, pausing before raising the gun back to her cheek. She slowly looked around the corner of the doorway and once again saw nothing. She sighed and exhaled. He was gone.

Heather backed up into the hallway and faced the bathroom.

That was when she heard the floor creak behind her. She felt her throat close and then turned around.

He was standing right in front of her.

"Freeze!" she yelled, quickly raising the gun toward his chest.

He stood perfectly still.

Heather wondered how she had missed him when she entered the house. He had to have been in the kitchen, or behind the couch, watching her the whole time.

Everything he had on—shirt, shoes, pants, gloves, and ski mask—was black. He was nothing more than a dark silhouette, standing at the kitchen end of the hallway with his arms at his sides.

Heather waited for him to move. Wanted him to move. He

didn't, and despite the darkness, she could see something in his right hand.

"Drop it!" she yelled.

He did, and it barely made a noise as it landed on the carpet.

"Put your hands in the air!"

He stared at her for a few seconds and his head leaned toward his left shoulder. And then he slowly raised his hands until they stopped slightly above his head.

Heather could hardly breathe. Her heart felt like a rabbit kicking at the inside of a cage, and what she wanted to yell only came out as a whisper. "Wh-what are you doing here?"

His head tilted from side to side in slow motion, and then it was still. He extended his right arm a little farther above his head, his gloved palm facing the ceiling.

"What are you doing here?" Heather repeated, louder this time. She sensed the desperation in her own voice and it weakened her. "Why them?"

The man just stared at her. He craned his neck forward, allowing the moonlight that came in from the window on the back door to add a shine to his dark eyes behind the mask. He now seemed less human, and as far as Heather was concerned, he was responsible for every nightmare she'd ever had. He took a step toward her.

"Stop right there!" she said, her finger sliding to the thin part of the trigger.

His right arm slowly lowered and he pointed right at her. He was unarmed, yet clearly unafraid. She imagined herself pulling ever so slightly on the trigger. It was the shot she had been waiting over twenty years to take. It was both the reason she always wanted to be a cop and the reason she'd feared being one.

The silhouette kept staring. He continued to point at her until he nodded and pulled his hand back slightly. He then tilted his fingers toward the ceiling and made what looked like a sign of the cross in the air between them.

Heather lowered the gun, feeling as if she were moving under water.

Who is this guy?

He brought his hands to his sides and then started to slowly walk down the hallway. He was coming right at her.

I can't shoot. He knows I can't shoot.

"Stop," she whispered, lifting her gun again.

But he ignored her and just kept striding forward. He didn't stop until he reached the back door, just a few feet in front of her, and grabbed the handle.

She pointed the gun at the side of his head. "Who are you?"

He said nothing, took another long look at her, and then walked out.

Heather lowered herself to a knee. She stared at the open doorway and tried to focus on breathing. Her hands were trembling so much she could barely hold on to the shotgun.

She wasn't sure how much time had passed before she finally rose and turned the lights on. Tentatively, she tightened her grip on the gun and made her way out of the house and down the driveway, out to the dark road. The woman and her children hadn't moved an inch.

"Did you hear anything?" she asked. "He didn't come back out front, did he?"

The woman and the oldest of the three kids shook their heads.

"He's gone now," Heather said. "Probably took to the woods. I'm going to have you guys stay somewhere else tonight, but I'll escort you back inside to see what was taken. Try not to touch anything."

The woman sprang to her feet. "Please, God. Please let our money be there."

"How much are we hoping is there?" Heather asked with trepidation. The burglar had to have taken it.

"Almost three hundred dollars."

Heather took the baby, Becky took her frightened children by the hands, and they all headed back to the house.

Once inside, she put the baby in the playpen, and the mother had the other two children sit at the kitchen table. Heather and the woman walked down the hallway, each a little spooked, as if the man might come back in the house. When they passed the back door, Heather chastised herself for letting the jerk escape.

Why did I bring them in the house? What if he does return?

They went in the bedroom, flicked the light on, and noticed the woman's purse on the bed. Becky pounced on it. The zipper on the top was closed, which on the surface appeared to be good news. Nothing else in the room seemed too far out of order. Was it a burglary at all? Maybe he was a previous renter, coming back for a stash. Or maybe he was just some freak, wanting to catch a peek at some innocent woman and children. *Some sign-of-the-cross-giving weirdo.*

Becky's eyes lit up when she looked inside. "The money is still here."

"Good," Heather said. "Let's go double-check the family room and kitchen and see if anything else is missing."

The woman led the way, but then bent down. "What is this?" she asked. She straightened, with her back turned to Heather.

"What is it?" Heather asked, coming around.

Becky's hands started to shake.

"What is it?" Heather repeated, squinting and taking a step closer.

It was a brown paper lunch bag. There was a tear on the side of it, exposing about an inch of what looked like cash.

"This has to be a couple thousand dollars," the woman said. There was hope in her eyes and her voice sounded different.

"Did you know that guy?" Heather asked, remembering the silhouette dropping something in the hallway. Again she thought about her idea of him coming back to find a stash . . .

"No," Becky said. "Had I known . . ."

She didn't have to finish her sentence for Heather to know what she was thinking. If anyone in Benning Township needed a couple thousand, this girl was the one. "I take it this isn't your money?" Heather asked.

"I wish it was."

"I admire your honesty," Heather said.

They walked into the family room, and Heather stopped next to the playpen and ran her hand across the top of the baby's head. He was holding an empty bottle and Heather smiled. "Looks like somebody needs a refill on his bottle."

"Okay," Becky said from the kitchen.

Heather heard a gasp.

"What is going on?" the woman said.

Heather looked at her. Becky was standing in front of the refrigerator, holding the door open, staring. Tears were welling in her eyes.

Heather rushed to her side. "What's wrong?"

"Are they real?" Becky asked.

"What?" Heather asked.

The woman pointed to the middle shelf. Leaning up against a gallon of milk was a stack of gift cards with a thick rubber band wrapped around it. The card that faced her was a dark green with the words *Food Village* centered neatly in fluorescent yellow.

"Is this some kind of sick joke?" Becky asked.

Heather grabbed a handkerchief out of her pocket and took

the cards out of the refrigerator. She removed the rubber band and carefully fanned through them. A matching bright yellow $100 marker was at the top-right corner of each card.

"There must be fifty cards here," Heather said, holding one up under the kitchen light. "And they look pretty real to me."

"Who put them there?" Becky asked.

"I'm guessing the same guy," Heather said.

"This doesn't make any sense."

Heather glanced around the house. It was a mess, but a mess made by kids, not an intruder. "Anything seem to be missing?"

"I don't think so," Becky said. She smiled and shook her head. "Can I go take another look in the bedroom?"

"Go ahead," Heather said. "Just try not to touch anything besides the purse. We pretty much compromised any prints that might've been on it. Let's not screw up anything else." She closed the refrigerator door and then followed Becky, feeling the weight of the gift cards in her hand. Who was that guy? Who went around dumping cash and stashing Food Village gift cards in fridges? It made no sense . . .

"Thank you," the oldest boy said as she passed.

"You're welcome, sweetheart."

Heather walked back down the hallway and into the bedroom.

"Nothing's missing," Becky said. "In fact, it seems like all he did was break in here to *leave* things."

"You *sure* you don't know anyone who would do this? Someone who might want to help you, but not be identified for some reason?"

"I hardly know anybody in this town," Becky said. "And I don't know anybody, anywhere, with this kind of money."

Heather stepped back into the hallway and looked at the door the intruder left through.

"I really don't know what's going on," Becky said.

"Me either," Heather said.

"But why would he do it this way?" Becky asked. "Come in here in the middle of the night. Freak us out and all. Why wouldn't he just give these things to me?"

"I don't know," Heather said, thinking about the way the intruder just stared at her and how he made the sign of the cross in the darkness between them.

And then she couldn't stop the creepy little thought that rolled over and over in the back of her mind.

He knows me.

TWO

Heather pulled her truck in the driveway and could see Judi Kemp cleaning the grill beside the freshly painted little red barn. Judi turned around as the truck rolled past the garage, and Heather rolled the window down and sighed. It had to be close to a hundred again, another freakishly hot day, with unbearable humidity.

Heather had been looking forward to going to the Kemps' to help Judi celebrate her son, Andy's, fourteenth birthday with a little barbecue, and then maybe have a glass of wine or two, to uncoil from a strange night and another long week.

"Where's Andy?" Heather called.

"Right there." Judi pointed at the white five-bedroom home that sat all by itself on the very end of what the locals called "Ripley's Field," a three-hundred-acre patch of trees and corn rows that spread across the northeast corner of Benning Township. The old farmhouse had been in Judi's family for the better part of a century, and its waterfront view from the rear deck was arguably the best, not just in Benning, but the whole county, with the only things separating the house from Canada being a few tiny islands and the thinnest part of Lake Erie.

Andy was on his minibike—a dinged-up old Honda 70—and was crossing the top of the gravel driveway. He was wearing a pair of jean shorts, a motorcycle helmet, and a light blue T-shirt soaked with sweat.

"Wow," Heather said. "Who got Andy the new helmet?"

"Rip," Judi said. She ran a hand along the side of her neck and dropped the wire brush on the top rack of the grill. She was long and lanky, like her son, and when Judi came out from under the shade, she looked thinner, and something about the sunlight made her dishwater-blond hair look the color of dry straw. "Rip said the old helmet wasn't worthy of the new dirt bike. Wait until you see it. It's unbelievable."

It was Andy's official graduation from a little kid's minibike to a real motorcycle—an old Kawasaki dirt bike that Rip had been souping up in private.

"Where is it?" Heather asked.

"In the garage," Judi said. "Andy has no idea."

Heather stuck her neck out the window for another look at Andy as he cut across the lawn before circling behind her truck. The new helmet looked like something from a movie set. It came down past the middle of his throat and was made of shiny black plastic. The visor that covered the small hole in the center of the helmet was equally dark, giving one of the shyest kids in town a tough-guy look.

"Where in the world did Rip get that?"

"He ordered it online," Judi said. "Cost him two weeks' pay."

Andy pulled the minibike up next to the truck and Heather continued to admire his new lid. "Aren't you burning up under there?" she asked.

Andy lifted the helmet off, and his shoulder-length brown hair was matted to his cheeks and neck, doing an extra fine job of what it was grown out to do—cover the scar on his face.

"Hey, Heather," he said quietly, pulling his earbuds out and pressing the power button on his iPod. Heather couldn't remember the last time he'd put more than two sentences together at once unless he and his mother were going at it.

"Glad to be out of school?" Heather asked.

Andy shrugged off her silly question. Summer vacation was only two days old. He put his helmet back on and pulled the visor down.

"How can you breathe with that thing on?" Heather asked.

"No big deal," he said, muffled by the helmet.

"Honey, it's too hot for that," Judi said. "Take it off and go wash your face."

"Whatever," Andy said, shaking his head. Even with the helmet on, his whole stance spoke of his routine indifference. It was the same stance that, for years now, had been eating away at whatever was left of Judi. And it made it tough for Heather to stay quiet.

"Don't *whatever* me," Judi said. She wasn't wearing any makeup, and it made her appear softer, younger, helpless in a way. "You can put it back on later when Uncle Rip gives you your gift."

Andy flipped the visor up and stared at her. His eyes seemed like a pair of lifeless, neon-blue marbles. "Whatever."

Judi bit her lip and tried to take control. "Go clean up. And feed Milo. Make sure he's got water too."

Andy revved the small engine of the minibike and Heather noticed the beat-up copy of *The Catcher in the Rye* tucked in the back pocket of his jeans.

"There's some light reading," Heather quipped, pointing at the book. "Don't you think that's a little depressing?"

"Nope," Andy said.

Of course it isn't, Heather thought. Asking Andy if the book was depressing was no different than asking a clown if he was uncomfortable at the circus.

"How many books a week are you reading now?" Heather asked.

Andy shrugged and then turned the throttle, spitting little pieces of stone from under the minibike's back tire as he rode toward the house. Surprisingly, he appeared to be doing what his mother asked him. Maybe he was hungry, Heather mused.

"Probably four or five books a week," Judi answered for him. "He gets them all from the library. Every time I go to clean his room, there are different ones stacked on his nightstand."

Heather could see Milo sitting in the shade of the barn's doorway. Milo was a six-year-old beagle that refused to eat dog food and wore a red collar that was meant for a dog twice his size. He was also a runner, and if a deer, car, bike, or anything else came down Judi's road, Milo was going to chase it away. One of those pursuits involved a milk truck a few summers back and cost Milo his back right leg.

"How is Milo dealing with this heat?" Heather asked.

"He doesn't mind it," Judi said. "He still thinks he's a puppy and swims in the lake at least twice a day."

"I wish I could too," Heather said. "By the way, where have you been? I've been trying to get ahold of you."

"Sorry," Judi said. "Cell's in the house and I've been out here all day."

"Oh. Well, I just stopped by to tell you I'm gonna be a little late," Heather said.

"No hurry," Judi said. "Rip won't be here until around six, anyhow."

"Good."

"Good?" Judi asked, arching a brow and casting her a sly look.

"Are you trying to get back with my little brother after all these years?"

Heather rolled her eyes and did her best to imitate Andy. "Whatever."

Judi smiled and it actually seemed real. "What time you gonna be here?"

"I need to do some paperwork on a break-in that happened in the middle of the night. You know Becky from church? The one who's a little rough around the edges?"

"Oh no," Judi said. "*Her?* They have to be the only people in town poorer than I am."

"Poorer than you?" Heather said, grinning and then biting her lip. Judi didn't make much as a secretary at Parsons Elementary School, but she did manage to keep her part of Ripley's Field in the divorce. She and Rip had inherited the property from their parents, who'd both died of cancer at a young age. *Bloodlines* it was called. Judi had even bought Rip out of his half of the land before he went to prison, making Ripley's Field, just like the house, all hers. Still, Heather knew what her friend meant whenever she talked about times being tough and guessed if an artist wanted to paint a picture of someone who was land rich and cash poor, Judi would make one heck of a model.

"What'd they take from her?" Judi asked.

"That's the weird thing," Heather said. "He actually *left* around $5,000 in Food Village gift cards."

"*What?*" Judi said. "Who does that?"

"I don't know," Heather said. "I had to take the cards with me, and the station is checking them out today to make sure they're not stolen or missing. If not, Becky gets them back."

"I don't get it," Judi said, shaking her head as if she was trying to puzzle it out. "Someone broke in and *left* something?"

"I don't get it either. What's even weirder is how long he stuck around the house. He could have been in and out of there in a minute, but he was still there when I showed up. Like he *wanted* me to see him. There are so many other ways he could have given the cards to that woman. It just doesn't make sense."

"Five thousand bucks worth of gift cards," Judi said. "Wow. That's a lotta dough."

"You're telling me," Heather said, glancing at her watch. "I gotta run. I'll see you later tonight."

"Okay. Feel free to bring some of those gift cards over for me."

Heather smiled and made a big U-turn in the driveway, thinking about the brown paper bag the intruder dropped. And how she had chosen to leave it with that Becky girl.

Not a penny of the $3,500 dollars in cash that was in the bag would make it into her police report.

Just the gift cards.

THREE

*G*od must be in prison.

Thirty-five-year-old Gerald "Rip" Ripley laughed out loud. He wasn't sure how many times he'd heard some variation of that while serving three years in the big house for selling weed. He'd also heard it a few times since he'd gotten out of prison, close to a year ago. As much as it seemed to bother him, he did his best to shake it off, mostly because there was a lot of truth in the statement.

But hearing it from Andy was different, particularly on the boy's birthday, and it was important that his nephew understood what people meant by it.

"God's everywhere," Rip said, taking his hand off Andy's shoulder as they walked across Judi's backyard and past the barn toward the garage. "But you already know that."

Actually, Rip wasn't sure if Andy knew it at all. His gut told him that Andy had pretty much tossed God under the same umbrella as the tooth fairy and Santa Claus, and it was number one on Rip's bucket list to try to change that.

"Where did you hear that God was in prison?" Rip asked.

"Mr. Hart," Andy answered quietly. "He's such a tool."

God must be in prison, because that's where so many people seem to meet Him.

Rip smiled, offering silent props to whoever coined the line. It was both clever and harmless, and despite the temporary urge to part Hart's forehead with his fist the next time he saw him, he didn't want Andy to make something bigger of it than it really was.

"Don't lose any sleep over what Mr. Hart has to say," Rip said, running his hand through the V of his thinning blond hair. "He's just poking a little fun at me because he knows that prison is where your Uncle Rip finally slowed down and found God."

Andy's eyes flashed, and there was something about those blue eyes that seemed to look right through Rip. It was as if Andy sensed he didn't care much for Kevin Hart. Rip had known Hart for a little over thirty years now, since they were in kindergarten, and now that he worked for him, letting anybody know that he also thought Hart was a "tool" wasn't his best move.

"We'll see how long it lasts, Ripley. I don't really think anybody's buying into your newfound faith or born-again spiel."

Rip had never argued with Hart about it. Sure, a lot of guys in prison talked about God. He also knew that most of those guys returned to their old ways the second they were released. But Rip had been set free while in prison, and he knew he didn't have to prove anything to anyone except the Guy upstairs, *the real Boss.* He also knew that he still had a lot of things to work on himself, so he decided to let his actions speak for him instead of his mouth.

"Check it out," Rip said, pointing out to the lake. A pair of jet skis were about fifty yards offshore, heading south at what had to be fifty miles per hour. Andy loved fast things and the noises they made, and Rip grinned, knowing in just a few minutes, Andy would be experiencing both in a new way.

"Those are cool," Andy said quietly. "Someday I want to try one."

"I think there is something else you may want to try first, bro."

"Like what?" Andy said. "And by the way, nobody calls anybody *bro* anymore."

"Not true," Rip said. "*I* do."

Rip put his arm around Andy and kissed his nephew on the top of his head. Andy's shoulders hunched in embarrassment before he looked around to make sure nobody had seen.

"What the heck, Uncle Rip?" Andy said. "You better not ever do that in public."

"Why?" Rip said. "You're my only nephew and I love ya."

"Seriously," Andy pressed. "Not cool."

"Okay, tough guy," Rip said, remembering the last time they upgraded Andy's mode of transportation. It was when they traded Andy's bicycle for the minibike. Rip shook his head, thinking that it seemed impossible for that to have been four years ago, particularly with three of those spent behind bars.

"Wait for us!" It was Judi.

Milo was in front of her, doing his three-legged race at her side. Whenever he ran, it looked like he was moving sideways, but the little guy was surprisingly quick, and what he lacked in limbs, he made up for in heart.

"C'mon, Tripod!" Rip yelled, sparking Milo into his highest gear. Judi actually seemed to move a little quicker too, her flip-flops smacking at her heels the whole way.

"I can't believe you were going to show it to him without us," Judi said, catching her breath and sounding miffed.

"Chill out," Rip said. "I was gonna have Andy put his new helmet on and pull it out in front of the house for you."

"Okay," Judi said, using that victim tone they'd all become accustomed to.

"Pull what out?" Andy asked, crossing his arms.

Rip kneeled down and grabbed the garage door handle, ignoring the pain in his lower back that had been bothering him for a while. He pulled up and the door swung open, leaving them all staring straight at Andy's birthday present. It was parked in the center of the garage, covered by an old white bedsheet.

Rip went into the garage and grabbed a handful of the cloth.

"What is it?" Andy asked, rocking back and forth on his heels.

Rip got jelly-legged and smiled. He couldn't wait for Andy to see it.

Under the sheet was the coolest dirt bike in the history of mankind. Kevin Hart had practically forgotten he'd owned it. Hart had worked about as hard for it as he had for his father's business, and it had been parked down in the factory's basement since Moses was a teenager. Rip had taken the motorcycle in lieu of pay for waxing Hart's boat, the forty-six-foot Cigarette Rough Rider—the fastest thing on Lake Erie. In fact, it was so fast, it could get his boss across the lake into Canada and to his little girlfriend's house before you could even say *affair*.

It had taken Rip close to a week just to get the bike's motor working. With the help of some spare parts he grabbed at the dump over in Carlson, some orange and black paint, and a few affordable decals he had found on the Internet, he had finished it two nights ago, and now the motorcycle was ready to roll.

"Put your helmet on," Rip said. "This is official business."

Rip grinned and he saw Andy hurriedly do what he asked.

"Happy birthday!" Rip shouted, yanking on the sheet. But his eyes were only on his nephew.

Andy smiled from ear to ear. Something that didn't happen too often.

"It's beautiful!" Judi said.

"C'mon, bro, get on it!" Rip yelled.

Andy ran toward the bike. "Can I start it?"

"Go for it," Rip said, handing Andy the key.

Andy got on, started the bike, and then gunned the throttle, revving the engine and filling the garage with a high-pitched zipping sound that reminded Rip of a new chain saw. Andy's head bobbed up and down in approval and he slowly lowered the visor. Rip put his arm around Andy and then looked back at Judi, who was smiling as well. And then her lips moved, but he couldn't hear what she was saying, so he reached over and cut the bike's engine.

"What the heck?" Andy said.

"Your mom is saying something," Rip answered, nodding at his sister. "What is it, Judi?"

She smiled again but it didn't last long. "It's so loud and so big. Is he going to be safe on that thing?"

"*Mom*," Andy said, lifting the visor.

"I'm gonna take him right now for a ride out to The Frank and Poet," Rip said. "I'll let him get used to it and then let him drive me back. What time is Heather coming?"

"You've got about an hour," Judi said. She crossed her arms and her eyebrows furrowed, clearly stressed out about the bike. "I still think that motorcycle seems too big. It's just—"

"Stay out of it, Mom," Andy said.

"Hey!" Rip said, rapping his knuckles on top of Andy's helmet. "Respect. Remember what we talked about?"

Andy pulled the visor down and turned his head the other way.

Rip looked back at Judi, and her shoulders were slumped. She looked as if she was about to cry and Rip closed his eyes, unable to stop the disappointment that stabbed at his heart in the midst of so much joy.

He knew he wasn't the only one who had things to work on.

✹ ✹ ✹

Rip and Andy had cut across the backyard toward the west side of Ripley's Field. They were halfway through the thick stretch of woods that ran away from the house and Lake Erie out toward the cornfields and The Frank and Poet Canal. Rip was helmetless with Andy perched behind him. Rip could feel the boy's impatience, waiting for them to make it beyond first gear as Rip slowly maneuvered around the tree limbs that had fallen and littered the old tractor path over the years.

"How come you don't have to wear a helmet and I do?" Andy asked.

"We ain't gonna go that fast," Rip said, knowing everyone had their own definition of *fast*. "I just want you to get an idea of what she feels like and then you'll bring us back."

"Still doesn't answer my question," Andy said.

"Really, smart aleck? We can always take the bike back to the barn and neither of us can wear a helmet. How's that sound?"

"Sorry," Andy muttered.

Rip spotted the end of the woods where the path widened between a pair of cornfields. "Hang on, bro. I'm gonna hit it here in a second."

Rip didn't feel Andy hanging on and he glanced behind him. Andy was just gripping the sides of the seat.

"I mean hang on to me," Rip said. "This isn't the minibike."

"C'mon, Uncle Rip."

Rip gunned the throttle and the bike lurched forward a little, clearly catching Andy off guard.

"Now you ready?" Rip said as they came out of the woods.

"Yeah," Andy said, wrapping his arms tightly around Rip's waist.

Rip gunned it, and they both leaned forward. The countless rows of short corn on both sides of them blurred as they headed straight toward The Frank and Poet Canal, one of a dozen canals that ran through Benning. Like a little finger that belonged to Lake Erie, The Frank and Poet curved around both the north and west sides of Ripley's Field and also served as a border between Benning and the abandoned McLouth Steel property, which was over in the town of Carlson. The water in The Frank and Poet was always cold and had a funny color to it. And despite all the rumors of toxic spills from the factory and the promises of cancer and two-headed offspring to anyone who ever went in it, the canal had always been a great place to swim.

Rip pulled back a little more on the throttle and the bike responded well. Almost too well. They hummed farther down the path until the deserted old factory came into view. He slowed the bike down as they came to the end of the cornfields and into the knee-high grass that ran about thirty yards downhill to the canal.

"What do you think?" Rip said, bringing the bike to a stop.

"Wow!" Andy said in a rare display of enthusiasm. "How fast you think we were going?"

"Maybe around sixty or seventy."

"I thought you said we weren't going to go fast."

"That isn't fast when *I'm* driving," Rip said, glancing over his shoulder and giving his nephew a subtle look of warning. "I know *you* won't go that fast, right?"

Andy didn't answer. He just lifted his visor and pointed across the canal at the McLouth Steel property.

Rip turned and couldn't believe his eyes.

"Where in the world did those come from?" Rip asked. "Weren't we just swimming out here a few days ago?"

"Yeah," Andy said.

Rip blinked and shook his head. It was around ninety feet from one side of the canal to the other. Beyond the far bank, the land had *always* been covered with the same kind of wavy grass they were standing in right now—grass so high and soft you could sleep in it. The grass ran about a football field back to a rusty old fence that was guarded by poison ivy so thick, you'd itch just looking at it. Beyond the fence were century-old railroad tracks, rusty chunks of abandoned equipment, and acres and acres of cracked concrete that led back to the dark walls of the deserted factory and its thousands of little, broken windows.

Every time Rip looked at the place, the first thing that came to his mind was the time he and a couple buddies, all around eleven or twelve years old, had pitched a pup tent in the tall grass over there. They were going to camp all weekend with just their BB guns, two bags of canned goods, and the three bottles of Mad Dog 20/20 Tommy Curtis had lifted out from under the passenger's seat of his older sister's white Camaro. The weekend didn't quite turn out as planned. They were all drunk and had passed out, only to be woken up by a pair of hobos who must have jumped off one of the trains that had stopped at the factory. The two men had helped themselves to most of the boys' food supply and were on their way back toward the fence when Rip came out of the tent. He remembered hurling a can of Franco-American macaroni and cheese, missing one of the men's heads by less than a foot. And then he remembered swaggering back down to the canal and hurling something else. Nothing like a little recycled Mad Dog adding to the lore of The Frank and Poet's toxicity.

But now it was different on the other side.

Just past the far bank, surrounded by the high grass, were four beds of wildflowers, each about the size of a tennis court. They were individually outlined in jet-black soil and in a neat row, creating an enormous stripe of color. On second glance, it almost looked like a giant garden—deliberately planted and cared for—with yellow, red, blue, white, and pink flowers that all seemed to be the same height.

"Look at that," Rip said. "Those four sections are carbon copies of each other. Who could've done such a thing?"

"Have you ever seen flowers there before?" Andy asked, clearly awestruck.

"No," Rip said. "I've been coming out here my whole life—thirty-two years, not counting my government-sponsored vacation. I'm telling you, I've never seen anything like that over there."

It was true. And even though Rip had never considered himself to be a nature buff, the garden's beauty was truly something to behold.

Andy got off the bike and walked down to the edge of the canal. He took his helmet off and tucked it under his right arm. "It's so weird, Uncle Rip. Wouldn't we have noticed it *growing* when we were out here? All I remember is grass."

Of course they would have. Had it been there. But it hadn't been.

"It is weird," Rip said. He wasn't sure if *weird* was the right word or not, and a little voice inside of him was begging him to remember this moment. And the longer he looked at the other side of the canal, the more he became convinced that there was *a reason* that garden was there, because just staring at it gave him a bizarre sense of peace he had never felt before.

Rip walked down to the water beside Andy. His nephew almost seemed like he'd been hypnotized, his eyes glassy and fixed on the flowers.

"Something's over there," Andy said.

"Even the early blooming stuff doesn't grow that fast," Rip said. "And look how those four sections are so neatly divided. You see it?"

Andy squinted and then nodded.

"And how in the world could somebody plant that many flowers, that fast?" Rip added. "Look how straight the edges of those beds are. It's almost too perfect, for crying out loud."

"Something's over there," Andy repeated. This time in a whisper. "I can feel it, Uncle Rip."

"I think I know what you mean. Feels good just looking at it, doesn't it?"

Andy didn't answer and they both just stared at the flowers in silence.

Rip finally shook his head, whispered, "Weird," and poked Andy on the shoulder. The boy seemed to snap out of his little trance. "You ready to give that bike a whirl?"

"Yeah," Andy said.

They walked up the bank, into the tall grass, and Rip turned back around and studied the wildflowers, wondering how he was going to describe them to Judi and Heather. "Looks like a little piece of heaven, doesn't it?"

Andy flipped the helmet in his hands and laughed. "If there was a heaven."

"Funny guy," Rip said. "Put your helmet on real quick. I want to test something before we take off."

Andy did and Rip smacked the side of the helmet with his open palm. The visor slid down over Andy's face and he took a couple steps the other way. "What the heck was that for?"

"Don't ever let me hear you say that again."

"Okay," Andy said. "Chill out."

Andy mounted the bike. Rip got on behind him and tapped Andy on the shoulder. "Who loves ya?"

Andy didn't answer and Rip knocked on the top of the helmet. "Okay, okay," Andy said quickly. "I *know*, Uncle Rip. *You* love me."

Andy fired up the bike, and before they had turned all the way around, Rip took one more glance across The Frank and Poet.

He couldn't stop his own words from playing over in his head as he looked at the garden.

A little piece of heaven.

FOUR

Rip was standing in the kitchen with Judi when he noticed Heather's truck pull in the driveway. Andy flagged her down to show off his birthday present.

"Look at him," Rip said, pointing proudly through the window. "He loves that bike."

"You sure he'll be safe on that thing?" Judi asked.

"He'll be all right," Rip answered, reaching over to pat Judi on her arm. "Why don't you let him give you a ride out to see those flowers? I'm telling you, they're unbelievable. You gotta see them."

"I've seen wildflowers before, Rip."

"Not like *this*, you haven't."

Judi walked closer to the window. "It looks way faster than the minibike."

"It is," Rip admitted as Andy zipped around the front yard for Heather. Little plumes of gray smoke puffed from the exhaust pipe and quickly disappeared. "But he'll be fine. Trust me."

Judi sighed. "I just don't want him to get carried away with the whole helmet and long hair thing either. I thought we were trying to get him away from covering up his scar."

"It's *fun* to him, Judi," Rip said. "Playing the whole motorcycle-riding bad-boy thing. Remember what it means to have *fun*?"

"Okay, Rip. Leave me be," Judi said, nodding toward Heather as she came toward the porch. "When are you going to fix up that other bike . . . the old one you got from the dump?"

"I was gonna bring it over and start working on it in a couple weeks or so."

"It would be nice if you and Andy could ride together," Judi said. "I'd feel better if you were out there with him."

"Gotcha," Rip said.

Heather came through the kitchen door with Andy and Milo right behind her. Andy peeled off his helmet the second he entered the house and Rip couldn't believe how tall he looked next to Heather.

"You are growing like a weed," Rip said, sitting at the kitchen table. "You sure you're not eighteen instead of fourteen?"

Andy slouched. The whole concept of being observed was something the kid got sick of a long time ago.

"How tall you think he is now?" Judi asked. "He and Heather were the same height just last year."

Rip tilted his head. "How tall are you again, Heather?" He knew, but he just wanted to hear her throw in that half inch.

"Five three and a half," she said.

Rip laughed.

"What?" Heather said.

"You must have measured yourself with roller skates on," he said. "And what is it about anybody under five five, that whenever you ask them their height, they always throw in the bonus half inch?"

"Shut up, Rip," Heather said, glancing up at Andy. "You have to be almost six foot, don't you think?"

"Who cares?" Andy said.

The kid was skinny as a rail, but considering it was only his first day at being a fourteen-year-old, Rip figured Andy was a shoo-in for the three to four inches he needed to catch up and then maybe even pass his favorite uncle.

"I'm glad he's getting bigger," Heather said. "He has to be for that bike. It's the coolest motorcycle I've ever seen, but it's not a toy, and it's not for little kids."

Rip knew each one of those words kicked at Judi's insides, but it seemed as if Andy liked the way that sounded, giving Rip a thumbs-up.

"Just make sure you keep it off the roads," Heather added. "Stick to the paths."

"You hear her?" Rip asked, looking at Andy.

"You think I'm deaf?" Andy said, pulling his hair forward over the sides of his neck. "I'm standing right here."

"Pound it," Rip said, holding out his fist.

"Pound it," Andy echoed, making a fist before their knuckles tapped lightly together.

"And the next time you get smart with me," Rip added, "the only thing I'm gonna be pounding is you upside your melon. Now go wash up for dinner."

Andy delivered one of his patented eye-rolls and left the kitchen.

"Tough day, Officer Gerisch?" Rip asked. "You seem a little out of sorts."

"Been working swing shifts," Heather said, joining him at the table. "I'm just really tired and was thinking about a strange call I went out on last night. We had a prowler."

"That's what I hear," Rip said. "Chasing off a prowler must be a nice break from speeding warnings and scattering teenage smokers out from behind the Dairy Queen."

"I had to take my gun out, Rip . . ." She gave him a long look.

Guns and break-ins were practically unheard of in Benning, and Rip knew that was the way Heather liked it. In fact, the only other one that Rip had ever heard of in the town's history had cost another cop his life. And Heather's father was that cop.

"I would like to ask you something, though," Heather said, facing Rip. "Sort of off the record, if you don't mind."

"Go for it," Rip said.

Heather rubbed at her temples. "Do you think there is any chance that Eric Bower is back in business?"

Rip squinted and then grinned at Heather. He and Eric had been the only two pot dealers of any consequence that Benning had ever known. Rip's career in that industry had come to a screeching halt when Eric got busted, because for Eric, his own future had pretty much come down to a simple decision.

"Tell us where you get your weed from or you are gone for twenty years."

After ratting out Rip, Eric didn't do a day in jail, and Rip ended up plea bargaining and getting a surprisingly lenient seventy months. Prison overcrowding and decent behavior had him out in a little less than half his term. Rip guessed that most of the town still figured it was just a matter of time before he attached some bricks to Eric and went for a late-night cruise out on Lake Erie.

Regardless, Rip was positive that Eric wasn't the type that was stupid—or *smart*—enough to get back in the dope game. Not without him.

"No way," Rip said. "He's all done. Why you asking?"

Heather paused. "I meant to ask you about it before, but last night just got me thinking."

"About what?"

"Nothing," she said. Heather was already the best-looking woman in Benning, but when she was distracted, something about her light green eyes made her even cuter.

"C'mon," Rip prodded. "Tell me."

She bit her lip and rested her palms flat on the table. "It's just that I saw Eric's kids over near the Dairy Queen on brand-new bicycles. And ever since he got busted . . ." Her eyes flicked to him nervously. "Well, you know. It's been hard on his family. They're not exactly rolling in the dough."

Rip laughed. "Did you chase them and their Marlboros away? Those may not have been Marlboros."

"They were on expensive bikes, Rip. Not the cheap thrift store ones. Eric can't swing that kinda money cutting lawns."

"Then ask him if he's dealing again," Rip said. "I'll ask him for you if you want."

"Yeah, right," Heather said. "Every time he sees you, he thinks you're going to cloud up and rain all over him."

Rip smiled. He hadn't used that line in years, but was pretty sure Eric was scared to death of him. "You should just ask him and see if he's dealing. Take his temperature and see how he responds. It's your job, isn't it?"

"I did," Heather said. "But he laughed at me. And then I asked him where he got the money for the bikes."

"What'd he say?"

"He told me he heard his kids yelling for him one morning. Said he went outside and the kids were on the bikes. Said someone just left them in the garage."

"And you bought that?"

"Not really," Heather said, giving him a frank stare. "The only place that sells those types of bikes within a hundred miles didn't report any stolen. They also said that they sell so many, no particular purchases stood out. But back to last night, did Judi tell you about the gift cards the prowler left?"

"Yeah," Rip said, glancing at Judi, who shrugged.

"The gift cards are worth a heckuva lot more than the bikes," Heather said. "But the way this guy left them for that woman sorta reminded me of what Eric said about the bikes just showing up in his garage."

"Who around here has that kind of money to just drop off at someone's house?" Judi asked, setting a plate of barbecued chicken on the table. Andy came back into the kitchen.

"The only person I can think of is Kevin Hart," Heather said.

Rip rolled his eyes the way Andy did.

"Seriously," Heather added. "Who else can toss that kind of money around?"

"No way," Rip said. "Kevin Hart wouldn't do that unless it was videotaped for the town to see. Either that or he would call a press conference and humbly announce what he did."

"He has done a lot for this town," Judi said. "More than he gets credit for. We should all be thankful. Particularly *you*, Rip."

"I *am* thankful," Rip said.

Hart had done a lot for Benning, and Rip really was thankful. But something about Judi and the word *thankful* being in the same room sort of reminded him of the old square peg in a round hole bit. Still, she seemed to be having a decent night, so he decided not to pick on her about it.

"No biggie," Heather said. "We'll figure it out. I'm sure the bikes and the gift cards are probably just a coincidence. Besides, Kevin Hart isn't exactly the type to go around breaking into houses."

FIVE

Judi had been up since dawn. She rarely slept anymore.

There was something about summer vacation that always made things worse. Andy had been in a hurry to get on his motorcycle, and the minute he finished his breakfast, he had taken off, leaving her in the lonely house.

She had vacuumed and dusted the entire downstairs before polishing the kitchen's wooden floor. She couldn't decide why she had never sold the big old house. Despite its beauty and location, it was easily four times the house she and Andy needed.

Moreover, it was the centerpiece of every bad memory she had.

She sat at the kitchen table and sighed. It was impossible for her to be in the kitchen and not think about the day Andy was burned. She stared dreamily at the door that led to the basement. She shook her head and sighed again. They had never been able to find hinges and paint that matched the doors in the rest of the house to repair it.

Judi stood and went to the kitchen window. It was sunny again, and she raised the screen, inviting the little breeze that came off the lake into the house. It felt good and she closed her eyes, hoping . . . *praying* that it would somehow push away the cloud that had hung over her for so long.

She took a deep breath and forced herself to smile, thinking about Andy when he left. His Detroit Lions T-shirt was on backward and when she pointed it out to him, he didn't even entertain the idea of fixing it. He just shook his head at her and put the new helmet on. Even though it was a long shot that he'd give her one, she asked him for a hug, he declined, and then he ran as fast as he could out the door, with Milo trailing him all the way to the garage.

She could still see him, crouched forward, as he jetted down the driveway and up the side of the road toward town, not having the faintest idea that Milo continued to chase him.

She stepped back from the window and noticed her breathing had gone shallow again.

Though school had only been out a couple days, she was already anxious to get back to work. Being around people helped take her mind off things. At least some of the time.

She and Andy hadn't seen Todd in over five years. When he first left, he called about once a week, then gradually once a month, and eventually, only on Andy's birthdays. But he hadn't called yesterday. Had Andy noticed?

She closed her eyes and thought about the way mornings used to feel. They even smelled different. Fresh orange juice, buttery toast, and the scent of Todd's aftershave that lingered after he kissed her and Andy good-bye.

They had tried to do everything right, according to the age-old manual. Have a high-school sweetheart. Go to college and graduate. Marry your high-school sweetheart. Have and raise healthy babies. Retire and ride off into the sunset together.

But things didn't work out as planned.

She turned and glanced back at the basement door. Then she tucked the memory under a rug somewhere in her mind, knowing it would come right back out tomorrow as it always did.

Heather had been the first to notice the bruises and put it together with Judi's growing unhappiness at home. She'd begged Heather not to arrest Todd. After all, he'd been under so much stress with work that year, and she had not been much of a wife to him, mostly just a mother to Andy. Raising a child took a lot out of her. But she should have done better.

Heather had kept her promise. She didn't arrest Todd.

She did something much worse.

She told Rip.

At the time, Judi had no idea that Rip suspected Todd was abusing her, before the day Andy was burned.

Judi pushed the images away again. She shook her head, exhaled loudly, then went and looked in the bathroom mirror.

Who'd want you? You're thirty-seven years old. Your life is behind you. You had your once-in-a-lifetime shot at love and a normal family. You blew it. It wasn't Todd's fault. It wasn't Rip's fault. It's all yours. Even the burn on Andy's face. No wonder he doesn't talk to you anymore. You were a bad mother. A bad wife. A failure.

The phone rang, forcing her back to the present.

"We have a little problem," Heather said, without a hello.

"What's wrong?" Judi asked.

"It's Andy's motorcycle."

"No," she said, her heart pounding in a cold thud. "Please tell me Andy's not hurt."

"He's fine," Heather said. "For now."

"Thank God," Judi said. And then she could hear the whining of the motorcycle. She headed to the front door and saw Andy coming back up the side of the road. "He's here. What's wrong, then?"

"It's too fast for him, Judi."

Judi exhaled another breath of relief and forced a laugh. "It's just an old dirt bike. He has been riding the little Honda for years now and hasn't ever gotten hurt."

"We clocked him near the park today," Heather said. "Believe me. Whatever Rip did to this thing, it's different."

"C'mon," Judi said. "It can't be that fast. What was he doing? Thirty? Forty?"

There was a pause. "Seventy-three."

Judi frowned. "I'm going to kill Rip."

Heather laughed. "Don't worry. I already called him."

※ ※ ※

Rip sat on the edge of the small desk inside the custodian's closet on the second level of Hart Industries. He closed his cell phone and snatched up the cheap cloth garden gloves he liked to wear while doing push-ups on the cement floor. Heather had called first, and then Judi interrupted him. If they thought they were going to get him to hobble Andy's new wheels, they had another think coming, because riding, listening to his iPod, and reading books were about the only three things that the kid enjoyed doing.

"Rip, it's too fast. They clocked him going seventy-three. He's gonna get hurt."

Seventy-three? Rip thought. *Not too shabby, Andy. Not too bad at all.*

Rip laughed out loud and then reconsidered. He knew the bike had a little kick to it, but seventy-three *was* pushing it.

He could hear someone coming down the stairs. He glanced at his watch. It was a few minutes before two. Only one person bailed this early—the one who didn't need permission. Though Rip had heard Kevin Hart's wife say at church that he normally didn't get home until around seven or eight o'clock, he was leaving a bit later today than usual.

"Have a good one, Mr. Hart," Rip said, thinking about Judi's comment from the previous day. Even though he was *thankful* for his job, something about calling Kevin "Mr. Hart" didn't sit well with him. But it was required on the premises.

"You too, Ripley," Hart said, stopping near the door. "How many push-ups today?"

"It's my lunch break," Rip said.

"I know," Hart said, holding out his palms like it was no big deal.

"I try to do around eight sets of fifty every day."

"Good for you," Hart said with a nod. "How does Andy like the motorcycle?"

"Loves it."

"Glad I could help," Hart said. "Not that your arms need to be any bigger, but would you mind boxing up those cans of food over in the warehouse? They're taking up too much space and I want to get them out of here today."

"Sure," Rip said, after a moment's hesitation.

Hart had offered up the space for a town-wide food drive, and getting the couple thousand cans that had been donated out of there today would've given some lucky employee about three hours of overtime. It was quite convenient that Hart didn't pick one or two of the hourly guys. Rip was salary. All three hundred and eighty bucks a week of it.

"I appreciate it," Hart said. "If you get a chance over the next week, see if you can hit the boat with another coat of wax."

Rip hesitated again. It was one thing to do the cans as an act of charity. But waxing the guy's boat again?

"I'll toss you an extra hundred if you can fit it into your

schedule," Hart said. "You know. Around your personal exercise program."

Rip studied him for a long moment. "No problem, boss," he said slowly. "I've got you covered."

"Good," Hart said, barely suppressing his gloating. "I'm heading out to Tecumseh for a few days next week. Gonna be down there ironing out the final details of the Phillips deal. Think you could have it done by the time I get back?"

"Sure," Rip said.

The details to buy out Phillips Corrugated Box had been settled weeks before. Rip guessed Hart was probably just rehearsing for the conversation with his wife before he was off to party with some young thing.

"Have fun," Rip said.

"Fun with what?" Hart asked.

"With the details." Rip grinned. He had a feeling Hart knew exactly what he meant.

"Let me worry about that," Hart said with a suspicious look. "Get those cans out of there. *Today.*"

SIX

Andy had been up in his bedroom, staring at the ceiling and listening to his iPod. He was also trying to figure out what would be the best way to get Uncle Rip to convince his psycho mom that his new motorcycle was safe.

Five years ago, Uncle Rip would have straightened Mom out in a second, but now Andy wasn't sure. Uncle Rip wasn't anywhere near as cool as he'd been before he went to prison. Now he'd probably just dish out some lecture on how going fast wasn't "the right thing to do."

The more Andy thought about it, "the right thing to do" looked more like finding out where Dad was and convincing him to let Andy live with him. Mom was nuts and he completely understood why Dad never came around much. His father had always kept it real, and Andy would never forget the "man-to-man" talk he and his father had at the Detroit Tigers game on his eighth birthday. Andy was sitting behind the Tigers' dugout, wearing his brand-new mitt and promising his father to never talk to Mom about the real reason they divorced.

That was when Dad told him it'd been because she had burned his face. No wonder she never wanted to talk about it.

Andy sat up in the bed and took out his earbuds. He got up, practically stepped on Milo, who quickly sprang up on all three legs, then walked over to his dresser and stared at the neatly framed picture of him with Dad and Mom. They were sitting at the picnic table in the backyard. Andy guessed he was about two years old. It was the only photo in the house where all three of them were smiling, and every time he looked at the picture, he wondered what had gone wrong, what terrible thing happened that made his mother do the things she did.

Why me? Why did Mom throw that water at me? I never did anything to hurt her.

Andy opened the top drawer and stared inside. To the left was the hardcover copy of *The Hunchback of Notre Dame* the library didn't know he had. To the right, sitting neatly on top of old comic books of *Batman, Captain America,* and *Spider-Man,* was the little mirror with the brown wooden handle. Andy wondered how many times in his life he had held it.

He pulled his hair forward and then took out the mirror to look at himself. He liked the color of his dark brown hair. It was the same color as Dad's and it made his eyes seem not just blue, but *really* blue.

He faked a smile. Andy really liked the shape of his teeth and then he studied the two tiny bumps on his forehead. So what if he had a couple tiny zits? Half the kids in middle school last year were playing connect the dots with their complexions.

But zits go away.

The fake smile faded. He grabbed a handful of hair and pulled it back away from the left side of his face and neck. Even after two surgeries, the scar still looked awful. It began just above the center of his ear. It was shiny and pink and covered with what looked like hundreds of thin white scratches. It widened as it went down his cheek, looking like a bell-shaped spiderweb that seemed to rest on his jawline. From there, three ugly streaks, about an inch wide and five inches long, reached down toward his collarbone like fleshy wet fingers.

Andy put the mirror back and pushed his hair forward.

Mom had always said that, despite the burn, he was beautiful and that God made him just the way He wanted.

What a flippin' idiot.

He would never forgive her.

※ ※ ※

Rip grabbed the pizza box off the passenger seat of his 1979 Pacer and looked straight through the windshield. Andy's dirt bike was centered perfectly at the top of the driveway—Judi's way of letting him know it was in need of some attention. He laughed and got out of the car.

Andy came bolting out the front door. He had his helmet on with the visor up and was halfway across the yard before you could say *Evel Knievel.*

"Mom's being an idiot," he said, coming to an abrupt halt. He then raised his arm and pointed at the motorcycle. "She says we have to slow it down or I can't ride it."

"I know," Rip said. He put his arm around Andy's shoulder, pulling him close. "But what's this I hear about you flying through town at the speed of sound?"

Andy looked out at the lake, then back to him. "Don't let her ruin this for me."

"Take it easy on your mom," Rip said. "She just doesn't want you to get hurt."

"But—"

"Don't worry, bro. You'll be back in the saddle before you know it."

"'Bout time you got here!" Judi yelled. She was wearing another boring white sundress that made her look around sixty instead of thirty-seven. Her hands were on her hips and she clearly wasn't too thrilled with him.

"I said I'd be here at seven," Rip said, glancing at his watch. He frowned. It was seven thirty. "Sorry. Hart had me working the one-man food drive program."

Judi took the pizza out of his hands, and he and Andy followed her to the side of the house. Milo smelled the pizza and joined them from the garage, suddenly Judi's best friend.

"When are you going to get Milo a collar that fits?" Rip asked. "It looks like he's wearing a red hula hoop."

"He has one that fits," Judi said. "But whenever I put it on him, all he does is lie in the corner, paw at his neck, and cry."

"He's a serial dater," Rip said. "Just get him fixed and then you don't have to worry about him running off overnight to romance, or for that matter, even wearing a collar at all."

"Yeah, right," Judi said. "Then he'll run off without his collar and tag, chasing a car instead of a lady dog, and we'll never get him back."

"Oh, that's right," Rip said with a sarcastic little laugh. "The people in town will mix him up with all the other three-legged beagles running around. My bad."

"We've got something bigger to discuss," Judi said. "The bike."

"Yeah, yeah, yeah," Rip said as they approached the picnic table. Heather stood and Rip pointed at the glass of wine she was holding. "Better watch it there, Officer Gerisch. Drinking and driving is frowned upon by the local authorities."

"So is a fourteen-year-old going seventy miles per hour on a motorcycle."

And so is a police officer dating a convicted felon.

Despite the couple years they'd dated in their early twenties, he'd never found a way to completely kill that puppy-love crush he'd had on her since he was about eight.

"Let's talk about the bike later," Rip said. "Plus, if Andy ever gets a speeding ticket, I know a cop who can get him out of it."

"It's too fast," Heather said. She looked at Judi as if to gain support and a little smile touched her lips. "It's faster than your Pacer, Rip."

"Don't hate on the Pacer," Rip said. "It's over thirty years old, and I only paid four hundred bucks for it. It's a classic."

"It's a real chick magnet too," Heather said, drawing a laugh from Judi. "Hey, remember those little rings that you could get in vending machines for a quarter?"

Rip nodded.

Heather snorted and was laughing so hard she could barely get the words out. "Your car looks like one of those plastic bubbles that the rings came in."

"That's pretty harsh," Rip said, studying the Pacer as Heather and Judi continued to laugh. It probably was the ugliest car in Michigan. But at the same time, it ran like a top and would last him at least another year.

"I'm just teasing you," Heather said.

"Who needs a fancy car when you have these babe magnets?" Rip said, smiling and then kissing each bicep. "Best guns in Benning."

"Oh, please," Heather said. "Let's get back to what's important. The bike. I'd cut the speed in half."

Rip shook his head and held his arms up in surrender. "Why don't we just put some training wheels on it?"

Judi pointed at the garage. "You heard Heather. Cut the speed in half."

"Not cool, Mom," Andy said.

"Not now, Andrew," Judi replied.

"What are you gonna do? Ground me?"

Judi crossed her arms and Rip could see the helplessness in her eyes. Still, she tried to take charge of the situation. "Fix the bike right now, Rip. Before we eat. I mean it."

Rip looked at Andy. His nephew meant the world to him and even more to Judi. Plus, he'd never forgive himself if Andy got hurt, so the bike needed an adjustment.

"To the garage," Rip said, taking the bike by the handlebars. "Off to chill out the motorcycle and hopefully your mom as well."

"This isn't fair," Andy mumbled, Milo at his side. About halfway to the garage, a semitruck hauling gravel came around the trees and sped past the house. Super-beagle Milo took off to show it who was boss, barking and chasing its dust until they couldn't see or hear him anymore.

Anytime Rip and Andy had ever worked on the minibike or fiddled with anything else in the garage, it was the ideal time to talk about life, things he learned in prison, and also about what Andy referred to as "boring God stuff."

"You reading that Bible I got you?" Rip asked.

"I can't get into it," Andy said.

"Why?"

"Too many family trees and too much unbelievable stuff. It's super boring."

"You didn't start with the book of John like I told you, did you?"

"No," Andy said. "Why not start on page one like every other book?"

"Tell me the five rules then," Rip said. "Take your helmet off first, though."

Andy did and quickly swooped his long hair forward. "You serious? The preaching stuff is getting a little old, Uncle Rip."

"Excuse me?" Rip said. "How about showing some self-control and trying to think before you run your pie hole and offend somebody?"

"More preaching?"

"Do it for Uncle Rip."

Andy looked at the garage floor and shook his head.

"C'mon, man," Rip said.

"Love God with all your heart and soul," Andy spit out quickly, as if the words were choking him.

Rip held his thumb up and waited the kid out.

"Two," Andy said quietly, "is love your neighbor."

Rip smiled. "Lay number three on me."

Andy tilted his head. "Rule number three . . . Help God make His house bigger."

"You got it!" Rip yelled. "Number four?"

Andy crossed his arms. "Don't mess with people who handle your food."

"Finish it with number five, bro!"

Andy lifted an arm and held up three fingers. "Number five. Only the first three rules count."

"My man," Rip said, holding out his arms for a hug.

"My man," Andy echoed quietly, avoiding the hug and accidentally dropping his iPod. As he leaned forward to pick it up, Judi appeared behind him at the garage door.

"You're not working on it yet?" she asked.

Andy turned around. Rip could tell that Andy's resentment for his mother was approaching a boil, and the possibility of an argument had just been upgraded to DEFCON 2.

"We just got in here," Andy said.

"I wasn't talking to you, Andrew!" Judi shouted, her face reddening.

"*Judi,*" Rip said sharply. "We *did* just get in here."

Judi crossed her arms and took a step back, exhaling loudly through her nose.

Andy crossed his arms to mock his mother. He exhaled loudly and took a step back. Rip heard the crunch and knew what it was.

Andy's head lurched down to the garage floor, and then he slowly kneeled down and picked up the iPod. Cracks ran across its tiny screen.

"Way to go, Mom," Andy bit out.

"What did *I* do?" Judi said.

"You couldn't leave us alone! I was about to pick it up and you came in here flippin' out!"

"Hey," Rip said. "It's not her fault."

"Is it broken?" Judi asked. "Let me see it."

Andy held it up and gave her a look of disgust.

"Oh, Andy. I'm sorry," Judi said, resuming her usual doubtful look again.

"No worries," Rip said. "If it doesn't work, we can fix it or get a new one."

Andy held it up and studied it like he'd never seen it before. He raised one of the earbuds to his ear. "Who . . . who is that singing?"

"Singing what?" Rip asked.

Andy just kept squinting at the iPod.

"Hey," Rip said. "No worries, bro. I said we can fix it."

Andy frowned.

"Give me that," Rip said. Andy handed him the iPod. Rip pressed the power button off and on and could see the screen light up behind the cracks. He couldn't hear anyone singing, but whatever kind of music Andy heard, he was going to have to get used to it, because there was no way he would be able to change anything with the busted touch screen.

"I could hear somebody singing something, Uncle Rip."

Rip handed it back to Andy and shrugged. "Isn't that what you normally hear in an iPod?"

Andy gave him another puzzled look. "But I didn't download that song."

"Don't know what to tell you."

"The song sounded weird," Andy said.

"All the music you listen to is weird," Rip said. "Looks like you are gonna have to get used to it until we get it fixed."

"Do you really think I can get a new one?"

Rip wasn't surprised that Andy was looking at him instead of Judi. "Let's see if we can fix this one before we go spending any money."

"Just make sure you fix that bike first," Judi said, leaving the garage.

Andy held one of the earbuds to his ear and made another strange face.

"Let's get to work," Rip said, grabbing the throttle on the bike.

"How slow you gonna make it?" Andy asked.

"Heather said it would probably be best to knock the speed in half."

Andy didn't say anything. He just looked at the ground.

"So if they clocked you going seventy-three near the park," Rip said, "I'm sure you were driving safe and didn't have it gunned all the way out, did you?"

"No, I didn't," Andy said.

Rip winked at him, and Andy smiled appreciatively.

"So what do you think the top speed is?" Rip asked. "About a hundred?"

Andy's smile widened. "Something like that."

Rip took a screwdriver and adjusted the governor on the bike's throttle and then looked at his nephew. "I'm thinking the top speed on this is now about fifty or sixty, but I have a feeling the fastest it will ever go outside of Ripley's Field is only about thirty. What do you think?"

"I promise," Andy said. "Thanks, Uncle Rip."

Rip held out his fist and they pounded knuckles. There was nothing better than seeing his nephew smile. And Rip knew he'd do about anything to see it again.

※ ※ ※

Even though it was only a few minutes past nine o'clock, Andy was exhausted and back up in his bedroom. He closed the Bible and placed it on the nightstand. He felt like he owed it to Uncle Rip to give the Bible another whirl. He'd been reading for a couple hours, skipping around different parts of the Old Testament, but the more he read, the more unbelievable it became.

Noah floated around in a wooden boat with two of every animal on it.

Abraham had a kid when he was crazy-old.

Moses parted the Red Sea and then he and his followers walked right through it.

"Phonies," he said to the bedroom ceiling, quoting his new friend, Holden Caulfield, from *The Catcher in the Rye.*

Those Bible guys and their stories were nothing but a bunch of garbage. Good things don't always happen to good people. In fact, in the world Andy knew, the good guy never won.

Never.

Andy had prayed to God about the scar on his face for as long as he could remember, and either those prayers had fallen on deaf ears, or God didn't care. So as far as he was concerned, the whole God-thing was a waste of time because bad things happened for no reason at all, and God didn't seem too interested in doing much of anything about it. Andy loved Uncle Rip and would repeat his rules if it made him happy. But it didn't mean he had to believe them himself.

Andy sat up in bed and glanced around the empty walls of his bedroom. There was just beige paint. No posters of rock stars, teen beauties, rappers, or other pretty people. He didn't bother with them either, because just like the Bible, those people also lived in a world he didn't know.

He rolled off the bed and woke up Milo, who was curled up on his yellow blanket. Andy went over to the dresser, pulled a couple pretzels out of a bag, flipped one to Milo, then opened the top drawer and took out the mirror. He pulled his long hair back off the side of his neck and studied the scar. And then he put the mirror back and took a long look back at the Bible on the nightstand.

"Why don't You talk to me like You talked to Abraham or Moses?" he whispered. "Am I not worth it?"

He closed the drawer and then went and lay back on the bed. He turned the lamp off and stared at the dark ceiling, looking forward to riding the motorcycle tomorrow.

Andy leaned over and patted Milo on his head. "Good night, boy."

He put his head back on the pillow, closed his eyes, and yawned. When he opened his eyes back up, he could see a little yellow flash beaming against a shadow on the ceiling. And then he could hear a song. The broken iPod was on top of his dresser. He and Uncle Rip had fiddled with it, unable to get the touch screen to change, and now it looked like the stupid power button was malfunctioning and the flippin' thing was turning off and on by itself.

Just my luck. I'll be up all night.

He stood again and stomped over to the dresser. He lifted one of the earbuds to his ear and the music immediately stopped. He powered it off and then went and lay down again. And then he closed his eyes and thought about Noah and how long he lived.

"Yeah, right," he mumbled in the dark. *"Nine hundred and fifty years."*

SEVEN

Rip liked Saturdays, but wasn't planning on spending most of the day alone. He didn't make it over to Judi's until about noon, and she and Heather had already taken off to the flea market over in Romulus to check out some antique sale. He knew there was no way Andy would have gone with them, so Rip figured the kid had to be out and about around town, getting his miles in on his new dirt bike.

Rip had decided since he was already at Judi's place that he'd make the most of his alone time, so he grabbed a box of Cheez-Its out of Judi's pantry and bribed Milo to come with him out to The Frank and Poet for another look at the flower garden. By the time they had walked out there, Milo had hit him up for half the box.

"Who in the world would plant that over there?" Rip said out loud as he sat on the bank and looked at the flowers. He'd been asking himself that question for the better part of two hours, and his best guess was that it was the work of some beautification committee, or some sort of whacked bio-art installation. But that made no sense because the only people who would ever see it would be those who happened to be on Judi's property or passengers on low-flying airplanes.

Regardless of the logic, Rip couldn't deny that he felt good just looking at it. Its dimensions were flawless and the gardener's work had left him feeling as if there was a presence or force in there waiting for him, *wanting* him. Even Andy had said *something* was in there. But then there was something else. Rip wasn't sure how he knew, but he was oddly certain that whatever was in the garden, he hadn't earned access to it yet. Kind of like when he was in prison for only a few months and tried applying for a furlough.

"What's over there?" he said.

Milo was down in the canal, wading in a foot of water and daring a pair of mallards to come closer. He looked back at Rip like he wanted to know who Rip was talking to.

"Let's go, Milo," Rip said, standing.

Milo ignored him and growled at the ducks.

"Treat," Rip said and shook the box of Cheez-Its. Milo shot up the bank and was at Rip's feet before he had the box open. "Tell me what's over in those flowers, Milo."

Rip tossed a handful of crackers on the ground and Milo went to work on them, putting them away in a matter of seconds. Milo looked up at him and Rip shook his head at the dog, whose pink tongue hung out the side of his mouth like a thick slice of ham.

"You are spoiled rotten, you know that?"

Rip dropped another handful of crackers on the ground and then looked back across The Frank and Poet at the flowers.

He knew it'd be trespassing to wander onto the old McLouth Steel property. But the drive to know more about the garden—and what was inside it—was too powerful to ignore.

❊ ❊ ❊

Kevin Hart stood in the darkness at the end of the dock. He looked out at the lake, and in the distance he could see lights gliding slowly across the water from the handful of boats that were out for late-night rides. Beyond them, more lights bunched together—as if stars had fallen and congregated on the ground, outlining the Canadian shore on the far side of the lake.

He sat at the edge of the dock and listened as little waves splashed against the shore, wondering if anyone knew what he'd been up to. He looked over his shoulder, back at his house. There weren't any lights on, but he could still see its mammoth silhouette, which made him smile in satisfaction. His house, the best and biggest house in town.

So big, even his dad would have been proud.

The thought warmed him, but then a light came on up on the third level, making his blood run cool. It was their bedroom. Carrie was home. Through the windows, he watched her walk across the room and then down the hallway. He'd have to wait until she fell asleep before he went out, but she'd probably been drinking over at the club, so he knew it wouldn't be long.

He stood and walked toward the house and another light came on up on the same level. It was to the right of the bedroom. Carrie was in the library now. He stopped and studied the two lights. They reminded him of something. It was as if the house were a head and the lights were the eyes of a crazy person looking down on him, watching his every move.

Gone was the pride. Here was the fury. The defiance.

He started walking again, maintaining eye contact with the lights.

And then he laughed.

No one knows what I've been doing. Not even you.

⚹ ⚹ ⚹

Heather watched as her mom, Sharon, thumbed the TV's remote control. *Wheel of Fortune* was about to start and if her mother ever missed a single episode or rerun that ran at eleven every night, End Times surely weren't far behind.

"I can't believe they haven't fired me yet," Heather said. "I never should have gone to the flea market today. Maybe I just didn't get enough sleep."

"When your daddy was on the force, police cars got dinged up all the time," Mom said. "You are getting yourself all worked up over nothing."

"I just backed into a dumpster between Mack's and the pharmacy," Heather said. "The car is brand new."

"That's why they call them *accidents*," Mom said.

"It's my fourth accident in the last three years alone," Heather said, thinking about two accidents ago. It was the middle of winter and hers was the *only* car to slide off of West Jefferson and into a ditch. Hundreds of passersby seemed to get their kicks out of the bumbling cop who had to stand there and watch a tow truck pull her cruiser out of four feet of water. She could still hear them laughing.

"You're making a big deal out of nothing," Mom said. "Besides, I have known Chief Reynolds since before you were born. I'd give him an earful."

Heather didn't want to keep her job because of her mother's and dead father's relationship with the chief of police. In fact, she wasn't sure she wanted to keep it at all, but opportunities for employment weren't exactly falling off trees in Benning.

"You want to go to church with me tomorrow?" Heather asked.

Mom found her *Wheel of Fortune* channel, but it seemed the volume wasn't quite cooperating. She was tapping at buttons and shaking the remote back and forth like she was trying to knock some good sense into it.

"Oh, you just go and say a prayer for me," Mom said.

Heather could've mouthed the response with her. Mom hadn't been to church in ten years, but Heather still asked her each Saturday night.

"Let's go for a walk tomorrow, then," Heather said. "I want to talk to you about something."

A commercial for life insurance helped Heather get her mother's attention. It was insurance just like the kind on the television, along with social security and a small percentage of her father's pension, that allowed Mom to sit in the family room and watch soap operas and game shows for fifteen hours a day.

Mom raised the remote and hit the mute button. It worked on the first try. "I could use a good walk. We'll go right after *Wheel* is over tomorrow."

"Great," Heather said, more than a little surprised Mom was up for leaving the house, not to mention missing the rerun of *Jeopardy* that was surely to follow.

"What do you want to talk about?"

Heather paused for a few seconds. It had never been a popular subject, the thing that had made them who they were.

"About what happened to Daddy and Mr. Hart. But mostly about Daddy."

Mom laughed humorlessly, her good mood fleeing. "Maybe we should talk about why you broke up with Mr. Hart's boy. You and Kevin would have made a beautiful couple and I wouldn't have to be up every night worrying about you. You should have been a teacher, like you wanted to be."

Heather shook her head. If she had a dollar for every time Mom reminded her of her failed relationship with Kevin Hart or how she should have been a teacher, she'd be a rich woman. Or at least have enough money to go back to school and finish getting her teacher's certificate.

"Kevin broke up with me, Mom. You know that. And that was a long time ago."

"Follow your gut."

"What do you mean?" Heather asked.

Mom pointed at the TV, which was still on mute. She had solved the puzzle a good thirty seconds before Vanna tapped on the *T* that completed both the phrase and the word *GUT*.

"Did Daddy ever tell you about any of the religious things he and Mr. Hart talked about?" Heather asked.

"Not really," Mom said. "Hart was quite the Bible thumper, though. He'd been after your daddy to get to church for years. Why you asking?"

Heather wasn't planning on telling her mother about the sign-of-the-cross prowler. She also had no intention of sharing how the intruder had somehow pulled a question out from the very back of her mind . . . *the very question* she'd been painfully asking herself for years.

Still, she needed to ask her mother.

"Mom," she said, already wanting—*needing*—the answer to be yes. She paused.

"What is it, Heather?"

"Do you think Daddy is in heaven?"

"Oh, there you go again," Mom said. "Drumming up the past. I'm not going to talk about this right now."

"Okay," Heather said, thinking about the only real conversation she and her mother ever shared about her father's death.

Heather was a sophomore in high school and had just walked in the door from an afternoon pool party with the other Benning

High JV cheerleaders. Her mom was sitting on the couch, watching the television, but the TV wasn't even on. Heather remembered knowing something was wrong and then sitting next to her mother on the couch without saying a word. Mom just stared at the TV without blinking, and when Heather put her hand on her mother's shoulder, Mom said it.

"A bad thing has happened to your daddy . . . a really bad thing . . ."

Mom had never quite made a comeback after that terrible day, and Heather wasn't sure if she had either. But knowing if her father was in a good place had become a question she needed to answer, and not having anyone to talk to about it bothered her.

Heather stood, disappointed that she didn't have the gumption to press the matter further with her mother. Once and for all. But she also didn't have time to push it now; she had to get back to work.

"See ya, Mom," she called, heading out the door to her car. The cruiser, the *freshly dented* cruiser, had been parked in Mom's driveway for close to a half hour and her night shift was far from over.

❋ ❋ ❋

He was a little disappointed that the Benning Township Recreation Center didn't have an alarm on its back door. But then again, he wasn't all that surprised. If they couldn't afford decent baseball equipment for the kids, there wasn't much sense in paying to protect it from would-be thieves or other types of crazies who may show up in the middle of the night.

He laughed out loud and adjusted the black ski mask he was wearing. It was way too hot to have the stupid thing on, but something about wearing it made him feel better.

He glanced up at the window above him. It had only taken him a few minutes to shimmy through it, and once he was inside, he had quickly determined that the best way for him to bring the new equipment in was through the back door. The rec center was right in the middle of the park, so earlier in the day he had dumped all the equipment over in the woods and neatly covered it with branches and a camouflage tarp, knowing it would take him a few trips to get it all inside when he came back tonight.

He opened the back door and gazed around the dark, heavily wooded park. Not a soul in sight. This was going to be too easy.

Or is it?

He could see headlights winding through the trees. He stepped around the corner of the building and waited as the car came toward him.

He smiled. It was a police car.

Maybe there's an alarm . . . Maybe there's a chance . . .

The cruiser drove right by and made its way toward the other end of the park.

Come back, he thought. *Come back.*

EIGHT

Judi lowered the leg rest on the old La-Z-Boy and glanced at the grandfather clock. She'd been up since four a.m. and if she went back upstairs, she wouldn't be able to sleep. She put one foot up on the chair and wrapped her arms around her leg. Then she rested her chin on top of her knee before closing her eyes.

Are things ever going to get better?

She slowly began to rock back and forth, wondering if Rip's idea of taking Andy for the rest of the summer was something she should consider. If anyone could ever bring Andy out of his funk, it would be Rip, and maybe it would be easier without her around.

Judi stood and walked to the window, looking out into the darkness of the front yard. All she could see was her own reflection in the glass, and she noticed the shine in her eyes. She had been crying and didn't even know it. She stepped back from the window, wiped at her eyes with the sleeves of her pajamas, and then she thought she heard someone talking.

She turned around and listened, waiting to hear it again.

73

She wandered into the kitchen and glanced at the small radio on the counter. That wasn't it.

And then she heard her name, but this time the voice sounded a little more familiar.

It was Andrew.

She took a step into the family room and faced the stairs, cocking her head toward the ceiling.

"Andy?" she said.

"Come here, Judith Ann."

Judith Ann?

He sounded more like her father than her son, and Judi walked quickly to the stairs and made her way up to Andy's bedroom door. It was open and he was sitting up in his bed with his eyes closed and his iPod in his hand. Only one of his earbuds was in and his head was perfectly still, his chin tilted up toward the ceiling. He was smiling.

For a moment, she just stared. How long had it been since she'd seen her son that open? That happy and content? Forever, it seemed.

"Judith Ann," Andy repeated, his eyes still closed.

"Why are you calling me that?" Judi asked.

Andy opened his eyes and looked right at her. It seemed like he was in a trance when his smile faded.

"I will forgive their wickedness and remember their sins no more."

"What?" Judi said, taking a little step toward him. A tiny finger of hope poked at her insides. He was talking to her and it was without hatred or sarcasm. But what was he saying?

Andy squinted at her and shook his head like he had just woken up. The familiar look of hatred returned to his face. "What do *you* want?"

Judi took a step back as if he had slapped her. "What did you just say to me?"

Andy lay down and pulled the covers over his head. "Nothing! Go away!"

She just stared at him, not really caring that he wanted her to leave. Had he been dreaming?

"Fine," she said, walking over and turning off the lamp. "I've just never heard you call me Judith Ann before. And it was good to see you smile."

"I have no idea what you are talking about."

"Fine. Pretend nothing happened. That's okay."

He ignored her.

She stepped back into the hallway. "In fact, I truthfully can't remember the last time anybody called me Judith Ann."

Andy pulled the covers off his face and stared at the ceiling. "*Truthfully?* Maybe someday we will sit down and really talk about what *truthfully* means."

"Let's do it right now," Judi said, going back into his room and walking to the edge of the bed. She didn't like his tone, but the fact that he was talking to her at all gave her hope.

Andy sat up in the middle of the bed, as if to let her know sitting on it with him would be a bad idea. "Seriously? We're really going to do this at four in the morning?"

"Hey, you were the one who called me up here," she said.

Andy sighed and ran his hand through his long hair. He stared up at her. "*Truthfully,* Mom. You and the truth don't even belong in the same room together."

Judi held her hands up in disbelief. "What are you talking about? I've never lied to you about anything, Andrew. Why would you say that?"

Andy leaned toward her and pulled his hair back, exposing the scar on his face and neck. "Even about this?"

Judi took a step back. It was almost as if he had shoved her. "What do you mean?"

"I know why I look like this," he said. "*I know.*"

Andy didn't know. They had all agreed it was in his best interest to never talk about that night. When he was little, he didn't seem to care. But now, it was as if *he really did know* how he'd been burned. She paused and thought about it again. It was impossible . . . there was no way Andy could know how it happened. Did he blame her? For the burn? That she didn't protect him on that terrible night?

"Your accident was an *accident,*" she said softly, miserably. She stared at him for a long moment. "Is this why . . . Is this why you act like you hate me?"

He didn't say anything. A few more seconds passed and Judi wasn't sure if she had *really* even asked him. But still, she wanted the answer. She wanted to hear why he'd changed. Hear it from him.

There is no good reason for hating someone, she thought.

There had been no progression, no warm-up event, nothing that had festered and grown until it popped. Just a simple flick of some cruel and mysterious switch that flipped on when he was eight.

And that was it.

Andy had gone from her lively little boy, her best friend, *her little pal* . . . to who he'd been for six years. Who he was now.

But he couldn't know what happened. They'd all promised. Sworn it.

"Tell me," she said. "I love you and deserve to know what I did that was so bad. Things were so good between us, and then one day, just out of the blue, they weren't anymore."

"You really want to know?" Andy said.

"Yes."

"This," he said, pulling the hair off the side of his face again.

She swallowed hard, looking at the scar. "What about it?"

"It's your fault."

"Why would you say that?"

Andy looked at the ceiling and then his eyes settled back on her. She reached out and gripped the doorjamb as the same thought rolled over and over again in her mind.

He does know. I failed to protect him.

His hatred reminded her of Todd's. And then more thoughts ran through her mind, the more familiar ones. How she failed at her marriage. How she had failed herself. How she had failed at *everything.*

Andy was right.

And then she said it. Her mouth moving without her thinking about it.

"You're right, Andy. It was my fault."

❄ ❄ ❄

"Nobody said being a Christian was easy," Pastor Edward Welsh said from behind the old desk in his office at St. Paul's Church. He scratched at his graying beard with big hands that belonged to someone who should have swung a hammer for a living. Welsh turned his head slightly, exposing some of the ponytail that ended beneath his shoulders. "In fact, being a Christian can sometimes be a challenge."

"Amen," Rip said, sitting in one of the two chairs across from the minister.

Rip did his best to spend a few minutes with Welsh every Sunday morning before service. Though he couldn't exactly put his finger on the cause, the men shared an invisible bond, and Rip appreciated Welsh's guidance in keeping him on track in his new walk as a Christian.

"And with it comes a great deal of responsibility," Welsh added, pushing his thick, black-rimmed glasses back up the bridge of his porous red nose, the kind of nose that was normally found on heavy drinkers. "Why does it bother you that Andy thinks you are preaching to him?"

"I think what he really means is that I *lecture* him."

"That's what I figured," Welsh said in a tired voice. He had just celebrated his seventieth birthday but looked closer to eighty. But Rip suspected that Welsh was one of those guys who'd always looked old. Welsh wasn't afraid to poke fun at himself about it either. Little jokes about having worked on the ark or being a waiter at the Last Supper were among his favorites.

"That's what you figured?" Rip repeated, frowning. "I keep telling myself I want my actions to show my faith, not my mouth. But it's tough."

"Sometimes we rush to judge others, or tell them how to lead their lives, because they sin differently than we do," Welsh said and smiled.

Rip smiled back. "I like that."

Welsh leaned forward and brought his hands to the sides of his face, covering road maps of broken blood vessels that littered his cheeks. "What do you think Andy thinks about you, Rip?"

"We are best friends," Rip said. "At least we used to be."

"That doesn't answer my question," Welsh said.

Rip thought about whether or not he really wanted to answer, but if there was anybody on the planet he felt safe with, it was Welsh.

"I really don't know," Rip said. "Other than knowing I sold drugs most of my life, I really don't know what he thinks of me. I just know he doesn't care for my lectures."

Welsh patted his palms against the desk. "Nobody likes to be lectured, Rip. And just about everybody in town is aware of the fact that you are a former drug dealer and that you were in prison."

"I guess that's probably true," Rip said.

"You still sell dope?"

"Of course not," Rip said, a little taken aback.

"Then who cares that other people know what you *used* to do?" Welsh said. "We all screw up. *All of us.* And I really believe you want to be a good Christian. But at the risk of *lecturing* you, stay focused on doing the right things and you won't have to lecture others. Focus on taking out the old parts of you and putting in the new. All of those bad things you used to do died with Christ, Rip. Let your behavior inspire, because that is where we can make the *biggest* impact as Christians."

"It's hard, letting my past go," Rip said. "I don't know what I have to do to wipe that slate clean, but I just want people to know that I'm not that person anymore."

"God knows it and you know it," Welsh said. "Don't worry what others think—even Andy—and just keep doing your thing."

"My thing?"

Welsh smiled. "That motorcycle you just gave to Andy isn't safe."

"Yeah, it is," Rip said, unsure of where the minister was heading with the sudden topic change.

Welsh stood and pounded his fist on the table. "No, it isn't!"

"Yeah, it is," Rip repeated with a frown, wondering why Welsh was acting so out of character. "I worked on it myself. I know the bike is all right."

"So then it doesn't matter what I think about the bike?"

Rip squinted for a few seconds and then smiled. "I get it."

"We better get going to service," Welsh said, stepping to the side of the desk. "Just like that bike . . . work on you, and you'll be all right. So will Andy."

❋ ❋ ❋

St. Paul's was both the oldest and the biggest church in Benning, and Rip was sitting in the very back pew with Andy, hearing but not listening to Kevin Hart as Hart flipped through the prayer request cards and made the week's announcements. When Hart was finished, Pastor Welsh would give them a nod to collect the offering.

"What are you looking at?" Rip said, nudging Andy's leg.

"Nothing," Andy said.

Andy had a peculiar look on his face. It also appeared he was having a hard time keeping his eyes off the Cochran family, about ten rows up. He was obviously checking out the teenage girl who had joined them for service.

"Hey, Romeo," Rip whispered. "Quit staring. Don't be so obvious."

"I'm not staring."

"And you don't call your mom by her first and middle name either," Rip said.

"I never did that."

"She said you called her Judith Ann. Let me guess. Mom's just being crazy again, eh?"

"Guess so," Andy said, shooting him a quick glance from the corner of his eye before looking back up toward Kevin Hart. As much as he didn't want to, Rip did the same.

Despite Hart standing at the lectern, Rip felt good at St. Paul's. Something about the place made it feel like home, and of all the houses God had, this was by far Rip's favorite. The two rows of dark wooden pews that gleamed with care and attention probably could have held three times the couple hundred people who were there now. Surrounding them, stone walls and stained-glass windows led to thick beams that supported a wooden ceiling that matched the color of the pews. Rip loved that ceiling. If he had to guess what the bottom of Noah's ark looked like, it would be the ceiling of St. Paul's. Maybe it had something to do with the fact that the ceiling *was* originally created to be the bottom of a ship by Detroit ship-builder Big Quincy Hart. Legend had it that Big Quincy sold the ship bottom to St. Paul's founders right before dying of a mystery illness in his midthirties.

Rip glanced back at the front of the church. He'd rather listen to Big Quincy talk about how he got his virus from Typhoid Mary than listen to Quincy's grandson's grandson, who was still spouting off at the lectern.

"It's important that we do the right things to strengthen the community," Hart said. "It's important that we give back."

Being one person on Sunday and somebody else the rest of the week wasn't that uncommon in the world, but Kevin Hart had taken it to another level. He truly was the master, so Rip leaned forward and propped his elbows up on the pew in front of him. He didn't want to miss the tail end of Hart's performance.

But as he talked, Rip felt a pang of pain, what Welsh would call a holy conviction. He knew what was missing from Hart's life. He knew because the same thing used to be missing from his own life.

And despite Hart's whispered claims of having more money than God, what was missing was something even he couldn't afford, because Someone else had already picked up the tab. And even though it was absolutely free, it was invaluable.

A relationship with God.

Rip bit gently on his lip, unsure of why Hart's behind-the-scenes behavior bothered him so much. But there Hart stood, speaking flawlessly with his $1,500 suit and his slicked-back brown hair.

"We will continue to collect nonperishables all week at the Hart

Industries parking lot, and our team will make sure your donations get where they need to be."

Our team? And I thought he wanted all those cans out of there . . .

Yep, Hart was the perfect husband. Mr. Community. President of the congregation. Model citizen.

If the town only knew.

Pastor Welsh gave Rip and Andy the nod and Hart took his seat next to his wife.

Rip stood and smiled at the poor woman who was sitting in the last row across the aisle. He wouldn't bother holding the offering basket out to her again this week, even though she had just hit the mother lode of gift cards. *Good thing*, he thought. *When you don't have to worry about your kids' next meal, maybe getting your life together will be a whole lot easier.*

Rip glanced at Judi and Heather and watched as Andy approached their row. Andy was holding his right arm out, his thin fingers holding the basket, waiting for Judi to drop the thirty dollars she and Andy gave every week. Dangling out of his back pocket were his earbuds. Rip smiled, guessing that was Andy's way of reminding him of the replacement they discussed. *Keep 'em visible 24/7 and maybe Uncle Rip will remember to buy you a new iPod . . .*

Rip reached the front row where Andy handed him his basket, and he caught Andy glancing back toward the Cochrans again. Rip smiled and gave Andy a little tap with his elbow and his nephew shook his head.

After service, Rip and Andy sat at a long folding table across from Heather and Judi. Rip guessed that at least half of the two hundred who attended were scattered around the fellowship hall, drinking coffee, sipping punch, and tentatively planning a fundraiser for the youngest of the Cochrans. Eight-year-old Marjo had a kidney disorder that had already emptied her family's piggy bank, and if the latest round of treatments didn't pan out, the last stop would be a six-figure surgery that would take deeper pockets than most of Benning had. Rip figured that Kevin and Carrie Hart would naturally be spearheading the event and that it would somehow turn into a black-tie affair. Rip quietly sipped at his coffee, knowing that he and a few other Hart employees would surely be invited. Valet and bartenders were usually a must at any event the Harts put on.

Heather had a distant look on her face. She was probably thinking about her armed encounter the other night. She wore very little makeup, and something about the way her dark brown ponytail rested on the front of her left shoulder made her look more like a schoolkid than a cop.

"Cheer up, Officer Gerisch," he said. "God loves you."

"I know," she said unconvincingly. "I need to talk to you later, Rip."

"About how you still aren't over me and have been trying to figure out a way to ask me out?"

"Seriously," she said. "I'm swinging by Judi's later and hopefully just you and I can chat for a bit."

"Cool," Rip said as Andy got up and walked over to the punch table. Andy was never big on Kool-Aid and cookies, but the table was a lot closer to the teenage beauty queen who had caught his eye. Rip tapped Heather on the arm. "Check out Casanova."

"Chelsea sure has grown up this summer, hasn't she?" Heather said. "Looks like Andy has found himself a little crush."

"That's Chelsea Cochran?" Rip asked.

"Sure is," Heather said.

The last time Rip had seen Chelsea, she was considerably shorter and was wearing a pair of glasses with lenses about as thick as Coke bottles—the type that you could burn ants with. Now she was in full charge of Cupid, and had apparently given the little guy orders to shower arrows on Andy.

Rip looked away from Chelsea and back to his nephew. The kid had a strange look on his face. He was holding his iPod in front of him and playing with one of the earbuds. He looked confused, so Rip joined him.

"You all right, bro?" Rip asked.

Andy just stared at the iPod with an expression Rip had never seen. Andy put the one earbud in his ear and said, "Who is singing?"

It was the exact same thing Andy had asked right after he had stepped on the iPod in the garage. Rip found the coincidence a little strange but dismissed it. "Is the iPod working?"

Andy didn't answer. He held the iPod in front of him, the cracked screen facing up in his open palm, and studied it. He poked again at the screen. Then he closed his eyes.

"What are you doing?" Rip asked.

"Un-Uncle Rip . . . who is that?"

Andy started to shake as he held the iPod.

"What are you talking about?" Rip asked. The entire fellowship hall had gone quiet, looking their way. He took Andy by the arm. "Let's step over here."

Judi stood. "Rip, what's happening?"

"What?" Andy yelled. He was squeezing his eyes closed.

The whole room waited in silence until Andy stopped shaking. His eyes were still closed, but his body seemed to relax. And then he removed the one earbud. His head slowly tilted back until he was facing the ceiling. And then a broad, Stevie Wonder–like smile spread across his face as his head swayed slowly back and forth. And then he became still again.

"Andrew?" Judi said, walking toward him.

Rip held up his arm for her to stop, and Andy opened his eyes.

"Kevin Frances," Andy said sternly. He was still smiling and facing the ceiling. It looked like he was almost squinting but his eyes were closed.

"Who are you talking to?" Rip asked, still holding Andy softly by the arm. Andy sounded like a schoolteacher taking roll. "Why are you—"

Andy brushed Rip's hand away and took a step back. He started looking around the room and his eyes hunted with a purpose Rip had never seen.

"You all right, Andy?" Rip asked.

Andy's eyes fixed on Kevin Hart and he walked straight over to him, then raised an earbud next to Hart's ear.

"You okay, buddy?" Hart asked, pushing away Andy's hand and then glancing around the room.

Andy stared at Hart for too long.

"Kevin Frances," Andy said again, this time calmer, yet still fatherly.

Hart looked uncomfortable. "What, Andy?"

"I have searched you, and I know you."

Rip couldn't believe what he had just heard. He turned to Judi, whose mouth gaped open. Rip swallowed hard. This wasn't going to end well. Whatever was happening, the boss wouldn't like being called out. At that moment there was no doubt in Rip's mind that Andy somehow knew about Hart's girlfriends . . . the cheating . . . the lying . . . but Rip was more transfixed by Andy himself. He sounded confident, and even the way he stood had a strange aura of authority and his words carried an almost parental tone. It was like he was someone else.

Hart smiled uncomfortably and looked around the room again. "What do you mean, Andy?"

Andy jerked, then looked confused. He took a step back and

shook his head. Then he looked at Rip. "What is Mr. Hart talking about?"

"I was gonna ask you the same thing Mr. Hart did," Rip said.

"Who told you to say that?" Hart asked Andy, shooting a glance at Rip.

"Say what?" Andy said.

Rip held out his hands and shrugged.

Andy held the iPod up in his left palm and then pressed on it with his right index finger. He lifted an earbud next to his ear and the room went completely silent again.

"Who was that?" Andy said. "Who was that singing?"

NINE

Mack's Café was one of Andy's favorite places to go. The brick, one-story diner sat on the corner of Old Main Street and Kingsbridge, right next to the pharmacy and kitty-corner from Benning's only gas station, Carl's, which still had a full-service pump for those too old or too lazy to get out of their cars.

Mack's was owned by a man named Ray McIntosh, an old dude with powdery white skin and dyed black hair that was always slicked to the side with some type of shiny hair goo. Mr. McIntosh had always been nice to Andy. He even gave him twenty bucks every Wednesday to climb the metal ladder and sweep the leaves and branches that fell from the big trees out back onto the building's flat roof. Mr. McIntosh had offered fifty bucks a week last winter for Andy to go up there and shovel the snow off, but in a decision that shocked no one, Mom quickly vetoed that, naturally saying it was too dangerous and that he'd surely fall off the roof and break something.

It only took Andy around thirty minutes to sweep, so it

actually came out to around forty bucks an hour, not to mention the fifty-percent discount Mr. McIntosh gave his family whenever they ate there. With that in the mix, they always came here after church—and on most other occasions—because tightwad Judi would never drive the extra three minutes over into Rockwood to go to McDonald's. Not when such savings were readily available at Mack's.

But this Sunday no one was talking about what they were ordering, their typical routine. No, this Sunday they were all about what had just happened at church. They wouldn't leave it alone.

"Kevin Frances?" Uncle Rip said, tapping his finger on the side of a saltshaker. "How do you know Kevin Hart's middle name?"

"I don't remember saying any of that stuff," Andy said. He thought about getting up and leaving the restaurant.

"You said it," Uncle Rip said. "Right to Kevin Hart."

Mom had her usual clueless look when she said, "You didn't remember talking to me like that either."

"I swear to God I'm leaving if you guys don't change the subject," Andy said.

"Don't say 'swear to God,'" Mom said.

"Then let's talk about your interest in Chelsea Cochran," Uncle Rip said, giving him a teasing smile. "She's grown up a little, eh?"

"Let's talk about your interest in Heather," Andy fired back. Chelsea had sure gotten pretty, but there was no way he'd tell Uncle Rip that. Besides, Chelsea wouldn't be interested in a kid who looked like he had a piece of pizza glued to the side of his face.

"Okay," Uncle Rip said. "Let's talk motorcycles. Now that yours is all fixed up, one of these days I'm gonna bring that other hunk of junk over. Want to help me fix it up so I can ride with you?"

"Yeah," Andy said. "That sounds good." It did sound good. What also sounded good was figuring out how to mess with that throttle on his own bike so he could see what it felt like to go close to a hundred.

"Cool," Uncle Rip said, glancing over at the booth across the aisle at a group of older kids.

Andy didn't recognize any of them and guessed they were from another town. What he did recognize was the stare from people when they noticed his scar. He quickly pulled his hair forward.

"What are you guys looking at?" Uncle Rip asked. It was kind of loud and Andy was embarrassed.

"C'mon, Rip," Mom said. "Just ignore them."

"Don't worry about it," the biggest one said in a deep voice. He had a brown crew cut and dark brown eyes. He had big arms like Uncle Rip, and Andy had him pegged as a football player or a wrestler. He finished off the last of his burger.

"Okay," Uncle Rip said. "I won't worry about it, then."

Andy was surprised at the way his uncle handled himself. He had never seen Uncle Rip fight, but he'd heard a lot of the stories about how he was the last person anybody wanted to mess with. Maybe he was showing some of that control he preached about.

But the football player's friends were jostling him, clearly egging him on. Almost pushing him toward Uncle Rip.

"You Scarface's guard dog or something?" the kid said. Andy winced inwardly but he held it together. Over the years, he'd heard just about every name possible.

Uncle Rip picked up his water glass and tilted it toward the kid like he was going to make a toast. "How old are you, son?"

"Nineteen."

Uncle Rip's baby finger came off the glass and pointed at the other two guys who were probably about the same age. "How about your two buddies there?"

"Twenty and nineteen. Why?"

Uncle Rip stared at the kid and it was clear he meant business. He looked like a guy who had just stepped barefoot on a Lego, maybe even a little possessed, and when he put the glass down and grabbed the metal napkin holder, you could see the muscles ripple in his forearms.

"Because I got out of prison about a year ago," Uncle Rip said. "And if you were under eighteen, I'd have no choice but to let your punk mouth slide. But seeing that you are an adult, I think me against you three sounds pretty fair. So why don't you and your two girlfriends go out in the parking lot and practice falling down. I'll be right out."

Andy could tell by the looks on all three of their faces that they clearly thought Uncle Rip was crazy; a normal person would never take on three people. And though Uncle Rip probably hadn't needed to mention it, the whole "I just got out of prison" bit had to have added fuel to the fear fire.

The kid who did all the talking was silent. His other friends seemed to be ready to wade into a fight, to see it through, but not Mr. Football. He finally said, "Sorry, sir."

"I admire your sense of self-preservation," Uncle Rip said, staring at the boys just long enough for them to abandon the rest of their food, grab their bill, and leave the table without a tip.

Uncle Rip stood, reached in his pocket, then went to their table and dropped a five-dollar bill on it.

"Thanks for having my back," Andy said as Uncle Rip sat back down. "But you know something?"

"What?" Uncle Rip said quickly, still clearly fired up.

"You really need to work on your self-control. How about trying to think before you act or say something that may offend somebody?"

"Preaching to me?" Uncle Rip said with a grin.

Andy didn't say anything. It felt kind of good to throw Uncle Rip's words back at him.

"You're right, Andy," Uncle Rip said. "I need to try harder."

※ ※ ※

Heather stood at the base of the worn wooden steps on the side of Rip's mobile home. The exterior of the place was a complete train wreck. It had to be the oldest home in the park, and it was the *only* single-wide she had seen while driving in. It sat in the far back corner, under the overhang of an enormous oak tree whose shade failed to cover the collection of makeshift repairs on the ancient metal roof. Kevin Hart owned the park along with Rip's single-wide rental. She took a step back and noticed the aluminum skirting that ran along the base of the mobile home was dented. Beneath it was a pair of Frisbee-sized holes in the ground that made the bottom of Rip's place look like a parking garage for whatever critters were in the area. Gophers, she guessed.

She looked through an opening in the drapes. She could see Rip near the far wall, sitting on the couch. His legs were up on the table in front of him and a book was on his lap. It looked like he was staring at his cell phone.

She went up the three steps and rapped on the door. She could hear the floor creak and then the drapes moved. He looked surprised and held his index finger up. She nodded and then grinned as she watched him through the window, scrambling to do a quick tidy-up on the table and small living room.

The last time she had showed up unannounced was close to six years ago at the luxury apartment he lived in off Humbug Point. It was a favor from the department. They had kept her as far away from the investigation as they could, and when the multi-city case against Rip had become a slam dunk, Chief Reynolds had called her into his office. It was probably out of respect for her father, more than for her.

"Go arrest Gerald Ripley."

It was the second toughest day of her life, one she would never forget.

"I have to put the handcuffs on you, Rip."

She remembered how he had just smiled at her and calmly put his hands behind his back. When she had gotten him to the station, it was clear she'd been crying, but she was glad she'd been the one to arrest him. Not just for her sake, but for Judi's, and for Rip's.

But that was all behind them. Back when Rip was . . . different. Now she needed help, and she couldn't think of a better person to talk to than the man Rip had become.

The door opened. Rip stuck his head around the corner and smiled.

"I thought you were meeting me at Judi's," he said.

"I need to talk, Rip," she said. "Can I come in?"

"You have a warrant?"

"Shut up. I'm serious."

Rip tilted his head and his eyes rounded in curiosity.

"C'mon in," he said, stepping aside and holding out an open palm. "Welcome to my humble abode."

There was no air conditioning and the mobile home was uncomfortably warm. Still, she was surprised at how neat he kept it. "It smells good in here, Rip."

"Gotta burn a candle most of the time," he said. "It helps keep that old-house smell away."

The living room walls were covered in thin brown paneling that shined as if newly polished. He only had a couple cheaply framed pictures on the walls and there was no television in the room. The carpet was a light brown, threadbare at the center and darker as it got closer to the wall, where an old and worn sofa sat. Resting on top of a beat-up coffee table was Rip's Bible, his cell phone, a half glass of what she guessed was water, and a tiny white oscillating fan that wasn't oscillating, just blowing right at where Rip had been sitting.

"Very tidy, Rip," she said. "I'm impressed."

"Thanks," he said, guiding her toward the small kitchen table that only had two seats. It looked like one of the old setups from the cafeteria over at Hart Industries.

"First the motorcycle," Heather said, sitting down. "And a kitchen table to boot? Kevin's been pretty good to you, hasn't he?"

"Okay, Judi Junior," Rip said. "I'm thankful, even if we both know he's a complete tool."

"Kevin Frances looked a little startled today by Andy's comment."

"No more than anybody else," Rip said. "It's weird how Andy spoke with such purpose and such confidence. I just don't get it."

"How *did* he know Kevin's middle name?" Heather asked. "I dated him and didn't even know it."

"I have no clue," Rip said. "If my middle name was Frances, I wouldn't broadcast it either."

"Why would Andy think he knows everything about Kevin?" Heather asked.

"Huh?"

"That's what he told him at church."

"Those weren't Andy's words."

"What do you mean?"

"He was sort of quoting a Bible verse. It's from Psalms."

"I don't remember Andy going around quoting Bible verses. Quoting anything, for that matter."

"He doesn't remember doing it," Rip said. "Judi mentioned he said something strange to her last night, but she wasn't sure what it was. She said Andy called her using her middle name as well."

"You sure what he said is from the Bible?"

Rip blew out the candle and went back over near the sofa. He picked up the fan with one hand and his cell phone with the other. He came back in the kitchen and placed the fan on the counter, directly behind her. Heather welcomed the breeze on the back of her neck.

"Close enough," Rip said. He opened his cell phone and turned it toward her. "Read Psalm 139."

Heather leaned forward and read it off his smartphone: *"You have searched me, Lord, and you know me."*

Rip pointed at the phone. "Pretty close to what Andy said to Kevin, right?"

"Yes. But *why* would he say that to him?"

Rip held up his hands and shrugged. "I grilled him about it over lunch. He said he just remembered hearing strange music from his iPod, but didn't remember anything else. I kept harassing him, and I think he was actually getting a little miffed at me."

"Andy's miffed at the whole world."

"He's a teenager. He'll be all right," Rip said. "So what's on your mind?"

"God."

Rip stirred for a second, as if he thought she was kidding. "Really?"

"Yeah," she said. "I've got issues, Rip."

"I appreciate that revelation."

"Shut up, Rip. I'm trying to be serious here."

"Sorry," Rip said. Then he grinned and hiked his thumb to his chest. "Everyone has issues, Heather. Believe it or not, even me."

"You're doing really good, aren't you, Rip?" she asked. "I mean, you really have never seemed happier than you do now."

He smiled again. "To be honest with you, I never thought living in a single-wide and working for Kevin were good life goals. But I'm good now. I have everything I'll ever need. Plus, I have a little set aside for a rainy day."

"I thought we wiped you out during the raid," Heather said.

"You just about did," Rip answered.

Rip was wrong. They did wipe him out. After she arrested him, officers and agents from four different departments seized everything he owned. And between the money from selling Judi his half of Ripley's Field and the funds he'd amassed over the years from selling pot, they'd taken better than $600,000, leaving him set to start at ground zero when he was released from prison.

But that was something to talk about another day.

"Look," she said, leaning forward. "I know your faith is the real deal. And that's why I'm here. To talk to you about God."

"Me?" he asked, his eyebrows lifting in surprise. Then that nice smile, the one she'd always loved . . . "That makes me feel good, Heather. Thanks."

"I mean it," she said. "Something's changed in you. I think God has done it and I want to know more about it."

Rip shifted uncomfortably. "You know you can talk to Pastor Welsh about God whenever you want."

"I know," she said, giving him a little shrug. "I just thought . . ." Maybe it'd been a mistake. Coming here. Thinking they could have a deep conversation like old friends.

"Wait," he said, bending his head to look in her eyes. "Let me start over. I'm happy you came to talk, Heather. I'm all ears. Where do you want to start?"

She mulled it over for a few seconds and then dived in. "I have doubts."

"Doubts . . . about what?"

"About my dad."

Rip ran his hand along the side of his face, like he was trying to find the right words. "I'm assuming our little prowler friend from the other night got you thinking?"

She nodded. "He came up from behind me. He wasn't armed, Rip. But if he had been and wanted to hurt me, he could have. I turned around and raised my gun. I could tell that he knew . . . he knew I couldn't pull the trigger. But God knows I wanted to. To prove it to my dad. To prove it to myself."

"Prove what?"

"That I'm a good cop. That I'm honoring my dad's memory."

Rip seemed to consider her for a long moment and then looked down to his hands. "Heather, I think it's more than that. I think you think if you could just stop one bad guy, shoot him before he shoots someone innocent—"

"No, no, that's not it," she said, frowning.

"I think it is," he said gently. "I think you put such pressure on yourself—to be able to pull that trigger—so you'll feel like you're ready to find your dad's killer."

Heather swallowed hard. A tiny part of her admitted it. *He's right.*

Rip leaned forward and covered her hands with his own. They were warm and broad, encompassing hers, which were suddenly cold. "Sweetheart, it's not your job—or Kevin Hart's—to settle the score with the man who murdered your father. You need to lay that to rest and let God take care of it, in His time."

Heather took a deep breath and thought about the prowler, standing in that hallway and making the sign of the cross.

"Do you think my dad's in heaven, Rip?"

Rip brought his hand to his chin and paused for a second. "Why don't you tell me?"

"My gut tells me he is," Heather said, oddly remembering the *Wheel of Fortune* puzzle her mother had solved: FOLLOW YOUR GUT. "I tried to talk to my mom about this, but you know how she is."

Rip nodded.

"When it happened, when my dad died, I really don't know where he was. Spiritually speaking."

"Wasn't that why he was at Mr. Hart's house that night?" Rip asked. "Mr. Hart was a good man and a good Christian leader. You used to tell me that your dad went there to pray and read the Bible with him."

"I guess, but I still don't know what he believed."

"I'd say it's a good bet," Rip said. "Maybe we should pray that you can feel a sense of peace about it. And that you realize every bump in the night isn't the man who killed your father."

"Easier said than done."

"Okay," Rip said. "But I still think you should talk to God about it. I know He will help."

"Really think so?"

"Of course," Rip said. "I still struggle with all kinds of things."

"Like what?"

"You know . . . Mostly about my temper and how I can be a little judgmental."

"Like about Kevin?" she said. "He's not the bad guy you think he is, Rip."

"Yeah, right," Rip said and then laughed with his mouth closed. "But you know what? Every time I struggle and my baggage gets a little heavy, I pray about it. I talk to God like He is sitting right next to me. And guess what happens?"

"What?"

"That baggage gets lighter."

Heather forced a smile and leaned back in her chair. There was a sign above the door that caught her attention. Rip had taken a piece of cardboard and thumbtacked it in place. Written on it in black Magic Marker, in big thick letters, were the words SERVANTS' ENTRANCE.

"I like that," she said, pointing to the sign. She liked it a lot better than the answer Rip had just given her about her father. A simple *Yeah, I think he's in heaven* would have worked just fine.

"The words on that sign are true," Rip said. "Every time we step outside into the world, we can go serve God and serve others."

"I just wish I knew my father was in heaven," Heather said. "I want to be sure, you know? I think that ever since it happened, I've felt hollow, almost like I can't be entirely happy."

"What better smile could there possibly be than knowing someone you love is in heaven?" Rip asked. "That would be the best of smiles."

"Yes, it would," she said, glancing at her watch. "Oh. I've gotta hit it."

"That was quick," Rip said.

"Sorry," she said, knowing her departure was abrupt. "I guess I'm just in one of those moods. You gonna be at Judi's later?"

"Not a whole lot of other choices on my budget," Rip said. "But I kind of like hanging out with that nephew of mine."

Heather went to the door. She glanced back up at the sign and thought again about the prowler, and the way his hand moved, making that cross. And then a sickening thought ran through her head.

"What about next time?" she asked.

"Next time, what?" Rip said.

"What if the next bad guy has a gun, and he's not leaving gifts?

What if he intends to hurt me or someone else? What if I can't shoot?"

He held her gaze for a long time, and she thought he saw a shadow of worry. "Is it safe to assume the department doesn't know about your inability to pull the trigger?"

"*I* didn't even know about my inability to pull the trigger," she said. "I freaked out and blew all kinds of procedures. I swear I'm the worst cop ever."

"Then quit. I've been telling you that for years. You don't have to be on the force to honor your dad's memory."

"Great. And do what?"

"Teach. Everyone sees how good you are with the kids at Sunday school, except for you. It's what you want to do and were meant to do."

"Yeah, I'll just quit tomorrow and move in with my mom until I finish up my degree."

"Why not?"

"I can't afford to do that," she said. "I'm gonna be a cop forever. Unless I actually meet up with a bad guy and he pops me."

Rip didn't laugh. "How long you been a cop, Heather?"

"Twelve years."

"This isn't Detroit," Rip said. "Seriously, how many times have you pulled your gun out and aimed it at someone?"

"The only time I ever pulled my gun out was last week."

"Exactly. And did he have a gun?"

"No."

"*Let it go,*" Rip said. "And if you do ever run into someone who has a gun, I know you'll be able to shoot. I'm sure of it."

TEN

Rip peeked over the dashboard of the police car as Heather unlocked the front gate of the main entrance to McLouth Steel. The police from Benning and Carlson were the only ones who had keys to the fence, and since he and Andy had made such a big deal out of the flower garden again last night, Heather insisted on seeing it the second Rip got off work.

"This better be good," Judi said. She and Andy were ducking in the backseat of the car. "What if somebody sees us and Heather gets in trouble for this? For crying out loud, I feel like I'm sneaking into the drive-in movies."

"It's not our fault you and Heather are too lazy to walk out through the corn," Andy said.

"I don't even know why we have to hide," Rip said. "We're the only ones out here."

Heather opened the driver's side door. "Stay down until we get past the fence. I can't risk having anybody see me take you guys in there. I'm already on Chief Reynolds's nerves."

"Maybe we should go back to the house and slap on some black face-camo," Rip said.

"Shut up," Heather said, giving him a little smack on the back of his head as he crouched on the passenger's seat.

"How do you like getting hit?" Andy snickered.

Rip looked back between the two front seats at his nephew, who was still ducking. "Like it when Uncle Rip gets knocked on the head, eh?"

"Yeah," Andy said as Heather pulled the car forward. "Dose of your own medicine."

"I've never hit you without your helmet on," Rip said. "Pansy."

"Hang on to this," Heather said, putting a closed hand next to Rip's head.

"What is it?" Rip asked, lifting his chin to see what she was holding.

Heather opened her hand and gave him another little smack on the cheek, drawing another quick laugh from Andy.

"Hey!" Rip complained.

"Quit being such a lightweight," Heather said with a playful grin. "Okay, we're clear. You guys can sit up now."

"I remember when you were a lightweight," Rip said.

"What's that supposed to mean?"

"Nothing," Rip said.

"You calling me fat?" Heather said. "I'm not fat."

"I never said you were."

"I remember when you had hair."

"Ouch," Rip said, sitting up straight and getting a really good look at the building that served as the old blast furnace for the plant.

"This place is cool," Andy said, his face right up against the window.

"I think it's spooky," Judi said.

Rip agreed with his sister. The place was a ghost town and it gave Rip a sick sense of déjà vu. The feeling that he'd never get back to the other side of the fence, the same feeling prison had given him. What was left of McLouth Steel looked like the ideal place for something bad to happen, or where the FBI would finally corner some mass murderer at the end of a movie. Behind the blast furnace was the main part of the factory. They could see the upper half of it over the trees from the main road, but Rip had only been this close a handful of times and had forgotten how big it was. It was easily seven to ten stories high, blackened everywhere by soot and ash. And it was long. It ran away from them like the walls of some haunted fort as far as he could see. At the top of the building, about every hundred feet, dark smokestacks stood guard, like ancient cannons from a war long since over.

They continued to drive over the cracked cement that surrounded the plant. They made it past the blast furnace and Heather carefully maneuvered the car around uncovered manholes, piles of broken glass, and scattered pieces of scrap metal that could put a serious hurt on some tires.

When they finally approached the rear of the main building, he noticed a sliding door—about the size of an entrance into an airplane hangar—had been left open. Even with all the broken windows, it was black inside.

"Let's go in there," Andy said.

"I don't think so," Heather said quickly as they weaved around a series of short metal poles that stuck out of the ground. "It's probably radioactive in there."

"Radioactive?" Rip said.

"Yeah," Heather said. "The EPA wasn't real busy when this place was running. Hey, there's a sign over there," she blurted, gesturing over her shoulder. "Maybe we—"

"Watch it!" Rip said.

Somewhere between *watch* and *it*, Heather did her part in lowering the pole population by one. She flattened it and then slammed on the brakes, sending her passengers up and forward.

"Oh my gosh!" Heather said. "Please don't be bad."

"Hang on," Rip said. Heather ignored him and by the time he made it out to the front of the car, she was looking at the same thing he was.

"Two accidents this week," Heather said. Her hands were on her head and she was looking at Rip like she wanted him to tell her she wasn't going to get fired. "You think it's bad?"

"It could be worse," Rip said.

The front bumper was smiling at them like a kid who had lost his front teeth. There was a two-foot hole in the plastic, right in the center of it. The grill was broken in half and the top of the hood had a jagged V-shaped dent. This wasn't one of those quick-fix dings where you could rush it to a buddy at a collision shop. The whole front end of the car needed to be replaced.

"I'm going to have to tell them where this happened."

"So?" Rip said. "You're allowed to be here."

"What reason will I give them? Some crazy hunt for a secret garden?"

"I dunno," Rip said with a shrug. "Maybe."

"Oh man, it's smoked!" Andy said. He and Judi had joined them.

Rip cocked his head toward Andy. "You're lucky you don't have your helmet on."

"Think it's okay to drive?" Heather asked.

"I don't know why not," Rip said. He kneeled down in the catcher's position and studied the damage. And then he stood and nudged the bumper with the tip of his work boot.

The whole bumper fell off.

"Then again, maybe it isn't," Rip said.

They all stared in silence. Rip glanced to his left at Judi and Andy, and then they all turned and looked over at Heather. Rip half expected her to take out her sword and perform the honorable duty of doing herself in. She looked at him and closed her eyes.

"Don't you dare say something smart, Gerald Ripley."

Rip held up his hands, signaling that he wouldn't.

"I am so toast," Heather said, followed by silence.

"Oh boy," Judi cried, studying the bumper. Something about the way she said it forced Rip to look the other way. He was struggling not to burst out in laughter until Heather snorted and giggled. By the time he turned around, all four of them, even Andy, were laughing uncontrollably.

They agreed that Heather's best play was to leave the broken parts, as none of them were salvageable. They also figured that since they were out there, they might as well still check out the flowers, so they all got in the car and Heather drove them toward the back fence.

There were three separate gates at the rear of McLouth Steel, and the one that was closest to the flower bed happened to be the one in the middle. Heather stepped out of the car again, unlocked the gate, and then returned. They drove past the poison ivy that surrounded the fence and down to a small clearing. She stopped the car. Then they all got out and made their way toward the canal through forty yards of high grass, spooking a pair of deer that jumped up and almost gave Judi a heart attack. Not too long after, they could see the back side of the flower bed.

"Isn't it awesome?" Rip said, walking quickly in front of them.

"Stop, Uncle Rip!" Andy yelled. "Don't get near it!"

Rip turned around and glanced at Andy. Heather was standing about ten feet behind him, and Judi another twenty feet farther back.

"Why not?" Rip asked. "You okay?"

The kid looked a little pale. "There's something in there. You aren't ready to go in there yet."

Rip flipped him a *you're crazy* look and walked toward the flowers, and with each step he took, little shots of adrenaline fired through his body, causing something to flutter on the inside of his stomach. Andy was right. Something *was* in the flowers, and whatever *it* was had him feeling better the closer he got. It was like it was calling to him. And the call was a song of such peace, such joy, such love . . . it was unlike anything he'd ever experienced before. He walked to the edge of the garden and studied the dark soil that separated the four sections of flowers. He reached down to take a handful of dirt.

"Stop, Uncle Rip!" Andy shouted. "Please!"

Andy walked toward him, his eyes never leaving the flower bed.

"It's okay," Rip said. "They're just flowers."

Rip noticed Andy was trembling.

"When I look at those flowers," Andy said, his eyes wide and wild, "I feel the same way I did after Mom told me I called her, using her middle name. The same way I felt with Mr. Hart after church. I'm not sure how I know this, but you're not supposed to go in there yet. Don't get too close to it. Please."

"Okay, okay," Rip said, putting his arm around Andy. His nephew didn't flinch or make his normal fuss about being touched. He just stared at the flowers.

"Rip?" Heather said. She had her arm around Judi. "Come here."

Rip walked back to them and Judi had her arms crossed. She looked dazed, her eyes fixed dreamily on the first section of the flowers.

"What did he say to me a few days ago?" Judi whispered. "When he called me Judith Ann? I need to know."

"That's the third time she's asked that in the last two minutes," Heather said. "Come here, Andy!"

Andy didn't move. He was still facing the flower garden like it might leap up and grab him.

"What did he say to me?" Judi said, louder this time.

She moved out from under Heather's arm and walked quickly down toward Andy. Rip and Heather followed her, and Judi stopped halfway, her eyes clearly still on the flowers.

"What did you say to me?" she yelled. "I need to know!"

Rip and Heather shared a look. For the first time, an arrow of fear shot through Rip. Maybe Heather was right and the old place was toxic . . . maybe this garden was some freakishly weird side effect of factory poison that was already seeping into all of them. A whole different kind of weed from the one he used to favor, with an entirely unique effect. And yet he couldn't deny that he felt *great* being here. Better than he'd felt in weeks. And it wasn't a bio-high. It was deeper. More *internal*. Like part of his soul . . .

Rip tried to see *exactly* what Judi was looking at. "Who you talking to? I thought you were talking to Andy."

"It's okay, Judi," Heather said, wrapping her arm around her friend's back. "It's okay."

Rip could see the tears working their way down Judi's cheeks. Judi started walking again and stopped next to Andy. Then she looked right at him. "You said it to me, Andrew. Right after you called me Judith Ann. What was it? I need to know!"

"I don't remember," Andy said.

Rip made his way down to the very edge of the flowers. There was something he wanted to know as well. Something he'd find out if he just—

"Don't go in the garden, Uncle Rip. You aren't ready."

"Okay," Rip mumbled. He somehow knew Andy was right.

But everything in him wished he wasn't.

ELEVEN

What Kevin Hart lacked in sincerity, Rip mused, he made up for in boat and boathouse. The two nicest boathouses in Benning were both owned by him. The one behind Kevin's house was big enough for a family of six to live in, and the one on the lake behind Hart Industries was arguably the nicest one in the state, complete with a game room, Jacuzzi, and state-of-the-art home theater.

Rip sat in the driver's seat of Kevin's Cigarette boat, which rested on a trailer near the boathouse's main entrance, and tried to catch his breath. He held a towel dipped in lake water against the top of his hand. He'd been waxing like the Karate Kid for the better part of three hours and had bloodied a knuckle, banging it off the edge of a vent that led down to the boat's cabin. His back was killing him and his left rib cage felt like he had a porcupine inside trying to get out. It sucked getting older, because lately it seemed he suffered one sore body part after another.

Rip lifted the towel off his hand and wondered where he could find a ten-cent bandage on a half-million-dollar boat. He figured he'd go below and see if one of the thirty-six keys on Kevin's ring worked on the medicine cabinet down in the head.

He'd fiddled with at least thirty of the keys before one didn't just go in but also turned. Inside was a little plastic box with the words *First Aid* stenciled in white on its side. He pulled at the lid for what seemed like forever and couldn't get it to open. He leaned over and tapped the edge of the box against the wall and noticed a little panel had moved next to the toilet.

When he was done bandaging his wound, he locked the medicine cabinet back up and went to straighten out the panel that had shifted. When he did, he could see what looked like the barrel of a pistol pointing straight down, so he pulled the panel off.

"Whoa," he said, immediately noticing that it was a large pistol with an unusual orange rubber grip.

"Quite a gun, isn't it?"

Rip spun around and thought he was going to add a coronary to the sore back and ribs. Kevin Hart had climbed up on the boat and joined him in the cabin. Rip figured he might as well toss in being deaf to his ever-increasing list of ailments.

"Sorry," Rip said. "I cut my hand and came down for a bandage and couldn't get the first aid kit open. I tapped it on the wall and here we are."

"No problem," Hart said, and smiled as if he understood. "I don't broadcast the fact that that gun is there. Remember about seven years ago when those drunks came on my boat out in the middle of the lake and ripped me off?"

"Yeah, I remember," Rip said. One of them had a gun and held it to Kevin's wife's head.

"Not fun," Kevin said.

Rip glanced back at the pistol. It was huge—an absolute hand cannon. "Next time somebody comes on the boat uninvited, just pull that bad boy out and watch them start walking the plank."

"Exactly," Hart said. He hesitated. "Please keep the gun between us, though, Rip. I don't want anybody thinking I'm the gun-toting type."

"No problem," Rip said. *Messes with your golden boy image, huh?*

"I appreciate it," Hart said.

"Hey," Rip said. "I haven't had a chance to apologize to you about what happened with Andy at church."

"Yeah," Hart said. "What was that all about? And how in the world did he know my middle name?"

Not sure, Frances.

"I have no clue," Rip said with a shrug. "Kids sometimes have minds of their own." He also still didn't have the faintest idea what happened with Judi out at McLouth a couple days ago either. But Hart didn't need to know about that. "I'm sure he meant no harm, though."

"No worries," Hart said. "Boat looks great, by the way."

Rip slid the panel back over the gun, and when he turned around, Hart was holding out four hundred-dollar bills.

"That's way too much, Kevin. I appreciate it, but it's not necessary."

"Seriously, Rip, take it. A few extra bucks for a great job, and I also appreciate you keeping the gun thing under wraps."

"Well, thanks," Rip said. He took the money. It was more than he'd made all week and Andy needed that new iPod . . .

But he couldn't shove down the feeling that he'd just taken something he shouldn't have. Money that was meant to pay for more than the job.

Kevin Hart was a rich man. He'd been attacked on board

his boat before. Rip thought he'd want the world to know he was armed . . . to keep others from coming. So why the big secret?

※ ※ ※

It had taken Andy a little longer than usual to sweep off the roof at Mack's, but he had expected it to. Whenever he carried Milo up there with him, the dumb dog always got in his way. Most weeks he left him behind, whining at the base of the ladder, but today Andy had relented.

When he finally finished sweeping, Andy decided to stay up top for a while because the roof was one of the quietest places in town to read. Mr. McIntosh didn't mind if he and Milo sat up there all day and Andy liked the heat, so he figured over the next hour or two he'd forget about the crazy things people said he'd been doing and get through the rest of his latest book. But first he wanted to take another glance at that article in the copy of the *Benning Weekly* he'd brought with him. He thought it was pretty cool that some guy wore a black mask and showed up places, leaving things for people.

Andy took the three hamburgers out of the bag that Mr. McIntosh had given him, sat down, and leaned his back against the brick chimney that stuck out of the roof. Milo lay at his feet and Andy unwrapped two of the burgers and gave them to the dog. They were gone by the time Andy had his out of its wrapper and Milo begged for more, but Andy only opened the newspaper and read:

Santa Vacationing in Benning?

Brianna Bruley—TBW Reporter

Benning—Officer Heather Gerisch of the Benning Police Department has confirmed that they are continuing to investigate a pair of bizarre break-ins that have taken place within the township over the last couple of weeks.

The first incident occurred on the morning of June 8th out on Old Parker Road, and the second on June 13th at the Recreation Center. Both police and the victims of the first break-in describe the suspect as a six-foot-tall male wearing all black and a ski mask.

"Early indications seem to suggest we are dealing with the same perpetrator," Gerisch said. "In both cases, the suspect seems to have entered the premises in the middle of the night without damaging or taking anything. It seems the sole intent of this person was to drop off items of value. In the first location, our perpetrator dropped off grocery cards. In the second, sports equipment. Regardless, this individual should be considered a threat, and we are taking these investigations very seriously."

Anyone with any information regarding these incidents involving the "Summer Santa" is being asked to contact the Benning Police Department or the *Benning Weekly*'s anonymous tip line.

Andy folded the paper and looked around him. To his right, he had a clear view of the rear parking lot for Mack's, and then the fields and trees that ran out toward the lake. To his left and beneath him were the front of the building and Main Street. It felt good to be up where he was, where he could see without worrying about *being seen*. Only a few cars moved up and down the street with most of them heading to the gas station. Right across the street, through the glare on a window, he could see a red-and-white barber pole spinning and old man Backus sitting in his barber's chair, waiting for a customer. To the right of the barber shop was McNair's

Sporting Goods with a sign in the window that read "Arrows Half Off." Bow season was still close to five months away, but everyone in Benning quietly knew that poaching over at the McLouth property had no season. *"Shoot them during the day and drag them off at night"* was what the old-timers always said. Next to McNair's was the oldest building in Benning, a dark brick structure that used to house the old IGA, a grocery store that went out of business when all the people like his mother started to go to the Walmart over in Woodhaven to save a few bucks. Uncle Rip had been a bagger at the IGA when he was about Andy's age and supposedly got fired for smoking pot on his break.

Andy glanced past the roof and beyond the abandoned grocery store, across the field behind it. He could see the back of the Dairy Queen. He had a fresh twenty in his pocket, and the idea of taking Milo over there and tossing a few bucks at a banana split sounded pretty good.

Andy looked back at the gas station and could see Eric Bower, the guy who squealed on Uncle Rip, getting out of an old white van. The only thing whiter than that van was the look on Bower's face the last time he saw Uncle Rip. A few months back, Andy and Uncle Rip were down below in Mack's eating breakfast. Bower walked in and when he saw Uncle Rip sitting there, his Adam's apple did a funny little dance, and then he turned around and went right back out the door. It reminded Andy a little bit of a white rat he had seen a couple years ago at a pet store over in Flat Rock, moseying happily around the aquarium until it rubbed noses with a boa constrictor in the corner.

Andy heard the back door slam and Milo sprang up. He tilted his nose up in the air like he smelled something, and then he walked over to the edge of the roof and started wiggling his backside as he looked down below. Andy knew one of the employees had just tossed a garbage bag of scraps in the dumpster and Milo was hoping to score.

"Come here, Milo," Andy said.

The dog ignored him. His tail and backside just waggled faster and when he leaned a little closer, over the edge he went.

"Milo!" Andy yelled, jumping to his feet, his heart pounding. He raced to the edge of the roof and looked down.

Milo's neck and collar looked like they were caked in mashed potatoes, and he was standing on top of a pile of loaded trash bags, pawing at the one he had just landed on.

"Milo, you idiot!"

Even though the dumpster was emptied three times a week, Andy had never seen it so full, and Milo's lucky butt just happened to go off the edge on a day when he could survive the fall. Had it been just about any other day, Milo would have had four legs again and would be chasing and *catching* cars up in puppy heaven.

Andy climbed down, fished Milo out of the dumpster, wiped him off with some napkins that were in the burger bag, and had him up on the roof again, this time with his leash on and attached to an exhaust fan. Milo wasn't happy about it and cried for a few minutes before giving up and rolling over for a midday snooze.

They hadn't been back up on the roof for more than ten minutes when Andy heard another door slam. He looked back behind Mack's and down into the parking lot. His heart beat about as fast as it had when Milo played stunt beagle and leaped off the roof. Chelsea Cochran was getting out of the car with her mom, dad, and sickly little sister, Marjo, who looked more like she was four years old than eight. Other than at church, Andy hadn't seen Chelsea in over a year. Ever since Marjo's kidney issue had come up, Chelsea had gone to live with her aunt and went to a different school, because her parents were gone so often. She looked like a completely different person than she did a year ago, and as she and the Cochrans walked toward the back entrance of the diner, Andy carefully slid around the side of the chimney, hoping he wouldn't be seen.

She'd never want to talk to somebody like me anyway.

Chelsea was beautiful and she belonged with somebody else who was beautiful. Maybe a football player or someone popular, like a class president. Certainly not the kid with the ugly scar on his face.

When Andy heard the back door open beneath him, he stood up and took a deep breath. He walked to the edge of the roof, and when he glanced back to where he'd been sitting, he couldn't help the wave of sadness that overcame him. The title on the worn binding of his book said it all.

The Phantom of the Opera.

❈ ❈ ❈

Kevin Hart leaned back in his office chair and studied the oil painting of his father on the wall. The old man had spent a fortune on it. In the painting, he was sitting on his dock, looking out at the lake, with the old house behind him. It had to have been done from a photograph, unless the artist sat in a boat on the lake. Hart smiled. He wouldn't be surprised if the old man paid the guy to sit out there and paint it over a couple hundred sittings.

Hart stood and walked to the window, wondering if his father would have been proud of what he had done with Hart Industries. Sales had never been better, the company was still growing, and with Phillips on board, the sky would be the limit.

He looked back at the painting. "What do you think, Dad?"

Hart bit his lip, practically expecting his father to look up from the lake and answer.

Yes, son. You are doing an amazing job. Keep up the good work, kid.

Hart's thoughts then skipped over to the gun. If Ripley went public with the fact that Kevin Hart carried a gun, what would people think?

After all, the gun was just tucked away for safekeeping, a memento of things that could happen. And God forbid he ever saw another need to possibly use it.

He pushed the idea away and then smiled, thinking about the night ahead.

※ ※ ※

"Andy hates me with a passion," Judi said as she and Heather walked on the path that separated the cornfields. They'd both felt the urge to go and check out the flower patch again from Ripley's Field.

"First of all," Heather said, "he doesn't hate you."

"And now Milo hates me too. It's spreading."

The two old friends shared a rueful smile.

When Andy brought the dog home, Milo had a minor skirmish with a skunk and it had become a major problem for the little guy. Judi had quarantined him to the outdoors until later, when Rip was coming over to clean him up. When Judi had taken his food bowl outside, Heather couldn't stop herself from laughing. Milo looked at Judi like she was about to put him down.

"When I'm feeling like the deck is stacked against me," Heather said, "it always helps me to think about all that is going right. You know how many people would trade places with you in a minute?"

"Yeah, right," Judi said. "Come trade places with the lady with a big, empty house and a son who hates her."

"Not a big, empty house. A big, beautiful house full of history, set on all this beautiful land we get to walk through like it's our own private park," Heather said.

"A private park? More like wasted land. I don't make squat off leasing all these acres of corn to part-time farmers."

"But it's land that remains open, preserving the prettiest view in Benning. And you have a *healthy* son," Heather added. "Even if he's being a pill right now. Just look at the Cochrans and what they are going through with little Marjo."

"That's true," Judi said, nodding.

"Just be thankful *you can have* kids," Heather added. "I can't."

"Sorry," Judi said. "You're totally right. I'm giving in to my own pity party again. It's just that with Andy . . ." She shook her head. "I have no idea how to cross this valley that just keeps getting deeper and deeper between us."

"It's okay," Heather said as they approached the end of the corn. She looped her arm through Judi's. "Remember what Welsh has told us about a hundred times . . . about how things we take for granted, someone else is praying for?"

"You're right," Judi said.

"Plus, don't forget, Andy's at that age."

Judi's eyebrows huddled again, as if they were saying, *Thanks for the pep talk, but Andy's been at that age for a long time.*

And then Judi pointed.

Heather turned her head and when she saw the flowers, it looked like the strength went right out of Judi's legs and she fell to her knees. Heather took her hand and tried to lift Judi to her feet, but she couldn't. Judi was still pointing and her mouth was gaped open. Heather had a feeling her own mouth was open as well. There'd been a part of them both that almost wondered if their experience on the McLouth side of the canal had been a dream. A crazy, fantastic, weird dream.

But there the flowers were. Bigger and brighter than before.

The garden seemed different from this side. *Safer.* It was

more like a painting or a photograph, impossibly perfect. It was like the flowers had been Photoshopped into the most incongruous place on earth, right behind the dark, ghostly factory.

She looked up toward the bright sun and squinted, a big part of her expecting to see a hole in one of those puffy white clouds. Like that beautiful flower bed had simply fallen out of the sky and landed across the canal, a piece of heaven snatched away.

And then Heather realized she was smiling and didn't have the faintest idea why.

"What did you say to me?" Judi said, her arm finally lowering. It was the same thing she was saying when they'd been over on the McLouth side.

But she wasn't speaking to Heather. She was talking to the flowers.

Heather's smile faded and her heart pounded. What was going on here?

They'd tried to talk about what had overcome Judi that day over at McLouth. Heather and Rip had figured it was just stress leaking out over Judi's relationship with Andy, and they'd thought a return visit might help resolve it. But whatever it was, it looked like it was trying to rear its head again.

"I need to know what he said to me," Judi called over to the garden. "I still need to know."

Heather kneeled next to Judi and didn't say anything. When she looked back at the flowers, gooseflesh riddled her arms and back. She felt like she was standing next to a window on a bright winter day and the sun's reflection was warming her entire body. She looked away from the flowers and the feeling disappeared. She turned back to the flowers and it returned. Off and on. Off and on.

"They are all gone when I look over there," Judi said.

"What's all gone?" Heather asked.

"My worries," Judi answered, turning to face Heather. "When I look over there, I feel like I don't have a care in the world."

Heather knew exactly what Judi meant. They stood and the two of them walked up to where the grass led down to the canal and sat there for close to half an hour, silently staring at the wildflowers, only taking little breaks to glance at each other and smile.

Heather didn't have the faintest idea what was going on, but whatever it was, no matter how much it scared her, she couldn't bear to look away. Because . . . it was *good*.

✹ ✹ ✹

This was a lot harder than he thought it would be. It was way too dark out and by the time he got the second tire off, he wished the police had declared old Mrs. Coventry too old to drive. She was ninety-three and never left Benning, but if she was ever going to go faster than twenty and quit creating the only traffic the town ever saw, the bald tires had to go. The new tires were an odd prayer request, particularly for somebody her age, but he was glad he could resolve this one.

He lifted the mask off his face, stood, and thought he heard a car coming. He removed his right glove, rubbed at his eyes, and then laughed quietly. Nobody was coming out here at two in the morning. He shook his head and then walked around the other side of the car to change the other two tires.

TWELVE

They are almost ready for us!" Heather yelled as she walked back into her Sunday school class. "About three more minutes."

Heather kneeled on the carpet next to Marjo Cochran, who lay on her stomach with her left palm propped under her chin and a red crayon in her other hand. Marjo would be delivering the final line in the skit they were about to perform for the congregation.

"You ready, Marjo?" Heather asked.

"Yes, Ms. Gerisch," Marjo said. "All I have to do is yell 'amen' when you look at me."

"That's right, sweetheart," Heather said, standing. "If anybody filled out a prayer request card, let me have them and I'll give them to Mr. Hart before we start the skit, okay?"

Marjo sat up and handed Heather one of the cards. It had been folded in half.

"Can you see if I spelled everything right?" Marjo asked, pointing at the card.

"Of course," Heather said, opening it.

DEAR GOD I DON'T WANT TO GO THE HOPSITAL ANYMORE I
DON'T LIKE NEEDLES AND JUST WANT TO BE HELTHY LIKE THE
OTHER KIDS THANK YOU MARJO

Heather's heart sank and she felt selfish, thinking about her own prayer request card. Here this little kid was fighting for her life and all Heather asked God was to give her the discipline to save the seventy-five hundred bucks she needed in order to go back and finish her teacher's certificate.

"Did I do it right?" Marjo asked.

"It's the best one I've ever seen," Heather said. She hesitated. "I don't know about you, Marjo, but I'm praying your family gets the money you need for one last hospital stay. One last round of needles. So I'm praying that your request is answered with a big *yes.*"

"Really?" Marjo said, her eyes lighting up with hope.

"Really," Heather confirmed, leaning over and holding out her hand for a high five, which Marjo gladly gave before hugging Heather's leg.

"I guess I could go one more time," Marjo said seriously. She looked up at Heather. "You think God will help us pay for my doctor and make me better?"

"I'm going to pray hard for that," Heather said, picking the little girl up. "Let's go, guys!"

Heather marched the kids out the door and to the entrance of the sanctuary. They stood near the last pew, waiting for Rip and Kevin Hart to collect prayer requests, and when Rip approached them, she put the kids' prayer request cards in the basket and gave him a little smile. Rip didn't smile back. He just crossed his eyes and stuck out his tongue, drawing a laugh from a few of the kids.

Heather led the Sunday school class up the main aisle for children's time in front of the entire congregation. She was holding

Marjo's little hand and smiling inside, admiring how cute the girl's short brown hair looked with the shiny white ribbons pinned in it. Heather hoped Marjo was going to hit her one-word part in the skit.

When they passed the first pew, all fourteen kids made their way up the three steps that led to the landing next to Kevin Hart, who had made it back to the lectern to introduce the skit.

The kids all sat and Heather made sure she sat next to Marjo. That way she could whisper "amen" as a reminder in the event a case of stage fright overcame her.

Heather nodded at Kevin and he gave her a little wink.

"And as we like to do once a month," Kevin said, gripping the sides of the podium, "we are fortunate to have our Sunday school classes perform a skit. Today they will be doing one called 'The Truth Shall Set You Free.'"

"Go ahead," Heather whispered to eleven-year-old Dennis James to start the skit. Dennis had a nice shiner, compliments of a line drive he had caught in the eye as he was trying to steal home last week in a Little League game between second-place Dino's Pizza and first-place Benning Rotary.

Dennis stood and glanced out at the congregation. Heather watched as he adjusted his clip-on tie and could see him take a deep breath before he started.

"All of the children were before the king and—"

"*Kevin! Kevin Frances!*" The voice sounded like it belonged to a concerned parent, one who was calling a child in from the backyard to discuss a broken vase that had been found. The voice practically sounded like it came from out of the ceiling. But it hadn't.

Heather knew it was Andy, or what sounded like a more mature version of Andy. She turned and could see him, the only person standing. He was in the last pew, right next to Rip, who was looking at his nephew like he had just stepped off a spaceship. The iPod was hanging out of Andy's left hand, dangling by the earbud cord and teetering back and forth almost hypnotically. Andy's chin was tilted toward the ceiling and his eyes were fluttering but closed. He had a peculiar smile on his face and he looked like someone peeking while counting for hide-and-seek.

Heather glanced back at Kevin, who bit his bottom lip. He stood back up and walked to the podium, and before he could say anything, Andy's words were filling the church.

"People who conceal their sins will not prosper, but if they confess and turn from them, they will receive mercy."

Heather wasn't sure, but she wagered those words came from the Bible. Maybe Andy had been reading the one Rip had bought for him, and perhaps he'd inherited some of that judgmental personality from the guy he was sitting next to. Whatever was happening, Kevin wasn't likely to take another round of this sitting down. Rip took Andy by the arm and moved to rush him out. Heather looked back at Hart, who lowered his mouth next to the microphone.

But before he could say anything, little Marjo Cochran stood up next to her. She faced the congregation and pulled her little shoulders back before she yelled her one line at the top of her tiny lungs. "Amen!"

❊ ❊ ❊

"Look at your hair," Judi said, passing another open photo album across the couch to Heather.

"Nice," Heather said, studying the photo. "This has to be like ninth grade. Definitely the early nineties."

Rip leaned over the back of the couch and laughed. "You're kidding me, right? You had that haircut until you were in your twenties. And when you finally decided to put away all your heavy metal albums to become a cop, I think half the hair spray companies in the country went broke."

"Yeah, right," Heather said. "Wasn't that about the same time you traded your mullet in for Rogaine?"

"Whatever you say, Adoohana," Rip said.

"Adoohana?"

Rip nodded. "It's the language of my ancient people. It's what they would have called you."

Heather shook her head. "Thrill me. What's it mean?"

Rip paused and had a straight look on his face. "She who sits on much ground."

Heather bit her lip and felt her eyebrows hunch together. "Second fat joke within the last week. You really think I've put on weight, don't you?"

"You're just perfect," Rip said, plopping down on the couch next to her and Judi. "It's interesting, though. I didn't start losing my hair until you dumped me for Kevin."

"Good thing I didn't lose my hair when he dumped me for the bimbo."

"True," Rip said. "But you came away from it a bigger person."

"Not funny," Heather said, elbowing him in the shoulder. Rip laughed and grabbed a handful of popcorn out of the plastic bowl on her lap. He tossed some on the floor for Milo who, despite three different tomato soup baths, still smelled slightly of skunk. Rip then pointed out the living room window.

Andy was coming up the road on his motorcycle and Heather thought about what he had said to Kevin. "Did you get that new iPod for Andy after church today?"

"You kidding?" Rip said and shrugged. "I offered but he wants to stick with the broken one."

"I think he likes it better broken," Judi said. "And he still doesn't remember anything he's heard from it or the things he's been saying, assuming they are related."

"Any ideas why he would say what he did to Kevin *this* time?" Heather asked.

"Nope," Judi said distantly. "Rip and I both tried talking to him about it today, but he just got upset. Like I said, he has no recollection whatsoever."

"He's probably no more upset than Kevin," Heather said. "The fact that Kevin didn't say anything after church leads me to believe his feathers were a bit ruffled, but I could be wrong. He sure is being a good sport about it."

"Yeah," Rip said. "But I guarantee you he pulls me into his office tomorrow."

"What are you gonna tell him?"

"The truth," Rip said. "It's from the Bible, and Andy doesn't remember reading or saying it at church."

"C'mon," she said. "He has to be reading it."

"I hear you," Rip said. "But he said he didn't and I don't ever remember that kid telling a lie."

"So if he didn't, and he's not lying, what's going on?" Judi asked. "Do you think I need to get him to a psychologist or something?"

"No," Rip said slowly. "It seems whacked on the surface, but deep down, don't you feel like it's something important, what's happening to him? Something's shifting in the kid . . . and it's a good thing. Kinda like the flowers. Inexplicable, but good."

Judi and Heather nodded, in complete agreement.

"What do you think Kevin will say?" Judi asked.

Rip shrugged. "Who knows?"

"What is happening around here?" Heather said. "Between the iPod and those flowers out there at McLouth . . . something's up."

"Wow," Rip said. "You should be a detective."

"Shut up, Rip," Heather said and nudged Judi. "Andy say anything else strange today?"

Judi didn't answer. She was just staring at a different album, and Heather could see that the page was loaded with old pictures of Judi and Todd. She looked over at Rip, who just shook his head.

Heather leaned over and closed the album on Judi's lap. "I think we need to have us a little bonfire and ditch some bad memories."

"Amen," Rip said. "But again, that would make too much sense. And we don't trade in good sense in this household."

Judi smiled mirthlessly. "You minding your own business would probably make sense too." She pointed at the basement door. "As it would have then. We'll never find hinges that match."

"What I did was wrong," Rip said. "I've said it a hundred times now. I screwed up that night. But you didn't. That is the truth, and the sooner you realize—"

"Hang on," Heather said, regretting what she was about to say before she said it. "I'm not all that sure what you did was wrong, Rip. Judi was getting hurt."

"Great!" Judi yelled. The only fight Judi seemed to have left in her came when she defended Todd. "I was getting hurt, yes, but what followed has hurt way worse than that!" She pushed away the albums and stood up, walking to the window.

Heather cringed and then she said carefully, "If I didn't tell Rip what was happening, Todd would've continued to hurt you. Eventually he would've left, or you would've finally left him. Why don't you understand that?"

"Did you see his face, Heather? What my brother did to my *husband's* face?" She shook her head, eyes bright with tears, as if she were reliving that terrible night.

Rip stood and walked up right behind Judi. "How about what he did to Andy's face?"

Rip had a good point. The only point. But Heather had also seen Todd's face. She saw it well before Judi did. Even before Todd was in the hospital.

When Heather told Rip about Judi's bruises, Rip had planned on waiting for a time when Judi and Andy wouldn't be home, but when he saw Andy get hit with the boiling water and Todd holding the pan, things changed.

Nobody except Rip and Judi, maybe not even Todd, knew exactly what had happened that day.

Heather arrived at the scene and rode with Todd in the ambulance. When he finally woke up in the hospital, Todd said he could only recall running down to the basement to hide from *someone*, and then hearing *somebody* kick in the basement door.

Heather wasn't all that surprised that *somebody* had convinced Todd that it probably wasn't in his best interest to press charges against Rip or even have the matter looked into further. Rip hung with a little different crowd in those days, and she couldn't recall any of them carrying Bibles.

"How many times are we gonna go over this?" Judi said, covering her face with her hands. She started to cry in earnest.

Heather got up and went to Judi. She put her arm around her and whispered, "It isn't fair what you have been doing to yourself. Blaming yourself. Almost *reveling* in taking the blame. It's been out of control for years and is only getting worse. You aren't happy anymore unless you are unhappy."

Judi sucked in her breath. "What are you talking about?" she asked between her fingers.

Heather took her hand and looked at her. "I love you like a sister. But I can't watch you play the martyr anymore. You aren't to blame for that terrible night. For not protecting Andy. Not even for not protecting Todd."

"But if Rip hadn't—" Judi began.

"If Rip hadn't beaten your husband, would he still be here? Think about that, Judi. Would that be good? Really?"

Judi tore away from her and sat down again.

"When are you gonna let Rip off the hook?" Heather asked.

Rip came over and kneeled in front of Judi. He had compassion in his voice as he touched her knee. "When are you going to let yourself off the hook?"

"Enough!" Judi said as Andy came through the door. The poor kid was so used to Judi's drama that he didn't even flinch.

"What's going on now?" he asked.

"Nothing, Andrew," Judi said. "Go wash your face, honey."

"Go wash yours," Andy said as he walked by. But when he approached the staircase, he came to a dead stop. Heather noticed the odd way in which he was looking at his iPod. Like he was protecting it. He put in an earbud and headed up the stairs.

"Look at this one," Heather said, grabbing an album again, trying for a quick subject change until Andy was out of hearing distance. She tapped on a photo. "Isn't he cute?"

In the photo, a group of kids, including her and Judi, surrounded a blindfolded Rip. They were all under ten years old and were in the backyard at the Harts' house, celebrating little Kevin's birthday. Rip was smiling and two-handing a wooden bat, standing under a Scooby-Doo piñata.

"I still *am* cute," Rip said, pointing at the two men who were sitting at a table in the background of the picture. It was her dad and Walter Hart, Kevin's father.

Heather touched the photo again and nudged Judi, relenting. She knew her friend had had enough pressing for one night. "Did your baby brother tell you that I visited him last week?"

"No," Judi said, a little surprised. "About what?"

Heather smiled at Rip. *Thanks for keeping it between us.*

"About them," she said. Her finger was right beneath her father and Mr. Hart. "Mostly about my dad."

"What about them?"

"Tell her, Rip," Heather said.

"We were talking about her father being in heaven."

Heather liked the way that sounded. She wanted to believe that all of those chats her father had with Mr. Hart had finally made him a believer. But how much progress Mr. Hart had made . . . only Dad and God knew, so that big block of doubt sat in her gut like a rock.

"Of course, you'd have to talk to Rip about that instead of me," Judi said. "He's *Mr. Advice* about everything lately."

"Hey," Heather said. "He's trying to help you. We just want you to get on with your life."

"I'm just fine," Judi said as Andy came back downstairs, one of the earbuds of his iPod in, as usual. He was wearing his light-blue pajama bottoms and maize and blue T-shirt that had *Michigan Wolverines* on the front. He walked around the couch and stopped directly in front of Heather. He had a glassy look on his face when he pointed down at the album.

"That's when we were little kids," Heather said, grinning at Andy. "Right there is your Uncle Rip."

Andy leaned over and placed his finger on the picture and said, "They are able."

"Huh?" Heather said. "That was my daddy and Kevin Hart's daddy."

Andy just stared at her. He dropped to his knees in front of her and placed his finger on the photo again, right beneath her father and Mr. Hart.

"*Heather Marie*," he said.

"Here we go," Rip said.

"What is it, Andy?" Heather asked.

Andy's eyes were closed. A peaceful smile quickly came and went and then he opened his eyes and tapped on the photo again.

"They are able."

Heather looked at Judi. It was only a three-word sentence, but Andy sounded like someone else.

"They are able to what?" Rip said.

Andy's eyes blinked quickly. He looked around the room and suddenly came across dazed, reminding Heather of someone who had just come out of a concussion.

"I just did it again, didn't I?" Andy said.

"Yeah," Rip said, glancing over at Heather, then back to Andy.

"What did I say this time?" Andy whispered.

"More importantly," Rip said, "who told you to say it?"

"I don't know," Andy said. He showed the iPod in his open palm and then held up an earbud. "But whoever it was told me through this."

✵ ✵ ✵

Kevin Hart stared at the bottle of scotch and wondered what in the world could possibly be in it that made it worth nine hundred dollars. Probably not his smartest purchase ever, but he got a nice charge out of the heads that turned at the country club when he outbid Jack Summers for it at the Benning Scholarship dinner a few weeks back.

"Try to outbid me, Jacko," he said and laughed. He opened the bottle and poured a half glass of it onto a few ice cubes before walking out the door and onto the deck outside his master bedroom.

He enjoyed alone time, and other than the door being closed

at the office, he got little of it. He glanced out over his backyard and onto Lake Erie, where the moon and stars cast smears of light on the water, giving it a glass-like effect. A little breeze came in from the east and he took a deep breath, reminding himself of the busy night ahead and the one thing he absolutely couldn't afford to do.

Get caught.

After all, what would people think?

He knew nobody would ever suspect him of it, particularly Carrie. Even after ten years of marriage, she still looked good, and he would pay whatever it took to keep her that way. Still, she was dumber than a bag of hammers and didn't have the faintest idea what he was up to. Nobody did, and he planned on keeping it that way. Still, he couldn't help himself from thinking about what Andy had said to him *this time* at church.

Does Ripley know what is going on? How? And has he been telling that little nephew of his to say these things to me . . . things that he doesn't have the guts to say to my face?

He shook it off. That type of nuance would have been long lost among the tar and bong resin that caked Ripley's brain. Still, the thought of pink-slipping the pothead danced through his mind like a happy little dream. But as good as it sounded, it wouldn't *look* good. Too many people were buying into Ripley's born-again spiel and it would ruin all the goodwill he had gained from being the only employer in the county to give Ripley anything that even resembled a real job.

Regardless, that ex-con wouldn't dare call me out on any funny business, because credibility is on my side . . . and the whole town loves me.

He sipped his scotch and closed his eyes. It tasted amazing.

He turned around to look at the bottle and saw Carrie entering the bedroom. She looked like a million bucks and he laughed under his breath. *I probably put half that amount into her.* It was worth it, though. At least some of the time.

"We're having dinner at the club on Tuesday," she said, catching sight of him.

"For what?"

"Some preplanning for the Cochran girl's fund-raiser. The insurance company isn't even considering coverage for that surgery she needs. Poor thing."

"I'll probably be working on Tuesday night."

"I'm going to pick up a dress for it." She said it as if she hadn't heard him, and even if she had, it didn't matter all that much.

Hart shook his head. "You mean buy another 'one and done' dress to go with the other three closetfuls?"

She gave him a long, doleful look. "It's less expensive than thirty million, isn't it?"

He didn't say anything. He'd never hit a woman in his life, but a big part of him wanted to backhand that smirk right off her face. Besides, she was right. He was pretty sure that Michigan divorce laws split everything down the middle and she'd clearly been paying attention to their monthly statements.

"I've got to run to the office for a little bit," he said.

"Working late again on a Sunday?" she said, her tone slightly more conciliatory. "You've been at it quite a bit lately."

"What's that supposed to mean?" he asked.

"Nothing," she said, giving up. "See you in the morning."

"I'll be back in a bit," he said.

"No hurry," she said.

No hurry, he thought. That was good, because he had another busy night carefully mapped out in his head.

Another one where he wouldn't get caught.

❋ ❋ ❋

It was going perfectly.

The door on the side of the garage had been left partially open, and picking the lock that led into the house from there was a breeze. He shook his head and laughed under his breath. *I'm getting pretty good at this, but soon it will all be over.*

He carefully stepped into the house and listened. At their age, he was certain they were fast asleep. No lights were on. He adjusted his black ski mask and pulled the tiny flashlight out of the pocket of his black pants. He twisted it, and a tight little cone of light cut through the darkness, giving him a decent view of the kitchen—a small table, a tiny island counter, and the reflection of his light off the shiny wood cupboards. He stopped and waited, listening for any movement upstairs. He heard nothing and smiled. He backpedaled into the garage and picked up the wheelchair. He hoped it would make a difference. He carefully walked back into the house and placed it right in the middle of the kitchen. He stepped back to the door and lifted his arm, watching the black glove on his hand move slowly through the darkness as he made the sign of the cross.

And then he left.

THIRTEEN

Would you consider him to be dangerous?" she asked.

Brianna Bruley was clearly just out of college and close to six feet tall. Despite being so young and new at her job, Heather was just as impressed with her as she was the first time they had met in the small office the station called the "media room." The reporter actually sounded more like an employee from the *Wall Street Journal* than the *Benning Weekly*, whose couple thousand readers were probably going to eat up this story about Benning's dark-clothed prowler just as much as they had the last one.

"Of course he's dangerous," Heather answered, studying the playing card–size tape recorder that sat on the desk in front of her. Something about the little red light that flashed made her nervous. She picked her words carefully before answering. "Anytime someone enters a house uninvited, it should be perceived as a threat."

"It's almost as if we have a Robin Hood among us," Brianna said. "First, $5K in gift cards, then the Little League equipment, and now a custom wheelchair?"

Heather didn't mention the new tires that magically showed up on old Mrs. Coventry's car or the bicycles that Eric Bower's kids were now riding. If this story got too big, it wouldn't look good for the department, and it wouldn't look good for Heather, who was already skating on thin ice with Chief Reynolds for her car "looking like it was in a demolition derby." She reconsidered Brianna's statement.

"No Robin Hood here," Heather said. "At least in the stealing-from-the-rich-to-give-to-the-poor sense. These things weren't reported stolen." She narrowed her gaze. "But that still doesn't give this person the right to break into people's houses."

"Right. But you agree that he is more of a Santa Claus, per se? Shows up at night and *only* leaves things?"

Heather shrugged. "Looks that way." She knew Brianna was gunning to bolster her Summer Santa moniker. Heather couldn't blame the kid. It was kinda catchy.

"Now the obvious question," the reporter said. "Why not just give these things to people, instead of doing it the way he is?"

"That's the question everyone is asking," Heather said, standing. It was time to end the interview. Short and sweet, that's the way Chief Reynolds liked it. "What's important is that we catch him, and we will. Because whoever this person is, despite his generosity, he is still breaking the law."

"Maybe this person *wants* to get caught," Brianna said.

"What do you mean?" Heather asked.

"It's the only thing that makes sense."

Heather thought about it. "Why?"

"Just thinking out loud," the woman said. She crossed her arms and Heather got a good look at the Rolex. *Nice watch for a rookie reporter.*

"Something makes you think that," Heather said. "Please share."

"Just a hunch," Brianna said. "Kind of like he is trying to do some good to make up for some bad. Maybe it's this person's way of balancing some scale in his personal life. That's the type of person I'd be looking for. Oh, that and the fact that this person also has to have some pretty deep pockets. Just saying."

Heather smiled. "You ever thought about being a cop?"

"No."

"You should," Heather said.

"I don't like guns."

Me either, Heather thought. She was also thinking about scales and deep pockets. Make that one deep pocket.

Kevin Hart's.

※ ※ ※

Rip took the change and dropped it in the tip bucket that rested against the serving window at the Dairy Queen. He grabbed his butterscotch sundae in his left hand, Andy's banana split in his right, and turned toward his nephew, who had been peeking over his shoulder the whole time. Now that Andy was out of school for the summer, Rip wanted to make sure that he and Andy got together at least a couple times a week during Rip's lunch hour, and today Andy had hit the lottery.

Chelsea Cochran was the girl behind the counter.

"Here you go, Rico Suave," Rip said, handing Andy the banana split. "Why don't you say something to her?"

Andy looked at him like he was crazy and Rip laughed. They went and sat at a picnic table that was shaded by a pair of trees at the edge of the parking lot.

"Uncle Rip," Andy said. "What's up with this Santa dude?"

"What do you mean?"

"I read about him in the paper. And then Mom was talking about him with Heather," he said, stabbing at his banana split with his spoon. "I think it's pretty cool what he's doing. You know, wearing a mask and giving people stuff."

"Nothing wrong with helping people out."

"I heard Mom say she thinks it's Mr. Hart, but she's probably just being weird like usual."

"Your mom's just being weird like usual, eh?" Rip said. He paused and then shook his head. "When you gonna lay off her, bro?"

Andy rolled the iPod earbud between his fingers and waited a few seconds before he responded. "Whatever."

Rip tugged on Andy's shirt. "That may fly with your mom, but you don't talk to me like that. Am I clear?"

Andy didn't answer and lifted his helmet as if he were about to get on his motorcycle and ditch his Uncle Rip, as well as his sundae.

Rip laid his hand on the helmet. "Am I *clear*?"

"Sorry, Uncle Rip," Andy said after a long moment, holding up his fist for a knuckle tap. "What am I supposed to do about the things I'm saying? I'm freaking out about it. How would you feel if you were saying stuff you couldn't control and don't remember saying?"

Rip grinned. "Before I went to prison, I had quite a few of those episodes."

Andy didn't seem to find Rip's pot reference all that funny.

"You sure you haven't been studying that Bible?" Rip said. "And maybe somehow zoomed in on a handful of quotes?"

"I'm positive. I'm telling you the iPod is telling me to say those things."

"Let's just give this a little time and see what happens," Rip said. "We'll figure it out. But speaking of Santa, you know what would be a great present for all of us?"

Andy looked at him and shrugged.

"And you don't even have to wait till Christmas," Rip said, leaning over and putting his arm around Andy.

"What's that?" Andy said.

"Seeing you and your mom getting along better and seeing each of you smile more."

Andy stared for a second and then said, "Smile about what?"

"There are lots of things to smile about. C'mon, man."

"Like what?"

Rip stuck his spoon in the middle of his sundae and set it on top of the picnic table. "Some things *have* to be funny to you, Andy. Some things *have* to make you happy."

"Lots of things make me happy."

"Name some," Rip said.

"Milo, my motorcycle, you, and—"

"Chelsea Cochran?" Rip edged in, nudging Andy with his shoulder.

"I think she's pretty," the kid admitted.

"That's something to smile about."

Andy shrugged. "I know I smile inside sometimes. But I guess a lot of my smiles just get smothered by the time they reach my ugly face."

"Hey," Rip whispered. "Don't be obvious, but turn around. She's looking at you."

Andy quickly spun around, and Chelsea Cochran, who had her head halfway out the server's window, retreated.

"Way to be subtle," Rip said, shaking his head. "Anything in particular about *don't be obvious* you didn't understand?"

"She would never go for me," Andy said.

"Why?"

"Because she is really pretty, and I look like someone who answered the iron when the phone rang."

Rip had heard Andy say that before. He also remembered Andy crying on the phone when he called from prison. Andy had told him about some of the names he had been called. *Pizza face. Freddy Krueger. Crispy Critter.*

Rip had never felt so helpless, not being able to stick up for Andy. He remembered praying about it. A lot of that harassment, from the locals anyhow, came to an end when Rip was released from prison. One of the few benefits of being a felon on the streets was the tough-guy stigma that came with it.

"So you're just going to give up on the idea of talking to Chelsea without even trying?"

"I just don't like . . ." Andy stopped and scooped a spoonful of his banana split.

"Don't like what?" Rip repeated. "C'mon. You know you can tell me anything."

"I want to talk about something else."

Rip didn't want to talk about something else, but he understood. "We can talk about whatever you want."

"Uncle Rip," Andy said. "Why did you sell the wacky?"

Rip spit out a little bit of ice cream and laughed. "Where did you hear it called that? The iPod?"

"No," Andy said. "I read it in a book once."

Despite being a loner and having just turned fourteen, it was clear that an answer to Andy's question, without too many particulars, was in order.

"I made a mistake, Andy. I let you down. I let your mom down. I let the community down, and most importantly, I let God down. But you know what? It's over and I'm forgiven."

Andy looked like he was about to cry. The kid had always been so good at masking his tears. His shoulders hunched and he leaned against Rip. Rip could feel his nephew shaking, but he couldn't see any tears. After a while, he sat up straight and turned toward Rip.

"I hate the burn on my face," Andy whispered. "And I don't know what to do about it."

Rip wasn't sure what to say, and the hopelessness in his nephew's eyes threatened to poke a hole in his heart. He gave Andy another squeeze and looked back at the server's counter.

Chelsea Cochran was looking at them again.

That You, Lord? Rip asked silently, taking a bite of his ice cream. *You mean to use Chelsea in this kid's life? Give me words, Father. Words this kid needs. Words I can't come up with on my own.*

And in that moment, Rip knew he would kill for the iPod to speak to *him* for once, instead of Andy.

❈ ❈ ❈

Kevin Hart walked across his office and glanced at his watch, wondering what was taking Ripley so long. He grabbed his phone, hit the pound sign, and Lynn, his secretary, answered.

"Yes, Mr. Hart?"

"Where's Ripley? I paged him, like, ten minutes ago."

"He's coming, sir."

"When?" he asked, thinking about the way Lynn had said *sir*. He liked the ring it had to it, but didn't want anyone thinking his employees were *supposed* to call him that, even though they were. He glanced at his watch again.

"I tried to buzz you when you paged him, but your phone was set on private," Lynn said apologetically. "Your door was closed too, so I didn't want to disturb you. He was still at lunch with Andy. I just saw him out on the floor and paged him again."

"Sorry about that," Hart said. "I didn't know the phone was on private. Have him knock first when he gets here."

"Yes, sir," she said.

"You're the best, Lynn. Thanks."

She really was the best. He'd seen old photos of her from company picnics. She was quite the looker back when his father had hired her, but even if she were about a hundred years younger, he still wouldn't dare go fishing off the company dock.

There was a knock on the door.

"C'mon in," he called.

Ripley opened the door and took a few short steps into the office. "You looking for me?"

Hart leaned forward and rested his elbows on top of the desk. He nodded at the chair to his left. "Have a seat."

Ripley pointed at a fresh oil stain on the side of his beige work pants. "I don't want to get any of this stuff on your nice chair."

"Good call," Hart said, standing. "You know, Rip . . . I don't know how else to say this, but I've really tried to be good to you."

"And I appreciate—"

"Your job, your home . . ." Hart paused and then exhaled powerfully, wondering if he was being too theatrical. "And what I get in return is being insulted by your nephew in front of half the church."

"C'mon," Ripley said. "Andy has no reason to insult you."

"Exactly," Hart said. "Not without coaching, anyhow."

"Coaching?"

"I don't stutter, Ripley."

Without being asked, Ripley turned and quietly shut the door. He looked back at Kevin, hands on his hips. "You are insinuating I got him to say that?"

Hart tilted his head and didn't answer. *Insinuating* was a pretty big word. *Maybe Doper still has some of his smarts left.*

"I didn't coach him on anything," Ripley insisted. "He's referencing things from the Bible, Kevin."

"I didn't know Andy was a big Bible reader," Hart said. "In fact, I've never heard him quote scripture before. What I don't care for is that he walked up to *me*, in front of *everyone*, and quoted them like they were a *lecture*."

Rip held up his hands. "I don't know what's going on. Seriously. Andy doesn't know the Bible that well, but he did the same stuff last night. With us, not just you." He shook his head. "I'm pretty sure Judi has him going over to Doc Strater's later in the week to see if everything's okay."

"I'm glad to hear it." Hart came around the front of the desk and sat on it. "But let's keep this simple. I really don't think it would be good for anybody if this sort of thing happened again, Ripley. Another *word* from Andy, to me."

"But—"

He held up his hand. "Ripley," he said, "you may have seen or heard things around town that might have given you the wrong impression about me."

"Kevin, I'm not trying to—"

"You familiar with the food-chain concept, Ripley?"

"C'mon, Kev. You serious?"

"Keep that Andy on a short leash. I'm warning you."

Rip straightened. "Excuse me?"

He didn't like the way Ripley was looking at him. He waited patiently and stared at Ripley's fists until they uncoiled. He loved that he could make the thug back down. He knew he'd hit a hot button, particularly with the pothead's history of getting physical with anybody who messed with his family.

He finally grinned, making it clear who was in charge. It would only take seconds for Ripley to understand that if he started huffing and puffing, he would only end up blowing his own house down. *Three . . . two . . .* "I'm not kidding, Ripley. Don't let it happen again."

One . . .

"Anything else?" Ripley asked, turning partially away, as if to remind himself of his boundaries.

"Nope," Hart said. "It's probably best that you keep this little chat between us. Other than that, thanks for stopping by, and I'll see you at Bible study tonight."

✖ ✖ ✖

Rip sat between Heather and Andy, listening to Jimmy Keeler give his weekly commentary on how it was practically impossible for anyone over sixty-five to survive on just social security. Jimmy then asked the group to pray that the cost of his monthly prescriptions stop going up, and then finished by asking God to soften the heart of "that crook down in Monroe," his dentist, so he would lower the $3,600 price tag on his new dentures. Jimmy figured if the Lord really wanted him to pay that much for new teeth, he'd ask for forgiveness and then just be happy eating bread and soup for the rest of his days.

It had been a pretty decent turnout for Bible study. Andy had, for some reason, decided to tag along. Rip hoped Heather would ask the group to pray for both her and her concerns about her father, but he wasn't all that surprised that when her turn came, she didn't bring it up. Still, it had been a good night of sharing, mostly among the regulars, with a few new faces there who asked for prayers.

The new woman in town, Brianna, was the reporter Heather had invited. She seemed like a nice girl, asking for prayers that God watch over her in her transition as she moved from Ann Arbor to Benning.

The rest of the group mentioned sick relatives, expressed some agreement with Jimmy Keeler's financial woes, and all nodded obediently as Kevin Hart asked for the community's prayers in handling the food drive and the fund-raiser for little Marjo Cochran.

Pastor Welsh then looked to Rip expectantly. Rip knew what he wanted. They'd talked about it. And Rip had no problem talking about how he'd come to know Christ and was looking forward to sharing tonight. *If only Kevin wasn't here.*

Keep him on a short leash.

Rip looked at Andy, who was sitting next to him, and then at Hart, who was right across the circle. He was proud of himself for the control he'd shown in Hart's office. In his previous life, the only thing that would have beaten Hart to the hospital would have been the front bumper of the ambulance. Now it was pretty simple. Despite the temporary urge to introduce Kevin to Mr. Knuckle Sandwich, he didn't do it for one reason, and it had nothing to do with the food chain. The reason he didn't lay a finger on Hart was simply because it was the wrong thing to do.

"I think Rip was going to share his testimony tonight," Pastor Welsh said, as if Rip might've forgotten his promise. "Rip?"

Rip took a deep breath and nodded at Welsh.

"I remember sitting in court, waiting to be sentenced," he said, without preamble. He leaned forward and rested his elbows on his knees and looked at the floor. "It's a lot easier to accept guilt when you've been caught. My eyes were closed and the world seemed so small to me. Judi, Andy, and Heather were behind me with Pastor Welsh. I didn't have much support from anyone else, and frankly, I didn't deserve it. I was the type who only talked to God when I needed something. And right then I needed Him more than ever. My plea agreement was for a sentence of somewhere between sixty-two and eighty-four months, but the judge had discretion to go above or below those guidelines, including the possibility that I'd only get probation. I prayed. I asked God to keep me out of prison and give me just one chance to turn my life around. I promised Him that I would be a better man, better uncle, friend, brother—a better Christian. I knew I could do better. All I wanted was to stay out of prison."

Pastor Welsh leaned forward and his voice was low, like he was doing a side commentary in a movie. "We can always do better. Every one of us."

"True," Rip said, glancing at Kevin Hart. "And you know what? In His infinite grace and wisdom, it only took God about ten seconds to answer my prayer. He said no."

He reached over and squeezed the nape of Andy's neck, and for some reason, Andy didn't shy away in his normal sea of embarrassment.

"Prison was God's way of putting me in time-out. Even though I always had the time, prison gave me some patience. It taught me to slow down, and it taught me to look for what I needed. What had been there all along."

"What was that?" Hart asked with just enough conviction to come across as sincerely interested.

"God," Rip said quietly.

"Amen," Pastor Welsh said. "Too many of us are in a hurry."

"You're right," Rip said. "We get into our routines. We wake up, take a shower, eat breakfast, kiss the kids good-bye, come home, eat dinner, kiss the kids good night, then get up and do it all over again. We don't make time for God, when in reality, it's the only time we really need."

"Keep going," Welsh said.

"I was like that," Rip continued. "Always in a rush, and I always needed everything right now, even results from God. And every time I talked to Him, I expected heaven to immediately open up, rain manna, or give me whatever else I wanted. But it doesn't work that way. Sometimes we get what we need, instead of what we want."

"Hmm," Hart said, nodding, his brows furrowed, pretending he was truly absorbing Rip's words. Rip tried to ignore him.

"God has been good to me," Rip said, bowing his head and slowly shaking it. "So anyhow, I started praying while I was in prison. I prayed about the things I had done that I was ashamed of. And then, instead of being impatient, I waited, listened, and most importantly, watched . . . watched what was happening around me. And then I started seeing things that could only be coming from Him. And in time, *His time*, I just knew."

"Knew what?" Hart asked. He honestly sounded sincere this time.

"That God is who He says He is, He's going to do what He says He is going to do, and that we all have access to Him." Rip paused and locked eyes once again with Hart, then patted Andy on the arm. "We aren't here for our own good. We are here to glorify God."

"What does that mean to you, Rip?" Pastor Welsh pressed. "Glorifying God?"

Rip considered the question. "For me, it's doing all we can to reflect Him. Making amends for the ways we screw up." He shrugged. "I feel like I owe Him . . . *we all* owe it to Him to do what He tells us to do. To live the way He wants us to. It's not always easy and we will certainly make mistakes. *But we should at least try* . . . and I guess that's sorta what I've been trying to do."

Pastor Welsh nodded and smiled. "Thanks for sharing, Rip."

Andy immediately stood up and walked away from the circle. Maybe it had been too intense, but that was okay. Andy went to the counter and held up an earbud and fiddled with the iPod. Rip looked over at Hart and back to Andy, who was smiling with his eyes closed as if he were trying to look into the sun. Rip tensed. Another word for Hart? It'd be the end if—

"*Gerald Michael*," Andy said.

Rip stood as if he were told to. He knew what was coming was for him. Who else referred to him as Gerald Michael?

"Yes, sir," he said without thinking about it.

"Love your enemies and pray for those who persecute you."

Everyone there except the reporter knew Andy, and they all just stared in silence. Hart broke it.

"Who taught you that, Andy?"

"That's also from the Bible," Rip whispered, turning the words over and over in his head.

"Who taught you that, Andy?" Hart asked again.

Andy made a fist and lifted it to the ceiling. His fingers splayed, as if stretching, reaching. But his head came down, his blue eyes completely focused on Hart.

"I'm not sure why He'd pick me, Mr. Hart, but I think it was God who told me to say that to Uncle Rip."

❇ ❇ ❇

He stared out the window at the moon, shuffling through the prayer request cards, wondering which ones he could maybe help God come true.

Heather wants the "discipline" to save $7,500 so she can go back and get her teacher's certificate . . .

Adam Vitale wants another promotion . . .

Marjo wants to be healthy . . .

Mrs. Miller wants a new puppy . . .

Maybe we should look after old Jimmy Keeler's teeth first . . . but what would be the best way to do that and when?

Nah, let's take care of Heather first.

FOURTEEN

Kevin Hart tossed the latest copy of the *Benning Weekly* on top of his desk and laughed as he studied the headline on the front page: "Santa Comes Early Again."

He leaned back and took a nice long look at the painting of his father.

"I don't like the things this Andy kid has been saying, Dad. What would you have done about it?"

He wouldn't have done it to me, Kevin. Just you. And he did it to you again because you let him get away with it the first time he did it. Now it's my turn to ask you something. What are YOU going to do about it?

Kevin pushed away from his desk, walked to the window, and then turned around and sneered at the painting.

"Thanks for the help, Dad. I'll figure it out on my own."

❄ ❄ ❄

Heather could tell Chief Reynolds wasn't happy. For him to come into the station and call a meeting on one of his days off, some heads were probably going to roll. And she suspected hers may be the first on the chopping block.

"Where's Ruthenberg at?" Reynolds barked, clenching his teeth. A little vein peeked out of his salt-and-pepper crew cut across his left temple.

"He's got the flu," Ray Blankenship said. "He's going to be out a few days."

"Who is covering for him?"

Heather glanced at Blankenship and then at Allen Dunning. They had each been on the force for around five years longer than she had and both gave her the same look that said, *Not me.*

"I'll do it, sir," Heather said.

"Good," Reynolds said, patting nervously at the side of his face and then grabbing a mint out of a glass jar on his desk. He took it out of its plastic wrapper, popped it in his mouth, and then threw the wrapper at a trash can behind him, missing horribly. "And see if you can make it a week without playing demolition derby."

"Yes, sir," Heather said. *Nothing like a little humiliation among peers to brighten a girl's day.*

"I got a call at home from the mayor this morning," Reynolds said. "He was at a conference up in Lansing and there were a few jokes made along the lines of *ho-ho-ho.* Does anybody want to guess what that's about?"

Dunning leaned against the wall. His hobbies included golf, pulling over attractive women, and covering his butt with both hands if there was ever a problem. "Our little Santa friend hasn't done anything on any of my shifts."

"Shut up, Dunning," Reynolds said. "We are a team here. And *we*—regardless of public sentiment—need to catch this clown and catch him soon. I've got two years left to retire and I'm not going out as the head of the laughingstock department in the state."

"We are doing everything we can," Heather said. "We'll get him."

Reynolds stood. "Heather, I want you to keep this little news reporter in your back pocket. Make sure she understands this guy is breaking the law. And make sure she realizes that we don't appreciate speculation in our newspaper. Only facts."

"She does," Heather said.

"And also make sure she understands this isn't cute, and it certainly isn't funny."

"Yes, sir."

"And if you three can't bring this guy down—and pass this along to Ruthenberg when you talk to him—I'll find some cops who will. That's it. Now go and make things right for the citizens of Benning Township."

FIFTEEN

There has to be an explanation," Rip said, sitting next to Judi. They were inside Pastor Welsh's office, weeding out all the things that *couldn't* be responsible for Andy's newfound ability.

"I heard what he said to Kevin during service," Pastor Welsh said. He ran his hand back through his straight white hair and a few strands fell back across his forehead. "And I also heard what he said during Bible study. And how that eloquently delivered little pearl of wisdom was aimed at you, Rip."

Rip held up his hands in surrender.

"Where is all of this coming from?" Judi asked. "Andy has that Bible Rip gave him, but he said he's only read a little bit of it. And I've never heard him talk about anything he's read, let alone walk up to somebody and start quoting it in their face."

"Andy said that it may be God telling him these things," Welsh said. "Why not?"

Rip and Judi looked at each other and Judi shrugged. "Doc Strater said nothing seemed unusual about Andy. All he said was that the mind can surprise us sometimes." She paused and shrugged again. "And to see if his behavior seems any different beyond the odd things he has been saying."

"Does it?" Welsh asked.

Rip said yes at the exact time Judi said no, and they quickly looked at each other. Rip was sure of it, and was also pretty certain Andy's wasn't the only person's behavior to have changed. They hadn't even told Welsh yet about the flower garden or how Judi wigged out over at McLouth.

"I haven't noticed anything," Judi said.

"C'mon," Rip said. "Just the idea of Andy acknowledging God is unusual behavior for him. I don't ever remember him even saying he *believed* in God."

"Andrew believes in God," Judi said as if he had insulted her.

Rip didn't respond to that, but there was something else he wanted to talk about. "Why can't he remember any of these things after he says them?"

"I don't think that's what we're supposed to be focusing on," Pastor Welsh said.

"What do you mean?" Rip asked.

"Maybe it's *who* he is saying these things to," Welsh said slowly, fiddling with a pencil. "If they're scriptural, I think we ought to pay attention."

Judi shook her head. "What about the thing he said regarding Heather's father and Mr. Hart?"

"Oh yeah," Rip said. "Andy pointed at a photo of them and said, 'They are able.' I couldn't find that anywhere in Scripture."

Pastor Welsh put a finger to his temple. "Let's just see what happens for a while. Maybe it will end here. Or maybe, if it keeps going, we'll learn more. I wouldn't lose much sleep over it."

"I still don't get it," Judi said.

"Me either," Rip added.

Pastor Welsh stood. He had that fatherly expression on his face he liked to use during certain sermons. He always paused and let you absorb it for a few long seconds, letting you know he was about to say something to remember.

"Rip and Judi," he said, "the Lord works in great ways. Unexpected ways. I'm telling you to just be thankful that Andy is giving credit to God."

❋ ❋ ❋

Asphalt cut the shore, outlining the edge of Lake Erie like a thin scratch of black ink on an old map. The path was brand new and so much easier to ride on than the leaves and hardened dirt it had been paved over.

Andy smiled and sped up. He had figured out how to adjust the governor on the throttle to return the bike to its original speed. It felt good to go fast, and he flipped up the visor, welcoming the oily scent of hot tar that filled his nose. Faster and faster he went, the sun's glare bouncing off the trail, wrapping around him, warming his face and neck.

It was getting too hot out, and he'd have kept going, but he spotted the new water fountain that had replaced the old pump. He remembered when he was little how he always liked cranking the rusty handle of the old pump. Up and down, up and down it went. And then he'd wait for the iron-smelling water to come, finally spilling out on his open palms for him to sip at and then slap on the sides of his face.

He pulled up next to the fountain and got off the motorcycle. He kneeled down and ran his finger across the top of the seat, thinking about how Mom had taken him to Dr. Strater's earlier and how they had sat there for what felt like forever before Dr. Strater came in the room. Mom had babbled on about how Andy had been saying some strange things, not caring in the least how much she was embarrassing herself and him. Then Mom actually seemed happy when Dr. Strater told her that nothing was wrong with him. She reverted to her normal and miserable self, of course, when it came time to pay the bill. Shocker.

Andy laughed about the doctor's visit. So what if he didn't remember the things he supposedly said? All he could really remember was how *good* he felt right before and right after he said those things.

Andy took a sip of water from the new fountain and then thought about all those times he used to ride his bicycle out here near the lake when he was younger. He remembered how he used to adjust the baseball card that Uncle Rip had clothespinned to the bike's frame. He liked the card there. The faster he went, the more the card rattled off the back spokes, making a sound just like a motorcycle. And now here he was, on a real motorcycle. It made him almost smile.

He stood and turned to the lake, thinking about what had been happening with the iPod again. Maybe Uncle Rip's God-lectures were finally rubbing off on him. Whatever it was, he could feel something happening inside of him, and he knew—he just *knew*—it was God. He smiled and took in a deep breath, watching the waves and enjoying how the sun glistened off the water.

A car horn beeped behind him and he turned to face it. A beautiful car approached. Shiny and red, with that loud purring sound that all fast cars made. A man was driving. It was hard to tell who it was because he was wearing dark glasses.

"Hey," Andy said, taking a step toward the car, wondering if the dude needed directions or something.

The driver revved the engine and Andy felt his eyes widen in approval. He moved closer to the car and then stopped, hoping the man would rev it again. He spotted the little silver horse on the side of the car and how it stood out against the red. A classic Mustang.

The driver turned the engine off and stuck his head out the window. Andy still didn't recognize him under the sun's glare and took off his helmet.

"Hear anything good today through your headphones?" the man asked. Andy recognized the voice then. It was Mr. Hart.

"Not today," Andy said slowly.

"How old are you now, Andy?"

"I just turned fourteen," Andy said.

"It's a shame how long you've been walking around with that face of yours, isn't it?"

Andy froze, wondering if he'd heard him right.

"Look in the mirror lately?" Mr. Hart said.

"Yeah," Andy answered. Of course he did. He looked in the mirror every day. *Several times a day.*

"You care about your Uncle Rip?" Mr. Hart asked. "About his home, about his job . . . about his freedom?"

Andy figured he had to say something. "Yes, Mr. Hart."

Mr. Hart put his hands on the steering wheel and looked out at the lake. "I know you don't do all that well in school, but I still think you are smart enough to know what will happen if you ever mention this conversation to your Uncle Rip or try to embarrass me in front of a group of people again."

"I don't even know what I said, Mr. Hart."

"I'm not an idiot, Andy."

"I don't remember saying that eith—"

"You tried to say that God told you to say those things, but God would only give a gift like that to someone He loves. God doesn't love you."

"I don't know, Mr. Hart," Andy said, feeling a surge of frustration. "Uncle Rip says He does."

Mr. Hart took his hands off the wheel and looked right at Andy. Then he took off his sunglasses and started to laugh. "Your Uncle Rip said that?"

Andy nodded.

"Really?" Mr. Hart said, laughing again. "If God loves you, I wouldn't want to see what He does to people He hates."

Andy took a step back and dropped his helmet. He lowered his head and covered his face with his hands, unable to do anything but that—something he used to do when he was a little kid and others shamed him.

Mr. Hart started the car and then it made a terrible sound and gray smoke came out of the tires. Little pieces of rock started hitting his arms and legs as the Mustang spun away.

When he couldn't hear the car anymore, he slowly took his hands away from his face and felt himself trembling. He opened his eyes and could see the little red welts that were rising on each of his arms. He clenched at his shorts and then lowered himself to one knee, squinting at matching cuts that were about an inch apart, halfway down his right shin.

He was glad that nobody else was around to see him. Not his arms and legs—but the side of his face.

A tiny droplet of blood was heading down his right shin. He dabbed at it with his thumb and then stood and faced the lake. He took a deep breath, ran his hand along the side of his face, then looked at the sky.

Maybe Mr. Hart is right . . .

He wiped the tears from his eyes, unable to remember the last time he cried. And then he picked up his helmet, got back on his motorcycle, and headed for home.

❋ ❋ ❋

Andy pulled the motorcycle back in the garage and could see Uncle Rip and Heather sitting out on the picnic table near the lake. He lifted his head to the sky, wondering if he had it in him to pretend that everything was all right.

"Your ears must be burning," Heather said as he walked out of the garage. "We were just talking about you."

"Shocker," Andy said, sitting Indian-style in the grass next to the picnic table. Milo got in his lap and rolled over for a belly rub. He still smelled a little of skunk, but it was bearable.

"What happened to your legs?" Uncle Rip asked.

"Nothing," Andy muttered, ignoring the urge to tell him. Mr. Hart had warned him what would happen if he said anything. "Why were you guys talking about me?"

"We were talking about some of the things you've been saying," Heather said.

"Here we go again," Andy said. "Like what?"

"Like what you said to Mr. Hart at church," Heather answered.

Andy froze at the mention of Mr. Hart's name and stopped petting Milo.

"And what you said to me and your mom," Heather added. "About the picture of my dad and Mr. Hart's dad. And what you said to your Uncle Rip at Bible study too."

"I seriously don't remember," Andy said, wishing he could. He had already told Uncle Rip the only thing he could recall was how good he felt when he was done saying those things and how he sort of felt the same way looking at the flower garden.

Then he wished he couldn't remember what Mr. Hart had told him.

"You've got us thinking we've lost our marbles," Uncle Rip said.

Andy tried not to think about anything that had to do with Mr. Hart. All he wanted to do right now was pet Milo, who looked like a little baby in his arms. He liked the way Milo's only back leg moved while he scratched his belly. The faster he scratched, the faster that paw pedaled at the air while his tongue hung out the side of his mouth like a big piece of wet gum.

"Sorry I'm driving everybody crazy, Uncle Rip."

"No worries, bro," Uncle Rip said. "We'll figure it all out."

Figure it all out, Andy thought. One thing they would never figure out would be why Mr. Hart would want to say those mean things to him. He swallowed hard, trying to forget the words that rang through his head as if on repeat.

"The truth isn't always easy," Andy blurted, surprised the words came from his mouth. "But I know whatever I hear in the iPod *is* the truth."

"The truth isn't always easy?" Uncle Rip said. He looked about as surprised as Andy felt. "That's not from the Bible and I don't see an earbud next to your ear. Where did that come from?"

"That's just from me," Andy said. He didn't have the faintest idea why, but he had never been so certain about anything in his life.

Uncle Rip stood. He came over and took the iPod out of Andy's hand.

"I just don't get it," Uncle Rip said, studying the iPod. "You hear *scripture* through this? Not, like . . . Christian music or something?"

Andy shook his head. "It's music, but nothing like you've ever heard on the radio. All I know is I hear a song and a voice. I guess I'm just repeating what I hear."

Uncle Rip held one of the earbuds to his ear.

Heather had a funny look on her face. "What do you hear, Rip?"

"Nothing," Uncle Rip said. He seemed to be thinking. "But whatever Andy is hearing seems to be generally scriptural. And what he said at the Bible study about loving your enemies and praying for those that persecute you . . . it was really something I needed to hear. It's something I need to do."

Heather also stood. "But what about what he said when he pointed at the picture of my dad and Kevin's dad? He said, 'They are able.' Is that from the Bible?"

"Yes, it is," Andy said. He wasn't sure why he said that either, but he had no doubt about it. "It's the truth too."

"They are able?" Uncle Rip said. He looked at Heather, shrugged, and then looked back at Andy. "I'm clueless on that one, bro. Haven't found it in the Bible yet."

"You guys ready to go?" It was Mom.

Uncle Rip held up the earbud to his ear again and smiled. "I still don't hear anything. I'm jealous."

Andy stood and Milo sprang up on all three legs. "I know why, Uncle Rip."

"Really?"

Andy took the iPod from his uncle and squeezed it tightly in his hand.

"Because you and Heather . . . Mr. Hart and Mom . . . you're not listening."

※ ※ ※

Heather and Judi sat on Judi's front porch. They had returned from dinner at Migliore's Steakhouse over an hour ago. Rip had gone home and Andy went to bed.

"Is this the hottest summer ever?" Judi asked.

"Feels like it," Heather said. She wasn't thinking about how warm it was. She was thinking about Rip.

Judi smacked a mosquito on her arm. "Why are you acting so weird? You seem mighty quiet."

"Everybody's acting weird," Heather said. "I kinda feel like I'm having a midlife crisis."

Judi laughed. "Heather, you're only thirty-five."

"And I'm a cop," she said. "I've never been married. Can't have kids. I live alone and there are no prospects of any of those things changing."

"You could always quit your job and move in with Rip."

"Shut up."

"Oh, please," Judi said. "You two should just get over yourselves and start dating again. What have you got to lose?"

"My job, for starters. What would the department say? And what would people think of a cop who dates an ex-con?"

"Not sure," Judi said. "Why don't you ask a few people at the department?"

"After letting the Summer Santa run? After screwing up my new squad car? They're already about to fire me. Are you crazy?"

"Maybe a little," Judi said. "But the more I think about it, I'm starting to think that we are all a little crazy."

Heather straightened up in her chair. She wasn't exactly sure what Judi meant, but something about what she said made her feel better.

"What do you mean?" Heather asked.

Judi laughed again. "I've been thinking about some of the things we've been talking about. Like what's been happening and what Andy's been saying. Mostly how we don't listen and how we ignore the truth. We ignore it and try to move forward to lead that perfect life, that TV-life that we think is normal. And you know what I think?"

"What?"

"There is no such thing as normal," Judi said, shrugging. "Maybe I'm wrong, but if there is, it sure wasn't me and Todd."

"Ain't me either," Heather said. "You ever figure out what was going through your head when we were over at McLouth, looking at those flowers?"

"No," Judi said, laughing again. "But I just know God is trying to tell me something, through Andy and through that garden. But when I was out there, it was kinda like God was right there in the flowers and I didn't need the middle man. The more I looked at the garden, the more I felt I needed to know what He was trying to tell me. Right then and there."

"You'll figure it out."

"Why don't you date anybody?"

"That was kind of random," Heather said. "Why don't you?"

"I asked first," Judi said. "I know why you don't. You still love Rip after all these years."

"Nah. I'm still hung up on Kevin."

The two shared a good laugh, then Heather sobered. "You know something, Judi? I don't know if Rip and I ever had what it took. We went out for two years and he never told me he loved me."

"So you're curious about round two?"

Heather thought about it.

Rip is a former drug dealer.

He lives in a beat-up single-wide.

He can barely support himself.

He drives a Pacer, for Pete's sake.

Heather thought about what Judi said about *normal*. Rip was everything but normal, but she couldn't deny it. Loving him just felt right.

"Yeah," she said, tapping Judi on the arm. "I'd give it another round."

Judi turned to her and smiled. "I knew it."

Heather smiled back. "But if you dare tell him that . . ."

"You'll what?" Judi laughed.

"Seriously," Heather said.

"Okay, okay." Judi laughed again. "Your secret is safe with me."

SIXTEEN

She was sitting at the kitchen table in Walter Hart's house, watching her father and Mr. Hart. They each had their Bibles in front of them and Mr. Hart was smiling and nodding his head patiently, tapping on Dad's Bible at a verse as if he was trying to explain it. Dad nodded back like he understood and then spoke words she couldn't hear. She asked him to repeat himself, but he didn't. He didn't even look at her and the two men just went about their business as if she weren't even there. Heather's heart began to race. She wasn't sure how long she had been in the kitchen and it occurred to her that there was no sound. There also weren't any colors. And then she noticed something else.

Mr. Hart smiled again . . . and nodded his head patiently again . . . and tapped on Dad's Bible again . . .

How many times had she watched them do the exact same thing over and over?

Heather stood and put her hand on her father's shoulder. He turned and seemed to look right through her, as if she were invisible. He smiled and she felt herself smile back. But then Dad's smile slowly disappeared and he leaned to his left and looked behind her.

Heather slowly turned around and the man in the black mask was there. This time he wasn't holding a brown paper bag. He had a gun and was pointing it right at the back of Walter Hart's head.

Heather drew her pistol and quickly squeezed off two rounds at the man's chest. He didn't flinch. He just lowered his gun. Heather wondered why she hadn't heard the shots and realized she was only pointing her finger at the man. He just stared at her for a few seconds and then put the gun back up next to Mr. Hart's head and pulled the trigger. The shot echoed in her ears, reverberated in her chest—

Heather sat up straight on her couch, her heart still hammering. She closed her eyes, rubbed her face, and gradually caught her breath.

After a second, Heather knew she wasn't alone.

Slowly she opened her eyes and saw him, standing across the living room.

Worse, he was between her and her gun, stashed in her bedroom nightstand.

For a long moment, they stared at each other, Heather's heart pounding. Why was he here? What did he want?

He blinked slowly behind the black mask, then held his hands up, showing that he wasn't armed.

"You here to turn yourself in?" Heather asked, the vehemence of her voice surprising herself. "What's your name?"

He didn't answer. He only pointed at the coffee table in front of her. It was another brown paper bag.

Then he held his right hand up in the air and she knew what he was going to do before he did it.

He made the sign of the cross.

And then backed away and walked out the door.

SEVENTEEN

Shall I tell him it's official police business?" the secretary asked.

"Do that," Heather answered with a smile.

She couldn't think of the woman's name, even though she knew her face. She'd only been in the factory one time since she and Kevin had broken up over ten years ago, but she knew it was the same woman who worked for Kevin's dad.

Heather guessed that official police business wasn't announced over the phone. She watched as the woman knocked on Kevin's door before sticking her head in his office. She then opened the door a little wider and stepped aside for Heather.

"What'd I do now?" Kevin said, smiling and showing those perfectly white teeth of his. Not only was he the richest guy in town, he was still one of the best looking.

"It's been a slow week," Heather said. "And I'm working a double shift today, so it leaves me lots of extra time for a little police harassment." *A little time to figure out how in the world you got into my apartment last night to leave $7,500.* Oddly enough, it was the same amount she figured she needed to go back and finish school. The *exact* amount she had put on a prayer card at church. Prayer cards Kevin Hart read every single week.

"C'mon in," he said, leaning back on his heels and holding his arm out in invitation.

Kevin's office was state-of-the-art everything. Hardwood flooring that was impeccably clean. Flat-screen televisions on separate walls, set to different channels, that each had stock market quotes silently flowing across their bottoms. A glass case that was full of sports memorabilia. And a fully stocked mahogany bar to match his desk.

"Pretty spiffy office," Heather said, sitting at one of the two chairs that were centered in front of Kevin's desk. "Looks a little different from the way your dad had it."

"Thanks," he said, pointing a remote at the two televisions to turn them off. He then aimed it over his shoulder and did a no-look click that had the blinds automatically open, slowly exposing a view of Lake Erie that was second only to Judi's back porch.

She noticed that his desk was a little messy. This was unusual for a neat freak like Kevin. "Looks like you've been busy."

"Swamped," he said. "We are still working on an acquisition, along with a bazillion other things."

"Like little Marjo's fund-raiser?" Heather said. "It's nice of you and Carrie to put that together. Seems like she isn't doing too well."

"I guess not," he said. "Looks like surgery is gonna be the last resort. She needs our prayers."

Heather could see the latest copy of the *Benning Weekly* on his desk. It had been neatly folded to the article about the "Summer Santa." *Well now, that's interesting . . .*

"What do you think about that?" she asked, pointing to the newspaper. "Pretty weird, huh?"

"I guess so," he said dismissively. He picked the paper up and she heard it hit the trash can below his desk.

She gave him a suspicious smile. "Don't want to talk about that?"

"I'll talk about it," he said quickly, giving her a confused look. "Why?"

"Oh, it's all right," she said. "I was just curious what you thought." Actually, she was thinking about the sign of the cross he gave her in her living room.

"Can't dislike a guy for trying to help people out," he said, leaning back in his chair and looking her straight in the eye. Was he trying to intimidate her?

"I agree," she said, leaning forward. "But he is still breaking the law."

"Well, I'm sure one of Benning's finest will catch him," he said. He paused. "What brings you by, Heather?"

His question startled her. They'd actually been getting somewhere . . . "I need to talk to Rip about something." It was a lie. "You mind me chatting with him while he's working?"

Kevin paused. "It can't wait till quitting time?" He gave her a rueful look. "Company policy and all."

She knew he wasn't buying her story, and latched onto the first thing that came to her mind. "It's about Andy. Maybe he can take a break?"

"Andy, huh?" He rose and came around the desk and casually leaned on it. "If it leads to you figuring out how Andy thinks he has 'searched me and knows me,' come back and enlighten me, will you?"

"Will do," Heather said, standing. She studied Kevin, imagining him in all black. "Andy said something strange about a photo of our dads."

"Our dads?" He cocked his head, then lifted his hands. "Not that Andy's short of odd sayings of late, right?"

"But everything else has been directed to a person. You, Judi, and Rip. This was about a specific picture."

"What'd he say?"

"'They are able.'"

"Huh?" Kevin said. "I don't mean to be indelicate, Heather. But do you think Doc Strater has what it takes to examine the kid? Any chance he needs to head to a psych ward?"

Heather bristled. "Andy's not crazy. This is . . . something different."

"I'll say." Hart rolled his eyes and sighed. "Look, I'm sorry. I'm just not really in a mood to think about our dads, okay? It's too . . . painful."

"Okay," she said, regretting bringing it up. His pain seemed to elicit her own. "Sorry. Let me know if you see the Summer Santa, will ya? Chief Reynolds will have our hides if we don't collar him soon."

He stood and put his hands in his pockets. A funny little smile etched the corners of his mouth.

"Will do," he said. "And don't go shooting a guy that's just trying to help somebody out."

※ ※ ※

No secretarial clearance was necessary for Heather to visit Rip. When she walked by his "office," the door to the custodial closet was wide open, and he was sitting at a desk with a piece of cold, leftover pizza hanging out of his mouth and his Bible between his hands.

"A little early dinner?" Heather asked.

"Heather!" he mumbled, the pizza still in his mouth. He marked his place in the Bible with a pencil. "Cop a seat. No pun intended."

"Thanks," she said. "You heard from Judi today?"

"You mean the daily despair report?"

"Be nice, Rip."

"I actually haven't heard from her, even though I've rung her cell all day." He held up his phone and then put it on top of the Bible. "Maybe she's just out and about. Went shopping in the city or something."

"Judi doesn't go out and about by herself."

"Long shot, I know," he said with a small smile. "Hey, I've just been scouring the Internet on my phone, trying to see what Andy meant with the whole 'they are able' thing. I'm pulling up a big donut. I can't find *any* reference that makes sense. I wanted to see if Judi had thought of anything."

"I was just talking to Kevin about that . . . Well, sort of."

"I'm sure that went well," Rip said with a little laugh. "I've *never* heard Kevin talk about his dad's death, and he's certainly not a big fan of Andy's newfound ability. What'd he say?"

"Nothing much," Heather said. She fiddled with the corner of his pizza box. "I don't talk much about my dad either. Maybe Kevin's like me . . . it just hurts too bad."

"You been prayin' about it, like we talked about?"

Rip's question saddened her. She hadn't prayed about it, and she felt like she was somehow cheating her father.

"I just wish *I knew* where he was right now," she said. "I know it sounds weird, but I can't get him off my mind."

Rip nodded as if he understood.

Heather imagined her father in the best place. Just the thought of it took a little of the weight off her shoulders she'd been carrying around since the night he died.

"Take care, you guys."

They both turned toward the door. It was Kevin. He came off the stairs from the third floor and was on his way out.

"See ya, boss," Rip said.

"Bye, Kevin," Heather added.

Kevin was out of sight when Rip said, "When you gonna arrest him for busting into people's houses?"

"Shut up," she hissed, looking over her shoulder to make sure Kevin was gone. Five thousand in grocery cards. Three-plus thousand in cash for Becky. More than seven thousand for her. Regardless, one thing was for sure . . . Kevin could certainly afford it.

Heather wasn't going to tell Rip about last night. He'd freak out that the guy had broken into her house, insist on sleeping over or something. And that wouldn't be good, for a number of reasons.

Rip raised his brows, as if considering her words, and Heather glanced back at the stairwell, thinking again about what she'd seen. The newspaper that Kevin had trashed had been tucked under his arm when he walked by.

EIGHTEEN

Judi wasn't sure how long she'd been sitting on the bank of The Frank and Poet Canal. Her elbows were resting on her knees and she was cradling her head in the palms of her hands, staring at the first of the four sections that made up the flower garden. She had felt it the first time she'd seen the garden when she was over on the McLouth side. Then she felt it again when she and Heather returned here to the bank. Now it was something she recognized, welcomed. That little tickling feeling at the center of her gut had convinced her. There was no doubt in her mind that the first section of the garden was there specifically for her. And why did that dark little cloud that always seemed to follow her disappear when she looked at the flowers?

She heard someone walking up from behind her and instinctively knew it was Rip. He'd called her several times that day, but she didn't answer because she just didn't feel like talking. Not to him. Not to anyone. That's when she knew she needed to come here, to the canal. To the garden.

She didn't bother turning around, and she could hear him getting closer.

"I was worried when I couldn't find you today," he said. "Have you been out here all day?"

She didn't answer. She was thinking about how Todd used to wade out in the canal, encouraging little Andy to jump in and join him.

"I've got some Mexican food back at the house," Rip said, sitting down next to her. "We gotta make sure Andy doesn't give any to Milo. Last time he threw up on his yellow blanket and farted for two months."

She didn't say anything and Rip waved his hand back and forth in front of her face.

"Hellooo," he said. "Anybody home?"

"Sorry," she said. "We don't have to worry about Milo and the Mexican food. He took off last night and still hasn't come back."

"Ahh," Rip said. "Is that what has you upset? He's probably courting some poodle on the other side of town."

"You're probably right."

"Then why so sad?" Rip said. "Tough day at the theater, Mrs. Lincoln?"

She sighed and lifted her head from her hands. "I've been sitting out here practically half the day, trying to make sense of my life. I've been thinking about a lot of things. But mostly about something Heather said."

"'Bout what?"

"The thing about me not being happy unless I'm unhappy."

"She didn't mean anything by that," Rip said, running to Heather's defense.

"No. It's true, Rip."

Rip had always been a world-class smart aleck, but lately he'd been pretty good at knowing when to keep quiet.

Judi continued, "I've also been thinking about what Andy told you and Heather. That we haven't been listening. I was supposed to hear that. When you told me what he said, it was like a tiny light went on somewhere in the back of my mind. And it's been getting a little brighter all day."

Rip's smile made her smile too.

"It's so true," she said. She paused and stared at the ground, shaking her head. "I haven't been listening."

"I promise you, I *am* listening," Rip said. "I love hearing you say stuff like this."

"I've been ignoring that little voice inside of me," she said. "You know what I mean—the One that guides us. The One that *knows and tells* us what is right."

Rip smiled. "It's the Spirit, Judi."

"I've always heard it, Rip. *But I haven't been listening.*"

"It's not always easy," he said.

"Todd's not coming back," she said. The words just came out. They hurt for a few seconds, but then she could feel some of the pressure come off. "Not that I even want him to come back . . . It's just that I spent so much time wondering what went wrong, Rip. So many years knowing the truth, but I kept lying . . ."

"Lying to whom?"

She felt peace and a connection with Rip that hadn't been there since they were kids.

"I've been lying to myself," she said. She took what felt like the first full breath she had taken in months. "People lie all the time. But when we aren't honest with ourselves, when we can't trust ourselves—it's the worst feeling in the world."

"Been there and done that," Rip said.

They sat there in companionable silence for a while, staring at the garden.

"You know what can hurt just as bad as lying to yourself?" Judi asked.

"What?"

She shook her head and paused before saying it. "Telling yourself the truth."

Rip patted her on the leg and considered her words. "Do you remember what Pastor Welsh said about lies a few months ago?"

She hadn't paid much attention to anyone over the last few months. Heck, the last several years, for that matter. She shook her head again.

Rip put his hand on her shoulder and gave it a gentle squeeze. "Welsh said that all lies have to change or die, because they are constantly haunted by the truth. And as much as we sometimes want to convince ourselves that we can . . . we can't change the truth. Only *accept* it."

Judi glanced back at the flower garden and thought about the lies Todd had told her as well. But as she looked at all the different colors across the canal, the hurt was somehow gone.

"Accept the truth?" she whispered. "Kind of like admitting that I spent so many good years with the wrong person?"

"It's better than your *whole* life," Rip said. He stared at her and then squinted. "But I'm pretty sure that's not what you really need to accept."

"What do you mean?" she asked. "Tell me what you think I need to accept."

They could hear Andy's motorcycle coming out of the woods and into the corn. The sound of it reminded Judi of a bee that was getting closer to her ear.

"Talk to God about it," Rip said. "Then listen to that little voice. He'll tell you."

"I want you to tell me," Judi said as Andy came out of the corn and into the high grass. *He sure got here quick for a motorcycle that only goes around forty miles per hour.*

Andy parked the bike in the grass and walked down the bank to join them. He and Rip tapped knuckles.

"I can't find Milo," Andy said. He raised the visor and then took his helmet off. "I've been everywhere."

"He'll show up," Rip said. "Don't worry."

Judi didn't want the subject to change. She felt better than she had in such a long time.

"I've been blaming myself for everything," she said. *"Everything."*

Andy looked at her and she could see a rare look of concern in his eyes. She appreciated it.

"What did *you* do that was so bad?" Rip asked.

Rip's question pierced her. And then something about the look on Andy's face seemed to beg for a confession.

"Why don't you answer the question?" Rip said. "Now is the time, Judi. Tell me, tell your son, tell *yourself* what you ever did as a wife and mother that was so bad."

Judi just stared at Andy, thinking about what Pastor Welsh had said. Whether the truth made her feel good or not, it was still the truth. She could hear that little voice inside of her. She could feel it guiding her toward the answer. She knew exactly what she did wrong in her marriage and as a mother. She faced Rip and then looked back at that first section of wildflowers that so drew her, from the moment she'd first seen them. Something over there forced her to answer, but it only came out as a whisper.

"Nothing."

"Nothing?" Andy whispered fiercely, pulling his hair off the side of his face. "You're kidding me, right?"

"No, I'm not kidding," she said. It was the truth.

"Unbelievable," Andy muttered, taking a step back. "You think you didn't do anything wrong?"

"No," Judi whispered, as layers of weights seemed to fly from her shoulders. "I didn't."

She felt bad for not protecting Andy. For not taking him and running from Todd after the very first night her husband hit her. But it wasn't her fault that Todd had made the decisions he had on that fateful night. It wasn't her fault that he'd taken to drinking again. It wasn't her fault that he'd gone to other women.

The truth was, Todd was just desperate. Desperately seeking solace anywhere he could. Like Judi had so desperately sought solace in her guilt and her grief ever since.

I've been looking in the wrong direction, Lord. For so long. Clinging to the sins, the sorrow, rather than to You! The truth of it washed through her like a spring wind, washing away winter dust that clouded her vision.

"You're right," Rip said, kneeling next to her. He put his arm around her and she put her face on his shoulder, choking on sobs long buried. "You didn't do anything wrong."

"I can't believe this," Andy said. "I can't believe that you . . . What the heck?"

Judi looked up at Andy and his eyebrows were hunched together and he was squinting, almost as if it hurt, utterly lost in his confusion.

"What is it, bro?" Rip said.

"Look," Andy said, pointing to the other side of the canal.

Judi followed his finger and quickly stood.

There were now only three sections of the garden.

Hers was gone.

No high grass. No black soil. No flowers. What was there seconds ago was now just a bald patch of cracked and sunbaked mud that hugged unevenly at the rest of the garden like it wanted back in.

Imperfection seeking perfection, she thought. Oddly, she didn't feel a loss, even though it had been her section. She only felt peace. Wholeness.

"How did that just happen?" Andy asked.

Rip stood and craned his neck toward the garden. Then he looked around as if he wanted other people to have witnessed it before pointing across the canal. "Okay, we all saw that, right? All three of us? It was just there a second ago. That left section of flowers. Right?"

Judi and Andy nodded.

"It just happened," Andy muttered. *"It really just happened."*

Judi laughed. "Yes, it did."

Rip held his hands up and then let them drop against his sides. "There is only one possible explanation. And it's also the only explanation for what Andy's been hearing in the iPod."

"What is it?" Andy said.

"Him," Rip answered. He went farther down the bank and stepped into the water. And then he smiled and pointed at the sky. "I think we just found out who the Gardener is."

※ ※ ※

Heather had spent most of the evening doing exactly what she knew she'd be doing—sleeping on the side of St. Paul's for the better part of two hours with the window down, being eaten half-alive by mosquitoes—until Natalie came across the radio, telling her to get out to old Jimmy Keeler's house. Heather figured Jimmy must have had a heart attack from stressing out about that "crook" dentist of his down in Monroe and the ever-increasing price of his health care.

But that wasn't it.

Jimmy had had an encounter with an intruder.

By the time she reached his house three minutes later, Jimmy was waiting in the driveway and complaining about how long it had taken her to get out there.

"What if I'd had a stroke or the missus had fallen down?" he barked. "My tax dollars don't seem to be too hard at work."

"I got here as soon as I could, Jimmy," she said. "Just be thankful those things didn't happen."

"I didn't hear your siren," he added. "You couldn't have been in too much of a cotton-pickin' hurry."

"It's late. And dispatch said the intruder is gone," she said. "Are you sure he's not still here?"

"Positive," Jimmy said. "I was in the living room, looking right out the window at him. He was standing right about where we are now."

"He was standing out here?"

"Yes, ma'am," he said. "I think he knew I was looking at him too. My heart was beating so fast, I thought it was going to break my sternum."

"Which way did he go?"

"He went that way." Jimmy pointed to the woods near the end of the road. "Funny thing was, he *walked*. He didn't run. You figure he'd be in a hurry to get out of here. I think it may be that Santa fella from the newspaper. Whatcha think?"

"Tell me what he looked like."

"Just like the weekly paper said. He was all decked out in black. Face and all."

"Are you sure he was in the house?" Heather asked, for some reason thinking about the reporter from the newspaper. "*Maybe he wants to get caught.*"

"Positive," Jimmy said, making a fist. "I was getting ready to grab my bat and bust him up, and then I heard him leave the kitchen."

"Let's go inside and see if anything is out of order. I need to make a report."

"That's not necessary," Jimmy said. "I already looked around, waiting for you to show up. Nothing's missin'."

"Jimmy?" It was Mrs. Keeler. Her head peered around the front door. Her gray hair looked blue under the porch light. "There is a booby trap in here."

"Good Lord!" Jimmy cried. "Call the bomb squad!"

Heather rushed to the door and Mrs. Keeler opened it.

"Where is it?" Heather asked.

"It's in the kitchen."

The light was already on and Heather tiptoed to the edge of the room. Jimmy and Mrs. Keeler were behind her. She couldn't see anything out of order. They both looked at Mrs. Keeler.

"It's right there," she said, pointing a blue and shriveled finger at the cupboard above the kitchen sink.

"Good Lord!" Jimmy said. "It's a trip wire!"

Heather wasn't sure if it was a trip wire, but there was definitely some type of line that stretched from the cupboards into the refrigerator door. She slowly stepped closer and pulled out her flashlight. She went to the edge of the sink and studied the line.

"Be careful," Jimmy said. "Some of that stuff is motion sensitive."

"It's dental floss," Heather said, running her finger across it to where it was tucked inside the cupboard. She opened the cupboard door and a little wooden cross fell out. The dental floss had been taped to it. She picked it up and studied the balance of the line that went into the refrigerator. *These people don't need gift cards to Food Village. What are you up to now?*

She followed the floss, wrapping it around her finger until she reached the refrigerator. She slowly opened the refrigerator door, and directly in front of her, on the top shelf, the dental floss ran to a toothbrush that was on top of an egg carton.

"A toothbrush?" Jimmy said, peeking over her shoulder. "He's lucky I didn't get down here while he was in the house. Sicko is making fun of me not having any teeth?"

"I don't think so," Heather said. She lifted the toothbrush off the egg carton and it popped open. The eggs were gone, but they had been replaced with something else. "Uh . . . Jimmy . . . the other day at Bible study . . . How much did you say your new dentures were gonna be?"

"Thirty-six hundred big ones," Jimmy said. "Money I don't have."

"I'm not sure about that," Heather said.

Inside of each little space where the eggs had been were three neatly folded one-hundred-dollar bills. Exactly thirty-six hundred dollars. She held it up and showed it to Jimmy and Mrs. Keeler.

"Good Lord," Jimmy whispered. "He was an angel."

Mrs. Keeler nodded. "That explains why he did this when he was out in the driveway . . . right before he walked away." She made the sign of the cross.

"He did that?" Heather asked.

"Yes," Mrs. Keeler said excitedly. "Jimmy couldn't see it. He was hiding in the closet, yelling at me."

"Quit babblin', woman," Jimmy said, shaking his hand dismissively at his wife. "Pay her no mind, Heather. You know how the mind goes when you get to a certain age."

NINETEEN

Andy leaned back against the worktable in the barn and waited
for Uncle Rip to try to start the old motorcycle they'd been working on for the better part of the day. Uncle Rip had picked him up
in the Pacer and they went back to his mobile home and hooked
a chain up to the old bike. Andy had gotten on it and steered it as
they slowly towed it all the way back home and to the barn. The
bike was a little bigger than the one Uncle Rip had fixed up for
Andy's birthday, and according to Uncle Rip, in much worse shape.

Uncle Rip had already tried to start it around ten times, and
Andy could tell he was growing impatient. He even swore a couple
times, but Uncle Rip said this time it was going to start.

Uncle Rip coughed and winced. He seemed to have a hard time
catching his breath before he jumped up and came down on the
kick-starter. The motorcycle sputtered to a begrudging start and a
sickly puff of blue smoke came out of the exhaust pipe.

"Nice," Andy said with a laugh.

"I should be on the cover of *Master Mechanic* magazine," Uncle

Rip shouted over the noise, with the first smile he'd seen from him in hours.

"Never heard of that magazine," Andy said.

"Me either," Uncle Rip added. "But I should still be on it for getting this old girl going. Get on your bike and let's take a little spin. Let's go out on the road and then we'll cut back up along the canal. If this thing dies, we're leaving it out in the field for good and I'm riding back with you."

"If it dies, you gonna swear at it some more?"

Uncle Rip wiped the sweat off his forehead and bit his lip. "You preaching to me?"

"How's it feel?" Andy said.

Uncle Rip smiled. "Sorry about the language, bro. You just made me think of something Pastor Welsh told me. Just like this bike, I still need a lot of work."

As they went down the driveway toward the road, Andy didn't want to go too fast and give away the fact that he had figured out how to adjust the governor on the throttle, reversing Uncle Rip's work to slow the bike down. Andy charged out in front, but when his helmetless Uncle Rip passed him, Andy buried it, zipping past his uncle down the road toward the bridge that ran over The Frank and Poet.

Uncle Rip yelled and Andy pulled the bike over.

"Maybe *you* should be on the cover of *Master Mechanic*," Uncle Rip said, shaking his head.

"Why you say that?" Andy asked, trying to hide a smug smile.

Uncle Rip looked like he was hiding his own smile. "I didn't think it would take you long to figure that throttle out. Keep it between us and be careful, okay?"

Andy grinned. It was a secret he didn't mind keeping.

"She's running pretty good," Uncle Rip said, tapping on the side of the older bike as if it were alive. "Before we hit the bridge, let's hang a right and run along the canal until we reach the flowers. I want to take another look."

This would be the fifth time in the last couple days he and Uncle Rip had gone out to the flower garden to make sure what they thought happened, really happened. Mom had even gone with them on a couple of those trips, and they figured it would be best not to tell anyone other than Pastor Welsh and Heather how the garden had changed. Andy was pretty sure the reasoning behind the decision was to prevent people from thinking they were flat-out nuts, so he was cool with it. They already thought he was crazy, what with all the iPod stuff going on.

"Let's race," Andy said.

"Wake up, little boy, you don't have a chance against your Uncle Rip."

Andy gunned it and laughed, knowing he had to have sprayed Uncle Rip with a fair amount of dirt and gravel as he peeled off toward the bridge. They were halfway there when he heard Uncle Rip catching up to him. Andy leaned forward and pulled back on the throttle as far as he could, but Uncle Rip still passed him.

He was laughing.

Despite its lack of upkeep, Uncle Rip's bike was clearly more powerful, and Andy watched as his uncle beat him to the bridge before jumping down into the high grass that ran the length of the canal. Andy followed and they were flying alongside The Frank and Poet toward the lake. When they approached the sharp bend in the canal that would take them toward the cornfields across from the flower bed, Uncle Rip pulled on the brakes and slid around twenty feet, almost straight sideways, before stopping only inches from the bank that led down to the water.

Andy slowed down and pulled up next to him. "I thought you were gonna get wet for a second."

"Checking the brakes at that speed wasn't real smart of me. Good thing they work."

Andy nodded. "How did she feel?"

"Not bad," Uncle Rip said. "Still needs a little work, though."

Uncle Rip turned his engine off and Andy did the same. They pushed the bikes along the edge of the canal, neither of them saying much, until the side of McLouth Steel came into sight through some trees on the other side of the canal.

"You really think God put that garden there?" Andy asked.

"What else could it be?" Uncle Rip said. "You saw the same thing I did."

They had talked and talked about it, and Uncle Rip offered his theory—more like another lecture—that maybe God was trying to tell Mom something through the garden. And when she finally learned the lesson she needed, "her" part of the garden disappeared.

As they continued to push the bikes, Andy thought about how that section of flowers disappeared right before his eyes and it scared him. Because the only thing that made any sense was that it had to be God. But then Uncle Rip's theory couldn't be true because God would know that Mom *did* do something terrible. And Mom knew it too. She burned him. So why would God let her get away with that? Without admitting it? God didn't like a liar, did He?

"Wow," Uncle Rip said.

"What?" Andy said.

"It's changed again."

Uncle Rip stopped walking and nodded across the canal, up to their left. The flowers were now in sight. They were a good fifty yards away, but Andy could tell something looked different.

"Let's get up there," Uncle Rip said, jumping back on his bike and firing it up. They rode slowly along the bank and stopped directly across the canal from the flowers.

Andy got off his bike again and looked.

It has changed.

The dried muck that had remained from what Mom thought was her part of the garden was now covered with high grass.

"If that one section of the garden was Mom's," Andy said, "who are the other three sections for?"

"Don't know," Uncle Rip said. "Other than your mom, the only people you've nailed with iPod Bible quotes are me, Kevin Hart, and Heather. Maybe they are for us."

Andy wasn't sure about that, but the longer he stared at the garden, the more he could feel his stomach fluttering with new sensations. Things like fear, awe, and a whole lot of confusion, to name a few. But surrounding all of these things was a feeling of something stronger. Something bigger. What?

"I feel weird, looking over there," he said.

"It's not weird," Uncle Rip said, his lips parted in wonder. "That, Andy, is pure love."

"I don't think so," Andy said. "I think it's God."

"Same thing."

"What do you mean?"

"I'm gonna let you figure that one out, bro."

Andy's legs felt rubbery. Whatever was in the garden, he wanted to be closer to it, and closer to it right now. And then a cool idea crossed his mind.

"You think I could jump the canal?" Andy said.

"What do you mean?"

"On my bike."

"That's what I thought you meant," Uncle Rip said. "You been puffin' the wacky?"

"No," Andy said and laughed. "I'd like to try to jump it, though. Seriously."

Uncle Rip looked at him. "You ain't gonna try it with your bike, my bike, or any bike. Even if we had a ramp."

"I think I could do it."

"Just be sure to let me know when you're getting ready to try it. That way I don't have to worry about you getting hurt."

"Why?"

"Because I'll kill you first."

Andy laughed. It was a long way to the other side and he agreed it probably wasn't the best idea he'd ever had.

"Let's get back before your mom has a stroke," Uncle Rip said, jumping up and coming down on the kick-starter of the old bike. "If we don't return, she'll think the worst."

"Imagine that," Andy said.

Uncle Rip tried the kick-starter again, but the bike didn't respond. At all.

"She's spent for today," Uncle Rip said.

Andy toed the tire. "You gonna leave her for dead like you said?"

"Changed my mind," Rip said. "I think she's worth saving."

"So you can show me up while racing again?" Andy said.

"Maybe more," Uncle Rip said with a glint in his eye as he glanced back toward McLouth Steel. "Who knows? With a little bit of work, maybe this dog could make that leap to the other side."

Andy did a double take. "So you get to jump it, but I can't?"

"We'll see, bro. We'll see."

❋ ❋ ❋

Heather was just pulling in the driveway when she saw Rip and Andy come around the corner of the house, pushing their bikes toward the barn. She waved Rip toward the car and he held up his index finger for her to wait a minute.

When he finally reached her, Rip got in.

"Ahh, AC," he said. "It's hot as blazes out there."

"You can say that again," Heather said. "Hey, I need to pick your criminal mind for a second."

"Well, it's good to see my dark days getting put to good use. What's up?"

"The Summer Santa. Something about him is driving everyone bonkers."

"He ain't driving me bonkers."

"Seriously," she said. "Why wouldn't he just give these people these gifts instead of doing it the way he is doing it? Any guesses?"

"Your guess is as good as mine. Why you asking . . . other than the fact you guys can't catch him?"

"Because I'm in trouble with work, Rip. And now I'm in even deeper."

"What do you mean?" Rip said slowly. "You his elf or something now? You're about the right height."

"Rip. He came to my apartment and left $7,500."

He lifted his chin and his mouth closed abruptly. "With you in it?"

"Yeah."

Rip exhaled loudly. "Were you scared?"

"Heck yeah. For a minute. But then I realized he wasn't going to hurt me. He's all about doing good. It's almost as if he wants me to *see* him doing these things."

"By giving you $7,500?" Rip asked. "I might be convinced myself, if I were on the receiving end of that." He eyed her. "But just in case, I don't think you ought to be alone tonight. You know, in case he wants to come back and make it an even ten grand or something."

"Thanks, but I don't need any company. If he shows up again, I'll just call him by name and the jig will be up."

"You know who it is?"

"C'mon! Who else has this kind of money to toss around? And who else has access to all our prayer cards—prayers that are so specifically getting answered?"

"Okay," he said slowly. "So you think you know who it is. Why would that put you in trouble at work?"

"I didn't tell Chief Reynolds about the $7,500," she said miserably. "And if I do it now, it will look even worse. I'm such an idiot."

Rip shifted in his seat. "Trust me on this. It's always best to turn yourself in. Otherwise, someone you care about can show up at your door with handcuffs and everything is far worse."

They shared a long look.

"I guess I was kind of thinking the money was like an answered prayer," Heather said. "Like God was telling me to go back to school, just as clearly as my mom likes to."

Rip put his hand on her leg. "If the money isn't traced to anything bad, don't you get to keep it? Eventually?"

She shrugged.

"Why don't you pray about it?" He turned to face her. "I love the idea of you as a teacher, Heather. You're so great with kids . . . it'd be perfect."

They stared at each other for a long moment, their eyes saying so much more than their talk about the Summer Santa and money and careers . . .

"Rip," she whispered. "Why didn't you ever tell me you loved me when we dated?" It was out before she'd thought it through. But now she really wanted to hear the answer.

Rip faked a laugh and looked out the window, breaking their intense stare. He took a long time to answer. "I guess I was emotionally unavailable at the time."

"Seriously," she said. "You never even said it once. Why?"

"C'mon," he said. "Why are we talking about this?" He looked as if her questions physically pained him.

"Did you ever *love*-love me?" she pressed. "It's okay if you didn't. I just . . . need to know."

Rip started to say something and stopped. He licked his lips and then looked out the window again.

"Heather . . . you were—and still are—way too good for me. Please, it's best if we never speak of this again."

TWENTY

The parking lot and grounds at St. Paul's hadn't been this packed since President Reagan's campaign stopped by during the 1980 election in an effort to rally southern Detroit's autoworkers.

It was ninety-five degrees, and after just fifteen minutes, Rip felt like he needed a shower.

A few thousand people gathered, mostly out-of-towners, moving shoulder to shoulder, yet still enjoying the Benning Fourth of July Festival along the lake.

They were fortunate that Pastor Welsh was given a complimentary table under the biggest tent next to the church, and even more fortunate that the minister had invited them to sit with him. At the table were Rip, Andy, Judi, Heather, and Heather's mom, who—much to the town's surprise—was out and about, rather than home watching endless episodes of *Wheel of Fortune*.

Sharon Gerisch might as well have been Sasquatch or Nessie sitting across the table, because over the last dozen years, the town had seen her only on a couple occasions.

"Look who's here," Rip said to Andy. He nodded toward the makeshift dance floor at the edge of the tent.

Andy turned around and Rip watched his posture stiffen when he spotted Chelsea Cochran. She was watching the dancers on the floor and leaning against the band booth and a sign for "DJ Allen." *Good call getting a DJ,* Rip thought, remembering how last year's live band spent too much time in the beer tent before the show. Besides, this guy sounded like he chose good tunes, at least.

"Go ask her to dance," Rip said.

Andy looked at Rip as though he'd asked him to run around the parking lot naked. He glanced quickly around the table, then looked back at Rip and shook his head.

"I really think she likes you," Rip said, nodding toward Chelsea, who'd clearly discovered Andy's arrival. "In fact, I'll bet you a Coke she does."

"Why don't you ask *Heather* to dance?" Andy said.

Rip laughed and pointed at Heather. "Because she couldn't keep up with Uncle Rip."

"Ignore your uncle," Heather said. "He doesn't like spending much of his time in a place we call *reality*." She still seemed edgy after their intense conversation a few days ago. As if she was ready to take him on again.

"Don't tempt me," Rip said. "I'll bust my dancing shoes out right here and now and put on a little clinic."

"Let's go," Heather said, standing.

Rip laughed under his breath, stood, and did a dizzying three-sixty. His back was feeling pretty good today and it'd been years since he'd last danced. And the chance to dance with Heather? He knew it wasn't wise, but he couldn't resist the temptation.

Rip pretended to need a drink before he tore up the dance floor, as Chelsea Cochran sidled up next to the table. *This, I gotta see.*

"Hey, Andy," Chelsea said.

"Hey," the kid answered. Andy's eyes looked like a pair of cue balls and he looked to Rip for guidance.

"Ask her to dance," Rip said.

"He doesn't have to," Chelsea said confidently. "I'm asking him."

Andy's eyes widened farther and he double-checked to make sure his hair was pulled forward. "I-I don't know how," he said.

"Who cares?" Chelsea said.

Andy swallowed heavily and looked back at Rip. Rip guessed Andy was hoping the tent had an emergency exit.

"Let's hit it together," Rip said. "I'll show you my killer moves."

Andy shot him a look of horror.

Chelsea held out her hand and Andy looked at it like she was holding a stack of hundred-dollar bills. But he stood up. Chelsea finally took him by the hand and led him toward the dance floor, ignoring the fact that Andy looked like he was being led to the gas chamber. Rip and the rest of the table just stared at them. Rip smiled, happy for Andy and for himself, because DJ Allen had just put on a slow song.

By the time he and Heather had made it to the dance floor to join them, Andy and Chelsea were already dancing like a couple of mannequins on a skateboard, never changing the way they were facing, just swaying slowly back and forth.

"Hey, Fred Astaire," Rip yelled to Andy's back.

Chelsea patted Andy's shoulder and pointed at Rip.

Andy turned around. "What?"

Rip smiled. "You owe me a Coke."

❊❊❊

"So how's your summer been going?" Chelsea asked.

"Good," Andy answered, thinking he liked the sound of her

voice. Summer had just gotten a lot better, but he had no idea how to tell Chelsea that.

"I see you at my brother's baseball games," she said.

"I've seen you too." Actually, she was the only reason he went.

"They are off this week," she said. "His next game is a week from Wednesday at three o'clock. You want to meet me there?"

"Sure," Andy said. The game was actually at two, but he didn't want to correct her. That would seem creeperish.

"I've been gone a lot with my little sister being sick with her kidney and all," Chelsea said. "They are using my room for supplies for her, and they were gone all the time, trying to find the right doctors. I was over at my aunt's house in Carlson for a while."

"I know. Didn't see you around school this year." He gave her a quick, nervous glance. "You look different," Andy added. He wasn't quite sure how that sounded.

Chelsea smiled shyly. "In a good way?"

"Yeah," he said, too fast. He wanted to kick himself for sounding too eager.

"You look taller," she said.

"I am. Grew almost six inches this year."

"Wow. That's a lot," Chelsea said.

She knows about my scar. And she still asked me to dance . . . The thought made him feel good, but he held back his smile in case he was wrong. *Maybe this is just a mercy dance. We'll finish and she'll run back to her friends and they'll whisper behind their hands, talking about me . . .*

"How's your sister doing?" Andy asked. It was a lot easier to talk about something other than the two of them.

"She's gonna need that surgery for her kidney," Chelsea said. "Thank God Mr. and Mrs. Hart are doing the fund-raiser for her. And they haven't charged my mom and dad any rent on our house in like four months either. We're lucky."

"He owns my uncle's house too," Andy said. *But he doesn't let him live there for free.*

"I think they own a lot of houses. Hey, me and my family are going to Mack's on Tuesday. I'll ask my dad if you can come with us."

He stared at her. *She likes me.* The thought left him feeling a little dazed.

"Yeah, sure," Andy said. He wasn't sure how long he was nodding before the song ended. The DJ started another song and it was a lot faster. Uncle Rip and Heather neared them and Uncle Rip started dancing.

"C'mon, you guys!" Uncle Rip yelled. "Let's boogie!"

Chelsea looked at Andy and smiled. He gave her an embarrassed, shy smile and shook his head.

"We were just gonna go sit and talk for a bit," she said to Uncle Rip.

Andy took a deep breath.

I don't think I just like this girl. I think I love her.

TWENTY-ONE

Rip sat in Pastor Welsh's office for close to an hour, privately agonizing in his chair while explaining to the minister what was going on with the flower garden. It had been a particularly brutal day for his lower back; the throbbing pain he'd grown accustomed to felt like it'd grown claws and attached itself to the rear portion of his left rib cage. *Probably from trying to get that dang bike started. Or my killer moves on the dance floor.* Regardless, he'd obviously sprung something loose and it was getting hard to breathe.

"You mind if I stand?" he asked. "Every once in a while, my back acts up."

"Of course," Pastor Welsh said. "Just wait till you're my age. Something new acts up every day."

"Yeah, I need a job like yours," Rip said, stretching and wincing. "Sitting around, listening to people like me yammer on. Telling them about God. It'd be a heck of a lot easier than working at Hart Industries."

"Think so, huh?" the pastor asked with a wise smile. But then he became serious. "You should think about it, Rip. If you're called, you'd be a great pastor."

Rip looked at him in surprise. "God doesn't mind felons working for Him?"

"Felons are His specialty," Welsh said with a smile. He leaned back in his chair and lifted his hands. "We're all felons, right? By grace we've been saved."

"Amen to that."

Welsh's smile faded. "I think your passion for sharing what you learn would make you a good minister, Rip."

Rip laughed. "I wouldn't mind getting paid to preach at people rather than handing out my vast wisdom for free. You got it made, my man."

Welsh lowered his head. "I wish you were serious about it."

"What made you think I was kidding?" Rip asked. He liked what Welsh said, and the idea of talking to people about God thrilled him. What a great way to spend the second half of his life . . .

"You serious?"

"Yeah. I think I am."

"Then let's sit down and talk about it one of these days."

"Sounds good," Rip said. He folded his arms. "Something's been bugging me, though. Something that would hold me back from that particular conversation."

"What?"

"I-I really don't know. I guess I feel like I'm doing my best to lead the right life, but there's something still missing, something to help me put my past behind me once and for all."

"Any guesses what it is?" Welsh said.

"No clue," Rip said. "But it's driving me a little nuts."

The pastor nodded and pursed his lips. "I've been thinking about what you said when you shared your testimony."

"And?"

"And you said that we're to glorify God, and you'd set out to do just that, which was admirable."

Rip waited, lifting his eyebrows.

"But there's a balance, Rip. Between accepting that God is glory, and allowing ourselves to be open enough to reflect that glory. It's not so much about what we do—what we do to try and make up for past mistakes, or try and live a life that is exemplary."

"So . . . you're saying I should just throw in the towel? Sin now, pray for forgiveness later?"

"No," Welsh said, sharing his grin. "In time, God will make what you're after known to you. Just be patient and realize that it may not be something you need to *do*, as much as how you may need to *think*. It's about perspective."

"Hmm. I've got to chew on that one for a bit." Rip pressed the heel of his palm just beneath his ribs. "Do you mind if we take a walk? Maybe my back will loosen up."

"You've been grabbing at that back of yours for a few months," Welsh said, rising. "You should let Doc Strater check you out. Back problems normally don't just get up and go away on their own. At least not without some rest, anyhow."

Rip agreed. "I'll give him a buzz. Either that, or I'll go see that new chiropractor over in South Rockwood. I'm hoping a quick adjustment will put me right back in business."

"Maybe so," the minister said. "Our walk is gonna have to be a short one. These old bones don't quite behave like they used to."

They made a quick pass out to the street where Pastor Welsh popped a couple birthday cards in the mailbox. He had done a pretty steady job, as long as Rip could remember, of sending them out to members of the congregation. Rip had even received a couple of them during his three years behind the fence.

They walked along the side of the church and through the parking lot to head out to the lake. The parking lot was a mess from the festival; city workers were probably pulling double shifts in order to finish sweeping up the piles of rubbish.

"Milo show up yet?" Welsh asked.

"Not yet," Rip said. "Judi and Andy are worried about him, and though I'd never tell them, so am I."

"He's been gone how long, about a week now?"

"Too long," Rip said. "Even for him."

"Lots of coyotes around here nowadays," Welsh said. "Judi doesn't seem to get many out near the farm, though."

"A Cadillac will get Milo before a coyote," Rip said. "If a couple more days pass by and he doesn't show up, we'll start putting flyers up for the handful of people around town who don't already know who Milo is."

"I'd be glad to help," Welsh said.

Rip's back was feeling better already and he found himself consciously slowing down so Pastor Welsh could keep up with him. They had walked fifty yards down the bike path that ran along the lake without either of them saying a word. Even though he enjoyed their shared silence, Rip had something on his mind.

"I've been thinking about what you said about Andy's little words of wisdom from the iPod—about how we should pay as much attention to who he says them to as what he says. Judi thinks God is speaking to us through Andy. In fact, I think we all do."

"What's so hard to believe about that?" Welsh asked. "God does stuff like that every day. Most just don't catch it."

Because we aren't listening, Rip thought. And then he asked Welsh something that had been niggling at him. "Why Andy?"

"Why not?"

"Isn't it a little crazy thinking we're getting divine guidance through an iPod and a surly teenager?" Rip grinned. "Apple should work up an app. They could make a fortune."

"Moses did some pretty interesting things with his staff," Welsh said, a peculiar grin spreading across his lips. "What's the difference?"

Rip laughed, imagining Andy standing at the shore of Lake Erie as God parted it, leaving a dry trail over to Canada. *Or Andy standing in front of The Frank and Poet Canal as God made a flower garden appear and partially disappear behind McLouth Steel . . .*

"It's funny how we know about things that happened in the Bible," Rip said, "yet it's so hard to swallow things that are even remotely similar today."

"Quite true," Welsh said.

"But if Andy's really hearing these things through the iPod, why can't we hear anything when we hold the earbuds to our ears?"

"I'm assuming you've tried?"

"Heck yeah," Rip said.

"I have no clue," Welsh said. "That's very strange."

"Hey, have you come across any specific Bible verse with the words 'they are able' in it? Could it be a different translation or something? All the other things Andy's been saying seem to fit."

"No, I don't believe so," Welsh said, bringing his hand to his chin in recollection. He squinted against the lake, and the wind moved his white hair over his eyes. He brushed it aside and let out a little laugh. "I even Googled it, thinking of that translation option. There's no individual verse in the Bible that says 'they are able.'"

"I didn't think so," Rip said. "That's the thing that Andy said about Heather's and Kevin's dads. Does that make anything click for you?"

"Are you sure that's what he said?"

"Positive," Rip said. "He specifically pointed at a photo of them and said that."

"Hmm," Welsh said. "I'm afraid it may be a little late for Mr. Gerisch and Mr. Hart to benefit from Andy's new ability."

"True," Rip said and nodded. "But remember what he said to me at the Bible study about loving my enemies and praying for those who persecute me?"

"I do," he said.

Rip pulled to a stop and the little pain in his lower back returned, making it feel like he had just taken a deep breath of broken glass. "Let's say there was someone in town who everybody thinks is a certain way, but you know they really aren't. And the town's perception of him is completely wrong and you know this person is actually a scumbag. Do I owe it to the people to expose him?"

"No," Welsh answered quickly.

"Really?"

"You need to expose him to himself."

That wasn't exactly the answer Rip had been looking for. He imagined himself sitting in one of the chairs in front of Kevin's desk, sipping on a cocktail and pointing out all of Kevin's wrongdoings.

"Hey, Kev, about those little girlfriends of yours. You know, the two or three I've seen you making out with back on the loading dock while I was working in the warehouse after everybody else had gone home? I may be a touch off base here, but I'm thinking both God and your wife may not be a big fan of that."

Right. Good-bye job and good-bye home-sweet-mobile-home. That conversation would be a one-way ticket to unemployment and sharing one of Judi's spare bedrooms with Milo. If Milo ever decided to return.

"Before you confront this person," Welsh said, "ask God if your heart is in the right place."

"What?" Rip said, teleporting from Kevin Hart's fantasy office back to the lakeside.

"If you think someone is your enemy and he is persecuting you, pray for yourself first. Ask God to help you look at your heart, to make sure it's in the right place. And if that doesn't work, pray for Kevin and then go talk to him."

Rip bit lightly on his lip and then gave a closed-mouth smile. "I never said I was talking about Kevin."

"Right," Welsh said with a smile. "But you should know by now that pastors *know* things."

TWENTY-TWO

There you go, Brianna," Heather said, placing the cup of coffee on the desk.

Despite the young reporter's good intentions, there was something about her that was getting under Heather's skin. Besides, they'd already talked for twenty minutes and Heather had said all she had to say. Now the girl wanted coffee? How long was this going to drag on?

"Thanks for the java," Brianna said, tapping her finger on the side of the Styrofoam cup, then lifting it for a tiny sip. "You know, there are other things happening regarding the Summer Santa that seem to be sliding under the radar of the Benning Police Department."

"Really?" Heather said, glancing past the reporter and out the open door at Chief Reynolds.

One thing Little Miss Rolex and her Louis Vuitton bag didn't know was that in small towns, everybody knew everything everyone else was doing, and even some things they *weren't* doing.

Heather knew a lot of what hadn't made the paper yet, like the yellow lab puppy that was left in the Millers' living room to replace

Finnegan, whom they had to put down only a few days before. She had also heard about the bag of toys that had been left in the Ansons' kitchen. Besides that Becky girl out on Old Parker Road, they were the poorest folks in town, and thanks to the man in black, their twin boys had a birthday to remember. And last but not least, word was traveling fast about the Summer Santa's biggest gift yet— the fifteen thousand in cash that had been left over at Mick Solack's food bank just outside of town. But still, Heather was curious what Lois Lane thought she knew.

"Like what?" Heather asked. "What's sliding under the radar?"

"Oh, I don't know," Brianna said. "Just little things. I'm not here to report things you don't know about. Was just curious if you've heard anything."

Something about the way the reporter was talking almost had Heather feeling that she was supposed to pry.

"The first time we chatted," Heather said, "you mentioned that you thought the Summer Santa wanted to get caught. I still don't completely understand why you would say that."

"Just a hunch," Brianna said.

"You said that last time. You also suggested that he may be trying to balance some scale in his personal life. Or something like that."

Brianna paused and seemed to consider what she was going to say. "I think it's like he's easing his conscience about something. He wants to do good, but seems to enjoy an unnecessary risk while doing it."

"Why even bother taking that risk?" Heather asked. It was the billion-dollar question that nobody seemed close to having the answer to.

"I don't know," Brianna said. "But regardless, he is making some pretty good news."

"True," Heather said.

"It's also kind of interesting that he only seems to work on the nights that you do."

"It's probably a coincidence," Heather said, thinking, *How would she know that?* "We are a small department."

"Mind if I ask you something?" Brianna asked. "It may be a little personal."

"I guess it depends on how personal."

"It's about your dad," she said. "I was curious if you were comfortable talking about what happened."

Heather swallowed a quick retort about sticking to new news, not old news. "It's interesting that you mention it. I was thinking about talking about my dad at the next Bible study."

"I'm planning on going again," she said. "I'll be there to hear it."

Heather stood. "I told you I didn't have much time today. And I'd appreciate it if you wouldn't speculate about anything you've heard about the Summer Santa in your articles. Let's just stick to the reported cases, cool?"

"Gotcha," Brianna said. "I'm sorry to bring up your dad. I guess I'm trying a little too hard to get familiar with the town."

"It's okay," Heather said, walking her to the door of the station.

"Can I ask one more question?" Brianna asked.

Heather had to admire her persistence. "Go for it."

"Thinking of Jimmy Keeler and his dentures," she said. "Doesn't it make sense that a suspect could be somebody at the Bible study? We share our needs there."

Or someone named Kevin who collects the prayer cards.

"Not necessarily," Heather said. "Keep doing your homework and familiarizing yourself with the town. I'm sure *everybody* knew how much money Jimmy Keeler needed for his teeth."

Brianna laughed. "Come to think of it, he does have kind of a big mouth."

"See ya later," Heather said, looking out at the parking lot at Brianna's BMW.

Blond hair, blue eyes, six feet tall, and what looked like more money than she probably knew what to do with. *It must be nice, being a new college grad riding on Daddy's money . . .*

"Thanks for your help, Heather," Brianna said.

Heather watched her get into her car and drive off. She went back to her desk and, before she sat down, stopped. She turned around and walked back to the window and watched the BMW disappear out onto West Jefferson.

Six feet tall and more money than she knows what to do with.

And Brianna was right, wasn't she? The Summer Santa was making pretty good news. Which was really convenient for a cub reporter, trying to make a name for herself . . .

Heather returned to her desk and the second she sat down, she thought about what Brianna had said earlier, about the department missing some of what the Summer Santa was doing.

And then a sickening thought ran through Heather's mind.

Does she know about the $7,500 the Summer Santa left for me? And will she soon report on it?

✖ ✖ ✖

Andy jerked forward and sat up quickly. He felt like he'd just pulled a muscle in his neck and his heart was pounding. He'd been dreaming Milo was licking him, but the smell of barbecue-flavor chips seemed like it was everywhere.

He looked to his side. In the grass, next to a water bottle and a couple of comic books, was a punctured and empty bag of chips.

And Milo.

"Milo!" Andy yelled, throwing his arms around the dog and hugging him. "Where you been, boy?"

He was covered in burs and looked like he'd lost a few pounds. Andy gave him another squeeze and gripped the sleeve of his T-shirt to wipe barbecue slobber off his face.

"Milo, you idiot. You're disgusting."

Andy yawned and took his earbuds out, wondering how long he'd been asleep on the bank of The Frank and Poet. There hadn't been any gasoline in the barn or garage for the motorcycle, so Andy had spent a few hours on foot looking for Milo. The second he spotted the flowers, he sat down and popped in his earbuds, and the next thing he knew, he had a face full of Milo-spit.

Andy yawned again and then rubbed at his eyes before glancing over at the flower garden on the other side. It felt familiar, close. Like he'd been standing in it a few seconds ago.

He shook off the idea as just a part of his whacked dream and stood up, brushing the grass and dirt off his jeans and shirt.

"You ready to go home, boy?" Andy said. "Everybody's gonna be glad to see you."

Milo shot quickly back toward the path and stopped, doing a frantic little doggy dance, waiting impatiently for Andy to follow.

Andy put the iPod in his pocket and started walking toward the path back to the house. When he hit the corn rows, he stopped and turned back around.

"I *was* just over there," he said.

It had to have been a dream, but it felt so real . . .

In the dream, a beautiful presence was trying to tell him there were two things he had to do. One of them had to do with his mom. And the other one had to do with a man Andy was standing near. He couldn't see the man's face, but the man told him to *come back* and to *let her see*. But the man wasn't talking about Mom. He was talking about Heather.

"Crazy," Andy said, shaking his head and making his way back through the corn toward the house. He couldn't wait to go eat with Chelsea and her family over at Mack's.

When he was about halfway through the knee-high corn, he turned around again and studied the three remaining sections that made up the flower garden. There was no doubt in his mind that he'd been standing in the section to the far left.

Heather's section.

※ ※ ※

Andy sat in a corner booth at Mack's between Chelsea and little Marjo. Straight across from him were Mr. and Mrs. Cochran, who insisted on being called Teddy and Cierra. Chelsea's little brother, Patrick, was taking his turn staying at the aunt's house for the week.

Mom had said that she graduated from Benning High with the Cochrans and that Teddy and Cierra had been together since eighth grade. Even though they were the same age as Mom, Andy thought they looked a lot older. Both had a bunch of gray hair for people in their thirties, and they each had puffy blue semicircles under their eyes. Andy guessed they had to be stressed out about Marjo, who looked to be in worse shape than she had been on Sunday. Her face and hands looked swollen, but it still seemed like she was getting smaller every time he saw her. She could easily pass for a kinder-gartener, with her skinny little arms that were riddled with bruises and needle holes from IV lines. Her sunken eyes were accented by purplish skin and she had a voice that reminded Andy of a munch-kin from *The Wizard of Oz*.

"What are you gonna get, Andy?" Marjo asked. Andy sounded

like "Annie" and when she looked up at him, he noticed that the whites of her eyes were kind of yellowed.

"I'm getting that," Andy said, tapping on the picture of the burger and fries in the menu she was holding. The menu looked the size of a newspaper in her doll-size hands.

"I'm gonna get these," she said, pointing at a picture of chicken strips.

"So how's your mother and uncle doing?" Mr. Cochran asked.

"Doing good, Mr. Cochran," Andy said. He had no intention of calling Mr. Cochran "Teddy." It'd just be too weird.

"It's good to see your uncle at church," Mrs. Cochran said.

Andy nodded and caught Marjo staring at his scar. He pulled his hair forward and looked away.

"How did you do that to your face?" she asked.

"Marjo!" Chelsea said.

Marjo recoiled and Andy cringed.

"Where's your manners?" Mrs. Cochran said.

Marjo's shoulders hunched together and she leaned her cheek against her shoulder. "Sorry," she said in that tiny voice.

"It's okay," Andy said. "I got it when I was little. I got burned."

Marjo gave him a sad look.

"Hey," she whispered, pulling on the sleeve of his T-shirt, prodding him to lean over to hear her.

"What?" Andy said.

As she started to talk, Mr. McIntosh showed up at the table with an order pad in his hand.

"Hello, Andy," he said, giving him a little wink, approving that he was sitting next to Chelsea. "Sorry about the wait, folks. We're missing a waitress tonight."

They had to be, because Andy had never seen Mr. McIntosh play waiter before.

While they ordered, Andy noticed the guy who had called him "Scarface" walk in with another dude. The second he spotted Andy, he glanced warily around, said something to the other guy, and they left. Andy laughed under his breath. *Thanks, Uncle Rip.*

By the time the food came, little Marjo had tried and failed twice to tell Andy something. And when she tried a third time, the final interruption came from Mr. Cochran.

"Excuse me?" Andy said, *praying* he'd misunderstood Mr. Cochran.

"Would you like to say grace, Andy?"

Andy's mouth felt like it was filling with sand. He'd heard Uncle Rip say grace about a million times, but Andy couldn't seem to find any of the words. It was like his brain went on vapor lock until he felt Chelsea's leg bumping against his.

"I'll do it, Dad," she said, coming to the rescue.

Chelsea said grace and as they quietly ate, he thought about her asking, in prayer, that they all be thankful for what they had. The family seemed game to try, which impressed him. Even with all they had to deal with . . .

Little Marjo nudged his shoulder. "Sorry again for what I said earlier about your face," she said. "But you should be thankful you don't have what I have. I heard Dr. Shepherd tell my daddy that I could die."

Andy wasn't sure how long he and Marjo stared at each other. Her little eyes seemed to look right through him. "You're right, Marjo," he managed to say. But as they all resumed eating, he realized that with each second he passed with the Cochrans, his own problems did fade in comparison.

He sneaked a look at Marjo, partly appreciating her, partly irritated by her. The little girl's bravery was raining on the party, *his own pity party,* that he'd been throwing for himself for a lot of years.

When Mr. McIntosh came back to the table with the bill, Andy reached in his pocket to retrieve the twenty he'd stashed there. He figured that with his employee discount, he could at least help the Cochrans with the bill, but Mr. McIntosh beat him to the punch.

"Dinner is on Andy and the staff here at Mack's," Mr. McIntosh said, giving Andy another little wink and plucking the twenty from his fingers.

Mr. Cochran looked at Andy, then Mr. McIntosh, while reaching for his wallet. "We don't expect you guys to pay for our meal. We appreciate it, but—"

"Andy and I insist," Mr. McIntosh said, holding up his hand, putting what Uncle Rip would call the "kibosh" on any money coming from the Cochrans.

"We can't tell you how much we appreciate this," Mrs. Cochran said. "What do you girls say to Mr. McIntosh?"

"Thank you," Chelsea said.

"Thank you," Marjo echoed. "And thank you too, Andy."

Andy had a hard time looking away from her again.

"No, Marjo," he said, running his hand across the top of her head. Her courage had him feeling like a complete tool, but a *thankful* tool. "Thank you."

TWENTY-THREE

Do You Believe in the Summer Santa?

Brianna Bruley—TBW Reporter

Benning—He comes silently, swiftly, and does so in the night, providing for those who are in need.

Grocery store gift cards for a struggling young mother.

A custom wheelchair for an elderly war veteran.

A paid dental tab for a new set of teeth.

Who is responsible for these things?

Benning Township Police and two of the "victims" have described the "Summer Santa" as a six-foot-tall male with a penchant for all black clothing, including gloves and a ski mask.

Officer Heather Gerisch has confirmed that the department has made little progress in solving these cases, which, in a small town like Benning, raises an entirely different set of questions.

Are police turning a blind eye to this anonymous benefactor, aiding him in his flight?

The *Benning Weekly* has been made aware of similar incidents, including a woman reportedly waking to find new tires on her car, the Benning Little League miraculously starting a day with a storage bin full of new equipment, and a massive cash donation appearing at a local food bank.

Why are police not investigating these incidents further?

Is it because they approve of what's happening, or is the Summer Santa truly that elusive?

Is their handling of these incidents right or wrong? Let us know what you think, but until then, maybe you just need to ask yourself another question, and we'd love to know your answer to that as well . . .

Do you believe in the Summer Santa?

The Benning Police Department sure seems to.

Anyone with any information regarding these incidents involving the Summer Santa is asked to contact the Benning Police Department or the *Benning Weekly*'s anonymous tip line.

Heather tossed the paper down on Judi's kitchen table, and Rip thought he heard her swear under her breath.

"Pardon me?" he said.

Andy was on his way out the door and stopped. "Heather said that—"

"I heard her," Rip interrupted.

Andy put his helmet on and then glanced at Rip. "When you goin' to the park, Uncle Rip?"

"Pastor Welsh and I are meeting at five thirty, right after I get off work. You want to join us?"

"Okay," Andy said on his way out the door. "I'll meet you near the baseball fields."

Heather had picked the newspaper back up. "Sorry about the cursing."

"No worries," Rip said, watching Andy as he headed up the road. "I actually used to teach that language in my previous life."

"It's just irritating," Heather said. "I specifically asked that Brianna girl from the newspaper not to mention any of the Summer Santa rumors that we haven't made official reports on yet. I look like a complete idiot."

"Exactly why haven't you looked into those rumors?" Rip asked, raising one brow.

"Shut up, Rip," Heather said.

"I'm being serious," Rip said. "Why aren't you looking into the rumors or making reports on everything you hear about? You know, besides a certain seven thousand dropped in somebody's family room . . ."

"Could something be going on between Brianna and Kevin?" she asked, clearly in another world.

"It wouldn't be his first trip outside the corral," Rip said and laughed.

"And we are checking out every story. It's just that the Summer Santa is too good at what he does," she said. "No fingerprints, no clues, no nothing. The only evidence he leaves is whatever gift he is giving. I already told you about the gift cards and how they were bought on several different occasions. None of the local banks have had any major cash withdrawals, all four tire shops have no leads for us, and there are twenty-nine sporting goods stores within a fifty-mile radius we have called that *didn't* sell the Little League equipment. However, we did track down the wheelchair by its serial number and I went today to the store that sold it up in Detroit."

"And?" Rip asked.

"They sold it to some homeless guy who came in and paid $6,200 in cash for it. Obviously, our man in black took care of the homeless guy so he would go in and get it."

"How about identifying the homeless guy and taking it from there?" Rip asked.

"Medical supply stores aren't exactly a hotbed of criminal activity. They don't have any surveillance cameras at the store, and good luck finding a specific homeless guy up in Detroit. Needle in a haystack."

"True that," Rip said.

Judi came back in the kitchen with two handfuls of burs and Milo at her side. He was dragging his yellow blanket in his mouth and looked like he was ready for a nap.

"I think I got all the burs out," she said. "When he came back from his little vacation, he was loaded with these things."

Rip reached down and scratched the top of Milo's head. "I was starting to think that you'd finally bought it, Milo. Gone and off to canine heaven."

Heather stood abruptly and rushed out the kitchen door to the porch.

Judi held up her arms as if to say, *What was that all about?*

"No idea," Rip whispered, walking to the kitchen door to look outside. Heather was down at the left end of the porch, standing up against the railing, looking away.

She was crying.

"Hey," he said, walking toward her. "What's up?"

"Nothing," she whispered. "No biggie. Just thinking about my dad again."

"What do you mean no biggie?" he asked. "I haven't seen you cry in about a million years."

She wiped a tear from her cheek and studied it. "I thought I cried myself out when my dad was killed. I haven't cried much since then."

Rip had gone to her father's funeral. Closed casket. Rumor had it that the intruder had shot both him and Mr. Hart in the head, but Heather's dad had taken it in the face. Mr. Hart's funeral was the day after her father's. Open casket. Fifteen-year-old Kevin had to be medicated and sat like a zombie in the first row.

"I know a cool place we can pray about this someday," Rip said.

"You want to pray with me?" Heather asked.

"Yeah," Rip said, "I was thinking we could pray over near the wildflowers."

"Back at McLouth?" Heather said. "I'll admit it feels great just looking at those flowers, but I am not going back over to the McLouth side. If all those chemicals from the plant are making those flowers come and go, who knows what it can do to us?"

"Then we'll stay on this side of the canal," Rip said. "And you can believe what you want, but I don't think chemicals have anything to do with what's going on with those flowers. I'm tellin' you, it's a good place to pray."

"You really think praying about my dad will help?"

"It won't hurt."

"Okay," she said, sounding like a little girl. "I'm sorry about this, Rip. I feel like an idiot, getting so worked up about something so long ago."

"Hey, it's okay," he said. "Obviously you have some unfinished business."

"I wish I could get a little of that magic out of Andy's iPod," she said. "A nice little word that would maybe give me some direction."

"If you did, it'd be wise to pay attention," Rip said. "I think Andy's messages are from God."

Heather dabbed at the corners of her eyes with her index fingers. Rip put his arm around her, and for the first time in over a decade, she leaned back against him.

"God is using Andy to help us," Rip added. "He's putting things in Andy's heart to share with us."

She looked up at him with those pretty, light green eyes of hers and they stared at each other for a long moment. If they had been talking about something else, he might have planted that kiss on her that had been floating in the air between them for as long as he could remember. But between her dead dad and Andy's odd new gift, the moment—no matter how intense—just wasn't right. But man, if she kept looking at him like that . . . he didn't know if he'd have the self-control to avoid it. He forced himself to concentrate on what she was saying, rather than thinking about her lips.

"You really think it's God who's talking to Andy? To us?" Heather asked.

"Judi and I had a nice talk about this," Rip said. "And I talked about it with Pastor Welsh too." He tapped lightly at his own chest. "You've heard the Spirit's voice inside of you, haven't you?"

She nodded. "That's the voice that keeps asking me where my father is, what I'm gonna do about that seventy-five hundred bucks I didn't tell the department I was given, why I'm still a cop, and also about . . ." Heather stopped and frowned.

"What?" Rip said.

"About us."

"What about us?"

"Nothing," she said.

"We'll pray about all of that stuff," Rip said shyly. "Just keep talking to God, but most importantly, listen, and I think you may get the answers you're looking for before you know it."

"I hope you're right," she said.

"Heather," Rip said. "What would it take for you to be certain your dad is in heaven?"

Heather was silent. The question clearly had her wheels turning. He was surprised that, for as much as she seemed to think about the subject, she didn't have an answer ready that didn't include actually seeing her dad taking harp lessons on a fluffy white cloud.

She went out from under his arm and took a few steps down the porch, toward the front door. She crossed her arms and then turned back around. "How can any of us be certain that someone we love is in heaven?"

"Faith," Rip said.

Heather looked away as if the word were a fistful of pebbles he tossed at her. "Are you saying I don't have faith?"

"I don't know, Heather," he said gently. "Do you?"

"I have faith," she said quickly.

"I believe you," he said. "Answer the question, then, because it's pretty hard to hit a target you can't see. What would it take for you to know your father was in heaven?"

"A miracle."

"That's not what you need," Rip said, smiling and shaking his head. "Let's just see what happens."

"What's that supposed to mean?" she asked.

Rip didn't answer. He just thought about the iPod and the flower garden . . . and what fueled them. What seemed to be at work all around them this summer. He pointed behind her to the far end of the porch. Three deer had come around the corner of the house and were just standing there, staring right at them.

"What do you mean when you say 'Let's just see what happens'?" Heather persisted.

"It means be patient," Rip answered. "Because God works in mysterious ways."

※ ※ ※

Andy didn't really care that the blue team was losing 8–0 or that Chelsea's little brother had struck out twice and made an error that cost the team three runs. Her brother could have been abducted by a UFO during the national anthem and Andy wouldn't have noticed.

He didn't care because he was sitting next to Chelsea in the bleachers and nothing else in the world mattered.

"Can you believe we are going to be starting *high school* in September?" Chelsea asked, giving his leg a playful bump. "I'm looking forward to going to school in Benning again."

"It's crazy," Andy said, noticing how neatly polished her pink fingernails were.

What was even crazier was the fact that out of all the pretty girls he knew who would be in high school, he couldn't imagine a single one he'd rather be sitting next to than Chelsea. And here she was, sitting right next to the friendless kid with the burned face.

✖ ✖ ✖

Rip closed the driver's side door of the Pacer and then grabbed the Dairy Queen bag off the roof of the car. It was another hot one, about three hundred degrees in the shade, so he figured Andy wouldn't put up too much of a fight if he asked him to knock down a banana split.

Lakeside Metropark was one of the skinniest, yet longest, parks in the state. It started about twenty miles south of Detroit, up in Trenton, then trickled down through the townships of Gibraltar, Carlson, Benning, and then Huckabone, before ending on the border of North and South Rockwood. Rip liked the park, and so did Andy. He figured his nephew easily spent three-quarters of his time there during the summer, riding on the winding trails that cut throughout the woods, hanging out near parts of the park that ran along the lake, or even watching Little League games, which he seemed to be doing a lot more of lately.

It didn't take Rip long to spot Andy. His nephew was sitting on the motorcycle and leaning up against the backstop of the ball diamond, talking to Chelsea Cochran.

Go, Andy.

By the time Rip had walked the fifty yards or so to reach them, he was surprised at how winded he was, and how that nagging little hack he had developed was starting to sound like the kennel cough Milo had picked up from the vet's office when he was just a pup.

"Pound it, bro," Rip said, walking up behind Andy.

"Pound it," Andy echoed, immediately eyeing the DQ bag before tapping knuckles with his uncle.

"How are you, Chelsea?" Rip asked, glancing at the scoreboard. He wasn't sure which team was home or away, but the home team had been punished, 15–1.

"I'm doing good," Chelsea said. "But my brother's team got killed."

"Crushed," Andy added, and Rip laughed. It didn't seem like a word Andy would use. It seemed like it was part of the vocabulary of someone much more confident.

"I'll leave you two alone," Rip said. "I'm gonna go sit in the car and wait for Pastor Welsh."

"That's okay," Chelsea said. "I have to take off. I'll see you around, Andy."

As Chelsea walked around the backstop to meet with her little brother, Andy stared at her like he'd never see her again, and Rip felt a little bad.

"Sorry about that, bro," Rip said, opening the bag and handing Andy the banana split.

"About what?" Andy said, glancing back at Chelsea.

"Nothing," Rip said, shocked that Andy wasn't miffed at him. "Let's go find Pastor Welsh. I'll push your bike."

"Okay," Andy said. Chelsea was officially out of sight and he started shoveling down the banana split like the world was about to end.

As they walked behind the backstop, Kevin Hart pulled up next to them in his Mercedes.

He powered down the driver's side window. Hart was wearing sunglasses, and something about the way he looked had him more suitable for a Hollywood movie lot than the park in Benning.

"Hi, Rip!" Hart said in a purposefully cheery, yet phony voice.

"Hey, Kevin," Rip muttered, glancing over at Andy. The boy had taken a couple steps away and stopped eating. Rip looked back at Hart. "What brings you up here?"

"I was just watching a game over on one of the other fields."

"Didn't know you were a baseball fan," Rip said.

"It's a nice break for me," Hart said. "Reminds me of being young."

Hart glanced at Andy and then Rip.

"I'm glad I caught you both here," Hart said. "I just want to make sure we are all on the same page."

"What page is that?" Rip asked.

"The only page," Hart said and his fake smile disappeared. "If you and Andy ever try to railroad me in front of a group of people again—"

"We've already been over this, Kev."

"Somebody is going to get *burned*."

Rip looked back at Andy and he was holding his hand up to make sure his scar was covered. And then Andy gave him a look that said, *Please do something.*

Rip put the kickstand down on the motorcycle and felt his hands balling into fists as he took a step toward the car.

Pastor Welsh's car was pulling up next to Hart's, and when

it did, Hart rolled down the passenger-side window and gave the minister a friendly wave as if he were just there to make a donation to the park fund.

Hart looked back to Rip and whispered, "Be smart, pothead. Jobs aren't growing on trees."

Rip didn't say anything as Hart backed his car away and Welsh parked. He turned to Andy and saw the look of disappointment on his face.

"What?" Rip said.

Andy just shook his head and said, "Thanks for having my back. But I was kind of hoping you'd drag him out through the window."

"I restrained," Rip said. "I figured you'd be proud of me." Rip kept looking at Andy and knew there was something else going on between his nephew and Hart. "What is it that you aren't telling me?"

"Nothing," Andy said distantly.

"C'mon," Rip said. "Let's go."

They greeted Welsh and followed him to a picnic table that was tucked back in the trees and sat on the opposite side from the minister.

"Guess who Andy was chilling with when I got here?" Rip said.

Welsh shrugged. "No clue."

Rip nudged Andy. "Tell him, Romeo."

Andy rolled his eyes and talked with a mouthful of vanilla ice cream. "When you gonna marry Heather?"

"Maybe we could make it a double wedding?" Rip said. He laughed and gave Andy another nudge.

Andy pulled his hair forward over the sides of his face and exhaled loudly. Rip knew he was thinking about what Hart had just said.

"What was Kevin doing here?" Welsh asked.

"Taking in a little baseball, apparently," Rip said.

"Speaking of Kevin," Welsh said, nodding to Andy. "I saw you talking with him out near the lake not too long ago."

Andy looked away and Rip said, "What? Where? You guys talked?"

"It was no biggie," Andy whispered. "It was near the new fountain."

Rip could tell by Andy's voice that it *was* a biggie, but Welsh gave Rip a nod to back off.

"The fountain," Welsh said. "That's been a favorite spot of yours for some time now."

"Yeah," Andy said. "I remember when Uncle Rip used to put baseball cards near the spokes on my regular bike to make it sound like a motorcycle. I was thinking about that right when Mr. Hart showed up that day."

Rip wondered what collectors would have paid for the hundreds of baseball cards the spokes on Andy's bicycle had torn through. He pointed at the motorcycle and said, "We don't need them old cards anymore, do we?"

"You didn't need them with the minibike either," Welsh said.

Andy plopped his elbows on the top of the table and he lowered his chin to his fists. His eyes kept shifting back and forth. He'd look at the ground, then Rip, and then back to the ground. He was anxious about something, and Rip was pretty sure he knew what it was.

"What did you and Mr. Hart talk about near the fountain, Andy? It's okay, you can tell me."

Andy's shoulders sagged and then he slowly looked away. "He said something about my face."

"That handsome face?" Rip said, now wishing he *had* dragged Hart out through the driver's-side window of his Mercedes. It would have been even more satisfying putting him back in the car through the windshield.

"Doesn't matter," Andy said. "The way I wear my hair, people can't see it anyhow."

Now Rip wanted to get in the Pacer and drive to Hart's house and beat him up in front of his wife. Hart had obviously made another *burn* comment to Andy.

"Why would you care what Mr. Hart says about your face?" Rip asked.

"That's a dumb question," Andy said.

"No, it's not," Pastor Welsh said, clearly understanding where Rip was going. "You don't have to wear your hair long, Andy. Unless you're trying to hide something."

Andy shook his head and pointed at the minister. "I don't think there are any women in town that wear their hair as long as you do."

Welsh laughed.

Rip really didn't care if Andy wore his hair long and over the scar for the rest of his life, but the fact that Andy thought he *had* to wear it that way wasn't working for Rip. Particularly to avoid comments from scumbags like Hart.

"Do you feel like you have to hide your face because of what Mr. Hart said?" Rip asked.

"Wouldn't you?" Andy said, quickly turning his head and pulling his hair back to expose the scar. He spoke quickly and anger filled his voice. "*Wouldn't* you?"

"Take it easy," Rip said, seeing the tears form in Andy's eyes. "Let's just—"

"If your mom burned you with boiling water and you didn't want everyone reminding you of it with their comments? Wouldn't you hide your face?"

If your mom burned you?

Rip couldn't believe what he had just heard. He wasn't even sure Andy knew he said it, he was talking so fast. Rip and Welsh shared a glance, and he knew the minister caught what Andy had said as well. Rip waited for Welsh to say something, but neither of them said a word, each waiting for the other.

Rip had a coughing fit and raised his hands over his head to stretch out his lower back. It hurt like a bear, so he lowered his left arm to press firmly at that aching rib cage with his fingertips. When the cough entered the equation, he'd made an appointment to see Doc Strater instead of that chiropractor he'd considered.

"Andy, we need to talk more about how you got burned and what that means for you now." Rip shrugged. "Or doesn't. But first, we gotta talk to your mom."

"*Mom?* Why?" The boy was backpedaling, looking like he regretted saying anything.

"Because she's the only one who can straighten this out."

✖ ✖ ✖

"So you are gonna spend a little time tomorrow with Heather?" Judi asked. "Praying?"

"Right after I get off work, I'm gonna take her out to the flower garden," Rip said, passing a bowl of mashed potatoes to Pastor Welsh, who had joined them for dinner. "There is some good mojo out there. You want to join us, Andy?"

"Sure," Andy said. It was the most they'd heard from him since they returned from the park.

"You need to get me out there one of these days," Welsh said. "Feel like I'm missing out on something special, but I don't know if this old body is up for too long of a walk or a motorcycle ride."

"Anytime you want," Rip said. "Just say when and we'll figure something out. We could take one of the cars out there, but it'd be pretty bumpy."

Judi took a sip of her water. "Heather said she was going to ask her mom to go to the cemetery tomorrow before you guys go out to The Frank and Poet."

"Good luck with that," Rip said. "You think she'll go out of the house twice in the same month?"

"Be nice," Judi said. "Mrs. Gerisch has problems."

"Sorry," Rip said.

As refreshing as it was to hear Judi talk about problems other than her own, saying that Mrs. Gerisch had problems was the understatement of the century. Rip still couldn't believe that Heather had gotten her to come out of the house for the Fourth of July festival.

"I'm done eating," Andy said, scooting back from the table. He hadn't touched half his plate. He set it on the floor and it took Milo less than twenty seconds to make Andy a member of the clean plate club.

"Okay," Judi said.

Andy made a beeline for the upstairs, and Rip was relieved that Andy had left.

"We need to keep it down," Rip said.

"For what?" Judi said.

Rip lifted his hand and cocked his head, finally hearing Andy's bedroom door close.

"Pastor Welsh and I were talking about Andy's burn earlier," Rip said.

Judi frowned and her eyes darted between the two men.

"What about it?" she asked.

"May I?" Pastor Welsh asked.

"Go for it," Rip said.

Welsh laced his fingers together and practically whispered.

"Judi . . . I've known you guys your whole lives, and we've all been through some interesting times over the years."

"I agree," Judi said.

"And I respect your decision to not tell Andy what happened to him when he was younger, but—"

"Why does it matter what happened? We can't change anything about it."

"He said today that he knows how he got the scar," Rip said.

"I've heard him say the same thing," Judi said. "But it's impossible. Nobody knows what happened except me, Todd, Rip, Heather, and you, Pastor Welsh. The hospital didn't even know what really happened."

"But," Pastor Welsh said, "maybe it's time Andy needs to hear the whole story, and hear it from you."

"Why?" Judi said. Rip could see the dread in her eyes.

Pastor Welsh put his hand on top of Judi's and whispered, "It's not what happened, it's *who* Andy thinks did it to him."

"What?"

"He thinks you burned him, Judi, not Todd," Welsh said. "And we think you should set the record straight."

✖ ✖ ✖

Heather wasn't surprised her mother didn't want to go to the cemetery, but she still needed to know *why*.

"Because," Mom answered, calm but firm. She threw her elbows up on the patio table and then took a sip of her tea. "Unlike you, I don't want to be dredging up all those funeral memories. I want to remember your daddy the way he was when he was alive."

Heather leaned back in her chair and took a deep breath. It was good to see Mom out in the sunshine, even though it was just on the back patio. Still, there was no good reason she couldn't go to the cemetery with her tomorrow.

"When was the last time you went to see him?"

"He's not *there*, Heather," Mom said. "And exactly how does visiting his grave make you feel better about things? Tell me that."

"I'm not sure," Heather said. She was having second thoughts about her idea. "Maybe it would make us both feel better if we went. We never talk about our loss, Mom. Maybe we need to."

"And maybe we don't," Mom said, closing her eyes. "If visiting that grave is going to somehow convince you that your father is in heaven, go do it. But it's not what I need."

"It's not going to convince me of anything, Mom," Heather said. "I just thought it would be nice for us to share some time out there with him."

"I want to share time with you, Heather," she said. "But not in a field full of dead people."

Dead people, Heather thought. She closed her eyes and tried to get the image out of her mind. A corpse lay in the ground, long rotting away. What she needed, *wanted* to know was that her father was more alive than ever.

In heaven.

TWENTY-FOUR

"That joint is way too nice to be a cemetery," Rip said, passing the screwdriver back to Andy as they worked on the old bike in Judi's barn. Heather had just showed up and he was hoping the bike would start again so the three of them could take both motorcycles out to the wildflowers. Rip was sure that taking Heather out to visit it again would help her deal with her dad-issues. Maybe once and for all.

"I agree," Heather said. "It's way too nice to be a cemetery."

It was common knowledge that if you lived in southeast Michigan, and had more than two nickels to rub together when you punched your ticket, Southeast Memorial Cemetery was the place you wanted to go for the big lay down.

"I always forget how big it is," Heather added. "It would have made a *great* park, instead of some gigantic landing zone for a bunch of dead people."

"It would have made an awesome park," Rip said. "I wonder if they still give people those little maps."

"They gave me one," Heather said, reaching into her shorts

pocket and pulling out a folded piece of paper. "Without it, I would have been lost."

"Those swans still out there?" Andy asked.

"Not sure," Heather answered. "I think they hang out on the other side of the lake."

Rip didn't like thinking about the swans. The couple hundred of them that normally hung out in the man-made lake were pretty close to the plots his parents were buried in. Though they'd been dead a long, long time, thinking about them made him feel melancholy.

"How did it go?" Rip asked, putting a fresh spark plug in the bike.

Heather shrugged. "I took some flowers with me and straightened up the grave a little. Nothing like flowers to cheer things up, so I guess it went all right."

"Good," Rip said, standing and crossing his fingers before putting his foot on the kick-starter.

"C'mon, baby," he said to the bike, pressing his foot down quickly. It started right up and he smiled.

"*Master Mechanic* magazine," Andy said.

"You still gonna go with us?" Rip asked Andy as he turned the bike off. "Your mom should be back from that summer inventory-taking thing up at the school in a little while, but I'm guessing we got about an hour."

"Okay," Andy said, walking across the barn to hop on his own bike.

Rip grabbed an old helmet and handed it to Heather. He sat on the bike and patted the seat behind him and she got on.

"I'll follow you, Rico Suave," Andy said.

They pulled out of the barn and the sun was high in the sky, another scorcher. It was supposed to be over ninety all week, and as an added bonus, the air conditioner in the Pacer had petered out on him earlier in the day. The thought of riding the motorcycle to work crossed his mind, but it wasn't exactly road-ready.

"Burning up under that helmet, bro?" Rip asked.

"I'm okay," Andy said.

"Let's take it slow," Rip said, turning the throttle. He looked over his shoulder at Heather and she looked cute as ever with the old helmet on. She wrapped her arms around his waist and Rip squinted. "You getting fresh with me, Officer Gerisch?"

"Shut up, Rico Suave," she said, getting a little laugh out of Andy. She rested her chin on Rip's shoulder and they pulled around the back of the house.

They were riding side by side, about halfway through the woods, approaching the cornfields and not going any more than fifteen miles an hour. Rip was rehearsing what he was going to say, or how he was going to pray with Heather without coming across as "preachy." The truth of the matter was that he didn't have the faintest idea how he was going to ease her mind about her father's spiritual whereabouts.

Lord, please help me make a difference. Please give me the words to comfort her. The words to give her strength and—

"Is this as fast as this heap goes?" Heather asked.

Rip tilted his head toward her. "You serious?"

"I feel like I'm on a kiddie ride," she said. "Let's move it."

"Yeah!" Andy yelled with a little burst of speed before slowing down around fifty feet in front of them. He looked back. "Let's move it!"

Rip knew the bike still needed a lot of work, but he figured he could give Heather what she was after. He pulled back on the throttle a little and pulled up to Andy and gave him a little wink.

"Sorry your bike doesn't go any faster than forty, bro!" he yelled, hoping Andy wouldn't try to keep up and get the women all riled up again about his bike being too fast. He pointed up the path that separated the cornfields. "We'll wait for you up near the canal!"

Andy gave him a thumbs-up and Rip patted Heather on her leg.

"Hang on," he said. He liked the way she tightened her grip around his waist. When he gunned it, the front tire came about a foot off the ground and they took off.

By the time he spotted the wildflowers, they had hit close to eighty miles an hour and he started to slow down. They passed the last row of corn and Rip pulled off the trail into the grass that ran all the way down to the canal's bank.

Heather lifted her head off his back and let go of his waist. "Are you crazy?"

"What?"

"Driving that fast without a helmet on this heap? I wanted to go faster, not die."

"Don't ever call this sweet ride a heap," Rip said and laughed. He glanced back down the path into the corn. Andy was a good hundred yards back, doing a brilliant job of acting like his bike was still hobbled.

Rip and Heather got off the bike and Rip cringed, feeling like his left rib cage had been run over by a truck. *What is going on?* Suddenly, his visit to Doc Strater couldn't come fast enough.

Heather didn't say anything. She walked in front of him, down to the bank, and just stared at the other side of the canal. Rip joined her. The flowers seemed even more incredible today, amplifying that perfect sense of peace that drew him. And despite Andy's repeated warnings, more and more he wanted to be over there and *in* the flower garden. *I wonder if Heather would drive us in again . . .*

Andy pulled up behind them. Rip looked back and saw his nephew hold his arms up as if to say, *What do you want me to do?*

Rip walked back up the bank and had to stop and act like he was checking his shoelace, when what he was really doing was privately gasping for air. He needed to get on some type of cardio program, and in a hurry. Maybe it was his lungs. Maybe all this growth was making him allergic or something, and made it harder to breathe. He finally stood and managed to make it up to where Andy was.

"Nice work riding slowly," Rip said.

"She all right?" Andy asked, looking down at Heather. Rip could see the earbuds for his iPod hanging out his front pocket.

"Not sure," Rip said. "Give me a few minutes."

He walked back down the bank.

"You okay?" he asked, staring at Heather's profile.

She didn't say anything.

"Heather?" Rip said. "What is it?"

"Just thinking about the dates on my dad's headstone," she said. "He was born in 1956 and died in 1992."

"Other than today, when was the last time you were out there?" Rip asked.

"It was like a month before we broke up," Heather said.

"When I had hair?" Rip joked.

Heather didn't smile. She started to say something and then stopped.

"What is it?" Rip said again.

"He was only a year older than we are now, Rip."

Rip did the math. It was hard to believe that Mr. Gerisch was only thirty-six when he was killed. His generation certainly seemed a lot more mature.

Rip felt a little pain in his side, as if somebody pushed the wind right out of him. He coughed a couple times and struggled to take a breath of air.

Heather finally looked at him. "Rip, your face is beet-red. You okay?"

"Feeling a little off lately," he said. "But I think I'll probably make it. You want me to leave you alone so you can collect your thoughts?"

"I don't want you going anywhere," she said. "Will you sit here with me?"

"That's why I'm here," Rip said.

She pointed at the grass where she wanted them to sit and there was something about her hand that warmed his heart. Her fingernails were colorless and chewed, as they'd always been. Then Rip looked at her face, and her natural beauty more than compensated for all of the toughness she had always tried to project.

"They think the killer may have known my dad and Mr. Hart," Heather whispered, sitting down in the grass with her knees pulled up close to her chest, right next to him.

Rip tried to kneel, but it made the pain in his lower back easily double, so he quickly sat just like Heather did.

"How long you known that?" Rip asked, mulling over her words. "You've never told me that before."

"Couple years," Heather said. "All the records from the case had been shipped up to a warehouse in Detroit around five or six years after it happened. I had a few days off and went up there and snooped around for a bit."

"Why didn't you tell me?"

"You were in jail, loser."

"C'mon. I mean since then."

"Because it's ugly," she said, glancing back at Andy. "Talking about a murder."

"He can't hear us," Rip whispered.

Heather rested her chin on top of her knees and stared absently across the canal again.

"The whole town knows they were both shot in the head," she

added. "And yes, just like everyone had always thought, my dad got it in the face."

"We don't have to talk about that," Rip said.

"I want to," she said. "That's why I was crying out on Judi's porch. Because when I was up in Detroit, checking on that place that sold the wheelchair, I swung by the warehouse and looked at the file again. I knew the picture was in there the last time, but I just couldn't look. This time I did."

"What picture?" Rip said, regretting his question by the time it came off his tongue. He knew.

"My dad's body," she said, closing her eyes. "It wasn't pretty."

"C'mon, Heather," he said. "We don't have to—"

"But the thing is, what was kept pretty low was the fact that they think it may have been my dad's service revolver that killed them. I guess it even looked like there was a possibility my dad killed Mr. Hart and then shot himself in the face."

"There's no way your dad would've done that, Heather."

"They didn't think so either," Heather said. Something about the way she was talking made her look ten years younger.

"How do they know that?" Rip asked gently.

"Because my dad's gun was missing. It's kind of hard to kill yourself and then get rid of the gun."

Rip glanced back at Andy, who was sitting Indian-style next to the bike. He was twirling the iPod around by the earbud cord. He held his finger up for Andy to be patient and Andy nodded.

Rip looked back at Heather and then held up his hands. "I still don't understand why they think the killer knew them."

"That's just a comment that showed up in two of the reports," Heather said. "There was no sign of any struggle at the Harts' house. None. It was like somebody was handed my dad's gun, took two quick shots, and then vanished into thin air."

Rip didn't know what to say.

Heather looked right at him. "You know what?"

"What?" Rip asked.

Her head didn't move an inch. "I wish I never dug into those files, Rip. I can't get that photo out of my head." She paused and closed her eyes. "A .357 is a pretty big gun."

Rip felt helpless, only imagining the freeze-frame of whatever was left of her father's head in Heather's mind.

She finally put her face in her hands and her shoulders began to slowly bob, unable to fight the tears. A big part of that feminine side she'd always meant to hide had come pouring out again and it made Rip melt, feeling even more helpless.

Rip shimmied over a few inches to be right next to her. He put his arm around her and whispered, "Let's pray about your dad. That's what we came here for, isn't it?"

She looked up at him and her eyes were filled with tears. "I'm tired of thinking about it, Rip. I'm tired of worrying about him."

Rip lowered his chin to the top of her head and then closed his eyes. *God, give me the words, ones that will offer her comfort . . . like right now if You don't mind . . .*

"Uncle Rip," Andy said.

Rip opened his eyes and held up his finger for Andy to be patient. Then he closed his eyes again and focused on God.

"Uncle Rip," Andy repeated, louder this time.

"Shhh," Rip said, glancing back at Andy. "I'm trying to help Heather here. Sit and pray with us if you want, but I need you to hush, just for a little bit."

Rip closed his eyes again before praying, "Lord, we ask that You look upon us, and give Heather—"

"*Heather Marie.*"

Rip looked back at Andy again. Andy's eyes weren't shut this time and he wasn't looking upward. In fact, he was staring straight across the canal at the flowers.

"To be absent from the body is to be present with the Lord," Andy said.

Rip stood and Heather didn't move.

"Say that again," Rip said, quickly approaching Andy.

Andy ignored him and walked straight toward Heather. He handed her the iPod.

"I don't know what I said," Andy whispered. "But I do know that *God is over in the garden.*"

Rip looked across the canal and then Heather started humming.

Her head was swaying slowly back and forth and she had a peaceful smile on her face. She was holding one of the earbuds up to her ear. And as she hummed, shifting flawlessly from note to note, Rip decided it was the most beautiful music he'd ever heard. The same Heather who never sang a single word in church was humming a song that was every bit as beautiful as the wildflowers.

She sounded like an angel.

And he could tell by the smile on Heather's face that she now had a good idea where her father was. Because it was the *best* of smiles they had talked about.

As he stared at her, Andy's words from Corinthians played over in his head.

"To be absent from the body is to be present with the Lord . . ."

It was perfect for Heather. Those words were just for her.

Andy was right.

Mr. Gerisch was with God.

Heather opened her eyes and looked at Rip and Andy.

"My father," Heather whispered, that smile still painted perfectly on her face. "Rip, my fear is *gone.*"

Andy tapped on Rip's shoulder and pointed across the canal. Rip turned and looked.

Heather's fear wasn't the only thing that was gone.

So was another section of the garden.

� ✖ ✖

"I can't describe it," Heather said, sitting on the couch in Judi's living room. "It was the most beautiful music I had ever heard, except it was more than music. *He was in* the music."

Judi was smiling from ear to ear. "And you think it was God?"

"It was Him," Heather said.

"You could see God?" Judi asked, nodding, as if eager to share the experience.

"Sort of," Heather said. "But I could definitely *feel* Him."

"You should have heard her," Rip said. "She could have sold tickets."

"I don't remember doing any humming," Heather said, "but I remember seeing my dad on the other side of the canal, standing right in the wildflowers. And something . . . someone was standing behind him, and I couldn't see a face, but it was God. I'm sure of it. And then I remember a feeling of being protected, accepted, and completely loved."

"Like God was holding you in His hands," Andy said.

Heather thought about that for a second. "That's exactly how I would describe it, Andy."

"The last time I went out to the canal," Andy said, "I fell asleep and remember seeing someone just like you described and hearing a voice telling me to bring you there so you could see. But Uncle Rip beat me to the punch. He asked you to go out there first."

"My dad is in God's hands," Heather said. Grinning, free. Just saying it gave her goose bumps and she smiled, knowing the truth at last. "I listened to you, Rip. When we were sitting out there I prayed and prayed and prayed. And He answered. Big-time." She couldn't stop smiling.

"What is happening?" Judi said, looking at Rip.

"*God* is what's happening," Rip said. "God dropped us a little gift basket on the other side of The Frank and Poet and it's filled with miracles, just like in the Bible."

"You are wrong," Andy said. "It's more than a gift basket."

Rip laughed and casually took the iPod out of Andy's hands and held it to his ear. He looked at Andy and then at Heather.

"When do *I* get to hear what you and Andy heard? Every time I hold this thing to my ear and try to listen, I get nothing but dead air."

"I can't wait to tell my mom," Heather said, ignoring him. "And the people at church and at Bible study. But they're going to think we've flipped our lids."

"Just tell your mom for now," Rip said. "I really don't care what anybody thinks, but let's not tell anyone else about this until we get this figured out. I don't think we want this turning into a *Field of Dreams*."

"It's bigger than some baseball game," Andy said without hesitation.

Heather agreed with Andy, but what Rip said made sense as well.

Rip coughed into the bend of his arm and it sounded like it hurt.

"You gotta get to a doctor," Heather said. "Your coloring seems a little funny and you sound like you have the croup."

"Croup?" Rip said. "I haven't heard that word since third grade."

"Seriously," Heather said. "You've been coughing for quite a while now."

"I hear ya," Rip said. "I already made an appointment to see Doc Strater. My back's been killin' me too. It stinks getting old."

"Not for me," Heather said. "I just keep getting more beautiful."

Rip laughed and winced. "It's crazy. We are going to blink our eyes and be forty. Can you believe it?"

"Shut up, Rip," Judi said. "I'll hit it before you guys do."

"Getting older is okay if you're a guy," Rip said. He coughed a little again and seemed to have a hard time catching his breath. "Men are like wine and women are like heads of lettuce."

"Whatever," Heather said. "At least you don't have to worry about going gray." She cast a heavy look to his balding head.

"You would take me back in a minute if I asked," Rip said. "I know you've struggled without me."

Heather nodded and a little smile creased her lips. She made sure Judi couldn't hear. "You know what?"

"What?" Rip said.

"Maybe you're right."

Rip laughed. "About *us*? That'd go over well with the department."

"I'm not worried about it anymore."

"Don't even joke about it," Rip said. "Not smart."

"Doesn't matter," Heather said. "Something in those wildflowers told me that there was something I needed to do about my job."

"What's that?"

"Quit," Heather said. "I'm going to give Chief Reynolds my notice soon."

TWENTY-FIVE

Kevin Hart waded through the stack of papers on his desk, wondering what it would be like to not have to worry about business anymore. Sure, the Phillips acquisition eliminated a major competitor, but the thought of being the seller instead of the buyer and leaving the game entirely had often been on his mind of late.

He glanced at his watch. Nine forty-five p.m.

He stood and walked over to the window, imagining himself living in California or even Florida. After all, sixty million dollars made somebody relatively portable. *Make that thirty million,* the number Carrie always tossed in his face, if they were to split ways.

One thing he knew for sure—if he was going to make that leap, he wouldn't be taking Carrie along for the ride. Thirty million would be enough for a lifetime.

But where would that leave me? Who would take my place as the one they all looked to?

The longer he thought about that, the bigger that wave of sadness grew.

The truth was that he didn't like who he had become. But he loved himself for who he was to other people. The man with everything that everyone else wanted.

He could see the headlights approaching from beyond the south entrance, so he aimed his remote at the window and opened the gate.

"It's going to be another long night," he said, clicking the remote again to close the drapes. He locked up his office and went downstairs.

By the time he was outside, she had already parked the BMW on the lake side of the dumpsters and was halfway across the parking lot, walking toward him in the dark.

"Hello, Brianna," he said, leaning over. He wrapped a hand around the back of her neck and kissed her.

"We've got some company," she said.

"What do you mean?"

"When I got out of the car, there was somebody standing on a loading dock back around the corner."

"At this hour?"

"Yeah," she said. "And he definitely saw me."

"Why didn't you turn around and leave?"

"I didn't see him until it was too late," she said. "He must have opened that big door to the warehouse, or whatever it is, right after I pulled up."

"It's gotta be Ripley," Hart said. "I can't believe he is here at this hour. I left him a note to organize some more cans we got in for the food drive and he's obviously got nothing better to do. You sure he saw you?"

"Positive," she said. "He was standing there with his arms crossed, staring at me, almost like he knew what we were up to."

"Not a chance," Hart said, giving her another kiss. A bit longer this time.

She pulled back. "This is unbelievable."

"What?" he said.

She pointed over his shoulder and he turned around. Ripley was standing on yet another loading dock, looking right at them. He stared back at Ripley and neither of them moved for a few seconds. Finally, Ripley went back inside.

"That's a problem," Brianna said.

"He's nothing," Hart said. "I own him. You'll just have something else to write about now."

"What do you mean?" she asked.

"You've got a deadline on a different story. The reason you are here is to interview me to write about how generous Hart Industries is to the community. Maybe the Summer Santa is getting too much coverage of late."

She smiled and ran her long fingers down his silk shirt. "That'll be easy. I know more about your generosity than anyone."

"Thatta girl," he said, giving her a little wink. "But we may just have to be a little extra careful tonight."

※ ※ ※

He stood in the middle of the kitchen, thinking.

Things were going well.

Again.

Nobody was up, and there weren't any police officers standing five feet away, pointing a gun at him.

He cocked his head and listened, hearing nothing.

Gifting cash was so much easier than pushing around a wheelchair and bicycles, and way easier than changing tires in the middle of a driveway at two in the morning.

Dropping off the Little League equipment in the middle of the night, out at the park, had been a no-brainer, but of all of his gigs, he was still most surprised that old Mr. and Mrs. Nelson hadn't said anything about the lost wedding ring he'd replaced. She'd been barking about it at church for a good three months and he'd left it right in the middle of their living room, attached to the base of their wedding picture.

Maybe they don't look at it, he thought. *Isn't anyone happily married anymore?*

He placed the paper lunch bag on the counter and thought he heard something. He turned his head toward his left shoulder and waited.

He heard water running and then the light went on near the staircase. He walked quickly toward the corner that led to the garage.

Footsteps. Heavy ones.

Someone was coming down the stairs.

He crouched and waited, hand on the doorknob that led to the garage. He'd be able to run if he had to.

The footsteps were closer and he gripped the doorknob a little tighter.

Mrs. Kelly came around the corner. All three hundred pounds of her, wearing only the T-shirt that was made for someone half her size.

She didn't turn the kitchen light on and walked over to the refrigerator. When she opened it, the light spilled out and he could see the paper bag on the counter.

She just stared in the refrigerator, but apparently nothing caught her fancy. She then closed the refrigerator door and walked back in front of him and toward the stairs, but then paused, spotting the paper bag on the counter. "What is this?" she asked.

He smiled.

It's enough for those back taxes. You don't have to move now.

He watched as she opened the bag. The look on her face was worth the trip all by itself.

And then he made the sign of the cross and left.

TWENTY-SIX

Rip and Andy were in the back pew, waiting to collect the week's offering. Kevin Hart was up at the lectern, covering the announcements. Hart had tried to explain to Rip that the little cutie from the newspaper was over at the plant just for an interview. Rip was pretty sure that Hart knew he wasn't buying it, but even with foul play going on, Hart didn't seem overly concerned about it, because that Brianna girl was parked right next to Hart's wife up in the front pew.

Rip leaned over and poked Andy on the shoulder. "Quit starin' at Chelsea."

"*Pfff,*" Andy said. "Just make sure I'm the best man when you and Heather get married."

"Anybody have anything they are thankful for this week?" Hart asked. He must have been riding a pretty serious guilt trip. He had managed to do both readings, the week's announcements, and had now created "thankfulness announcements." Still, Rip liked the idea and there was a lot to be thankful for, so he raised his hand.

"Mr. Ripley," Hart said, pointing at him.

"I'm thankful for my sister and my nephew," Rip said.

Heather went next. "I'm thankful for resolutions to old problems . . . and for my friend Gerald Ripley."

Judi turned around with a look that said, *What's going on with you and Heather?*

Hart went next. "I'm thankful for my lovely bride and for Ms. Brianna Bruley for the kind piece she will be doing on Hart Industries for this week's paper."

Nice, Rip thought. *A little preemptive strike in case anybody else saw you sucking face last night.*

Mrs. Kelly got up and thanked the Lord for saving their house with an unexpected windfall.

Mrs. Cochran stood up and gave thanks to Kevin Hart and the whole church for their support and prayers. Then she mentioned the price of little Marjo's experimental surgery.

One hundred and eighty thousand dollars.

Rip shook his head. It seemed impossible. But again, if each Benning resident showed up at the country club for the fund-raiser and ate around 4.8 of those twenty-five-dollar dinners, little Marjo would be golden.

There were a lot of people who were still giving God thanks and Rip was thankful for that too.

After service, Rip and Andy were putting a pretty significant dent in the peanut butter cookies that the poor girl, Becky, had brought in. She seemed to be getting quite a charge out of people eating her cookies instead of her and her kids eating everyone else's. They'd been bringing the goodies for three weeks straight.

"That was a nice service," Heather said.

Rip smiled at her. "I want you to know that I'm thankful that *you're* thankful for me."

"I *am* thankful for you, Rip."

"Thanks, Heather," he said. "I really think that we—"

"*Kevin Frances.*"

Rip froze and then slowly turned around. Pastor Welsh approached Andy. The hundred other people who were in the fellowship hall had all gone quiet, listening for what was next.

Andy opened his eyes and lowered the earbud from his ear. He looked around and then quickly spotted the man.

Rip was pretty sure that Hart was already on edge; he seemed to brace himself, expressionless, as Andy walked toward him.

"Why do you call Me Lord, Lord, and not do what I say?"

"Oh boy," Rip whispered. This was not going to end well.

Pastor Welsh sidled over and took Rip by the arm. "Remember that little talk you wanted to have with Kevin? Why don't you go talk to him, like, tomorrow?"

"Before he tosses my butt to the curb?" Rip whispered.

"Yeah. Before then," the pastor whispered back.

They both waited for Hart to say something to Andy.

Hart didn't. He just walked over to Rip and took him by the arm. "Busy tomorrow, Rip?"

"Nothing out of the ordinary," Rip answered.

"Good," Hart said with an insincere smile. "I think you should stop by my office *the minute* you get in."

"No problem, Kevin," he said. "I was actually going to stop by anyway."

TWENTY-SEVEN

Kevin Hart guessed that Ripley thought things were going a little better than expected. After all, the stoner had made it twenty-five seconds into their meeting and was still employed.

After a restless night, Hart was perfectly calm as he sat behind his desk. He didn't like the idea of being unusually friendly with Ripley, but he had come up with just the right plan to butter him up in exchange for some sort of vow of silence about the whole Brianna thing.

"You said that you were going to stop by anyway," Hart said. "Let's get that out of the way before we talk about your possible promotion."

"Promotion?" Ripley said slowly.

Hart nodded, taking care to school his expression into something hopeful, encouraging. "I'm assuming you want to talk to me about why I was being interviewed so late the other night."

"Interviewed?"

"Yeah," Hart said. "That's pretty much what I was thanking Brianna for at church. I thought it was going to be in this week's paper, but it won't run until next week. She is quite thorough and I think it's going to make all of us at Hart Industries look pretty good. We are very fortunate."

"You *are* very fortunate, Kevin," Ripley said. "I mean *Mr. Hart.*"

Hart smiled. "We've known each other a long time, Rip. Call me Kevin whenever you want."

Ripley sat up in his chair and it looked like he was in pain before he rubbed at his lower back. "It's good to hear you call me Rip, instead of Ripley."

"I apologize for that," Hart said. "I call just about everybody around the plant by their last name. That way, when I call somebody by their first name, ten people named John don't turn around at the same time."

"I guess that makes sense," Ripley said.

"So on to what you wanted to talk to me about," Hart said, thinking, *This ought to be good.*

"Kevin, I guess I want you to know that this isn't an employee to boss conversation, or even man to man."

"What else could it be?" Hart asked. *What a complete moron.*

Ripley looked at him and hesitated for a few seconds. "I guess I kind of wanted it to be like brother to brother—you know—as Christians?"

Hart smiled and it appeared to make Ripley comfortable. That was a good thing.

"Lay it on me," Hart said.

"You have been blessed," Ripley said. "More than you'll ever know."

"Thank you, Rip," Hart said. He nodded and a little smile etched the corners of his mouth. Of course he'd been blessed. Blessed to the point where he could wave his hand and Ripley would be cutting lawns and cashing unemployment checks.

"But . . . ," Ripley said, hesitating.

"It's okay," Hart said, doing his best to sound like he meant it. "Tell me."

Ripley pointed at the ceiling and then lowered his hand. "The Bible sort of says I'm supposed to talk to you about some things I've seen. That I'm supposed to come to you and—"

"Like what?" Hart said.

"Those blessings," Ripley said. "I guess that maybe . . . maybe you aren't really using them for Him . . ."

"For God, you mean?"

Ripley's confidence seemed to pick up and he held up his hands as if to encompass the whole factory. "All of this means nothing, Kev." Then Rip pointed at his own chest. "Unless this is in the right place."

"You think my heart is in the wrong place?"

Ripley looked away and seemed to be struggling to find the right words.

"Don't get me wrong," Ripley said. "I still have a hard time with my temper. I'm judgmental. I sometimes preach a little . . ." He sighed. "I've made so many mistakes in my life," he added. "And I'm still paying for a lot of them, but I'm better than I've ever been because God is in my heart, and my life is running on all cylinders for Him. And if just one of those cylinders is not filled with the truth, things don't work. Things can't work. It all gets clogged up."

"I'm not sure what you're saying."

"I'm saying that everything in our lives has to go toward God. And when something doesn't, when we screw up, we should ask for His forgiveness and let His love straighten us out."

Hart didn't say anything. He didn't nod, blink, or twitch. He was perfectly still. *This idiot actually believes this bunk.*

"And if we don't see our problems," Ripley said, "hopefully we can trust that someone who cares about us will."

"And that's why you're here?"

Ripley was clearly hesitant to answer. But he did. "Yeah. Your threats against my nephew . . . I think they're born out of a knowledge inside you. You know you're doing something wrong, and it hurts to be called out on it. I'm sorry if Andy's embarrassed you. It's not how it's supposed to go." Ripley gestured in the air between them. "But *this* is how it's supposed to go. Between brothers, in private, so a guy has a chance to get it straight first."

Hart shifted in his chair and blinked slowly. *Brothers.*

"There's nothing going on with me and that reporter, Rip."

"But, Kevin, I'm not sure we are on the same page here. I think most people would think that what I saw—"

"I would never risk what I have for something like that."

It was clear that Ripley didn't have the guts to tell him what he saw, but he kept yapping anyhow. "You understand the Twenty-Third Psalm, Kev?"

Hart frowned. "The Lord is my Shepherd? You've lost me."

Ripley leaned forward and rested his elbows on his knees. "David was basically saying that he was okay with God managing his life. He admitted that God's management was all he needed. Period."

"I'm okay with that too," Hart said.

Ripley held up his hands again. "Possessions mean nothing, Kevin. You've already heard that you can't take them with you."

"We all have." *But you can have a lot of fun with them while you're here.*

Ripley continued, "Do you know that David's equivalent modern-day net worth was around $700 billion? He could have taken out Bill Gates and Warren Buffett with his pocket change. Still, he knew his most valuable possession was his relationship with God. Fortunately, that is something that applies to both of us as well."

"Amen," Hart said. It felt like the right thing to say.

"Amen?" Ripley asked. "God loves you, Kevin. He loves us all. But one of these days He is gonna cut His losses, clean out His closet, clean out our closets. And I'm here because I want you to be on the right side of the table when that happens."

It was time to know the truth. "What have you seen, Rip?"

"It doesn't matter what I've seen."

"I do a lot of good for this town. Even some things others don't know about."

"I believe that, Kevin."

"I'll ask again," Hart said, his boss volume rising. "What have you seen?"

"And I'll answer again," Ripley said. "That doesn't matter."

"Why not?"

Ripley pointed to the ceiling again. "Because He has seen it all."

An awkward silence hung in the air. Hart stood and went to the window. He looked at the floor and tried to act ashamed. And then he finally spoke. "You're right. I should do better."

"That's the only reason I wanted to chat," Ripley said. "I've been on the cover of *Sinner Magazine*, like, a hundred times. And I'm hoping that you'll straighten me out whenever you see me straying."

"I want to be comfortable with God managing my life," Hart said in an appropriately somber tone. "Just like David."

"Me too," Ripley said.

"I appreciate you coming to me, Rip. For being someone I can trust." He picked up a pen, as if mulling something over, and then peered back at Ripley. "In fact, I need a guy I can trust with confidence to manage the new facility down in Tecumseh when we change the name on the building from Phillips to Hart. Pay would be around three times where you are at now."

Ripley stared at him for a long moment, then shifted as if he couldn't get comfortable in his seat. "I have to say, Kevin, that I thought there was a good chance you were going to fire me today."

Kevin nodded. "I imagine. But I think this marks a new chapter of our relationship. *Brother to brother.*"

"I'm not qualified for it," Ripley said. "But I have to admit, I'd like a shot at it."

"We'll get you trained for it," Hart said, smiling. "You'll be fine."

Ripley coughed into the V of his arm. Probably coughed up a nice wad of tar from his smoky-smoky days.

"It'd be an honor," Ripley said. "I really appreciate it."

"And I appreciate you coming to me, as a man, and as a fellow Christian."

"That's a bigger honor, Kev. The best honor."

"I tell you what," Hart said. "Think Andy may want to make a few bucks?"

"Why?"

"Just thinking," Hart said. "I've been kind of slave driving you on those cans down in the warehouse. Maybe the three of us could finish the job together one night."

"I think Andy would be open to that."

"And maybe I could get him to quit calling me out with that iPod of his."

"God has chosen to give him messages," Ripley said with a shrug. "Messages that we're supposed to be listening to. But maybe if you and I are chatting in private, God will see that you're making an effort and leave you alone." He gave Hart a smile.

"I'm game for anything if it gets the kid to quit hammering at me."

"When do you want me to have Andy at the warehouse?" Ripley asked.

"Whatever time or day works for you guys."

"I'll let you know," Ripley said.

"One other thing," Hart said. "I like to keep spiritual matters private. What we've discussed . . . it will stay between us?"

"It stays between you and me, Kevin. I promise you."

Hart took his turn pointing at the ceiling, fully playing the part now that he understood what drove Ripley. "And Him."

"Now you're talking, bro," Ripley said.

Hart smiled. "Did you just call me bro?"

"I did," Ripley said, dropping his hand on Kevin's shoulder. "Because you are."

Hart nodded and smiled, but not for the reason Ripley thought.

Mission accomplished.

TWENTY-EIGHT

Y ou don't have to apologize," Heather said, sitting across from Brianna at the station's media room table. "We all make mistakes."

"I appreciate it," Brianna said. "You were probably wondering why you hadn't heard much from me."

"It's no big deal," Heather said. She really had forgiven Brianna about the article, but the odds of her commenting on anything she didn't want to be in the paper were next to zero.

"So about the arrest last night up in Carlson," Brianna said. "You think it's the Summer Santa?"

"You may want to talk to the Carlson Police Department about that," Heather said.

"I did," Brianna said. "They said they nabbed him at a house and he had the black gloves, shirt, mask—seems like the whole getup."

"Like I said. You may want to talk to them."

Heather knew it wasn't the Summer Santa. For starters, the Summer Santa was either Kevin Hart or Brianna herself. Secondly, a friend of hers at the Carlson Police Department had said the guy had a gun and was also apprehended with around $3,000 worth of jewelry on him. He did, however, claim to be the Summer Santa, most likely trying to gain some sympathy.

"Can I ask you a question?" Brianna asked. "Off the record?"

"Your record of keeping things off the record isn't exactly exemplary," Heather said, crossing her arms.

"This doesn't have anything to do with the Summer Santa," Brianna said, holding up two fingers. "Scout's honor."

"Since I'm a former Girl Scout," Heather said, "looks like I have no choice but to trust you."

Brianna didn't hesitate. "That thing that Andy kid said to Kevin after church a couple days ago. It's almost like somebody told him to say that. Do you think he knows about something Kevin did?"

Kevin? Heather thought. *Pretty personal for the new girl in town to refer to the most important man around by his first name.*

"Like what?" Heather asked. "What could Kevin have done?"

"Not sure," Brianna said, her eyes darting away. "I was just wondering what you thought."

Heather thought about what Rip had told her that day she was crying out on Judi's porch before she answered Brianna. "The Lord works in mysterious ways. But I'm not sure how much Andy is privy to about Kevin Hart."

"I was just curious," Brianna said. "It was a little jarring how the whole room seemed to go on pause right before he said it. He's good friends with Ripley, right? I saw them sitting next to each other at Bible study."

The only people who had referred to Rip as Ripley over the last thirty years were the police during his drug bust, Rip's teachers in school, and Kevin Hart. Heather found this odd, so she decided to lean on the reporter a bit.

"Andy is *Ripley's* nephew," Heather said. "They are best friends."

"Oh," Brianna said, clearly uncomfortable.

Heather stared her down. "Is there something about Kevin Hart that makes you nervous?"

"Not at all," Brianna answered. "Why?"

There was a little pause. Heather wasn't buying her answer. In fact, she wasn't even close to it.

"Brianna, I have to tell you something," she said, still staring right at her. She was trying Kevin's little intimidation secret. "I can't help but feel that you know more about the Summer Santa than you claim."

"Why do you say that?"

"Just a hunch," Heather said.

"You know as much as I do," Brianna said, looking quickly away.

"*As much as you do?*" Heather asked. "I would certainly hope so. I am the police."

"I know that," Brianna said, her eyes darting nervously back and forth.

"You okay?" Heather asked. "Sure there's nothing I need to know?"

"No," Brianna said. "I've just got a lot to do. I better get running. I promise you, Heather, Thursday's article won't be bad."

Heather had never been involved in any form of interrogation, but she did remember a few snippets of body language she had learned that let questioners know when someone was being untruthful, and Brianna was in prime form.

"I may want you to stop by again soon," Heather said. "If that's cool with you. Don't go too far."

"Oh. Okay," Brianna said slowly.

Heather stood and followed her to the door. She watched as the young reporter made her way toward that red BMW. And then Brianna stopped suddenly and glanced back at her.

By the look on Brianna's face, the idea of coming in for another talk was anything but okay.

TWENTY-NINE

Neither of them had said a word in close to ten minutes, but Kevin Hart had become used to quiet dinners. He was pretty sure that Carrie didn't care either.

"What happened to us?" he asked.

"What are you talking about?"

"You and I," he said. "Our marriage."

"Oh, please," she said. "Aren't we about five years too late for this conversation?"

Her answer didn't bother him.

He tapped his finger on the side of his wineglass and thought about his conversation with Ripley. He couldn't imagine not worrying about what people thought of him. Being *the man* with all the money and all the answers to everyone's problems was what he really lived for. Only worrying about what God saw sounded good, really good, and he tried to imagine the pressure it'd relieve if he quit worrying about what everyone else thought.

But there was a slight problem.

If there really was a God, He already knew the truth about every sin Kevin had ever committed.

"We already have over a hundred guests coming for the Cochran fund-raiser," Carrie said. She stood and walked over to the kitchen counter and held up the copy of the *Benning Weekly* that had come out that day.

"What part of the paper are you in this week?" Hart asked. "'The Only Socialite in Town' section?"

"And you wonder what happened to us," she said, with that irritating little smirk of hers. "I just wanted to show you the ad we have for the fund-raiser. It looks good and you usually like to see the ads *you* pay for."

"Great," he said. "You know the odds of us raising close to two hundred thousand? One hundred people at twenty-five a clip leaves us around one hundred and ninety-eight thousand short."

"The Cochrans will be paying that bill the rest of their lives if we don't do something," Carrie said. "That's *if* the hospital even does it without the money up front."

You mean if I don't do something, he thought.

"Besides, we can put in a good chunk of change ourselves, right?" she said. She gave him a curious look. "What's gotten into you? You've never worried about the success of our fund-raisers. You actually seem like you care."

She was probably right. At the end of the day it was just another fund-raiser for yet another cause. But something about getting the credit for it felt good. And deep down, there was something in him that wanted this to work for little Marjo. The kid was darn cute.

Carrie flipped the paper over. "How about this Summer Santa character?"

"What about him?"

"He sure seems to be getting a lot of attention."

He didn't say anything.

"I'm taking a shower," she said, dropping the newspaper on the table and leaving the room.

Hart picked it up and looked at the full-page ad for the fund-raiser: "Black Tie Optional. Choice of Entrée Selection. Entertainment."

Then he flipped the paper over and glanced at the headline of the latest article Brianna had put together on the Summer Santa: "What's Left in the Summer Santa's Sleigh?"

He took a sip of his wine and thought about what Andy had said to him. Not all of the boy's words made sense. But something about that first thing Andy had said played over and over in his head.

I have searched you, and I know you.

The words chewed at the back of his mind until they forced him to look at the ceiling and ask his dead father.

"Do you think anyone really knows what I've been doing lately, Dad?"

He waited, wanting the mighty Walter Hart to answer. He held his hands up in the air. And then he finally let them drop to his sides.

He lowered his head and closed his eyes.

Or the things I did a long time ago?

THIRTY

Rip was sitting in Judi's kitchen, thinking about what an uneventful week it had been since he'd had his little chat with Kevin Hart. That had made things better between them, which made life easier by taking a little of that awkward edge off things at work. Other than that, Andy hadn't had any further words from the iPod and the garden seemed unchanged. The only blip on the weekly radar was the battery of tests he hadn't quite planned on at Doc Strater's. When he told Judi how much weight he'd lost, she couldn't believe it.

"When I got out of prison, I weighed 205 pounds," he said, trying to ease her concern. "Then I put on a quick twenty, so I'm really just right back to where I started."

"C'mon, Rip," Judi said. "You've lost twenty pounds eating like a pig and not working out?"

"What are you talking about?" he answered. "I've been doing a million push-ups a week. Don't worry, Doc Strater took a bunch of tests and said the weight loss could be a lot of things."

"And the tests said what?"

"Not sure yet," Rip said. "I had to wait in his office forever before I got in to see him and was over an hour late getting back to work. The nurses said they'd call me if anything came up."

"You do look skinnier, Uncle Rip," Andy said, looking at him with worry.

Rip faced him. "C'mon, bro. Your mom is already freaking out on me."

"I'm surprised Kevin is actually gonna *help you* with the cans tonight," Judi said. She pointed at Andy behind his back. "And I'm really surprised he wants you-know-who to come along. Particularly after the last *Bible-versing* he gave him."

Rip thought about the way Kevin acted the day of their "talk." Rip hadn't mentioned anything about their conversation to Judi, just the fact that Kevin wanted to help out and that he asked that Andy come along. Andy hadn't wanted to go, of course, but Rip talked him into it, telling his nephew that Hart seemed really ready to change, and they might get to be a part of it.

He glanced at his watch, then looked at Andy. "You ready to go make the big bucks? I'm guessing you're gonna need some extra dough for all your upcoming dates with Chelsea."

"Shut up, Uncle Rip."

"Let's do it," Rip said, glancing at his watch. "We can head over a little early and get a head start."

※ ※ ※

Andy was a machine.

Rip knew that when the boy put his mind to something, it was hard to get him away from it, and in this case, that made him an excellent worker. Six or seven thousand cans still needed to be put on the trucks for the different shelters, and Andy was loading the boxes at a pace that was twice as fast as his own.

Rip wasn't sure if Judi's worrying had taken a little of the wind out of his sails, but he was gasping for air and felt like his strength had up and left. Throw in the added bonus that every time he coughed, he felt like one of his lungs was going to break in half and he was ready to call it a night.

"Let's take a break," he said. "You're wearing Uncle Rip out."

Andy stopped like somebody had hit his power switch.

"C'mon, bro," Rip said. "I'll give you a tour of the place."

"Okay," Andy said.

"You want to go out and see Mr. Hart's cool boat or you want to go in the haunted basement?" Rip tossed in a little spooky humming and he knew it wouldn't be much of a decision for Andy. He liked dark places, and Rip guessed it was for the same reason he liked wearing his hair over the side of his face and neck.

Rip led them off the end of the loading dock and over to the automatic garage door that, once opened, would expose the ramp that led into the basement.

Rip could see Andy's eyes widen as the door finished opening.

"It stinks down here," Andy said. "Like dirt and cheese."

"Hey, don't complain. This is where I got your motorcycle," Rip said. "There's a car down here I want you to see. No promises, but with my new raise, I may be able to put enough dough together over the next couple years to buy it by the time you get your license."

They started to make their way down the ramp.

"Hey," Rip said, pointing at Andy's back pocket. "The iPod is about to escape."

"I better watch out," Andy quipped. "It may break." The two shared a smile, but Andy pulled it out of his pocket and held it as they walked slowly down the ramp into the darkness.

"It *is* spooky down here," Andy said.

"Only for a little longer," Rip said, flicking on a whole row of switches, sixteen in all, the second they got to the bottom of the ramp.

The lights started out dim and then got progressively brighter, giving them a decent view of the whole basement. Rip coughed, and the pain in his lower back upgraded to a category five. Hopefully Doc Strater could prescribe something that would heal the strained muscles, because he seemed plagued by them. *It'll be good to move into management* . . . Maybe he was just too old for janitorial work.

Strater had said about the same thing Pastor Welsh said. If it was a pull, it wasn't going to go away without some rest, but time off wasn't an option. *Time off's for rich men.*

They walked along a row of discarded treasures that had been stored down in the musty basement since the dawn of man, including several sets of golf clubs, a motorized golf cart, and a pair of old jukeboxes. Farther up were a dozen victims of Old Man Hart's hunting excursions. Taxidermied heads of deer, elk, and a moose were surrounded by complete bodies of a bobcat, a pheasant, and a skunk, whose marble eyes drew a good stare out of Andy.

"Maybe this is what stinks," Rip said, lifting it by its tail.

Andy rolled his eyes.

Rip glanced at his watch. Hart was ten minutes late, so Rip figured he and Andy would hang in the basement until he showed up.

"I'm thinking you could fly down here for a few minutes with your hair in a ponytail," Rip said.

"Why?"

"Just until Mr. Hart gets here," Rip said, pulling a rubber band out of his pocket. "Do it for Uncle Rip."

"Why?" Andy repeated, lowering his head. "I don't want to."

"I think you'd look cool with a ponytail," Rip said.

"Then you'd see the side of my face. I don't want to."

"The side of your face doesn't bother me."

"Yeah, but—"

"And I guarantee you it doesn't bother Chelsea," Rip said. "Or your mom, or Heather, or Pastor Welsh, or—"

Andy stopped in his tracks. "But what about everybody else?"

"Who cares what anybody else thinks?" Rip cried. "What are they going to say that you haven't already heard?"

"*Whatever*," Andy said, snatching the rubber band out of Rip's hand.

Rip smiled, wanting Andy to smile with him.

Andy pulled his hair off the sides of his face. He put the rubber band over his index and middle fingers and formed a tight ponytail. "You happy?" he said, glancing around the basement, cautiously on the lookout for something that Rip knew didn't exist.

"You've never looked more handsome," Rip said, putting his arm around Andy and then kissing him on the side of his head. "Seriously."

"Uncle Rip," Andy said, holding a fist up. "If you ever plan on kissing me in public, you better make sure you've practiced falling down first, because I will knock you right out."

Rip laughed and they started walking again, coming across a portable basketball net. A lot of the guys used to come down and play during lunch until some union steward put the kibosh on it. Some even suggested Kevin Hart had finally called basketball a no-no because it was a threat to his workman's comp insurance.

"You probably never knew Uncle Rip was a basketball star, did you?"

"You never played basketball," Andy said. "You were too stoned to play."

"That doesn't mean I didn't have the tools," Rip said, grabbing the ball that sat on an old lawn chair beneath the hoop.

He shot the ball and it went over the backboard, landing in a stack of clay flower pots and breaking most of them.

Rip laughed. Andy didn't. He just stared at Rip like he'd missed a free throw to send the state championship into overtime.

"You're a scrub, Uncle Rip."

"Why the hatin', bro? I miss one shot and get this harassment?"

"What's that?" Andy asked, pointing to the very corner of the basement.

"Underneath that tarp is the car that I was telling you about," Rip said. "Mr. Hart hasn't had it on the road in years. It was his dad's and he only took it out every once in a while. But it's really fast."

"Can I see it?" Andy asked.

"You got it," Rip said.

They walked over to the corner, where the car had been backed in and covered up.

"Why don't you close your eyes?" Rip said. "I can't pull this off like the sheet on the motorcycle. It's too big. I'll tell you when to open your eyes."

"Okay," Andy said.

"You are gonna love this."

Rip unbuttoned the four corners of the tarp.

He slowly uncovered the Mustang and made sure to remember how the tarp went on so he could put it back. The car really was beautiful. Kevin didn't like driving it much because the old-timers called him by his dad's first name when they saw him in it. It seemed to bother him.

"Hang on," Rip said. "We're almost there."

Rip pulled the rest of the tarp off. The car still looked amazing. In fact, whatever maintenance it needed seemed to have already been done. It looked practically new with its candy-apple red paint shining under the basement light.

"Okay," Rip said. "I'll bet you double or nothing on that Coke you owe me that the thought of you driving this car will put a smile on your face."

"You're on," Andy said dully.

"Open your eyes," Rip said, stepping away from the car.

Andy did. But he didn't smile.

His neck slowly tilted back and his eyes widened. "Oh," he whispered.

"Andy?" Rip said, edging over to him. The kid looked like he was going to puke. "What is it?"

"Nothing," he said.

"Andy," Rip said again, standing in front of him and taking him by the shoulders. "Talk to me, bro. What is it?"

"You guys ready to get some work done?" It was Kevin Hart. He was standing about halfway down the ramp to the basement.

Andy looked quickly back at Hart and grabbed at the back of his head, tearing his hair out of the ponytail and pulling it forward over the sides of his face.

"What is it, Andy? Tell Uncle Rip."

"It's nothing," he muttered, but his eyes didn't leave the car.

"You guys okay down there?" Hart asked.

"*Andy*," Rip said, grabbing hold of his arm. "Tell me *now*."

"That's the car Mr. Hart was driving," Andy whispered harshly, wrenching his arm away. "When I saw him at the fountain that one day. That's when he said God didn't love me."

"*What* did he say?" Rip asked.

"He said if my scar is an example of what God does to people He loves, he wouldn't want to see what God does to people He hates. He said God doesn't love me."

"*What?*" Rip said. He spun Andy around and pointed at Kevin Hart, who was now only a few feet away. "*He* said *that?*"

"It's no big deal, Uncle Rip."

But something inside of Rip had already started to turn.

He thought about Judi's bruises. He thought about the cuts on his hand as he punched Todd's teeth until they weren't there anymore and how good that felt. *Vengeance.* He clenched his fists and looked at Hart.

Did you tell Andy God doesn't love him?

Rip was pretty sure he never asked the question, so Hart never had a chance to answer. He'd already elbowed him in his chest and Hart was on his knees. Rip grabbed a handful of Hart's hair and had his fist pulled back.

Hart's face came into focus. He was every bit as terrified as Andy.

"Did you tell my nephew that God doesn't love him?" Rip shouted.

Hart tried to lower his face but Rip pulled it back.

"Answer my question!"

Hart didn't answer, and that's when Rip heard Andy.

"*Gerald Michael.*"

Andy's eyes were closed. He was holding an earbud against his ear and his head was swaying back and forth as he looked at the basement ceiling like a person who was looking into the sun.

He lowered the earbud and walked up next to Rip. He eased Rip's hand off of Hart's head and Hart fell to his side on the basement floor.

Andy pointed at Hart and said, "He is Cain."

"You are history, Ripley!" Hart yelled. "You are fired and I'll do everything I can to make sure you're going back to jail!"

"Forgive him, Gerald Michael," Andy said. "For God will bring every deed into judgment, including every hidden thing, whether it is good or evil."

"Shut up, you freak!" Hart yelled.

"He is Cain," Andy repeated, pointing again to Hart. He took a step back and slowly lowered his hand. "And vengeance is mine."

THIRTY-ONE

H eather's here," Judi said, standing at the kitchen window.

Rip stood from the kitchen table and joined her. Heather wore her business face as she stepped out of the patrol car and walked toward the house.

"Hart didn't waste any time, did he?" Rip said.

"Guess not," Judi answered. "You sure you don't want me to go over to your place and get any of your stuff out of there?"

"No," Rip said. "I'll deal with that later. Stay here and keep an eye on Andy, and I'll have Pastor Welsh drop me off back here *if* I make bail."

Heather walked in and Rip leaned back against the sink and crossed his arms. "Looks like you didn't quit your job soon enough."

"What in the world were you thinking?" Heather asked.

Rip could see that she was puzzled, and a little part of him secretly loved her more because she looked so innocent. Heather was normally quite good at controlling herself, but Rip could also tell that the fraying process was well under way.

He held his arms up and then let them drop to his sides. Honesty really was the best policy. "I'm *thinking* Kevin told Andy his face is burned because God doesn't love him. I'm *thinking* Kevin is lucky Andy was with me when I found this out."

Heather didn't look satisfied.

"So, would Kevin really say that to Andy?" she asked. "Kevin is thirty-five. Would he really say that to a fourteen-year-old kid?"

"You think Andy made this whole thing up?" Rip said. "Have you *ever* heard Andy make anything up?"

The police radio on her hip made an annoying series of beeps and she ended it with a little turn of her wrist. "I'm just surprised at Kevin's behavior."

"I'm not," Rip said, sensing a tiny victory in the case. "Kevin Hart is a scumbag. This town has no idea what he's like. Just take my word for it."

"He said you hit him with a baseball bat in the chest."

"That's not true."

"I saw the bat, Rip," she said.

"There are a hundred baseball bats in that basement," Rip said. "Let me guess. I started hitting golf balls at him too?"

"Who do you think most judges would believe? A convicted felon or Kevin?"

"I elbowed him," Rip said. "If I hit him with a bat, he'd be sipping tea right now with his dad."

"*Nice,*" Heather said.

"Sorry," Rip said, giving himself a swift kick inside.

"He said you dragged him halfway across the basement by his hair."

"Right now, I'd like to drag him halfway across the planet by his hair."

"Did you have him by the hair?"

"Yeah," Rip said. "But I didn't drag him anywhere and that was the end of it. He was just sitting there on the floor of the basement, cowering like a scared little rat when Andy and I left."

"You okay?" Heather asked. Rip was disappointed that she was talking to Judi instead of him. He turned and looked out the window wondering what the next few hours were going to bring.

Nice little parole violation, Rip, you ding-dong. You are going back to jail. Do not pass Go.

"I believe Rip," Judi said.

"At least someone here does," Rip said, turning back around. "Thanks, Judi."

"I never said I didn't believe you," Heather said. "I'm just telling you what Kevin told me and—"

"Just take me in," Rip interrupted. His patience was growing thin, and at the moment, it really didn't matter what Heather thought. There wasn't a judge on the face of the earth who would take his word over Kevin Hart's. "But let me go up and talk to Andy for a second before we leave."

Heather shook her head. "You aren't going in."

Silence filled the kitchen and Rip squinted as if she'd suddenly hugged him.

"What?"

"You heard me," she said. "You are understandably out of a job, and he wants you out of the mobile home today. But *Scumbag* isn't pressing charges."

❈ ❈ ❈

"I don't understand why you didn't live at Judi's to begin with," Heather said, watching Rip as he took down the "SERVANTS' ENTRANCE" sign from above the door. She figured it was a good idea to follow him over to the mobile home and stick around until he got his stuff out of there. In case Kevin Hart showed up.

"Andy has asked me that a few times," Rip said. He put the sign on top of the kitchen table and opened the refrigerator. All Heather could see was a jar of mustard, some type of lunch meat, a loaf of bread, and a gallon of milk with only a couple inches left. He turned and smiled at her. "See anything in here you want?"

"I'll take the rest of that milk, if you don't mind."

"You serious?"

"No," she said with a little laugh. "That's disgusting."

Rip laughed as well, and it surprised her a little. "Sorry about putting you in the middle of this mess."

"Maybe I should have quit already," Heather said. "I'm still gonna."

"Good," he said with a smile.

"You sure seem to be in a good mood for a guy who just lost his house and job," she said.

"I've just been thinking about all of the things that happened and how God works," he replied.

"Why didn't Andy ever tell you what Kevin said to him that day?" she asked.

"No clue," Rip said, pouring what was left of the milk into the sink and dropping the plastic jug in the trash. "He told me that Kevin said something about his scar, but nothing about God not loving him."

"Unbelievable," Heather said. "What now? What's next for you?"

Rip shrugged. "Unemployment checks and me sleeping in one of Judi's spare bedrooms with Milo and his farts. But I'll be fine."

"I'll swing by Judi's tomorrow and make sure you're adjusting," she said.

"Good," Rip said, grabbing the two bottles of water out of the fridge and handing her one. "And I was hoping there was something you could maybe enlighten me on."

She took the cap off the bottle and took a quick sip. "What's that?"

He paused a few seconds before asking. "Why do you think Kevin isn't pressing charges against me?"

"Maybe he's just being nice," she said. "Giving you a break."

Rip grabbed at his lower back and gritted his teeth.

"You all right?" she asked.

"Yeah," he said, brushing aside her concern. "I can understand why I got fired and why he'd want me out of here, but I figured I was in real trouble today. He even told me I was going back to jail."

"But you're not. Be thankful."

"I am," he said, holding his hands above his head and leaning to his side like he was stretching out his back. "I have one more question about Kevin, if you don't mind."

"Go for it," she said.

He grinned. "Should I ask him for my security deposit back on this place?"

"You're such a dork," she said.

"I know," he said, holding up his arms in surrender.

She smiled and their eyes met. It was awkward at first, but then felt just right.

"But you're a cute dork," she said softly, stepping a little closer to him.

Rip looked at her and smiled. He'd never looked more handsome, she thought. He edged forward and leaned in toward her—for a kiss?—but right then, his cell rang. He slowly straightened, eyes never leaving her, and reached in his pocket to pull out his phone. Only then did he turn away.

The call didn't last long.

"Who was that?" she asked.

"Doc Strater," he said with a grim look.

Calling at nine o'clock at night?

"They want to see me first thing in the morning."

※ ※ ※

Rip checked in on Andy, who had gone to bed early, clearly wiped out by the day's drama. Then he headed downstairs to chat with Judi.

"You settled in?" she asked, sitting on the couch. On her lap was an open photo album, and it took Rip about half a second to notice the page was loaded with pictures of Todd.

"I think so," he said, plopping down on the couch next to her. "I don't think Milo is too happy with me. He's still upstairs sniffing around my things and trying to figure out how long I'm going to be here." He gestured to the album. "I thought you were done taking trips down memory lane."

Judi waved at it. "I'm gonna straighten things out with Andy. I think I'm finally ready. And having you here . . . Rip, I think I needed you here, in the house, to find the courage. And after what happened today with Kevin telling Andy he looks that way because God doesn't love him . . ." She paused and looked right at Rip. "It's time for Andy to know God does love him, and so do I. That I would've done anything I could to protect him. That I tried to, and failed. But it wasn't for lack of trying."

Rip reached out and wiped away a tear on her cheek with the pad of his thumb. "When do you want to tell him?"

She looked straight into his eyes and nodded. "Right now."

※ ※ ※

Judi knocked on the open door and Andy didn't move. Rip went in and shook Andy's shoulder.

He turned over and squinted at Rip. "What?" he said, half asleep.

"Your mom and I want to talk to you," Rip said, sitting down on the side of his bed.

Andy rubbed at his eyes and then sat up. "About what?"

"About *things*," Rip said.

"About what really happened to your face," Judi blurted.

Andy looked at her with contempt and lay back down.

"Hey," Rip said, giving Andy a little push. Andy rolled over to face him. "I think you need to hear what your mom has to say and we can put all of this behind us for good."

Andy sat up quickly. "Put it behind *you*, Uncle Rip?" He pointed at Judi and her heart raced. "It's her fault, not yours."

Judi stepped fully into the room. "It *wasn't* my fault, Andy!"

"I heard you say it, Mom!" Andy yelled. "You were standing right where you are now. It was the first night you heard me call you using your middle name. You said it was your fault."

"But, Andy—"

"I forgive you, okay?" Andy said. "I forgive you for everything that has ever happened in this house."

"C'mon, Andy," Rip said. "We've had a rare day and—"

"What do you mean?" Judi interrupted, Andy's words playing over in her mind. "What do you mean that you forgive me for *everything that has ever happened in this house*?"

Andy sat up again and looked at her like she was kidding. "With my face. With Dad. With everything."

Judi went to the other side of his bed and sat down.

"You were three years old," Judi said.

"Who cares?" Andy said.

"It was two days before Easter."

"I don't care," Andy said, a little louder.

"And I was boiling water on the stove for Easter eggs."

"I don't want to hear this!" Andy yelled, lying back down and covering his head with the pillow.

"Well, you're going to hear it!" Judi shouted, standing and yanking the pillow off him. The hair on the left side of Andy's face pulled forward and then fell back over his ear, exposing the scar. Judi couldn't take her eyes off it as she continued. "I had no idea you were standing right behind me, Andrew. No idea."

Andy didn't say anything and then Rip nodded for her to continue.

She took a deep breath and waited a few long seconds before whispering, "Your father threw the water at me."

Judi just stared at Andy and waited. Andy had become perfectly still, then, after a moment, covered his face with his hands.

"You were standing right behind me," she repeated. "We didn't know you were there. Your father was having one of his fits and was standing right next to the stove. When he quit yelling, you must have thought it was over, thought it was safe. You'd been sleeping on the couch. You came and grabbed onto my leg from behind and peeked around to look at your father at the same second he threw the water. The *exact* same second."

Andy looked at her from between his fingers and slowly sat up again.

"You're lying!" he screamed. "Dad told me you threw the water at *him* and it hit me! He told me that six years ago!"

Six years ago. Judi closed her eyes and thought about the switch that had been flicked on. The same one that had instantly turned Andy from being her little pal into a stranger who despised her.

"No, Andy," she said, shaking her head. "Your father never should have told you that. *Never.*"

"You're lying!" Andy repeated, the hair falling back from behind his ear over the scar. "You felt guilty! You said it was your fault!"

"For not knowing you were there, behind me!" she said. "For not keeping you from harm." Tears clogged her throat. "Every day since, I've felt the pain of that failure. But that's what God released me from. What I felt, looking at the garden. The guilt, the weight, all that was never really mine to take on. Don't you see?"

"Why didn't *you* get burned then?" he spat out, gesturing to the side of his neck. "If Dad threw it at you? Why didn't you get stuck with something like this?"

Rip looked at her for a second. "You don't have to—"

"Please don't ever ask me that again, Andy," Judi interrupted. "I've told you what happened, and it's the truth."

"Yeah, right," Andy said. "It's all really convenient, isn't it? To revise the truth when it suits you?"

He really doesn't believe me. And who could really blame him? For so long, I've accepted the blame. The guilt.

Judi stood and walked around to the side of the bed where Rip was. She flicked on Andy's bedside lamp, adding more light to the room. She looked at Rip and then back at Andy. Confident she had their undivided attention, she unsnapped the button on her jeans and turned her left side toward them. And then she quickly pulled her pants down to her knees, exposing the burn scar that ran from the bottom of her underwear down to her knee, covering the entire side of her left leg.

She met Andy's wide, blue eyes.

Then she yanked her pants up and left the room.

THIRTY-TWO

The generator came to life, waking Judi up. Something about its steady hum soothed her, and she closed her eyes again and thought about the previous day. It had been a *good* day, one that involved the truth and finally ended with a long overdue conversation with God. It was a nice prayer, and concluded with her asking to see just a little more of His glory, because the *truth* sometimes hurt, and she and Andy needed His help to accept it, then move beyond it.

She opened her eyes and stared at the dark ceiling. She noticed the off-yellow shadow that was pulsing against it and then turned to the alarm clock. A steady "12:00" flashed from it, confirming there had been a power failure.

She grabbed her watch off the nightstand and squinted to see the time. It was almost quarter past nine. She couldn't remember the last time she had slept in this late and wondered why it was still so dark. She glanced over at the wall to her left and could see the thick smears of rain that were pressed against each of the windows that faced the lake. She could hear the wind beating against the side of the house, and then some thunder that rolled not too far away, sounding more like someone sliding furniture across the floor in the attic above.

Judi stood and walked to one of the windows, pressing her hands flat against it and welcoming the coolness from the rain on the other side of the glass. She leaned back on her heels and put her hands behind her neck for a good stretch, then thought she heard music coming from somewhere in the house. She lowered her hands and her head tilted toward her right shoulder. It was coming from downstairs and she turned around to face the bedroom door.

It was Andy. He was humming. It sounded amazing.

She walked out of the bedroom and past the room Rip was staying in. He had already left for his appointment with Dr. Strater. Then she leaned over the edge of the staircase. She could see Andy sitting on the couch with one hand up near his ear, his head swaying slowly from shoulder to shoulder as he hummed.

She had to get closer.

She went downstairs and sat in the recliner across from him. He was wearing his tight white T-shirt and his dark blue pajama bottoms that were a little too big. His hair was sleep-tossed and his eyes were peacefully closed as his head continued to sway back and forth as he hummed. He had never looked more beautiful to her, and the only thing in the world more beautiful and perfect than Andy was that song.

And then he stopped.

"Judith Ann."

Judi stood and went to sit next to him. Andy didn't move and his eyes remained closed. His chin tilted toward the ceiling. Judi wasn't ready for the song to be over. She reached up and uncoiled Andy's fingers from around the earbud and held it to her ear.

She heard nothing.

Andy's eyes opened and he looked right at her. He waited for a few long seconds and said, "I will forgive their wickedness and remember their sins no more."

Now she remembered. It was the exact same thing he had said to her the first night she had heard him call her by her first and middle name. It's what she needed to know that day standing out at McLouth, staring at the garden . . . *her part* of the garden. She needed to hear it from God that day, but now it was God, talking through her son.

But this time the words hung in the air between them, and Judi felt them start to surround her. And then they somehow *filled* her.

"I know who that was," Andy whispered.

Judi knew as well. She couldn't say anything. All she could hear was ticking coming from the grandfather clock behind them.

"Do you know who that was?" Andy asked.

She nodded. "God was talking to me."

"I liked that song," Andy said.

"Me too, baby," she said, leaning over to hug him. As they held each other, first her heart, and then her entire body felt as if it were slowly being filled with warm water, gently bringing a smile to her face.

"Forgive, Mom," Andy whispered. "As you've been forgiven. It's your time to show others God's strength in you . . . and His ability to heal."

"I know, baby," she said, trembling in his arms. She wiped a tear from her cheek and then squeezed harder, holding him tighter than she had in a long time. These were the types of hugs they owed each other. The ones they'd been holding back for so long. They deserved so much better than what they had been giving.

"Forgive," he repeated.

"I just did," she said. She had never been more certain of anything in her life. Andy was talking about Todd, and it made her think of what Rip once told her. He said if she ever forgave Todd, she would really be letting herself off the hook.

He was right. She could already feel it.

"And forgive yourself too," Andy said. "You shouldn't have carried the blame."

She lifted her head off his shoulder and looked at him. "I'm sorry I waited so long, Andy. On all of it. I'm sorry for the way I've been."

"It's okay, Mom," he said. He ran his hand along the side of his face and then dropped his hands to her shoulders. "I forgive you. Will you forgive *me*, Mom, for treating you so bad?"

"Yes," she whispered, nodding and hugging him again. "Thank you so much, baby."

"You're welcome."

"And thank You, Lord," she said, tilting her head up toward the ceiling.

Nothing mattered more than forgiveness.

Her prayer had been answered.

※ ※ ※

Oh Where, Oh Where Has the Summer Santa Gone?

Brianna Bruley—TBW Reporter

Benning—Perhaps he has simply become too good at his craft.

Too silent.

Too swift.

Too elusive.

Or perhaps recent B&E arrests in Carlson, Huckabone, and New Boston have clipped the wings of Benning's Summer Santa, bringing an end to a most bizarre run of daring and kindness.

Or perhaps his recipients are simply clamming up, not in fear, but out of respect and concern that they may be jeopardizing the one who has had such a positive impact on so many members of their community.

Benning Police are still asking for the public's help in locating this criminal, who has been described as a six-foot-tall male who wears all black clothing, including gloves and a ski mask. According to authorities, this individual might be dangerous and has an extensive history of generosity as well as what appears to be a genuine interest in the well-being of his fellow man.

Anyone with any information regarding the flight of the Summer Santa is asked to contact the Benning Police Department or the *Benning Weekly*'s anonymous tip line.

Better yet. Don't.

Rip laughed and folded the newspaper back up. He'd been sitting in an examination room chair for fifteen minutes, waiting for Doc Strater to come in and give him the lowdown on his test results. He glanced up to the wall at a medical poster of a fleshless man with big blue eyes. Arrows and lines ran from points all over his body that identified bones, muscles, and organs. Rip leaned forward, studying the man's midsection, and tried to identify the parts of his own body that seemed to be getting progressively problematic.

There were three little knocks on the door, it opened, and the doctor came in. He wasn't wearing his white coat or his stethoscope around his neck and carried no chart. He looked like he was dressed to go out and play nine holes rather than deliver test results, and when he took his glasses off, something about the look on his face made Rip catch his breath.

Strater sat on the edge of the examination table, sending the long sheet of white paper beneath him into a fit. He placed his palms flat at his sides and then stared at Rip. The lines on the doctor's forehead looked deeper than Rip remembered, almost painted on.

"It's not good, is it, Doc?" Rip asked.

Strater took a few seconds to answer. "Why do I think you already know the answer to that question?"

"This cough hasn't even thought about going away," Rip said.

"It's gonna go away, Rip. It may take about six months, maybe a little less. But it's gonna go away."

Rip bit lightly on his lip and let Strater's words sink in a little further. He knew exactly what the doctor meant and was surprised at his sense of peace. "That long, eh?"

The doctor sighed. "I wish you'd come to see me when you first started noticing it."

"I know," Rip said. "You sure? Six months?"

"Tops," the doctor said. "I want to send you up to U of M to verify things, but I'm surprised you're functioning as well as you are."

"Really?" Rip said.

"Yeah," Strater whispered. "The cancer . . . it's everywhere, Rip."

✖ ✖ ✖

Rip was glad that Judi and Andy weren't at the house when he got back from Doc Strater's. Milo wasn't even home, so he decided to jump on the bike and do a little post-rain mud riding out to the canal for a little prayer. A prayer that would hopefully lead him to yet another path.

Acceptance.

He leaned forward and rested his elbows on the handlebars as he sat on the old motorcycle near the edge of The Frank and Poet Canal. He took a deep breath with what was left of his lungs and studied the wildflowers, thinking about what he was going to say to Judi, Andy, Heather, and Pastor Welsh. It wasn't every day that you rehearsed how to tell the people you loved that you were pretty much history.

Rip got off the bike and walked over to the spot where he and Heather sat when they came to pray about her father. It was too wet to sit, so he crouched into a catcher's position and laughed quietly at the mud that now caked his jeans from the ride out.

He laughed again, a little louder this time, wondering why he wasn't questioning God. Wasn't he supposed to be clenching his fists at the sky and shouting, *Why?*

Rip was also surprised he wasn't angry. Him, the guy with the short fuse, now all calm and accepting? Rip stood and glanced up at the gray sky and thought about what he felt.

Regret.

Mostly about Heather.

He'd blown it with her. Missed the big love of his life.

If he hadn't been so dang focused on making his own way, making a quick buck, he wouldn't have dropped out of college to pursue a career as a weed dealer. Sure, he'd made more his first year in the business as a twenty-year-old than just about everyone he knew who had a college degree, but in time, money became his god.

And when money became his god, he could only serve *it*. And *it* wasn't a big fan of competition, so Rip pretty much ignored the *real* God and took for granted one of the greatest gifts the *real* God had ever given him. Heather.

Rip touched the grass where he and Heather had sat. He

thought about her chewed-up fingernails again and then the question she had asked him not that long ago.

"Why didn't you ever tell me you loved me?"

He'd told her the truth. She really was too good for him. That little voice inside of him had *always* told him to stop what he was doing . . . stop selling drugs and do what he knew was right. But Rip knew it was just a matter of time before it all ended, before he was caught, and he couldn't risk Heather being involved when it happened. So he finally pushed her away for one reason and one reason only: he loved her.

He loved her when he dated her.

He loved her the day she broke up with him.

He loved her the day she arrested him. The day he got out of prison. Just as he loved her right now.

He wanted nothing more than to spend the second half of his life loving her and telling her he loved her, because he was so close to becoming the man he wanted to be, a man who was good enough for her. Rip crossed his arms and choked on the disappointment, realizing he'd already spent the second half of his life.

His cell phone chirped and he reached into his pocket and took it out.

It was a text from Judi. She and Andy were home.

※ ※ ※

"I'll be down in a second!" Judi yelled cheerfully. Rip noticed energy in his sister's voice he hadn't heard since she was about ten.

"Okay!" Rip shouted back from the laundry room, sliding into a clean T-shirt and jeans and out of his muddy grubs.

"There are some Cokes in the fridge," Judi shouted. "They may be a little warm. I just put them in there."

Lemon-water Judi has Cokes in her fridge?

Rip walked into the family room. Andy was over on the La-Z-Boy, holding and petting Milo like he was the Golden Goose. He noticed Milo had a little blue handkerchief attached to his collar and looked cleaner than he had been in a year.

"Did you guys take Milo to the vet?" Rip asked.

"Yeah," Andy said. "The groomer was in and they cleaned his ears and gave him a bath."

Rip cocked his head back. "And your mom didn't want to give ole Tripod the forty-dollar night-night shot?" Rip had used that line frequently since Milo had lost his leg. But this time it occurred to him that the phrase *night-night* wasn't all that funny.

"He's just a puppy!" Judi said, coming down the stairs. She walked quickly past him to fiddle with the drapes and her hair had a shine to it and was also out of its semi-permanent ponytail.

"What's going on around here?" Rip asked. "You hit the lottery or something? What's up?"

"I finally woke up," she said, turning around with a smile. "We also made an appointment to get Milo fixed."

"Sorry to hear about that, Milo," Rip said, but he couldn't keep his eyes off his sister. She looked great. It wasn't the fact that it was the first time she had makeup on since gas went over a buck a gallon. It was something about the look in her eyes. She seemed *alive* again.

"You got a date or something?" Rip asked.

"Yeah," she said.

"Really?"

"Yeah," she repeated, pointing at the couch. She smiled and it was a *real* smile, not the forced ones he was used to. "I have a date with my son and the best brother anyone could ever have. But first sit down and tell me what the doctor had to say."

"He said I've got about six months to live," Rip said.

"Oh, shut up," Judi said, passing by him.

Rip did not know how to respond to Judi's newfound brashness. But at the same time, shutting up, at least in terms of his doctor's visit, was his best play.

He looked at Andy and then hiked his thumb at Judi.

"Can you believe the change in your mom, bro?"

Andy shrugged. He was still rubbing the dog's stomach, and even old Milo seemed to be wondering what was going on. Milo jumped down, went to the window, and started barking his little brains out. Judi smiled, went to the door, and let him out. Rip could see him jetting across the puddles in the front yard toward a semi that was humming up the mud-soaked road. So much for Milo being clean.

Judi came back and sat next to Rip. He held up his hands in surrender. Something big had happened beyond Judi showing Andy her burn scar.

"What happened to you?" he asked.

"God's been helping me peel away the layers—the things that have kept me from life and from joy all these years."

"Nice," Rip said.

"Hell is other people," Judi added. She looked into his eyes and Rip could tell she was searching for the right words. "You remember how Uncle Ray used to say that all the time?"

"Yeah," Rip said.

"I'm thinking he was partially right," Judi said. "But mostly it's in our response to what other people do, or have done, and what we allow it to do to us. That was the misery I was trapped in. For so long." She lifted her brows and smiled. "But now I'm free."

"That's awesome," Rip said. "Let's celebrate with a couple of those Cokes." He went to stand and she touched his arm.

"I realize this isn't instant oatmeal," she said. "Change doesn't usually take place this fast. But, Rip, I prayed before I went to bed. And when I woke up, my prayer was answered."

"It sure seems that way," Rip said. "And you're right, change isn't always quick."

"If we don't keep making progress—moving toward God—there is only one other direction to go. And that's where I was headed."

Rip found it refreshing that *she* was actually encouraging *him*. He could listen to her all day.

He covered her hand with his own. "Sometimes it's just easier to be a victim, isn't it?"

Judi nodded. "I used to thank God every day for bringing me and Todd together. I waited and waited for Todd to come back." She glanced over at Andy and then whispered, "Guess what I thanked God for today?"

"What?" he whispered back.

"Today I thanked Him for taking us apart."

⁂

"She'll be home any minute," Kevin Hart said, holding his cell phone up to his ear while sipping at a scotch on the balcony outside of his bedroom. He glanced at his watch and then at the waxing moon that hovered over Lake Erie.

"I thought you would be here by now," Brianna said. "I've got a life too, you know."

"Just relax," Hart said. "I've had a couple days you wouldn't believe."

"Wanna tell me about them?" she asked.

"On or off the record?" He laughed, wincing at the pain in his sternum. It felt worse today than it did yesterday. Ripley had a pretty nasty elbow.

"Whatever you choose," she said.

Hart heard a door close downstairs. "Gotta run. I'll catch up with you later tonight."

"Okay," she said.

He powered off his cell phone and walked back in the bedroom. He had another big night planned and needed to come up with a good excuse to get out of the house. The whole Ripley thing had thrown him a bit off kilter, and his planning for that night's jaunt wasn't quite up to snuff. Still, he was confident he could pull it off.

Carrie was on her way up the stairs. She never stayed out this late and had to be exhausted. With a little luck, she'd be asleep before long.

"I'm surprised you're home," she said.

Surprised sounded more than a little slurred, and it was a bonus for him. Her band of lonely wives had obviously been hitting the cough medicine over at the club together. She'd be out like a light within a half hour, and his free pass would be in her open hand.

"How was work?" she asked, tossing one of her Louis Vuittons haplessly to the floor of her walk-in closet. The thought of locking her in there crossed his mind.

"It wasn't all that—"

"I want to get a kitten!" she yelled, interrupting him.

She was about as interested in how his day went as he was in telling anybody else what happened with Ripley. But if someone ever decided to ask why Ripley wasn't at the plant anymore, he had his answer down pat.

With Rip's history, it's probably best I don't discuss why he's no longer with us. I'm sure you can appreciate that . . .

It was quick, painless, and laid suspicion at Ripley's feet rather than his. After all, Ripley certainly wouldn't tell anybody what really happened, or he'd be back in the hoosegow quicker than someone could say his favorite two-word rhyme: *probation violation.*

"Maybe you should get a kitten!" he yelled back. Come morning, she would forget about both the need for a cat and the fact that he ditched her for a couple hours.

"What are you talking about?" she mumbled, almost tripping over the handbag she dropped. She walked right past him and plopped down on the bed.

Wow, he thought. *She is hammered.*

"You okay?" he asked.

She exhaled loudly through her mouth and put her palms on top of her head.

"I'm just gonna lay here for a few minutes," she said.

"Okay, honey," he said. "You do that."

She'd be snoring in seconds.

And in those same seconds, he'd be gone. Out for another big night of fun.

⚙ ⚙ ⚙

What a night. What a week, for that matter.

It was the first time he had made two stops in one night and was proud of himself. He actually *was* starting to feel a little like Santa Claus. It just happened to be that both houses were on the same street and both were gifts of cash, so it seemed most efficient.

He laughed under his breath, thinking about the article in the paper.

Oh where, oh where has the Summer Santa gone? Really?

He walked quietly down the sidewalk. A car was coming up the road, so he hid behind a tree until it drove by.

It was a police car, and he already knew who was driving.

291

"Hello, Heather," he whispered with a little chuckle.

"And hello, Summer Santa," a man said behind him. "Get your hands up."

His heart about jumped out of his chest. Slowly he raised his arms. He knew the voice. It was Chief Reynolds.

"You might have avoided Deputy Gerisch all summer," gloated the chief. "But I had a feeling I might find you out tonight. Turn around and take that mask off."

"I don't think you want me to do that."

"Oh yeah? Why?"

"Because you don't want to positively ID me."

"Quit messing around. Turn around slowly."

He took a deep breath. "If I do, things get very messy, very quickly, because you know where I've been pulling the cash to fund these gifts."

"You really think so?" Reynolds said.

"Yeah," he answered. "I'm taking it from the very same place you did, illegally, years ago. You're retiring soon, aren't you, Chief? Are you hoping to retire here, in Benning? Think the people will still feel so warmly about you when they find out what you did?"

He glanced over his shoulder at Reynolds and saw the man was faltering, his gun partially lowered.

"You arrest me, and I'm taking you with me," he promised. "You understand me?"

The chief was silent for a long time.

"I won't arrest you," Reynolds said. "But I want you to quit, now."

"I will. After one more delivery. Deal?"

"Deal."

He slowly edged away from Chief Reynolds, half expecting him to shout at him again, tackle him.

But the man didn't give chase.

He smiled, thinking about the chief's demand. Then he thought about his last gig and all the good that it would do.

Flight of the Summer Santa, he thought, chuckling under his breath. It was almost over with. Just one last visit remained.

The big one.

THIRTY-THREE

Rip had been upstairs most of the afternoon, praying and asking God to give him the right words. He hadn't said anything to Judi or Andy yet, and was glad Judi thought he was kidding about only having six months left. Once he had a grip on it himself, he could tell everybody. The right way.

He'd invited Heather and Pastor Welsh over and figured if he was going to drop the bomb, he might as well hit the four people closest to him with one shot.

Why am I not sad?

He shook his head and gave thanks.

And then he thought about what Judi had said last night, before he went to bed, about this being the weirdest summer ever. He kind of guessed it was now going to be a weird fall and winter as well. And then he thought about spring, which was about *seven* months away . . .

And then he thought about Andy.

Lord, help me to let him know that I'll be with You. Let that be a constant comfort to him.

He stood and went downstairs. Pastor Welsh was talking to Andy at the kitchen table, and Heather and Judi were at the kitchen window, speculating where Milo had spent the night this time. When they saw Rip sit in the La-Z-Boy, they all gathered in the living room.

Judi and Andy went to the love seat, opposite Heather and Pastor Welsh, who sat on the couch. Rip still didn't have the faintest idea how he was going to break the news, but figured God would guide him.

"Lay it on us," Heather said.

"Where have you been all day?" Rip asked.

"Nowhere special," Heather said. "So what's your big news?"

Rip couldn't find the right words and looked at Andy. For some reason, he looked more like ten than fourteen and it saddened Rip.

"You got a new job!" Judi blurted.

"Actually," Rip said, "I'm thinking about retiring within the next six months."

"Unemployment doesn't pay that much," Judi said, smiling like the new person she had become. Rip gave thanks again for that too and glanced back at Andy.

"I don't need unemployment," Rip said. "When Heather and the rest of the gang raided my place and thought they took all my money before I went to prison, they missed a spot. I hadn't planned on using any of it, but if need be, I'm pretty sure I'll have enough money to get by until I retire."

"We didn't miss any spots," Heather said. "What are you trying to tell us, Rip?"

"I'm telling you I'm leaving," he said.

"Where you going, Uncle Rip?" Andy asked. "Can I come?"

"You bet," Rip said. "In fact, you can all come. But I want you to wait awhile, though. Take your time."

"Where?" Judi asked. "Did you get a job out of state?"

"No," Rip said.

"Spit it out," Heather said, looking hurt. "Tell us where you're going."

Rip smiled and pointed at the ceiling.

"I'm going to heaven."

Heather laughed and pointed at Andy. "Did the iPod tell Andy, 'Thou shalt surely die'?"

"No," Rip said. "Doc Strater told me yesterday morning."

"Shut up, Rip," Heather said. "That's not even—"

"Cancer," Rip said. "Six months. I'm totally serious."

Three of the four of them got it then.

Judi leaned back and brought her hands to the top of her head and Andy just stared at Rip.

Welsh bit gently on his bottom lip and slowly nodded.

On the couch, next to Welsh, Heather leaned forward and put her elbows on her knees. She tilted her neck to the side and her eyes widened in anticipation. He'd seen that look hundreds of times before. She was waiting for a punch line.

Rip ran his hand along the side of his face and exhaled loudly through his nose. "I guess there's no right way to deliver that news."

Heather covered her eyes with her hands. And then she peeked at him between her fingers and squeezed them back together. Judi's eyes were now closed and Andy put his head on her shoulder.

Welsh asked the obvious. "What's the treatment plan?"

"I've got the first available appointment to go out to U of M and have some more tests run, but I really don't think I'm gonna spend my last six months doing the whole chemo and radiation thing if—"

"Yes, you are!" Heather yelled, taking her hands away from her face. He'd never heard her yell so loud. She was crying and rubbed tears away from both eyes with the back sides of her hands. "You've played tough guy your whole life, and you're not going to do it now! If treatment can make you better, *you are going to do it.*"

Rip couldn't look at her. Judi was crying now too. Rip was glad that Andy wasn't.

"We lost Mom and Dad to cancer, but we're not going to lose you," Judi said, standing and pointing out the window toward the lake. "I will sell this house and all three hundred acres and we'll find you the best treatment center in the world."

Rip knew only a miracle would save him, but his sister was broken, desperate. "Okay," he said. "Let's just see what the next round of tests say and then we can take it from there. Together."

※ ※ ※

Mr. McIntosh had never asked Andy why he wanted to go up on the roof of Mack's on a Friday. Andy only went up there on Wednesdays to clean and he'd told Mr. McIntosh that he just wanted to go up there and read for a little while. He had been leaning against the chimney for close to an hour and hadn't read a single page of *Flowers for Algernon.*

Andy also hadn't been able to get the power to work on the iPod since he found out that Uncle Rip was sick, but he still kept it close by his side. Not that the power mattered, he mused. If God was going to speak through it again, Andy supposed He could power it up.

But he still wished the power would come back on. To remind him that God was near. That He saw what was happening with Uncle Rip—what was happening to all of them. Andy looked up at the sky. *Don't take him yet, God. Don't take him!*

He didn't hear anything in response. Not that he expected to. In fact, if it weren't for the iPod or the garden, there wasn't a whole lot for him to believe about God. And now, when he needed it most, the iPod was silent.

Six months.

He'd be about halfway through his freshman year when Uncle Rip might *die.*

Just thinking about that last word saddened Andy and he closed his eyes and wanted to pray for his uncle, but he wasn't even really sure what that meant. Uncle Rip was always talking about the need to talk to God about things, but really, how did a dude pull that off, other than speaking into the silence? He tapped at the iPod's power button again. Nothing happened.

Thinking about Uncle Rip dying made him think about little Marjo. She, at least, had a long shot at life, with the surgery. It didn't sound like a surgery would give Uncle Rip a shot.

Six months.

A little flash of hope ran through him. Uncle Rip still had more tests that needed to be done, so maybe they weren't one hundred percent sure. So he tried to pray again. *God, please tell me my Uncle Rip is gonna be okay . . .*

He waited to feel something in his belly. That same good feeling the garden gave him.

Nothing.

"Please?" Andy said to the sky.

He still couldn't feel anything, but a clanking noise startled him and then he saw the top part of the ladder that was attached to the building start to shake. Somebody was coming up.

When Chelsea peeked over the edge of the roof, Andy wanted to smile, but couldn't.

"There you are," she said. "I called your house and your mom said you went to the Dairy Queen. I just finished my shift and waited for you to come up. If it weren't for Mr. McIntosh coming in for a Peanut Buster Parfait, I'd still be waiting for you to show up." She reached the top of the ladder and looked around. "I'm surprised he lets you come up here."

"Yeah, it's pretty cool." Andy slid over and she sat next to him with her back against the chimney.

"I thought you had to be sixteen to work at the DQ," Andy said. He'd always thought it'd be cool to work there and score free sundaes. But he had to admit, Chelsea looked so cute in the uniform, he wouldn't ever want to replace her.

"You do, but I just fill in some, when other kids go on vacation. My best friend's mom owns it."

"Ahh."

"What are you doin' up here?" she asked.

"Reading," he said, patting the cover of the book. He wanted to tell her he'd been trying to pray, but they weren't supposed to talk about Uncle Rip's cancer until his other tests were done. "How's Marjo doing today?"

"She's good," Chelsea said, and Andy realized how upbeat and positive she always seemed. He wished he could be like that.

"Why're you always in such a good mood?" he asked.

She smiled in surprise. "Why do you say that?"

"Because you are. I think it's great that you always seem to look at the bright side of things."

"I try," she said. "What good does moping around do for anybody? Did you know that a bad mood is the fastest kind of mood to spread?"

Andy thought about that for a few seconds and what she said made sense. It sounded pretty adult, almost like something Uncle Rip would say. He agreed with her, but it really didn't make him feel any better.

"Sorry if I'm moping," he said. "I'm such a tool."

"I don't think you are a tool," she said and smiled. "I wouldn't be here if I thought you were. Something wrong?"

"Just having a bad day," Andy said. "You mind if I don't talk about it?"

"Okay," she said. "Believe me, I understand that stuff happens and that it's not always good."

Stuff does happen, Andy thought. *You spend six years hating your mom for something she didn't do. It gets fixed. Everything is perfect. And before you know it, the person who has done the most for you in your life, the one you've taken for granted, is going away forever.*

"It's actually getting cool out," Chelsea said, crossing her arms and hunching her shoulders. "Kind of weird. It's been so warm this summer, I forgot what it feels like to be chilly."

She was right. The light was starting to drain from the sky and the temperature had to have dropped fifteen degrees in as many minutes. Andy crossed his arms, mirroring Chelsea, and looked at her.

"You know that saying 'You don't know what you've got till it's gone'?"

"Sure," Chelsea said.

"I heard a guy on television say that's not true."

"Why?"

"The guy said, 'You always knew what you had, you just never thought you'd lose it.'"

"Makes sense," Chelsea said, taking the iPod out of his hand. She ran the tip of her index finger across the cracked screen. "You can always get a new one, though."

"I don't think you understand," he said.

"Yeah, I do. Everybody at church thinks you are hearing God through this thing. Isn't that what you're talking about?"

Andy didn't want her to know he was talking about Uncle Rip, so he went along with it. "I don't even remember any of the things I hear through it."

"But the things you've heard and said . . . they've helped people, right?"

He shrugged. "Seems to. Mostly. That's if they're listening." He turned the iPod over in his hands. "But it looks like it's all over with now. The thing won't even take a charge."

"Andy, you can hear from God without a miracle iPod," she said, giving him a surprised look. "But I'm sure you already know that."

"Oh yeah, right," Andy said, nodding eagerly, as if he totally knew.

But the truth of the matter was, he doubted her words. Hadn't he already tried to listen?

THIRTY-FOUR

Andy couldn't remember ever being so tired, but at least his head-ache was gone. He figured he would have cried himself to sleep, thinking about Uncle Rip only having six months to live.

He sat up in his bed and pulled his knees up toward his chest. He rolled the iPod over in his palm and squeezed it tightly, wondering if it was ever going to work again. Then he yawned and stretched his arms out over his head before resting his arms on top of his knees.

He closed his eyes.

"Please, God," he whispered. "Please make Uncle Rip get better."

He wasn't sure what else to say. It was all he really wanted. He waited for a few seconds and when he opened his eyes, he was sitting at the bank of The Frank and Poet. It was so dark. There was no sound, no wind, and everything was perfectly still. All he could see were some clouds, a handful of stars, the full moon, and a thin strip of moonlight on the water a few feet away.

How did I get out here?

He squinted and tried to make out some of the shadows around him. That's when he saw the little hint of light between his fingers. The iPod. He opened his hand and the screen was brightly lit, accenting the crack in the plastic.

He held it up in front of his face and smiled. He could hear a buzzing sound and looked around to see what it was and where it was coming from.

The earbuds.

He lifted one and placed it in his ear. He immediately recognized the buzz as the sound of a motorcycle. It was coming from the direction of the house, cutting through the woods and heading into the corn.

Andy stood and faced it. It was getting louder. Closer.

The bike was quickly nearing the end of the cornfield and would reach the canal bank within a matter of seconds.

He craned his neck forward and still couldn't see it. The noise became unbearable. It was coming right at him. He dove to the ground and pulled the earbud out of his ear as the bike sounded like it flew right over his head.

And then everything went quiet.

Andy rolled over and then brought himself up to his knees, staring into the darkness across the canal. And then like a spotlight on a dark stage, the two final sections of the garden lit up.

In the section to the right, Uncle Rip was right in the middle of the flowers, sitting on his motorcycle, facing Andy and leaning forward on the handlebars. He was smiling and talking, but Andy couldn't hear him.

Andy stood and shouted, "I can't hear you!"

Uncle Rip held his hands up in the air and then dropped them to his sides. Then he pointed at his own ear and then the ground.

The iPod.

Andy turned around, picked it up, and put one of the earbuds in his ear.

"Uncle Rip?" he said.

"You won't believe it, Andy!" Uncle Rip said through the earbud. Andy had never heard someone sound happier.

"What are you doing in the garden?" Andy asked.

"It's okay," Uncle Rip said. "You were right. I wasn't ready to come in here. But then I figured it out and Pastor Welsh told me I was ready! You won't believe it, bro!"

And then Andy thought he heard barking and pressed the earbud a little farther into his ear. He recognized the bark and smiled as he could see the top of Milo's head as he scampered through the flowers toward Uncle Rip.

"What's Milo doing over there?" Andy asked.

"Don't worry about him!" Uncle Rip said. "Don't worry about me either. You wanted my cancer gone and it's gone! I'm healed! Everything is perfect here!"

Uncle Rip tapped the side of the bike and Andy watched as Milo ran up next to him. Uncle Rip leaned over and picked up Milo, and Andy saw that Milo had four legs again. He blinked twice, doubting what he saw.

"Look at the light, Andy!" Uncle Rip yelled as the garden lit up even more. "It's all coming from Him!"

"From who?" Andy shouted back.

Uncle Rip kissed the top of Milo's head and put him back down in the flowers. "Get rid of that iPod, Andy. Chelsea was right! You don't need that thing! Throw it in the water! You won't believe it here! I'm telling you, you don't need it! You don't—"

Andy sat up straight in his bed. His heart was knocking inside of his chest and sweat was rolling down the side of his neck. He needed to wake up Uncle Rip.

He was going to be healed.

❋❋❋

Andy didn't have to wake up Uncle Rip. He and Mom were already up by the time he had made it downstairs. Mom and Uncle Rip both looked tired. Mom's hair was a bed-head train wreck, but again, he wasn't used to seeing her without a ponytail. Uncle Rip hadn't shaved that morning and had circles under his eyes.

Uncle Rip glanced at the clock and then at Andy. "What are you doing up this early?"

"I have to tell you guys about the dream I just had!"

"Let me guess," Uncle Rip said, biting into a piece of bacon. "You were either dreaming about beating me in a motorcycle race or kissing Chelsea." He cocked an eyebrow. "Pastor Welsh said he saw you sitting up on top of Mack's with her yesterday."

"Hanging out with Chelsea is fine," Mom said, handing Uncle Rip a cup of coffee, "but I better never catch you two racing."

"What's the worst thing that could happen to me?" Uncle Rip said, winking at Andy. "I could die?"

"That's not funny," Mom said.

Andy agreed that it wasn't funny and told them his dream. When he was through, Mom and Uncle Rip just stared at each other and then Uncle Rip leaned closer to Andy.

"So I jumped The Frank and Poet on my motorcycle and my cancer went away?"

"Yeah," Andy said. "But I think going in the garden is what made your cancer go away."

"I'm all for getting better," Uncle Rip said, winking and giving him a thumbs-up. "I'm ready to go in the flowers. Maybe I'll swim over there today."

"No, you won't," Mom said. "For all we know, all the chemicals from McLouth seeped into the ground and water and that's why you're sick. Why Mom and Dad got sick too. The last thing you need is to swim over there."

"But you can't go in the flowers yet," Andy said. "In the dream, Pastor Welsh was the one who will tell you when you're ready."

"There you go again with that not-ready stuff," Uncle Rip said, frowning. He stood and went to the door and opened it. "Milo!"

They waited for Milo to come flying through the door, but he didn't.

"Hope he's not gone for a week this time," Mom said.

"Must be off romancing the ladies again," Uncle Rip said.

"Why would Milo have all four legs in my dream?" Andy asked.

"Don't know," Uncle Rip said.

"I think something happened to him, Uncle Rip."

"I doubt it," Uncle Rip said. "I think he was hip to the conversation about getting fixed and took off for his swan song. Why don't you tell me more about how the garden was lit?"

"Remember when I told you about how I fell asleep out near the canal that one day? And how I had a dream about a man out there, whose face I couldn't see, and how he told me to bring Heather to see the flower garden?"

"I do," Uncle Rip said. "But you never talked about taking her to the wildflowers until after she'd already gone."

Andy thought about it for a second. Uncle Rip was right, but that didn't change the fact that the man had told him to bring Heather to the wildflowers.

"I think it was Him," Andy said. "In fact, in the dream, you told me the light was all coming from 'Him.'"

Uncle Rip walked over to the sink and looked out the window. Then he turned around, started to say something, and stopped.

"What is it?" Mom asked.

"It's weird," Uncle Rip said, tapping at his own chest. "Something in here just told me that when I'm in those flowers, I won't be sick anymore. Like it's a certainty."

"Are you being serious?" Mom asked.

"Yeah," he answered. "It's that little voice inside of me. I think I just heard what Andy's been hearing. I'm supposed to go to the flowers, but not yet. I'm not ready. Pretty weird, huh?"

"How can you not be ready?" Mom asked, getting all excited. "Let's call Heather and have her open up the gate. If you really believe you are gonna get better, why wait?"

"Because I also just had the craziest feeling . . . I mean *really* crazy, and if I told you how I was thinking about getting to the garden, you'd have a stroke."

"Heather will let us in," Mom said. "She did it before."

"Nah, that's not the way it's supposed to go . . ." Uncle Rip looked to the window with a faraway expression and then laughed and shook his head. "Forget it. My imagination ran away from me there for a second. But it seemed *so* real."

"What?" Andy asked. "Tell us."

"Yeah," Mom said. "I really don't want you swimming in that water again, Rip."

Uncle Rip leaned back against the sink. He looked at Andy and the smile that came across Uncle Rip's face didn't look like it belonged to a guy who had only six months to live.

"You heard the motorcycle, right?" he asked Andy. "In your dream?"

"Right."

Uncle Rip's smile grew wider and he nodded. "When the time comes . . . I'm gonna take the *bike*," Rip said, his tone growing more confident. He shook his head. "It's *not* my imagination. I'm going to get the old bike ready and then jump The Frank and Poet. And when I land in that flower garden, *I will be healed*."

❋ ❋ ❋

"I will stay on until you find someone to replace me," Heather said, sitting at Chief Reynolds's kitchen table. "Sorry to spring this on you on a Saturday, but I didn't want to be too formal about it with a guy I've known my whole life."

"It won't be easy to replace you, Heather," Chief Reynolds said. "You are one of the best I've ever had."

"Yeah," Heather said and laughed. "The best at driving into things with my squad car."

He gave her a rueful smile. "Those things happen. Sometimes they happen more to *some* than others, but there's a lot more to being a good cop than never putting a dent in a vehicle. I wish I had more like you."

The conversation wasn't going anywhere near how Heather thought it would. She expected the chief to give her a pat on the back followed by a quick *seeyalaterbye*.

"You're just saying that, Chief, right?"

"Not at all," he answered. "You're committed, dependable, and care about people and the community. What else could I ask for? Your dad would be proud of you."

"My dad would be proud of me?" Heather whispered. She felt surprised and then saddened, a little lump climbing up the base of her throat. "Now, look. You're gonna make me cry, Chief. Maybe I should stay on."

Reynolds picked up his coffee cup and took a little sip. "I don't want you to stay. You've got one month."

"Didn't you just say I was a good cop?"

"The best," he said, grinning. "And I mean that."

"But you said—"

He reached over and put his hand on top of hers. "But you'd make a better teacher."

"Thanks," she said and smiled. She believed him. "Who knows? Maybe I can nab the Summer Santa before I go. Or should I say Kevin Hart?"

"I'm not sure about that," the chief said.

Heather laughed. "I doubt if anyone will press charges once we catch him, but it's just a matter of time before we do. Sure would be nice if we could set up twenty-four-hour surveillance on Hart and just get it over with."

"I don't even think it's Kevin," Reynolds said, drumming his fingers on the kitchen table before crossing his arms. "But regardless of who it is, Heather, I understand that this guy is going about his acts of generosity in the wrong way. But maybe . . ." He paused and looked to the window, then back. "Maybe we should look the other way. At least for the summer. Concentrate on other things."

She stared at him in mute surprise for a moment. "Look the other way? Chief, he's *breaking into houses.*"

"And changing people's lives," the chief said. "Do we really want to get in the way of that? Besides, all of Benning seems to love him. If we collar him, *we'll* be seen as the bad guys."

She continued to stare at her boss. "He's breaking the law."

Chief Reynolds sighed heavily and leaned back in his chair. "Sometimes, Heather, we have to concentrate on the peacekeeping part of our jobs, over the letter of the law. Has he hurt anyone?"

"Not yet, but—"

"Something tells me he won't. He'll finish this string of gifting and be done."

"Chief," she said slowly. She just had to ask. "Do you know who the Summer Santa is?"

He gave her a funny smile. "That, Heather, is a secret I intend to take to my grave."

※ ※ ※

"Are you coming?" Rip yelled as he walked toward the garage.

"Yeah!" Andy shouted back, coming out of the barn.

"Let's sit down for a second," Rip said, pointing at a pair of lawn chairs at the side of the garage.

They sat down together, and Rip could see the iPod in Andy's hand.

"So," Andy said, "what's up?"

"We haven't had much guy time lately. And a lot of our talk has been about me and my diagnosis. I just wanted to get your thoughts on what's going on with you and your mom since you found out how you got burned. It seems like it let you start over with her, in a way."

Andy shrugged and rolled one of the earbuds between his thumb and forefinger. "It's just been a weird couple days, Uncle Rip. A lot's happened."

Rip reached into his pocket for a couple sticks of gum. He handed one to Andy and said, "Now that we have set the record straight, don't you think life is gonna get better?"

Andy pulled his hair off his neck and slid his thumb across his scar, deep in thought. "At least Mom can hide her scar with long skirts. But some scars can't be hidden."

"What do you mean?"

Andy let his hair fall back over the side of his face and then ran the back of his hand up and down his chest. "I think we can get hurt inside too. Mom's different now," he said, glancing toward the house, "because of the healing she's found inside. Not because her scar on the outside is any different."

Rip nodded, his heart swelling with pride over his nephew's wisdom. "Sometimes scars are good. To remind us of where we've been. And what we've passed through."

"The way I've treated my mom," Andy said quietly, almost ashamed. "And the way I thought she was treating me. We were hurting each other for so long. Creating scars on the inside too."

"Yes, you were," Rip said.

"But those wounds have already started to heal."

Rip smiled with him. "Andy . . . that is one of the greatest things I have ever heard anybody say."

"It's true," Andy said. "Mom and I are talking more. It's gonna take some time to feel . . . like it's supposed to, I think. You know, between a mom and son. But I know we're gonna get there."

"It will come," Rip said, hoping he would be around to see some of it.

Andy dug the toe of his Converse shoe in the dirt. "Yesterday was the only time I could ever remember telling my mom that I love her. *Ever.*"

Rip tried not to react. No wonder his sister had been so unhappy . . . "What did she do when you told her that?"

"She cried."

Rip laughed, unable to remember the last time he felt such joy. Still, there was a more important item on the agenda.

"But don't forget there is someone who loves you more," Rip said.

"I know you love me, Uncle Rip," Andy said.

"I wasn't talking about me, knucklehead," Rip said. He pointed above his head. "I'm talking about God."

Andy ran his hand across the side of his face, and his fingers dove under his hair to the scar again. He stood.

"I'll take your word for it, Uncle Rip," he said distantly.

"What's that supposed to mean?"

Andy held up the iPod. "When I was sitting on top of Mack's, I was thinking that if it weren't for the iPod and the garden, I wouldn't believe in God."

"You don't need either of those to believe in God."

"Chelsea kind of told me the same thing."

"Smart girl."

The kid stared at him, as if trying to puzzle something out. "You even told me in that dream to get rid of the iPod. To throw it in the water."

"Go for it," Rip said. "You said it hasn't worked since you found out I was sick."

"I don't know about throwing it out yet," Andy said. "But what I do know is once you jump The Frank and Poet and land in the flowers, God is going to make you better."

"And where do you suppose that feeling is coming from?"

"God, I guess."

"Smart boy," Rip said. "And I've never heard anything through your iPod, but there's no denying the way I feel when I look at that garden. And what's even crazier than me being healed and me jumping that canal on a motorcycle is what that little voice is telling me about this leap of faith."

"What?" Andy asked, scrunching up his face in confusion.

"I'm not jumping it for me."

"Okay," Andy said slowly, probably thinking the cancer was overtaking Rip's brain now. "But do you think the bike can do it? Actually jump that far?"

"I think so, yes."

"It just doesn't make any sense. As fun as it would be to see you hit the water trying to jump the canal . . . why do you have to get to the garden that way?"

312

"I don't know," Rip said. "But does much of this summer make sense? At least the way we're used to things making sense?"

Andy shook his head slowly.

"I think we just gotta go with it," Rip said. "God has His reasons."

Rip's phone rang and he pulled it out of his pocket.

"Hello, Miss Heather," he said.

There was a pause. "I'm right down the road. Down near the east end of Ripley's Field, right near the bend. Come on out here. We've got a problem."

"What is it?"

"Just get out here. I don't know what to do."

"Okay," Rip said. "See you in a minute."

※ ※ ※

They took Andy's bike, but Rip was driving and Andy was on the back. The east end of Ripley's Field was less than a half mile away and it didn't take long before Rip could see Heather, who was standing in front of her truck on the side of the road. She had her arms crossed and her head was bowed.

When they pulled up alongside her, she looked up and Rip could tell that she'd been crying.

"What happened?" Rip asked. "You okay?"

"I didn't know Andy was with you," she said quietly, wiping at her eyes with the back of her right hand. "I'm sorry. I wasn't thinking."

Rip and Andy both got off the bike. Rip walked toward her, and when Heather used the back of her other hand to wipe her eyes again, Rip could see what she was holding. Even though it had been darkened from the mud and rain that covered the gravel road, he could tell what it was by the dirty blue handkerchief that was attached to it.

It was Milo's collar.

Their eyes met and Rip hugged her.

"Please tell me that's all you found," Rip whispered. "I think we've had enough hard news this week."

"He's seen him," Heather whispered back.

Rip turned around and Andy was standing at the side of the road. His shoulders were slumped and his arms were at his sides. He had a vacant look on his face and was just staring down into the ditch.

Rip took the collar from Heather and then walked over and stood next to Andy. He squeezed the collar in his hand, thinking about how ridiculously big it was for Milo and wondering how in the world the dog had made it this long without it ever falling off. But it was off now, and it was no mystery how it happened. The collar had been knocked off of him.

Actually, *he'd* been knocked out of *it*.

Milo's body was on the far side of the ditch, his upper half out of the water and his lower half in. He was lying on his side and was completely covered in mud. It looked like he was sleeping, but the nasty gash that ran from his shoulder blade down into his lower torso was something even Milo couldn't have survived. It looked like he had been clipped by a bumper.

There was an indentation in the mud on the far bank that was about the size of Milo's body. Around it, there were little claw marks. He'd clearly been hit and thrown into the far bank. He must have struggled, trying to claw his way out of the ditch, and died shortly thereafter, sliding down into the water.

"Say something, bro," Rip said to Andy, still looking at Milo.

"Like what?" Andy said.

"I don't know."

"Why don't you say something?"

"I don't know what to say either," Rip said. He glanced over at Heather and then back into the ditch. "Let's just get him out of there and get him home."

※ ※ ※

Heather put her arm around Judi and they both cried as they watched Rip place Milo in the hole behind the barn. Rip was still covered in mud from fishing Milo out of the ditch, but he'd cleaned Milo with the hose, towel dried him, and then wrapped him in the yellow blanket that Milo liked to lie on. Inside the blanket with Milo was his red collar and blue handkerchief, the new rubber chew toy that Judi had gotten him, and an unopened box of Cheez-Its.

Heather could see the tear that slowly cascaded down the side of Andy's face as Rip shoveled the earth back over Milo. Rip had to pause about halfway through the job and leaned over to catch his breath, trying to hide the pain. Andy took the shovel from Rip and filled in the rest of the dirt before patting the soil with the back of the shovel. When he was done, he and Rip kneeled and started placing the rocks they had collected from the shore of Lake Erie around the edge of Milo's grave. Then they both stood and stared at it.

"I knew this was going to happen," Andy said.

"I think everybody did," Rip said. "You can't weigh thirty pounds and go around threatening trucks for too long." He looked back to the grave. "Milo, you were a trip. I figured when you lost your leg it would've slowed you down, but you just went harder. You were only six, but lived more in that time than any dog I've ever heard of. You were a great dog, brought a lot of happiness to our lives, and I'm glad you were ours. We're gonna miss you."

Heather and Judi edged nearer.

"Bye, Milo," Judi said, choking on tears. "You were a good boy. Well, not so good. But we loved you anyway."

"Good-bye, Milo," Heather said. "I'm going to miss you."

Andy looked at Rip. "What I meant to say was, *I knew something happened to him.* Remember when I said that right after I asked you why Milo would have all four legs in my dream?"

"Yeah," Rip said, staring at the small grave.

"Maybe God wanted me to see Milo, whole, in the garden, so I'd be even more sure about you," Andy said. Heather noticed the troubled look on his face. "I just wish He could've let Milo live and still convince me."

"That would have been cool," Rip said.

"Good-bye, Milo," Andy said. Then he leaned over the grave and made a quick, almost sarcastic, sign of the cross. And then he turned around and quickly walked away.

THIRTY-FIVE

Andy needed to talk to somebody about God, the iPod, the garden, and why Uncle Rip and just about everybody else weren't taking his uncle's cancer more seriously. Though he and Pastor Welsh had never had a conversation with just the two of them, he was the only person Andy could think of qualified to answer all of his questions.

Andy had just come out of the woods on West Jefferson, about a quarter mile north of the church. He got off the motorcycle and pushed it on the roadside gravel for a little over a hundred yards, and then he took it across the street and onto the bike path that ran along Lake Erie. There weren't many people around, so he decided to jump back on the bike and head down the path toward St. Paul's.

When he approached the water fountain where Mr. Hart had told him God didn't love him, he slowed down and circled the fountain a couple times, almost wanting Hart to come back. Andy smiled, wondering how tough and mouthy Hart would be now that he knew Uncle Rip wouldn't hesitate coming after him. Between the lost job and the death sentence, there wasn't a lot to hold Uncle Rip back . . .

Andy laughed out loud, zipped the rest of the way down the path, and then cut across the road and into the back of the parking lot of St. Paul's.

When he walked in the church, he took a few steps into the sanctuary and was surprised how different it felt with the lights off and no people in there. Until recently, the only reason he ever went there on Sundays was to make Uncle Rip happy. Maybe there had always been too many distractions, but today, in the silence, he could feel something, something familiar. In the smallest part of his stomach was a tingle, a tiny sliver of that good feeling . . . the one he would get from the iPod or from looking at the flowers.

Not that he'd had that feeling recently.

The iPod was toast. And just that morning he had taken the bike out to the flower garden to talk to God and felt nothing. Not even a faint reminder of the healing dream and the hope he'd felt for Uncle Rip. Was it all just one big, fat lie?

Andy studied the stained-glass windows that ran the length of the wall to his left and then reached behind one of the pews and pulled a Bible out of the little wooden compartment attached to the backrest. He leafed through it and thought again about how long Noah lived and how short Uncle Rip's life might be in comparison. It didn't seem fair.

A door slammed behind him and it startled him, causing him to drop the Bible on the floor. The sound echoed near the church's wooden ceiling. He turned around and Pastor Welsh was standing in the entrance to the sanctuary. He was carrying a cardboard box and placed it on a table near the door.

"Hello, Andy," he said, taking a quick glance around the sanctuary. "Where's your uncle?"

"Home."

"I see. You mind giving me a hand with something real quick?" Pastor Welsh pointed at the cardboard box. In his hand was a pocketknife. He pulled out the blade and then ran it through the tape on top of the box to open it. He took out a couple handfuls of those self-help booklets and stacked them neatly on the edge of the table.

Andy walked back next to Welsh and read a couple titles on the booklets:

HAS A FRIEND ASKED YOU ABOUT CHRIST?

HOW CAN I HELP MY CHURCH?

Andy was pretty sure the booklet he was looking for wasn't in there:

IS YOUR FAITH A RESULT OF DREAMS, FLOWERS, AND TECHNOLOGY?

Welsh handed Andy a stack of each and pointed at a pair of clear plastic booklet holders that were mounted out on the wall next to the exit. Andy filled each one and Welsh closed the box back up and joined him.

"I had a feeling you'd be coming by one of these days," Welsh said.

"Really?" Andy said. "Why?"

"You've had a pretty full plate this summer and it's just gotten a lot fuller. Your uncle send you down here?"

"No," Andy said. "I want to talk about him, actually."

"I see," Welsh said, shifting the cardboard box from one arm to the other. He pointed down the hall to where his office was. "Shall we?"

Andy followed Welsh to the door of his office. "You like being a pastor?"

"What do you mean?"

"You know . . . coming to church and stuff."

"I do," Welsh said. "I like *being* the church, here and elsewhere."

Andy considered his words, trying to figure out what he meant, even as he nodded. They walked into Welsh's office, and he tried to remember if he'd ever been inside before.

"Have a seat," Welsh said, walking behind his desk and sitting in a big leather chair.

Andy sat down and wracked his brain on how to begin. There was an awkward silence.

"Your mom said you were thinking about getting another pup already," the pastor said.

Nice segue, Andy thought. He liked that word. Mrs. Mason taught that one to the class during the fifth grade. Welsh's segue softened the blow of the dying uncle conversation by opening up with a reference to the dead dog.

"Not sure if we're gonna get one or not. He's just been gone a few days."

"He was, what, five or six?"

"Almost seven," Andy said.

"We could all learn something from the way he lived his life. He didn't sit around too much. If he saw something, he went for it. Even though he was only six, he got his money's worth."

Andy nodded. "Suppose Uncle Rip doesn't get better. Did he get his money's worth?"

Pastor Welsh didn't answer.

"What do you think is gonna happen to him?" Andy asked.

Pastor Welsh pushed his glasses back up the bridge of his nose. "I'm really not sure, Andy. We'll wait and see what they say at U of M."

"What if they say the same thing Doc Strater said? Then what would you say?"

Pastor Welsh leaned forward, resting his elbows on the desk.

"You really want me to answer that, Andy? I think you're ready for an honest answer."

"Yeah," Andy said.

Pastor Welsh nodded. "I lost my father when I was about your age. He was a drinker, like I was after him. He used to embarrass us a lot. Showing up at the school drunk, coming out in the yard when I was playing with my friends and falling down, stuff like that. But I still loved him. Then one day Mrs. Nagy, my eighth-grade social studies teacher, came and got me when we were in the cafeteria. She told me my mother was in the office and that was it. My dad was gone."

"What happened?"

"Heart attack. Dead before he hit the floor."

"That sucks," Andy said.

"When it happened, it was almost like my head was in a fog. Like it hadn't really happened. Like it was a big dream."

"I know what you mean," Andy said. He'd felt that way for a long time after his dad moved away.

"And then my head filled up with all the things I wanted to say to my dad . . . that I should have said. I'd still give anything to spend six more months with him, Andy. Anything."

"Six months?"

Pastor Welsh nodded. "Your uncle loves you more than anything in the world. You are just about all he talks about. It's in God's hands, but make the most of your time with him, Andy. Treasure every day. Say all that's in your heart—don't hold back."

So the pastor thought Uncle Rip was going to die. It kind of took his breath away for a moment. But he didn't know . . . didn't know about Andy's dream.

"I just want him to get better, Pastor Welsh. And when he's ready to go in those flowers over by The Frank and Poet, I think God's gonna do it. Heal him."

"How do you know that?"

"I had a dream about the garden . . . a couple dreams, actually. One about Heather and one about Uncle Rip. And in the one about Uncle Rip I could see that if he went into the flowers, he'd be healed."

"I really need to get my keister over there and see those flowers. It must be some garden."

Andy stared at him for a second, checking to make sure he wasn't making fun. But the old pastor looked dead serious. "In the dream I had about Heather, there was a man in the garden. Do you think it could be God?"

"A man?" Welsh said, leaning a little closer. "What'd he look like?"

"I couldn't see his face. Heather saw him and said the same thing."

"Interesting," Welsh said, as if Andy told him something he already knew.

"Is it God?"

"I don't know, Andy."

"I want to see His face."

"You and everybody else. But God has blessed you and you're helping Him help others. Through that iPod of late, and in other ways in days to come, I'd wager."

"God needs my help?"

"God doesn't need anybody's help. But He wants it."

"Why me?"

"Why not? Keep reading that Bible your uncle got you and you'll find that God has chosen some pretty unlikely candidates to give Him a hand."

"I want to help. But other than that dream, it seems like God's left me."

"God never leaves. People leave Him, but He won't leave you."

"Ever since I found out Uncle Rip was sick, I don't hear anything in the iPod and I don't get that good feeling when I look at the flowers."

Welsh smiled. "That good feeling is the Holy Spirit, Andy. You don't need earbuds or a garden to feel that."

"That's basically the third time I've heard that," Andy said. "I sorta felt it when I came in here today. A little bit."

"You can feel it anywhere, anytime. Because *He* is everywhere."

"I have another question," Andy said.

"Fire away," Welsh said.

"When we went through the McLouth Steel side to get near the flowers and Mom saw the garden, she freaked out and kept asking me to repeat a Bible verse I told her. She kept asking, 'What did you say to me? What did you say to me?' But then I realized she wasn't really talking to *me*. She was talking to the *garden*." Andy stopped and waited for a response.

"So what's your question?" Welsh asked.

"Do you think it's possible that God is *in* the garden?"

"Like I just said," Welsh said with a playful grin, "He's *everywhere*."

"Uncle Rip said the same thing when I asked him what Mr. Hart meant when he said God must be in prison."

Welsh laughed. "He's right."

"I'm telling you, Pastor Welsh, that dream I had is right. When Uncle Rip is ready, he's gonna go into those flowers and he won't be sick anymore."

"What do you mean by *ready*?"

"You have to tell me. You're the one who's supposed to tell Uncle Rip when he's ready to go."

Pastor Welsh considered him. "According to your dream?"

"Yeah," Andy said, more convinced than ever that it was right.

"Well, you know I love you and your Uncle Rip, Andy. I'll do whatever I can. You can count on me."

"Thanks," Andy said, rising. "You know something, Pastor Welsh?"

"What?"

"Uncle Rip's right. You really are pretty cool."

THIRTY-SIX

Heather was amazed at how well everyone was doing at keeping a positive attitude about everything, so the little dinner get-together they had originally planned in Judi's backyard had turned into more of a barbecue. Heather even managed to convince her mother to come with her, after picking up Chelsea Cochran on the way.

Andy's gonna be so happy. Just the thought of another smile on the boy's face made Heather smile too. *What joy, Father! Thank You for the changes You've brought to Judi and Andy this summer, even in the midst of the fear . . .*

She got up from the picnic table the second she heard the side door close. Rip and Andy were walking toward her and she wanted to make sure there was room next to Chelsea for Andy. Not that Heather would mind sitting between Rip and her mother . . . *Mostly next to Rip.*

"Honey, can you get a tank of propane out of the barn?" Judi yelled to Andy from the porch.

"Okay," Andy said, separating himself from Rip and heading toward the barn without ever noticing Chelsea. He stopped at the small grave they had made for Milo and seemed to study it for a few seconds.

"Nice little group we have this afternoon," Rip said, shaking hands with Pastor Welsh and then patting Chelsea on the shoulder. He sat next to Heather and leaned forward to look around her. "And a special hello to you, Mrs. Gerisch."

"Hello, Gerald," Mom said.

Heather smiled at Rip and he did his best to keep a straight face.

"You can call me Rip if you'd like," he said.

"Then you can call me Sharon," Mom said. "I remember when you had really long hair."

Rip pointed at Pastor Welsh and then to Andy, who was on his way back, carrying the propane tank in front of him like a big pumpkin. "I don't see any other guys around here with short hair. I'm thinkin' maybe I should grow out what I have left of this fine blond hair to try and keep up."

"You'll be a cue ball before long," Mom said with a snort. Heather knew Mom didn't mean anything by it. She also didn't know Rip had cancer and that if he decided to do chemo, *when he decided to do chemo*, it would make him a cue ball for sure.

Heather looked over at Andy, who had obviously noticed Chelsea. He'd stopped dead in his tracks with a silly grin painted on his face.

"Hey, Chelsea," Heather said. "Lift that spell you've put on Andy for a second, or I don't think he'll ever make it to the barbecue."

Embarrassed, Chelsea waved at Andy in a *hurry up* fashion. "Come and take me for a ride on your motorcycle before the burgers go on the grill."

Andy glanced over at Rip with an expression like he'd heard

Chelsea speaking Chinese. Either that, or he was looking for Rip's permission to take her on the bike.

Rip gave Andy the thumbs-up. "Take it slow and just go around the yard. And make sure you both have helmets on."

Andy replaced the tank under the grill in record time and then he joined them at the picnic table.

Heather nudged Rip with her shoulder. "How ya doin'?"

"I'm unemployed, living at my sister's, and a dead man walking," he whispered. "Things are just peachy." He smiled and nudged her back. "Let's watch Romeo for a second."

Andy smiled shyly at Chelsea as he got closer.

"Well?" Chelsea said to Andy. "You gonna take me for a ride or what?"

"Yeah," he said, as if more than one word would result in his arrest.

"Ride slowly," Judi said.

Chelsea took Andy by the arm and everybody within thirty acres smiled except Andy. It looked like he had stage fright as she led him toward the garage. They all waited until they heard the bike start and then slowly pull out. Andy was wearing the old helmet, and Chelsea was wearing Andy's new one, which was covering her entire face and head. She had her arms wrapped around Andy's waist and Andy gunned the throttle a few times, a dreamy expression on his face. Clearly he was over the moon to have Chelsea on the bike with him.

"To be young again," Pastor Welsh said, raising his glass of lemonade.

Heather watched as Andy pulled the bike around the front of the house and disappeared. "Remember your old Harley, Rip?"

"Sure do," Rip said. "I thought I was pretty tough on that chopper."

"You thought you were a regular Hell's Angel," Judi said.

"Remember when you rode it to the Upper Peninsula and it died on you up there?"

"I'm guessing it's still up there," Rip said. "That bike wasn't a Hog . . . it was more like a pig."

"Ever think about getting another one?" Heather asked.

"I already have a bike," he said. "It still needs a little work done to it, but I've got big plans for her. If I did get a new bike, maybe I could finance it, you know . . . *six months* same as cash?"

"Shush," Heather said. She didn't like his jokes about his cancer, but knew it was his way of dealing with it. "I always liked riding on that Harley with you."

Rip looked at her and they seemed to share another intense moment. It went away as Andy and Chelsea came zipping around the back of the house. Andy stopped the bike next to the picnic table, and he'd clearly gone from outright shy to thinking he was *the man*.

"Go around again," Rip said.

Andy looked back and nodded at Chelsea. She had the visor up and was smiling from ear to ear before lowering it and leaning forward to rest her head against Andy's shoulder. Andy gunned it and they were off again, doing a little fishtail that the bike quickly recovered from.

"Slow down!" Judi yelled, red-faced. Rip guessed her blood pressure was going off the charts.

Rip glanced at Mrs. Gerisch, then turned to Heather. "Your mom sure has gotten quiet."

"You all right, Mom?" Heather asked.

"Just thinking," Mom answered. She was pointing at the lake. "I haven't been here in years, but didn't there used to be a big willow tree over near that dock?"

"I remember that tree," Pastor Welsh answered. "Rip and Judi would have been really little when that tree came down."

"I totally forgot about it," Judi said excitedly. "Dad had an old tire and rope attached to one of the branches as a swing. I remember they'd have people over to swing over the edge of the water. Everybody loved it."

"I don't remember it," Rip said.

"Me either," Heather said.

"I was only, like, four or five, so you guys would have been really small," Judi said.

"You ever go on that swing, Mom?" Heather asked.

"Every once in a while," Mom said. "But we did shoot the guns quite a bit. It was fun."

"I remember that too," Judi said. "They would throw those clay thingies over the water and shoot them."

"Clay pigeons," Mom said. "All you kids would sit right about where we are now with your fingers over your ears, cheering or booing if a target was missed or hit."

"I remember that gun with the big orange handle," Judi said. "I remember how loud it was."

Mom smiled and it quickly faded. "That was your father's service revolver, Heather. The one with the bright orange rubber pistol grip on it." She shook her head. "I used to tease him about getting such a silly color." She smiled. "They used to hang a paper plate on that old willow tree and shoot at it with that pistol. Your dad was an excellent shot."

"Why did they cut the tree down?" Judi asked.

"It was leaning," Pastor Welsh said. "It was just a matter of time before it fell over. Your mom and dad figured it was best to bring it down, particularly with kids all over the place."

"That tree was a whopper, though," Mom said, staring dreamily at the place where it once stood.

"It took the better part of a weekend to get it out," Pastor Welsh said. "Seemed like every man who owned a chain saw within a fifty-mile radius was here."

"I still don't remember any of it," Heather said, turning to Rip. "Do you?"

Rip had a peculiar look on his face. He was staring at the lake.

"You okay?" Heather asked.

He didn't say anything.

"Rip?" she said, waving her hand in front of his face. "You look like you just saw a ghost."

He turned to her and their eyes met. It wasn't that *we're connected* look she thought they shared earlier. He was clearly troubled.

"I kind of feel like I just saw a ghost," he said.

"What do you mean?"

"Heather," he said, before stopping and closing his eyes and rubbing them.

"What is it, Rip? Tell me."

He stared at her and his answer came in a whisper. "I've seen a gun like the one your mom just described."

THIRTY-SEVEN

So you're saying that Kevin Hart killed my father and *his own* father?" Heather asked.

It was about the fifth time Heather had asked that question over the last fifteen minutes, and Rip still wasn't prepared to answer. As soon as their little shindig ended, they had asked Pastor Welsh to meet them at St. Paul's for a powwow, and it was the first thing out of her mouth as they sat down in Welsh's office.

"All I'm saying is that I've seen a pistol, with an *orange* grip on it, in Kevin's boat."

"And it was a big gun?" she asked, panicked.

"Yes, Heather," Rip said. "You told me the investigators thought that the killer may have known your dad and Mr. Hart, right? And that they believe it was your dad's gun that killed them both?"

"Kevin was only fifteen when they were killed," Heather said numbly. "It's unbelievable."

"I'm sorry to bring it all back," Rip said. "I just figured you'd want to know. There's a chance that Kevin just has a very similar—"

"Of course I'd want to know," she interrupted, crossing her arms and shaking her head.

"I'm sure there's an explanation," Rip said, glancing at Pastor Welsh, who seemed uneasy. Rip figured Welsh had listened to just about every problem in the world from behind that desk.

But murder?

"What am I supposed to do?" Heather asked.

"Talk to the chief about it," Pastor Welsh said.

"Good idea," Rip said.

"And just to be safe," Welsh added, "you should probably step away from this and let somebody else handle it."

"No way. I want to go and talk to Kevin," Heather said. "Like, right now."

"Are you crazy?" Rip asked. "If we're right . . . Heather, tell Chief Reynolds about it and take a few days off. Maybe they can get a warrant to search the boat."

"It's been twenty years," Heather said, standing and walking to the corner of the office. She turned around. "There is no way it's the same gun. Are you positive it had an orange grip?"

"Yeah, but the more I think about it, the more I'm sure we're overreacting here," Rip said. "Kevin's a tool, but he hasn't always been. What reason could there be for *fifteen-year-old* Kevin to have wanted his father dead?"

"You're probably right," Heather said, rubbing her temples, looking dazed.

Welsh started to chime in and then stopped. Rip couldn't ever remember him hesitating before. He looked almost . . . *uncomfortable* again.

"What is it?" Rip asked.

"Nothing," he said.

"Tell us," Heather said, her eyes narrowing.

"Actually," Welsh said, looking like he regretted what he was about to say. "Kevin may have had millions of reasons."

"Don't say that," Heather said, shaking her head again.

"Lord, forgive me for saying this," Welsh said. "But Walter Hart, rest his soul, sat right where we are on numerous occasions. We had a lot of talks about Kevin, and most of them weren't too pleasant."

Heather winced. "I don't ever remember Mr. Hart saying anything but nice things about Kevin."

"In public," Welsh said. "That's what the Harts have always done. And I sort of feel like I'm violating confidentiality, but two men have been killed here and . . ." He paused and brought his hands to the sides of his face.

"And what?" Heather asked.

Welsh seemed to mull over his response. "And guns with orange rubber grips aren't all that popular."

"This is impossible," Heather said, pacing back and forth across the office. "But if it isn't, what Andy told Kevin at the factory won't be true. Vengeance will be *mine.*"

"Andy said that to Kevin?" Welsh asked.

"Yeah," Rip said. "He also called him 'Cain.'"

"What?" Welsh said, followed by an awkward silence.

"Cain," Rip repeated.

"Good Lord," Welsh said as if a light just went on at the back of his mind. He took his turn standing. "Cain?"

"What is it?" Rip asked.

Welsh looked at Heather. "Tell me again what Andy said about the photograph of your father and Walter Hart."

Heather glanced at Rip and then back to the minister. "He said, 'They are able.'"

Welsh sat back down and rubbed at his eyes. He took a deep

breath and his head teetered slowly back and forth. "Heavens. He was telling you who the killer is."

"By saying they are able?" Rip said.

Welsh glanced at Rip and then looked right at Heather.

"Andy wasn't saying they are *a-b-l-e*."

"I heard it," Rip said.

"So did I," Heather added. "It's exactly what Andy said."

"No," Welsh said. "Andy said that Kevin is Cain, and that your dad and Walter Hart are capital *A-b-e-l*."

THIRTY-EIGHT

Rip and Judi decided to meet Andy and Chelsea over at the park to watch a few innings of Chelsea's brother's ball game. The only reason they were sitting in the bleachers was because that's where Chelsea was. Rip would have rather been parked under a tree and some shade, because it was about a trillion degrees outside again and he had the mother ship of headaches docking between his ears.

Rip still hadn't heard from Heather. She wasn't working, wasn't at her mom's house, wasn't home, and he'd been lighting her phone up all morning with no luck. He was hoping she'd taken Welsh's advice and shared what she found out with Chief Reynolds.

He hadn't said anything to Judi about the gun. In fact, he, Welsh, and Heather agreed not to say anything to anyone about it, but Rip was still afraid that Heather was going to somehow confront Kevin Hart himself.

Judi elbowed him and then cocked her head toward Andy who was one row down in the bleachers in front of them. Chelsea and Andy weren't holding hands, they were holding pinkies. Rip winked at Judi and she smiled.

"Guess who's going over to Chelsea's tonight for dinner?"

"Someone that's holding pinkies with her?" Rip asked. "I may have to separate those two. It's getting *way* too physical."

"I had a nice little chat with Heather's mom last night," Judi said.

I'm thinking my chat with Heather last night was a little more interesting, Rip thought. "What did you guys talk about?" he asked.

"Mrs. Gerisch said that Heather's faith has inspired her to rethink her own," Judi said. "She seemed a little shy talking about it, but it's good to hear her bring it up."

"That's cool," Rip said, quickly praying that same faith of Heather's was guiding her, wherever she happened to be.

"For the most part," Judi said, "God has really been good to . . ." She paused and frowned.

"You can say it," Rip said. "God *has* been good to us."

Just the idea of Judi mentioning that, in itself, was a miracle compared to where she had been just a few weeks ago. Heck, a few *days* ago, for that matter. She and Andy were finally on the right path, but at the moment, that was the least of his concerns.

He took out his phone and tried calling Heather again. It went straight to voice mail and he didn't leave a message. He took a deep breath and a little pain shot through his side as only one thought repeatedly ran through his mind.

Where are you, Heather?

❈ ❈ ❈

Kevin Hart thought about telling Lynn to send Heather away, but if the whole Ripley-getting-fired thing ever got out of control, it would be nice to have her accessible as a potential mediator.

The door opened. Heather was in street clothes. She never was quite the slave to fashion that Carrie had become, which was a good thing, but at the same time, a personal shopper could do her wonders for the days she wasn't playing policewoman. She had a serious look on her face, and he would have bet Carrie's half of his fortune that Heather was there to lobby for Ripley to get his job back. Needless to say, if that were the case, she was about to waste everyone's time.

"Hello, Kevin," she said, sounding more businesslike than when she wore her uniform.

"Hi there. What's up?" he said, standing and walking over to the bar. "You're not working. How about a cocktail?"

"No thanks," she said. "I'm good." She didn't seem good. She seemed uptight.

"Have a seat," he said, gesturing to the overstuffed chairs on the other side of his desk. "You been busy keeping the criminals off Benning's streets?"

"Here and there."

"Out chasing the Summer Santa again?"

She gave him a benign smile. "The Summer Santa is an unusual guy. He seems to think that doing a whole lot of good makes up for a whole lot of bad."

"Interesting," he said. "You all right? You seem a bit out of sorts."

She shrugged. "I guess you could say that I've had a pretty strange twenty-four hours."

He poured himself a splash of scotch and returned to his desk. "How's that?"

"I was over at Judi's last night, and my mom was talking about how all of our dads used to shoot guns in Judi's backyard. I don't remember any of it. Do you?"

"No," he said. "I was never quite the hunter my dad was."

"I see," she said quickly. The way she said it was without that signature smidgen of fear that was usually sprinkled on the edge of her voice.

He figured he'd try to get that fear to resurface and take control of the conversation.

"Why are you asking?" he said loudly. A little too loud. He wondered if she saw through his intimidation tactics.

"Because my dad's gun came up in the conversation," she said, leaning forward. "The same gun—you know—that they thought may have killed our fathers?"

"I've heard that," he said. *Is that what this is about?* "But I can assure you I never thought your dad did it, Heather."

She gave him a hard look. "Me either. But do you remember seeing his gun, Kev?"

"No," he said. Of course he'd seen the gun. In fact, even though it hadn't been fired in twenty years, he still enjoyed looking at it once in a while. Holding it felt . . . empowering.

"Okay," she said. "I'll take your word for it."

He didn't like the way that sounded, nor did he like the way she was looking at him. He narrowed his eyes, remembering the last time he'd seen the gun. *Ripley.*

"What's that supposed to mean?" he asked. "Why *wouldn't* you take my word for it?"

"Just a hunch about something," she said. The way she maintained eye contact with him was completely unlike her. "Who do *you* think killed them, Kevin?"

I killed them. I capped my dad right in the back of the head. Greedy old pig never knew it was coming.

"How would I know that?" he asked slowly. "And why bring all this up again now?"

"Don't take it personally," she said. "It's just that I'm thinking about reopening the investigation and was curious what *you* thought."

She was on to something. He could see it in her eyes. But she wouldn't get far. They never got far.

Your dad saw it coming. I can still see the look on his face as I sent one right into his eye.

"Honestly?" he said, taking a sip of his scotch and lifting it. "I do my best not to think about it. You'd be better off if you did the same."

"I'm a cop, just like my dad," she said, quickly standing. She walked to the door and turned around. "I can't *not* think about it."

"Well, maybe you can bring our fathers' killer to justice," he said, raising his glass as if in a toast.

It was as easy as that, he thought smugly. *Boom and my dad was history. And boom, your father was—*

"I think I've already caught the killer," she said, giving him a little smile that gave him pause. She opened the door and looked over her shoulder. "And I'm pretty sure I can prove it too."

❊ ❊ ❊

"You are the best hide-and-go-seek player I've ever seen," Andy said. He was sitting in the Cochrans' backyard on a white plastic lawn chair, part of a cheap patio set whose umbrella had a dent in it about halfway up its pole. Mrs. Cochran came through the back fence and was carrying the two pizza boxes that had just arrived.

Marjo two-handed a Styrofoam cup of water and took a sip. He couldn't believe how big it looked as she held it, even though her little hands appeared to be even more swollen than the last time he'd seen her. She put the cup down and picked up his iPod again. Even though it was dead, for some reason the kid was having fun with it.

"What was my best hiding spot?" she asked in that tiny voice of hers. The whites of her eyes still looked funny and he guessed her weight at no more than forty pounds. A big part of Andy wished she could toss down half the pizza and put some meat on those tiny bones.

"The duffel bag," Andy said.

"I knew it!" Marjo said.

The Cochrans lived at the end of a cul-de-sac, and all of the houses on the street were three-bedroom brick ranches with basements. Chelsea and Marjo had agreed to hide on the main floor, which Andy thought smelled like a peppermint potpourri farm, and there were only so many places they could be. Andy had found Chelsea in less than a minute. She was hiding in the bathtub behind the shower curtain, and when he found her, she guaranteed Andy that he had no chance of finding Marjo.

She was right.

He looked for a good fifteen minutes, and when he'd finally given up, he was standing right next to Marjo in Chelsea's bedroom. She was laughing and he could hear her, but it drove him crazy that he couldn't see her. A little duffel bag on the floor started moving. Not the big kind, but a small one like the type you would take to gym class. He couldn't believe she was in it and still couldn't figure out how in the world she'd gotten in at all. If she ever got better, she could become a contortionist and try out for the circus.

"You guys want to eat inside or outside?" Mr. Cochran asked.

"Want to go inside?" Chelsea asked Andy. "It's kind of warm out here still."

"Whatever Marjo wants to do," Andy said. He looked at Marjo, whose eyes were closed. She had the iPod earbuds in and was smiling.

"You have a funny name," she said.

Andy stilled and stared at the little girl, then again at the dead iPod as she handed it to him. "What do you mean by that?"

"Let's go inside," Chelsea said, nudging Andy on his shoulder. "And don't worry, I'll say grace."

"Yeah," Marjo said, giggling again. "When Daddy asked Andrew Todd to say grace at Mack's restaurant, he didn't want to."

Andy's heart raced and he quickly lifted an earbud to his ear.

He heard nothing and was disappointed. No music, no words. But . . .

He put his hand on Marjo's shoulder. "Hey, did you hear something from that iPod? How did you know my middle name?"

Marjo gave him a flirtatious smile and shrugged.

"I don't know. I forgot."

❈ ❈ ❈

When Heather finally came to her door at five minutes past eight at night, Rip breathed a sigh of relief. He didn't think he'd ever been so glad to see her.

"Where have you been? I've been trying to—"

"I went to see him, Rip."

"Are you crazy?" he said, trying not to shout. "Stand aside, 'cause I'm coming in."

Heather was wearing a plain white T-shirt and blue yoga pants, and her hair was a haystack, as if he'd woken her. She held an open palm out toward the inside of her apartment. Rip headed straight for the recliner. He sat down and pointed at the little couch to his right. "Sit down."

Heather sat down on the front edge of the cushion. Her knees were together with her palms flat on top of her legs and her head bowed like a little kid who had just been scolded. "I know, Rip. I'm a terrible cop." She looked up at him. "But I had to know. Had to see it in his eyes, you know?"

There wasn't enough activity in Benning Township for cops to show their stuff. Speeding tickets for those who ignored her previous warnings, filling out a report for an occasional scuffle at one of the local bars, or talking to the elementary kids once a year on not taking candy from strangers. That was about it. So Rip didn't know if she was a good cop or bad cop. But he was pretty dang sure that approaching Kevin at this juncture was a really bad plan.

"I asked him if he'd ever seen it. The gun," she said.

Rip winced and closed his eyes. If Hart really had anything to do with killing their fathers, Rip knew that big gun with the orange handle was now resting peacefully in the mud at the bottom of Lake Erie.

Heather fell back into the couch and closed her eyes. "What was I thinking?"

"You were emotional. Sometimes it's hard to control yourself."

"I was angry," she said. "I *am* angry."

"Did you tell the chief about this yet?"

"Not yet," she said. "I'm such a moron. Kevin's probably chucked that gun into the lake by now."

Rip didn't have the heart to tell her he was just thinking the same thing. "Listen, Heather. We don't even know if Kevin did it. Like you said, why would a fifteen-year-old kid shoot his dad? Or your dad, for that matter?"

"I don't know." She straightened up. "But I *know* he did it, Rip."

"How?"

"*I just know,*" she said. "And I also know Kevin is the Summer Santa."

"Hmm," Rip said. "Maybe."

"It's Kevin," Heather said, "and in some twisted way, it makes him feel better about who he really is. What he's done. And I'm almost positive that he is in cahoots with that Brianna too on the Summer Santa thing."

"I think you need to step aside and let somebody else from the department look further into the murders," Rip said. "If you ever listen to any of my crazy preaching, *believe me* that I know anger can cloud your judgment, so it's best somebody else handles it. And once again, we don't even know if Kevin really did it. So pray about it and take a few more days to absorb all of this. Then tell Reynolds everything you know and then get out. Quit the force. He'll understand."

Heather tossed her hands up and her arms landed on her lap. "I just feel like my world is coming to an end."

"Believe me," Rip repeated. He reached over and patted her on the leg. "I know how that feels too."

"Shut up, Rip," she said. "Will you please quit making jokes about being sick?"

"I was dying to tell you that one."

"Rip!" she yelled, quickly standing and walking into the kitchen.

He followed her. She stood at the window, face in her hands.

"Hey," he said, walking up next to her. "I'm sorry."

She looked up at him and little tears spilled over from each eye. "What are Andy and Judi going to do without you?"

"Andy and Judi made it three years without me," Rip said. "And now they are better than they've ever been. They'll be just—"

"What am I gonna do?" she interrupted, wiping at her eyes with her index fingers.

"You are going to be—"

"I love you, Gerald Ripley," she blurted. "What am I going to do without you?"

Heather looked up at him and her eyes were filled with despair. Still, she had never looked more beautiful to him, because beneath that despair, he could feel her hope. Hope that he'd say four words back to her.

I love you too.

The words made it to the edge of his lips and then he choked on them for the same reason he always did. "You are wonderful," he whispered. "Your whole life is still in front of you and I know you will find that special someone who will know it as surely as I do."

Heather didn't say anything. And as she stared at him, he could feel her light green eyes lighting up the edges of his soul. It made him want to live. *To be with her.*

Rip swallowed and could feel something on his cheek. It was a teardrop. He wiped it away and gave her a sheepish grin.

"Looks like the tough guy has a heart after all," Heather said, leaning against him, her eyes never leaving his. "So tell me, Rip. Do you love me?"

Rip blinked slowly and could feel another tear weaving its way down his cheek. He ignored it. "You deserve way better than me," he whispered. "You are and have always been too good for a guy like me."

She pushed away from him and crossed her arms. "Shame on you, Rip," she said. "Shame on you. For never letting that be *my* decision."

❋ ❋ ❋

Kevin Hart sat in the dark and laughed at the moon.

He was parked out near the lake, at the very back end of the parking lot of Hart Industries. It was pitch-black, and he was sitting on the hood of his Mercedes. He and Brianna didn't have an *outing* planned for that night, so he thought it would be nice to just sit out there in the dark, smoke a cigar, look at the water, enjoy some alone time . . .

And laugh.

He only ever laughed when he was upset. And he only got upset when someone thought that they were ahead of him in the game.

Always stay ahead of them, son . . . always be out front . . . because life is a game and there can only be so many winners . . .

He *laughed*, thinking about his father this time, instead of the sudden Super Cop, Heather.

Kevin Hart had always tried his best at whatever he did. He had to. His dad expected it of him.

Five home runs in one Little League game.

Youngest Eagle Scout *ever* in the state of Michigan.

Nothing but As on *every* report card he *ever* had until tenth grade.

He could go on and on, but it was never good enough. Even for a kid whose socks were too short, ties were too long, talked too much, didn't talk enough . . . a kid who did nothing but *embarrass* his father.

He remembered sitting in his room, staring at the report card. He could still see that terrible grade, sticking out among the As. Madly, he'd tried to work up a good explanation for the B+.

Then more thoughts of life without Dad ran through his head. They had been coming more frequently and were stronger. But at the end of the day—of *every* day—there was no way out.

Talk of graduating from high school, going to college in a different state, and maybe starting his *own* business was always extinguished. There were no options, because if he *ever got his act together*, he was going to go to work at Hart Industries and be his father's protégé. And maybe, when he was fifty or so, his father would think about letting him take over the company.

It was never up for debate. Kevin was trapped.

He finally decided to tell his father about the bad grade with Mr. Gerisch there. He figured maybe Dad wouldn't be so hard on him with a police officer around.

By the time he made it downstairs and into the kitchen, he was too afraid to go through with it. He remembered the strange way his father was looking at him and then how Dad told him to quit bothering them. And as he was leaving the kitchen to go back upstairs, that's when he saw it.

It was an act of God.

For some divine reason, Mr. Gerisch had placed his service revolver on the kitchen counter.

"*Boom boom*," Hart said out loud, remembering picking up the phone and calling the police crying. He had told them he heard two shots and ran downstairs and found them. Then they spent the next three years looking for someone who didn't exist.

He looked at his watch. It was the one he had taken off his dead father that night. He took another drag off the cigar and then tossed it over the fence into the lake.

And then he thought about Heather and wondered what she knew. Obviously Rip and she had put two and two together, like Fred and Daphne on *Scooby-Doo*.

The gun had to go. Just like Heather. But not yet.

He smiled, thinking how he would use it just one more time, and how this little problem would soon go away.

THIRTY-NINE

I'm pretty sure that Heather is going to bow out and just let the department look into the whole Kevin thing," Rip said, sitting across from Pastor Welsh.

"Why in the world would she go and confront him?" Welsh asked. "We should have taken her over to meet with Reynolds right then and there. Either that or taken her over to Canada for a few days and let her clear her head."

"She still would have said something to Kevin when she got back."

"Maybe you're right."

"Maybe we're also making a big deal out of nothing. Maybe the gun's still in Kev's boat because he didn't *do* it." Rip leaned back and put his hands behind his head. "God talks to Andy through an iPod. God drops a funky symbolic garden out behind McLouth Steel for us. I am diagnosed with terminal cancer and there is a possibility that Kevin Hart is a murderer. There goes the neighborhood."

"Life sure seemed pretty simple a couple months ago," Welsh said. "How you doing with the whole six months thing?"

"It's surreal," Rip said. "I don't think this whole 'gonna die' thing has sunk in yet."

Welsh nodded and parted two stacks of books that were on his desk. "I think I know what you mean, Rip."

"How?" Rip asked.

"I'm seventy years old," Welsh said. "And I'm living in the body of a ninety-year-old. All the drinking I did caught up with me a long time ago. I could drop dead at any time. You think you're the only man who's thought about his mortality?"

"I hear ya," Rip said. "But I guess I wasn't planning on it for a few more years."

"How about Judi and Andy?" Welsh said. "They seem to be handling everything pretty well."

"Yeah," Rip said. "Even though I think Judi's holding on to a hopeful word from the U of M doctors. We've sort of made a pact to stay positive and not focus too much on it, but I guess I'm a little concerned about Andy's obsession with the flower garden getting me better. He figures it's a sure bet and doesn't think he has to worry about anything other than me working to get the bike ready."

Welsh smiled and nodded slowly. "It's good to see the boy be optimistic."

"Hey, I can use all the optimism I can get," Rip said. He tapped his fingertips together, thinking. "Are you ready for it?"

"For what?" Welsh said.

"Death."

"Absolutely," Welsh said with confidence. Then a peculiar, almost puzzled look crossed his face. "Why?"

"Because I'm dying and I don't *want* to be dying," Rip said. "I thought I'd be more . . . *settled* about the whole thing. You know, as a believer."

"Not many people want to die," Welsh said. "But many are ready."

Rip nodded. "How will I know if I'm ready? I feel like something's still missing. I know it's something simple too, and whatever it is that I'm supposed to do . . . I really think it will put my past behind me, once and for all, and make me *ready*."

"You've said something sort of similar before."

"I know, sack of flour, no bread." They chuckled together. "It's cracked that I'm also only thirty-five. Think my age is making me feel unready?"

"Let me ask you a question," Welsh said, leaning forward. "One hundred years from now, do you think you and I will be in heaven?"

"Yeah," Rip said.

"How about a thousand years from now?"

"Yeah," Rip said, not having the faintest idea where the minister was going.

Welsh tapped at his own chest. "So whether you are an old fart like me, ten years old, twenty years old, or thirty-five years old is irrelevant when you consider that we are only on this earth for a flash compared to the time we will be in heaven, which, by the way, is *a lot* longer than a thousand years."

"Like forever," Rip said.

"Exactly," Welsh said, smiling. "So in the big picture, there really is no difference in our ages, Rip. Our time here is a flash in the pan."

"Okay," Rip said, holding up his hands. "Age doesn't matter, but I still don't know how I'll know if I'm ready."

Welsh smiled again, but it was one of those smiles that normally accompanied disappointment.

"You've got a little work to do, Rip," Welsh said. "Go home and pray about it. And I'm confident you'll know when you are ready."

"*When I'm ready*," Rip said. "Andy even told me I'm not ready to go yet."

"What do you mean?"

"Into the garden."

Welsh had a puzzled look on his face. "You're not ready to die and you're not ready to go in the garden to be healed. Interesting coincidence."

"What do you mean?"

"Nothing," Welsh said with a suspicious grin. "Like I said earlier, you'll know when you're ready."

"For which? Death or the garden?"

The smile disappeared from the minister's face and a little chill danced across the side of Rip's neck.

"Both. Don't be surprised if they are the same thing."

FORTY

You are washing this car the second we get back, Andrew," Mom said, doing her best to weave their white Tempo around the mud puddles.

"Chill out, Mom," Andy said. She had gotten so much better recently, but she was still pretty much freaking out about a little back-road trek . . .

They were on the path that led back to The Frank and Poet Canal, and despite it being ninety and sunny again, the path was still muddy from another shower that morning.

"Chill out?" Mom echoed. "You are starting to sound like your uncle. What if we get stuck?"

"If Uncle Rip's Pacer made it out there, we will make it. Don't worry."

They had gone clothes shopping for a few hours up at the Southland Mall in Taylor, and even though school was close to a month away, Andy knew Bargain Shopper Judi would have him up there the first day the back-to-school specials started. Uncle Rip had called while they were gone and said he'd driven the Pacer out to the canal, and for them to join him when they got back.

"What's he up to?" Mom asked as they approached the end path, where the two cornfields gave way to the opening.

"Not sure," Andy said as they neared the back of Uncle Rip's Pacer. Andy laughed. The Pacer was covered in mud and looked like it had just finished some off-road event or competition. Probably how the Tempo looked now too.

Mom spotted Uncle Rip first. He was right on the other side of the Pacer. "Oh my Lord," Mom said. "He's really going to do it, isn't he?"

"Yes!" Andy yelled, jumping out the passenger door before Mom's car had even come to a stop. "It's awesome!"

Uncle Rip had built a wooden motorcycle ramp out of some two-by-fours and plywood. He was standing halfway up it, smiling, clearly proud of his work, with his chest puffed out and arms crossed.

The ramp was around fifteen feet long. It was as wide as the triple-stacked pieces of plywood that served as its surface, and Andy guessed it was maybe seven feet high at the far end.

It was aimed over the canal. Right at the two remaining sections that made up the garden.

"I've never seen anything like it," Mom said, obviously trying to hold back her freaking-outness. "How'd you build it so fast?"

"It was pretty easy to put together," Uncle Rip said. "It only took me about an hour to frame it up, then a couple more hours to reinforce it."

Mom walked right past Uncle Rip and put her hand up on the top corner edge of the ramp. She was looking across the canal and her eyes almost looked glassed-over.

"Go, Rip," she said quickly. "Go right now. Get over there."

Uncle Rip looked down at Mom. "What's gotten into you? Aren't you the same person who just warned me of every peril on the McLouth side of the canal?"

Mom had to brace herself against the ramp. Her eyes were still on the wildflowers and she wasn't blinking. She kind of had that same vacant look on her face as she did that one day they were on the other side, checking out the garden.

"Get over there," she repeated. "Get over there right now, Rip. And He will make your cancer go away."

"Who?" Uncle Rip said.

"Him," Mom answered, pointing at the flowers.

Andy stepped on the ramp and walked up next to Uncle Rip at the top. "What's He look like, Mom?"

"I don't know," Mom answered. "I can't see His face."

"It's Him, then," Andy said, wanting another look. He turned to his uncle. "How can Mom see Him and I can't?"

Uncle Rip shrugged. "Don't know."

"Go, Rip," Mom said. "Please hurry."

"I promise I'll go," Uncle Rip said with a little laugh. "But there's a little work left to do."

FORTY-ONE

I felt the exact same way as I did when Andy was calling me using my first and middle names," Judi said, exiting off I-94 toward the University of Michigan Hospital. They were on their way to get the second opinion, and Rip had no doubt they were going to give the same prognosis. He'd spent the better half of the morning coughing up some scary stuff.

"That's awesome," Rip said. His muscles tensed and he laughed, thinking about what he was going to say. "It's funny. I remember calling that flower bed a little piece of heaven when I first saw it. Wouldn't it be cool if I was right?"

"A little piece of heaven?"

"You were practically *begging* me to go across the canal yesterday, telling me I would get better if I did."

"I don't remember saying that," Judi said. "And I've decided you aren't jumping it on that old motorcycle. Even if you make it, the bike will probably bust apart on the other side, and you'll definitely be dead."

"Don't worry about that," Rip said. "But think about it, Judi.

What if it really was a little bit of heaven? Why not? If it is, I really will get better if I go in there. Anybody sick would."

"Then why haven't you gone over there yet?"

"I've got some work to do."

"On what? The ramp or the bike?"

"Neither," Rip said, thinking about his last conversation with Pastor Welsh. "It's what Andy has been saying. I just don't know if *I'm* ready yet."

※ ※ ※

Andy handed Chelsea a Coke and joined her at the picnic table behind the house. They had spent the early afternoon at the park, watching her brother's baseball team run through some drills. After all, losing every game by ten or more runs was pretty hard work and took practice.

It was another boiling day, and he and Chelsea were going to swim just off the dock on the lake, and then maybe he'd take her out to The Frank and Poet on his motorcycle to see the wildflowers and the new ramp Uncle Rip had built.

He still hadn't said anything to Chelsea about Uncle Rip's health, doing his part in keeping it a secret, not to mention that Chelsea already had enough to think about with her little sis, who'd spent the last couple days in the hospital. Mrs. Cochran was taking a break from the hospital and had also been at the park. She looked like she hadn't slept in about a year, and Andy was half tempted to tell her to take Marjo out to the wildflowers.

"What is the latest with Marjo?" Andy asked. "I didn't want to bring it up with your mom around."

"About the same," Chelsea said. "But we sure are lucky that Mr. and Mrs. Hart are doing the fund-raiser."

"I guess so," Andy said.

Andy figured Mrs. Cochran would think he was crazy if he told her about the garden, so he thought the second best idea he had all day was to not tell Chelsea what he really thought about Mr. and Mrs. Hart. But still, what they were doing was a good thing and he hoped everything would work out.

"Ready to go swimming?" Andy asked and gulped down some of his Coke.

"Yeah," Chelsea said.

Andy had put his swim trunks on when he had fetched the Cokes, and Chelsea was wearing a one-piece swimsuit under her shorts and T-shirt.

"I have a question," Andy said as they walked toward the dock.

"Go for it," Chelsea said.

"Everybody's telling me I can hear God, talk to God, and feel God's presence without my iPod. I went and visited Pastor Welsh at St. Paul's and could feel God a little bit there, but other than that I haven't felt anything and I really want to. How do I do it?"

"Lots of ways," Chelsea said. "Mostly by praying, though. When you open your heart, sometimes you can even hear and see God in other people around you."

"I know about praying," Andy said. "But there are so many things I want right now, I wouldn't know where to begin."

Chelsea stopped walking and so did Andy. She squinted and shook her head as if she was disappointed. "You might want to start by thanking God for what you have, instead of telling Him what you want."

"What if I told Him I wanted something I already have?"

"That doesn't make sense."

Andy clammed up. He wanted to hear God again through the iPod, to feel His presence in the garden. Heck, he even wanted Milo back. And those were all things *he had* . . . once. He really wanted Uncle Rip to stay alive, which was something *he had right now.*

"How about Marjo?" he said at last. "You already have her in your life, so if you pray that she will get better, isn't that basically telling God you don't want to lose her?"

"I thank God every day for giving me *that* day with my sister. And I mean *that* day."

Andy thought about what she said and realized he'd never thanked God for his Uncle Rip, or anything else, for that matter.

They started walking again, and when they hit the dock, Andy couldn't help but notice the scar near the top of Chelsea's leg, and she flat-out busted him staring at it.

"Dog bite," she said, sitting at the end of the dock and dangling her legs into the water. She ran her finger along the scar. "I was like four years old when it happened."

"It's not that bad," Andy said, sitting next to her.

"Seen worse, eh?" she asked, taking his hand.

Like, every day, Andy thought.

"How did you get yours?" Chelsea asked.

Not that we're comparing apples to apples, he thought.

"Me, my uncle, and my mom were just talking about this," Andy said, watching as a school of minnows passed beneath their feet. "I was a little younger when I got mine. I was three. It was a couple days before Easter and some boiling egg water kind of ended up on my face."

Andy waited, hoping he wouldn't hear that one word.

How?

Instead, Chelsea asked a more painful question. "May I?"

She had taken a handful of the hair that covered his scar and was asking to pull it back so she could look. Andy felt his heart starting to pound, and it felt like someone had just put his head underwater.

Still, he closed his eyes and said it.

"Sure."

She pulled the hair back off the scar. He fought to not jerk his head away. His eyes were still closed and he could feel her examine the scar. And then he felt something else. It didn't last long. It was quick. It was clean. It was painless. It was magical.

A kiss.

"All better," Chelsea said, standing and giving him a beautiful smile.

She'd kissed him. *On* the scar.

Andy quickly stood on legs that didn't feel like his own. She had tucked his hair behind his ear and he ran his hand across the scar, a part of him almost wondering if it *was* gone. In this moment, it didn't matter who could see it.

"You okay?" Chelsea asked.

Andy wasn't sure how much time had passed before he finally said, "Yeah."

"Good," Chelsea said as she laughed and pushed him into the water.

❈ ❈ ❈

Judi had dropped Rip off at St. Paul's and he was sitting in the first pew, waiting for Pastor Welsh to get back from volunteering over at Mick Solack's food bank. It was way too quiet and he was staring at the cross that hung against the back wall. It looked bigger today.

The tests from U of M didn't quite agree with everything Doc Strater had said. Strater had given him maybe six months. Today, they said they'd be surprised if he made it three.

They did, however, like Strater, seem to marvel at how well he was still getting around. Then they informed Rip that with or without chemo and radiation, his lung capacity was disappearing and he would slowly suffocate.

At least I have that to look forward to.

He heard the door open behind him. He already knew it was Pastor Welsh, and even if it wasn't, he didn't want to look away from the cross. It made him feel good.

Welsh sat next to him.

"I just got off the phone with Judi," the minister said.

"Still crying?"

"Yeah."

Rip thought about the way Judi's voice sounded as she encouraged him to go to the wildflowers. She was like a little kid. Innocent and filled with trust, knowing that the only thing that could make him better was just on the other side of The Frank and Poet Canal.

A little piece of heaven.

But still, he didn't want to go over there for one simple reason. The bike was as good as it was going to get and the ramp wasn't half bad. He figured that even with a bad jump . . . he'd easily clear the canal.

But could he make it into the flowers?

He knew that didn't have anything to do with the bike or the ramp. It was all about the operator.

"I prayed about it," Rip whispered.

"As we all have," Welsh said. "From the second we first knew you had cancer."

"No," Rip said. "You told me if I prayed about it, that I'd know when I was ready to die."

"And?"

"I've been staring at this cross for the last forty-five minutes, talking to God. And I was thinking about how you told me that sometimes it's not about what we have to do, but about how we have to think."

"And what'd you come up with?"

Rip swallowed heavily and pointed at the cross. "It starts right there. Life starts at the cross and it just *keeps* growing. I know what I've been missing. This whole time I've been acting like Joe Christian and doing my best. Trying to fix what I did wrong."

"There's nothing wrong with that."

"But it's not enough," Rip said. "It will never be enough. And the funny thing is that I've been lecturing people about how they could have a relationship with God for free because the price was already paid. But you know what? I never really thought about what that truly meant." He let out a breathy laugh. "And it's the only thing I needed to know. *The only thing.*"

"What do you mean, Rip?" Welsh asked.

Rip lowered his hand and bowed his head. "He died for me. He would've died for me alone. Regardless of what I've done or not done. Regardless of what I could do today or tomorrow. I've asked for forgiveness for all I've done wrong, and He's forgiven me. I'm covered. He covered me. He's always had me covered."

"Rip?" Pastor Welsh said.

Rip wiped his eyes and looked at the minister. "Yeah?"

Welsh smiled and put his hand on Rip's shoulder. "You're ready."

※ ※ ※

Something seemed different about downtown Benning. Rip opted to walk back to Judi's from St. Paul's, and instead of going down the lake side and cutting through the woods, he decided he'd go the long way, which took him right through town.

When he stepped into the shade under the awning of the old

IGA, he could feel about a thirty-degree difference in the temperature. He put his hands up around his face, as if he were holding binoculars, and leaned against the window, looking inside of the abandoned grocery store. It was dark and the whole space was nothing but empty floor. He looked over in the back left corner, near the exit, and remembered the day he got fired. He was sixteen, six foot three, and high as a kite. Mr. Schwartz looked up at him and told him that "smoking drugs" would stunt his growth. Rip pulled back from the window and let out a little laugh. Maybe old man Schwartz was right. He hadn't grown an inch since.

Rip turned around and walked across the street toward Mack's, and when he hit the sidewalk, he glanced back over his shoulder for another look at the old grocery store. Then he watched a few people walk in and out of the sporting goods, the barber shop, and then the gas station.

The barber shop, Rip thought. *How many haircuts do I have left?*

Rip smiled, but it wasn't a good smile, because being *ready* to die didn't necessarily mean you were *willing*. He thought about how he would trade places with any of the people he was looking at, because what was happening wasn't fair.

All the peace he'd felt the day Strater had given him the diagnosis, all the peace he'd felt in St. Paul's an hour ago seemed to up and leave him. The farther he walked, the angrier he became.

He had tried to turn his life around, tried to do everything right, and look what was happening to him! He could feel his fists clench and he wanted someone to be responsible for the fit of rage that ran through him. He shook his head and looked up at the sky.

"Is this what I get? I turn my life over, do my best, and this is what I get? I know I'm covered! I know I'm ready! But, Lord! I want to *live*."

Rip crossed his arms and looked at the ground, shaking his head again. He didn't like waiting. He remembered the only thing worse than going to prison was waiting to go to prison.

And now this. More waiting. Waiting to die.

He didn't want anybody to see him so he walked into the alley that separated Mack's from the pharmacy. Then he crouched down and covered his face with his hands, shaking with his anger.

"You okay, man?" someone said behind him.

"I'm cool," Rip said without turning around.

Whoever he was, he had just come out the back door of Mack's. "You sure?" the man said.

Even though he hadn't heard the voice in a while, it was a familiar one. Rip stood and turned around.

It was Eric Bower. The man who'd basically cost Rip three years, *almost ten percent* of his short life.

Rip clenched his teeth and started walking toward Bower, and when Bower recognized him, his eyes widened and he started walking backward so fast that he tripped over a parking block.

Bower was on his backside rowing himself backward on the gravel, using his hands as oars. "Please, Rip," he said. "I'm sorry, man. Please."

Rip walked faster toward him and his rage continued to grow.

"I'm sorry, Rip, please forgive me," Bower begged.

Rip stepped over the parking block, leaned over, and grabbed Bower by the front of his shirt with his left hand and then cocked back his right fist.

"Please!" Bower cried, holding up his hands in front of his face to protect himself. "I'm begging you, Rip!"

That's when Rip saw it.

The blood on Bower's palms.

Rip froze and struggled to control his breathing.

He stared at Bower, at those hands, for what felt like forever. *Please forgive me, Rip. I'm begging you.*

And then Rip thought about another set of bloody palms . . . and the peace he'd felt. Just an hour ago. *Lord, help me. I'm so weak.*

He let go of Bower and crouched down again, still trying to catch his breath. Bower still held his hands up and Rip was saddened by the fear in Bower's eyes. They continued to look at each other until Rip stood and held out his hand.

"I'm sorry too, Eric."

Bower's head tilted, almost as if he were unsure he'd heard Rip right.

Rip leaned closer and Bower took his hand. They made eye contact again but Bower was clearly still terrified. Rip pulled him to his feet.

"*You're* sorry?" Bower finally asked. "For what?"

"Lots of things," Rip said.

"What's that?" Bower asked, peering at him strangely. "You're crying, Rip. Sure you're okay, man?"

Rip wiped a tear from his cheek and could feel the breeze cooling it on the back of his hand. "I'm gonna tell you something, Eric. Something I want you to remember when I . . . leave Benning. I'd rather live for a year as a Christian than eighty the way we lived once. I mean that."

Bower dared to smile. "That church stuff has really affected you, huh?"

"Talk to Welsh. He's a good guy." Rip held out his hand again and Bower took it. "But know everything is good between us, Eric."

Bower smiled again and their handshake became a hug. "Thanks for forgiving me, Rip."

Rip's cell phone rang. It was Judi.

He answered it and it was actually Andy on Judi's phone. He was out of breath.

Another section of the garden had disappeared.

❊ ❊ ❊

"I think you were right about each section of the garden being for someone," Andy said. "Mr. Hart must have learned his lesson because the only part of the garden that's left is the section for you, Uncle Rip. The one that will heal you."

"I like your thinking, bro," Rip said, lying on his side on the garage floor next to the old motorcycle. He wasn't sure if it was the position he was in, or if it was the cold, cement garage floor, but he felt more comfortable than he did standing up. "Hand me that baby screwdriver over on top of the bench."

"I know you were right," Andy said. "First was Mom's piece of the garden, then Heather's, then Mr. Hart's. The last one is yours."

Rip smiled. "You seem pretty sure."

"Yes," Andy said, kneeling next to Rip and handing him the screwdriver. Andy looked a little dejected and it reminded Rip a bit of the old Andy. "Other than the dream I had, I *still* haven't felt or heard God since we found out you were sick."

Rip sat up and poked Andy on his chest with his finger. "Right there is the only place you need to feel God."

"He's right, Andrew."

It was Judi. She was standing just inside the garage. Her eyes were puffy and her cheeks were tear-soaked. She was holding her finger against her chest and started tapping at it.

"But Andy is also right, Rip. And I feel it in here," she said. "*I know*, just like Andy knows, that you will be healed when you get in those flowers. I don't care if you go through McLouth, swim through The Frank and Poet, parachute in, or jump over with that bike. Just get over there. Please."

"I need to do it on the bike," Rip said.

"Just do it," Judi said. "Go for it."

He looked at Andy, who nodded and smiled, looking eager.

"Maybe it *is* time. I think this old girl just may be ready for my little leap," Rip said, handing the screwdriver back to Andy and running his hand along the side of the bike. "Soon. Very soon."

FORTY-TWO

And we still want to encourage as many of you as possible to attend Marjo's fund-raiser tonight," Mr. Hart said. "She's been in the hospital for over a week now, and her family has been with her around the clock. Stop by tonight, and let's do our best to support this beautiful little girl and her wonderful family."

"Isn't Mr. Hart nice?" Chelsea said.

Andy didn't say anything. He just glanced at Uncle Rip, who winked at him.

Uncle Rip stood and went to help Mr. Hart collect the prayer request cards, but between Uncle Rip still not wanting anybody to know he was sick yet, and his refusal to make the jump to the garden, Andy felt like he had to do something. He pulled a card out of the back of the pew and grabbed one of the little pencils.

God . . . Thank You for everything You've ever given me. It's all I need. But if things aren't what I think and I'm wrong about the garden, can You please make sure Uncle Rip doesn't suffer before he goes?

Andy folded the card and when Mr. Hart came by, he put it in the basket. Then he pulled the iPod out of his pocket like a talisman and ran his thumb over the smooth surface. "Please, God," he whispered. "It's all I ask."

"Are you praying?" Chelsea asked, hope in her eyes. But the hope died when she saw the iPod in his hands.

"Yeah," Andy said, stuffing it in his back pocket. He didn't care what she thought about how he prayed. He was ready to pull out all the stops, whatever it took, to see Uncle Rip get better.

Uncle Rip returned and kissed Andy on the top of his head. And today it didn't totally embarrass him like usual. Today he was glad.

"I think they are ready for us to collect the offering," Chelsea said.

Andy looked at Uncle Rip, who nodded, indicating that Chelsea was right.

It was Uncle Rip's idea that he and Chelsea collect the offering that day, and that made him glad too. He wouldn't be seeing much of her for a couple weeks because she and her brother were going to be staying at their aunt's until Marjo's surgery was over and her parents were back home on a regular basis.

Andy and Chelsea walked up the aisle and took the two baskets from Pastor Welsh. When they turned around, he could see Uncle Rip smiling at him and he smiled back, suddenly feeling more sure than ever that God was going to make Uncle Rip better. *If he'd just get to the garden . . .*

And that's when Andy saw him.

As he waited for one of the baskets to come back up the first row, he glanced back at the last pew on the other side of the church and smiled again.

Eric Bower was sitting back there.

❋ ❋ ❋

Rip and Andy were sitting with their legs dangling over the edge of the ramp, staring at what was left of the wildflowers. What started out as four evenly divided plots was now just one section of flowers, neatly outlined in that beautiful black soil.

Rip also noticed that the cracked mud of the last section Andy had seen disappear was already thick with grass. But Rip wasn't focusing on the grass. He focused on *Him*.

Because Rip could finally see Him. That faceless being who was over in the garden.

That's God, Rip thought, grinning. And in seeing God, he inherently understood that what was left of the garden wasn't meant for him. He didn't want to tell Andy that, though, because the kid had still been right. Regardless of whom it was meant for, Rip knew that he was now *welcome* to enter it, and when he did . . . he wouldn't be sick anymore.

But why do I have to do it on the bike?

"You gonna jump it today?" Andy asked.

Rip smiled and kept looking at the garden, basking in that faceless fountain of love that had him completely forgetting he was sick. All that remained was to make a few minor tweaks to the bike, and he'd pretty much be ready to go. He guessed on the ride out he had her going easily over ninety, more than enough speed to get him to the other side. Then an odd little thought skipped in and out of his mind.

"What if I don't make it?" Rip said, pointing down into the canal. "What if the bike hiccups and I land right there in the drink or face-first in the other bank?"

Andy lifted his helmet up and gave it a peculiar look. "I noticed something's rattling around in here on the ride out, Uncle Rip. Can you put it on and move your head from side to side to see if you can hear it?"

Rip took the helmet and pulled it down over his head. Andy smacked him hard on the side of the helmet and it startled Rip.

"I don't care what you have going through your head," Andy said. "You're going to jump it and land right in that garden. And you *will be healed*."

Rip laughed. "A little dose of my own medicine, eh? Nice whap, bro."

"I also knew from my dream that Pastor Welsh would be the one to tell you when you were ready. And he's told you, right? That you're ready?"

"How did you know that?"

Andy shrugged. "I just knew."

"I see," Rip said, thinking, *Welsh didn't tell me I was ready to go in the flowers, he told me I was ready to die.*

"So I don't see what the big deal is," Andy said. "Go for it. Jump it right now."

Rip took the helmet off and ran his hand across the top of Andy's head.

"Tonight or tomorrow," he said. "I promise."

FORTY-THREE

Carrie Hart pointed at her feet. She had a different shoe on each foot. "Which one of these do you think looks best?"

It didn't matter which one he picked. She'd go with the other one.

"I like the one on your left foot," Hart said.

"I'm still not sure what type of turnout we are going to have tonight," Carrie said. "You should have told the church you were going to be late to the fund-raiser."

"What difference does it make?" Hart said, sitting at his desk in the far corner of the bedroom. "You and I both know we're going to end up carrying the majority of Marjo's surgery anyhow." He sighed. "Besides, I won't be down in Tecumseh that long. I just need to drive by and check something out on the grounds at Phillips before the deal closes."

"Just hurry and get back," Carrie said. "I refuse to look like a fool sitting at the head table by myself."

"I said I'd be there," he said.

He would be there all right. But first the Summer Santa had a little bit of work to do at the Cochrans' place.

Because like Heather said, doing a whole lot of good made up for a whole lot of bad. *But lately, the Summer Santa has been a little too good.*

❄ ❄ ❄

Judi was sitting next to Pastor Welsh at the Benning Country Club when Teddy Cochran approached their table. Teddy looked like he'd aged in the last few months, but made the effort to walk around and thank everyone for attending the fund-raiser.

"I'm sorry your brother and Andy couldn't make it," he said.

"Rip's feeling a little under the weather," Judi said.

"Andy home with him or is he not feeling well either?" Teddy asked. "Chelsea mentioned he didn't seem much like himself today."

Judi didn't answer. She glanced over at Chelsea, who was sitting as one of the guests of honor with Carrie Hart, who was dressed like she should be at the Oscars. They were at elevated tables that looked as if they were prepared for members of a wedding party or a celebrity roast. Chelsea glanced over and realized Judi was looking at her. She smiled and lipped, *Is Andy coming?* Judi shook her head and Chelsea's smile disappeared.

It seemed like it had been a night of apologies.

Carrie Hart apologized for Kevin's temporary absence but assured everyone he would be along soon. Teddy Cochran apologized for his wife and Marjo not being there, as the hospital was still keeping Marjo overnight.

Judi wondered where Heather was. She had to work but mentioned she was going to stop by. Judi grabbed her purse and took out her cell phone. She'd missed two calls from Rip.

She called him back and he answered after one ring.

"Heather there?" he asked.

"Not yet. Where's Andy?"

"He's right here," Rip said. "Can you tell Teddy and Cierra I'm sorry I couldn't make it?"

"I just talked to Teddy and told him you weren't feeling well. Cierra isn't here."

"Where is she? It's her daughter's fund-raiser."

"They're at the hospital, Rip."

"Chelsea there?"

"Why all the questions?"

"Just curious," Rip said. There was a pause. "Andy just wanted me to tell her hello for him."

FORTY-FOUR

Kevin Hart had already driven by the hospital to confirm that nobody would be at the Cochrans' house that night. It was truly unfortunate that things had come down to this. Carrie had already gone to the fund-raiser and he'd quickly changed into the black pants and shirt, while making sure the ski mask and gloves were tucked away in the duffel bag with the gun.

He pulled the gun out of the bag for a second and admired its beautiful orange grip, and as he held it, he could feel that extra sense of power it gave him. It was the gun that had put him in charge, and the thought of getting rid of it could never come to pass. He aimed out in front of him and smiled. He hadn't fired it since he'd taken out Heather's old man, and he thought it was rather ironic that Heather would be going bye-bye as a result of the same gun.

The plan was quite simple. He already knew she was the only cop working. He'd be at the Cochran house, then he'd disguise his voice and call in from the prepaid and untraceable cell phone he'd bought earlier.

I just saw someone break into the Cochrans' house at 303 Bayview. It looked like that Summer Santa that was described in the newspaper . . .

He'd be there waiting for her. No one expected the Summer Santa to be violent, so killing her would be quick and painless. He laughed out loud and checked his watch. It was just about time.

Then he smiled again and couldn't help the thought from dancing around in his mind.

Man, I'm good.

FORTY-FIVE

Heather was parked on the dark side of St. Paul's, still trying to think of the best plan to present her case against Kevin Hart to Chief Reynolds. In hindsight, she guessed she probably should have listened to Rip and Pastor Welsh and not gone to see Hart. Surely there was no way in the world that gun would still be around Hart Industries, or anywhere, for that matter. Regardless, the truth was the truth and she wondered, at the very least, what they could do to spark a legitimate investigation.

She glanced at the clock on the dashboard of the cruiser and yawned. The fund-raiser wouldn't be over for another couple of hours. She was exhausted and the thought of a little shut-eye for half an hour or so sounded great, but she knew there was no way in the world she'd be able to sleep.

Rip.

Judi said he was most likely going to forgo chemo and radiation and just stick it out as long as he could. He said he was all about the fight, but if there was no way the fight could be won, he wasn't going to spend his last couple months getting blown up by chemicals.

"Where are you, Heather?" It was Natalie, from dispatch.

"Chilling out near St. Paul's, as usual," Heather answered. "Probably gonna swing by the fund-raiser for a few minutes and then go park over near the elementary school."

The radio chirped and crackled.

"Sounds like we have an intruder over at 303 Bayview, dressed in black. May be our Summer Santa."

"Did you say 303 Bayview?" Heather asked, turning the key in the ignition. "Isn't that the Cochrans' house?"

"Affirmative."

"I'm on it," Heather said, turning the car around and pulling out onto West Jefferson.

"Be careful."

"Will do," she said.

Heather flipped the roof lights on and sped up. Before she knew it, she was going over a hundred along the lake, closing in on the Cochrans' place. She thought about the last time she'd gone this fast on this road. It was the night of her first encounter with the Summer Santa. The night he left the gift cards and cash for the poor woman from church.

But the Cochrans?

What are you going to do, Kevin? Leave little Marjo a new kidney in the fridge?

And then she thought about her father's gun, and by the time she reached Bayview Drive, a little part of her was actually hoping that Hart was armed this time and that she would be given the chance to serve up a little payback.

And then something else crossed her mind.

What if Kevin didn't kill them?

She slowed the car and flicked off the roof lights before parking a few houses down from the Cochran residence. She got out of the car and unbuttoned her holster. It wasn't until her hand was on her gun that her mouth went dry. She battled for air and glanced around at the five or six ranch houses that made up the very end of Bayview Drive. Naturally, they all had a light or two on inside with the exception of one. The Cochrans' house.

Heather started walking toward it and glanced up at the dark sky. She realized she was walking into a no-win situation.

What if he's leaving the money the Cochrans need for the surgery? Am I supposed to arrest him? Scare him away?

She was walking along the edge of the street, right in front of the Cochrans' neighbors', and she could see a young couple through the front window, sitting on their couch and watching television. They had no clue what was going on right next door to them.

Heather reached the edge of the Cochrans' yard. She started walking slowly, pistol in hand, to the right side of the driveway until she reached the attached garage and stopped.

Arrest him. That's what I'm going to do. Then I'll tell Chief Reynolds everything.

She could feel the tiny pool of sweat that separated her hand from the gun as she made her way closer to the backyard. She came to a fence and noticed that the gate was open. She stopped again and could barely make out a small, aboveground pool, a swing set, and a toolshed toward the rear of the backyard.

She walked through the gate and turned left, staying as close to the house as she could. She hadn't taken three steps when she saw someone. She quickly ducked.

He was standing at the back door, holding it open. Black shirt and pants. He was also wearing a mask and holding what looked like a duffel bag in one of his hands.

It was him.

She raised her gun and slowly stood, just as he dipped into the house.

She lowered her gun and waited, trying to make sense of what she had just seen.

Why would he be going back in? The call came five minutes ago.

Her own question frightened her. Her gut told her something was wrong here. Nobody breaks in, leaves, then goes back in. Nobody.

She walked quickly, still hugging the side of the house, and instinctively stopped before reaching what she guessed was a kitchen window. She would have given anything for a quick peek through the window, but it wasn't worth the risk. She ducked as she went by it, staying low until she made it to the door. She stopped and listened.

Nothing.

She stared at the screen door handle, which was on the far side of the door, and a sickening sense of trepidation filled her gut again.

Why did he go back inside?

She moved quickly to the other side of the door and leaned back against the house. The main door was wide open, so she only had to get through the screen door.

She peeked around the corner and made out what seemed to be the kitchen. She grabbed the screen door handle with her left hand and pressed the button at the top. It didn't make any noise, so she pulled the door open and stepped inside.

That's when she heard the shot.

Instinctively she let go of the door and ducked. Her ears rang and her heart began hammering in her chest as the echo from the shot filtered throughout the house.

Somebody just shot him. It was just a matter of time before it happened . . .

Adrenaline shot through her. *Get out of here, Heather,* she told herself. *You are quitting soon anyhow! Get the heck out of here!*

But she knew she couldn't. She had to see this through. Had to find out, once and for all, if Hart was the Summer Santa. She slowly stood and held her gun out in front of her with both hands, not surprised to see them tremble. She took a few steps across the kitchen and stopped. She knew the drill.

It is time to be quiet. It is time to be still.

She heard nothing and took a few more steps across the kitchen, the smell of peppermint filling her nostrils. She stopped just short of what she guessed was the family room.

Heather peeked around the corner and could see someone. He was standing in a hallway that led back to what were probably the bedrooms. He was facing the other way and appeared to be holding a gun. She aimed her gun at him.

Did he shoot somebody? This doesn't make any sense . . .

Her throat became even drier and her heart slowed into a series of hollow thuds that practically paralyzed her. Still, she kept a steady aim on his back.

She then took a deep breath and lowered herself to one knee. She let her thumb pull back the hammer of her pistol and the *click* made the Summer Santa spin around.

"Drop it," she said.

He didn't. He stared at her and Heather thought she saw him begin to raise his gun.

"Drop it, Kevin!" she shouted.

He jerked his arm upward and Heather pulled the trigger. Her mind struggled to register the sound of another shot. *Her shot.* It rang in her head as a little plume of smoke drifted slowly toward the ceiling.

The Summer Santa was down.

Heather struggled again to control her breathing, the gun still pointing to where he had been standing. Slowly she stood and adjusted her aim to where he lay on the floor. With her other hand, she reached back and flicked a light switch that offered just enough illumination to let her see the pool of blood forming in front of him. He was curled up and perfectly still.

On legs that barely supported her, she approached him and then crouched down, her gun still on him. She nudged him with her other hand, and when he didn't move, she gripped the mask. She peeled it upward, then paused to feel for a pulse. *Nothing.* She pulled the mask all the way off, and then slowly stood and stared at his face for a long moment.

Kevin Hart was dead.

She'd just noticed the orange pistol grip of the gun next to him when she heard a sound. She aimed her gun back down the hallway.

"Police!" she yelled. "Who's there? Show yourself!"

She heard what she thought might be somebody moving in a bedroom at the end of the hall.

"Teddy?" she yelled. "Cierra?"

He's at the fund-raiser and she's at the hospital. Her heart pounded. The floor squeaked, followed by the faint sound of something being dragged. Then she heard nothing.

Heather walked slowly to the edge of the bedroom doorway, stopped, and kneeled down. She waited and listened again.

Nothing.

She moved her head closer to the open door. She could hear someone breathing.

Heather stood and faced the wall, gathering her nerves. Then she raised the gun above her head and quickly leaned to her right, peeking around the corner of the doorway, dropping her arm and pointing the gun into the room.

She couldn't believe her eyes.

Another man. Black shirt . . . black pants . . . black gloves . . . black mask . . . *and unarmed,* just sitting on the floor, leaning back against what looked like a hospital bed. He was wheezing and cradling a duffel bag over his chest.

Or is it her *chest?*

"Freeze, Brianna!" Heather yelled, aiming right at her. "I knew you were in on it with Kevin!"

Brianna didn't move. She just held the duffel bag tightly and her head appeared to be teetering ever so slightly. Then Brianna's gloved hand came off the bag and dropped heavily to the wooden floor.

"I'm not kidding!" Heather yelled, extending her arm straighter. "Move another inch and I'll take you out, just like Kevin!"

Brianna's head shifted against the metal railing of the hospital bed and then she slowly raised her hand off the floor, as if intending to give herself up. But she was clearly hurt. Had Kevin shot her?

Heather cocked back the hammer on her pistol, hoping Brianna would stop moving.

She didn't. Brianna managed to extend her right arm toward Heather.

"Last chance," Heather said. "There won't be another—" She waited and watched as Brianna slowly made the sign of the cross in the air between them.

Heather paused. "It was *you* that night?"

Brianna didn't say anything.

"Take your mask off," Heather said. "Do it slowly."

Brianna's shoulder seemed to flinch and her hand dropped to the floor again with a dull thud.

Heather took a step forward and Brianna stayed still.

She took another step. And then another, right through a thin strip of moonlight that ran from the window and across the bedroom floor. She was now close enough to see eyes behind the dark mask. Brianna was staring right at her, blinking slowly.

She kept her gun aimed at Brianna's chest, placed her left hand on top of the mask, and slowly peeled it away. The first thing she noticed was the sweaty and thinning blond hair. Her heart felt like it leaped out of her chest. Her mouth gaped open.

It was Rip.

"*R-Rip?* What are you doing here?" Heather asked, still pointing her gun at him.

"I told you you'd be able to shoot if you had to," Rip whispered.

"*I need to know what you are doing here, Rip,*" she said, lowering the gun.

"*I need* you to make sure the Cochrans get this for Marjo," he said, patting his hand on the side of the duffel bag.

"What is it?" she asked.

"It's the rest of my pot-selling proceeds," Rip said. "It's a little over two hundred grand. That'll pay for her surgery and give the Cochrans a little bit of breathing room."

Heather just stared at him. "What pot-selling proceeds?"

"I told you that your boys missed a spot in the raid when I got busted," he said. "I wasn't kidding."

"You could have gotten in more trouble. You should have turned that money in." Her eyes narrowed and she kneeled beside him. "Are you hurt?"

He ignored her question. "They'd have kept the money for themselves. You know that six hundred thousand the newspaper said the authorities seized? They really took over a million from me. It's behind us now, but Chief Reynolds and a few of those other boys had themselves a half-million-dollar payday."

"What?" she said. "Are you serious?"

"Yeah," Rip said, and coughed. "I still had a little over three hundred thousand left that they missed . . . so I figured . . . when I got out of prison, I'd run around in the night, making the sign of the cross . . . and see if I could give the money away and do some good with it. Sort of help God answer some prayers."

"*You* are the Summer Santa?"

"Very good, Officer Gerisch," Rip said with a tired smile. "You should be a detective."

"How did you know what people needed?"

"Prayer request cards," Rip whispered. It sounded like it hurt him to talk. "Whenever I helped Kevin collect them, I'd pocket a few after service and take them home with me."

"Chief Reynolds skimmed money?" She still couldn't believe it.

"Don't rat him out," Rip said, coughing again. "Because you have some of the Summer Santa's money too, and I want you to keep it. Go back to school, Heather."

"He knew you were the Summer Santa, didn't he? How'd he know?"

Rip shrugged and he buckled a bit. "We had a little chat one night."

Heather's head was spinning. She pointed at the hallway. "What was Kevin doing here, then?"

"Not sure you're gonna like my answer to that," Rip said haltingly. "But that gun he was holding sure looked familiar. And he was already in here . . . when I came in the bedroom. It was like he was waiting for me . . . waiting for you . . . because he said your name before he shot."

"Rip, you need to get out of here. I have to call this in."

"I don't feel too good," Rip mumbled.

He tried to pull the duffel bag off his lap and failed. Heather helped him and when she pulled it away, she could see the wet stain against his black shirt.

"Rip?" Heather cried. She tried to grab her radio off her hip to call for an ambulance and then Rip reached over and squeezed her wrist until she let go of it. "What are you doing? You're shot. You're bleeding really bad. What am I *supposed* to do?"

"Tell Andy that his prayer was answered. He didn't want me to suffer. And then just tell the truth about what happened here tonight and you'll be fine. Reynolds knows where that money came from. He told me to hurry up and—and get it over with. He said he'd let me slide, and crazy as it seems, I believe him. Besides, I'm not heading to jail again. Not tonight."

"I want to call an ambulance," Heather cried. "Please let me."

"No," Rip said, leaning into her. "And promise me that you'll go back to school and be a teacher."

"Rip—"

"Promise me!"

"I promise." She was weeping now, tears running down her face.

Rip leaned his head against her and looked up at her. He was sweating worse and blood appeared at the corner of his mouth.

"Why did you do it this way, Rip?" she asked. "Why didn't you just give these gifts to these people?"

"A broke ex-con can't give away that kind of money." He forced a smile and a tear rolled out the corner of his left eye. He took a ragged, wet breath. "I wanted you to catch me, Heather. You sort of already did once, but I was just getting started. But I wanted you to finally see me do something good."

"You *are* good," she said, grabbing the radio again as her weeping turned to sobs.

Rip's hand was shaking when he wrapped his fingers around the bottom of the radio, pulling it away.

"I wanna tell you somethin' else," Rip said, his voice barely audible. "And don't you forget it."

"Okay," she said, trying to wrestle the radio from his grip. "Please just hang on, Rip. *Please.*"

Rip clicked the power switch off the radio and Heather knew then that she wouldn't make the call until it was far too late.

Their eyes met.

"I love you, Heather Gerisch," Rip whispered. "I always have. I always will. I'm sorry . . . I couldn't . . ."

She ran her hand across the side of his face, then clutched at his far shoulder and pulled him closer to her, feeling a pain so deep it left no sound, just a gaping, hollow chasm in her heart.

"I love you," she said, when she could at last take a breath. "I love you!" she screamed, her pain gaining sound, her keening cry filling the house.

But it was all too late.

Rip was gone.

FORTY-SIX

I was going to be leaving the department soon anyway," Heather said as she and Judi sat on the picnic table three days later, looking out at Lake Erie. "Besides, I really don't want to be involved in the investigation. It's pretty safe to assume that Kevin was planning to shoot me with the same gun he killed our fathers with. But instead he killed Rip."

"You know what's really weird, if you think about it?" Judi said distantly.

"You mean other than Rip making his final gift at the same time Kevin wanted to kill me?"

"Kevin actually ended up doing Rip a favor."

"I know," Heather said. "But I still can't believe he's gone."

Heather knew Rip's death hadn't hit home yet with Judi either, but it certainly had with Andy.

"Andy still out near The Frank and Poet?" Heather asked.

Judi nodded. "I think he's cried himself out. He's been out there almost all day. In fact, we should probably go check on him."

"That last section of flowers still out there?" Heather asked.

"Yeah," Judi answered. "Andy seems to think it will always be there."

"Why is that?" Heather asked.

"Because he believes that part of the garden was for Rip, and it was never used for what it was meant for."

"And he's sure the last part that disappeared was Kevin's?" Heather asked. "Why?"

"I'm guessing because you, Kevin, Rip, and me are the only people Andy relayed messages to from God. We'll never know what Kevin had to accept, but apparently he did. The *jerk*."

They shared a long smile. "God via the iPod," Heather said and shook her head matter-of-factly. "It was really Him, wasn't it?"

"It was also Him who Andy dreamed about," Judi said. "And He's also what you and I felt . . . what we *saw* when we looked in the garden."

"What do you think the garden is, Judi?"

"I think Rip was right. I think it was like God had dropped a gift basket over there for the four of us. The first section was for me. The second for you. The third for Kevin. And the last one was meant for Rip to be healed."

"I think the garden is more than a gift basket," Heather said. "I saw my father over there. And God," she added in a reverent whisper. "And the more I think about it, I'm not even sure that He was standing *behind* my dad, it was more like He *surrounded* him."

"I wonder what would have happened if Rip went over there before he got shot," Judi said.

"I don't know. I wish we could still find out," Heather said. The two women shared a thoughtful, knowing look of shared pain.

Judi shook her head. "I was right there with Andy in thinking Rip would have gotten better had he entered the garden. But now we'll never know."

Judi was right. They never would know and it was the coulda-shoulda-woulda that saddened her even more.

They both stared into the distance, thinking for a while.

"You're gonna bury him right next to your parents?"

"Yeah," Judi said.

"I like your idea for the headstone," Heather said. "*RIP* without the periods in between the letters."

"Won't be done in time for the funeral, but I think Rip would have liked it."

"We could have always put 'The Summer Santa' on there."

"I still can't believe it was him," Judi said with a sad little laugh. "So you originally thought that Brianna was partnering up with Kevin?"

"They were," Heather said. "But, uh, not on the Summer Santa thing."

Judi lifted her brows and leaned forward, plopping her elbows on her knees. "Just wait until the town gets ahold of *that* story."

"Rumors are already flying," Heather said. "And Brianna didn't waste any time getting on it. But lucky for me, Chief Reynolds insisted on handling this one. He didn't want the article coming out right away, but when it does, I'm pretty sure Rip's gonna end up looking like a saint."

FORTY-SEVEN

Y ou okay?" Judi whispered.

Andy didn't say anything back to her. He just continued to
stare down into the grave as Pastor Welsh spoke.

He had taken the news of Rip's death worse than any of them.
The fact that Rip was already sick and facing death hadn't seemed
to soften *any* of the blow for Andy.

Reverend Welsh finished his prayer and many of the fifty or so
who were there shared hugs and took turns throwing small handfuls of dirt onto Rip's casket before leaving.

Heather had been kneeling at the very foot of the grave with
her head down, and Judi watched as Andy went up beside her and
placed something on the grass in front of her. Heather picked it up
and then Andy dropped to his knees as well.

"Is he all right?" Chelsea asked as she and Judi stepped away
from the grave.

"No, but I think he will be," Judi said, watching Pastor Welsh
walk toward them.

"I enjoyed listening to you," Chelsea said.

"Thank you, sweetie," Welsh replied, pointing over at Andy and Heather. "Let's go visit with those two, shall we?"

When they approached the grave, Judi walked up behind Andy and put her hands on his shoulders. Andy opened his eyes and then stood and put his arm around her. Judi gave him a motherly smile and leaned into him.

Heather raised her arm and Judi immediately saw one of the earbuds dangling from her hand.

"Doesn't work for you anymore either?" Andy asked, taking the iPod from her.

"Thank you for giving it to me," Heather said. "But I don't need it. Neither of us do."

Andy bit his lip lightly and then took his arm out from around Judi. He started to say something, stopped, then held his hands up and let them drop to his sides in disappointment. "I was kind of hoping you'd hear or see something. Kind of like how you did with your dad."

"I already know your Uncle Rip is with God. But I want you to know that as well, and I want *you* to smile that best smile your uncle and I talked about, knowing someone you love is with God."

"I don't want to smile right now," Andy whispered. "I just want a sign. Something. Anything. I need to know that Uncle Rip's okay."

"I assure you that he is more than okay," Pastor Welsh said. "He is better than he has ever been because he is with God. He was ready to go, Andy."

"Ready to go in the garden!" Andy yelled, slamming the iPod to the ground. "And he was supposed to get better!"

"He *is* better," Judi said. "It's going to take some time for us to—"

"You don't know that, Mom," Andy interrupted, leaning over

and picking up the iPod. He held his open palm out over the grave and one of the earbuds dangled down toward Rip's coffin. "You better, Uncle Rip? You told me I don't need this to have faith. Why don't I feel anything anymore? Where is God right now? Why doesn't He show His face and make *me* feel better?"

Judi put her arm around him and he stepped out from under it.

"I'm outta here," Andy said. He stuffed the iPod in his front pocket and headed toward the rear exit of the cemetery.

Heather and Chelsea started after him and Pastor Welsh held up his hands. "Let him go. He needs more time."

"Let's just head back to the house," Judi said. "We'll give him an hour or so, and when the time comes, I think we know where we'll find him."

⬥ ⬥ ⬥

Judi didn't like her own idea of giving Andy an hour. They hadn't been back at the house for more than twenty minutes before they all piled into her Tempo, and by the time they'd driven halfway through the corn, they could see Andy down past the opening, sitting up on the edge of the ramp.

They pulled up behind him and got out of the car. Heather and Chelsea stayed back as Judi and Pastor Welsh walked around the front of the ramp and looked up at Andy.

"God never leaves. People leave Him, but He won't leave you," Andy said, his eyes firmly fixed on the remaining part of the garden. "That's what you told me, Pastor Welsh, and I believed you."

Pastor Welsh didn't look at Andy. He just took a step down the bank, crossed his arms, and stared across the canal at the flowers. "I'm glad you believed me, Andy. Because it's true."

"Where *is* God right now?" Andy asked. "I thought it was Him that I was hearing through the iPod. I thought it was Him in my dreams, and I thought it was Him that I used to feel whenever I looked at that garden, or whatever the heck it is over there."

"It was Him," Welsh said. "In fact, I can feel Him over there right now."

"Really?" Andy said. "I don't."

Welsh glanced over his shoulder and up at Andy. "And I can also feel God when I look at you. He was with you when He had a word for His people, just as He's with you right now, Andy."

Judi smiled when she heard that. Her first in close to a week.

"Yeah, right," Andy said. "I know you said God chose unlikely candidates, but *c'mon* . . . Why me?"

"I'm not out here to speculate with you," Welsh said firmly. "Why don't you tell me why God *wouldn't* pick you?"

Andy finally looked away from the garden and right at Welsh. His eyebrows huddled and then relaxed like he was going to answer, but he didn't.

"That's a good question," Judi said as Andy looked back at the flowers.

"God can do whatever He wants," Welsh said. "And all of those things you did and felt were real, from repeating what you heard out of that iPod to having a dream that told you I would be the one to tell your Uncle Rip when he would be ready to go in the garden."

"But he never went!"

"He's there now!" Welsh yelled back, pointing at the garden. "What do you think that is over there?"

"Nothing," Andy said. "At least, not what it was *supposed* to be."

Welsh came up the bank and stood right in front of Andy.

"Look at me," Welsh said sternly, and Andy did. "Hearing things through an iPod, a prophetic dream, and a *patch of flowers that come and go in the twinkle of an eye?"* Welsh let out a sarcastic little laugh. "What else in the world do you need to see, man? What will it take to make you realize this is all exactly how it's *supposed* to be? Stuff like this doesn't happen by accident."

Andy shrugged.

Welsh reached up and grabbed the top of the ramp. "Your uncle told me that when he bought you a Bible, you laughed off a lot of the things you read in the Old Testament."

Andy shrugged, a little irritated, a little embarrassed. "Sure. The crazy stuff."

"Crazy stuff?" Welsh repeated. "Why is it that people think God could only perform miracles two thousand years ago? Where is it written that He was going to stop?"

"They could write whatever they want in that Bible," Andy said.

Welsh laughed and this time Judi could tell it was because he thought what Andy said was funny. "Whether you like it or not, Andy, just like Noah, Moses, and Abraham, God used you to make a big difference in people's lives."

"Says who?" Andy asked, looking back over his shoulder at Heather and Chelsea, who were leaning against the hood of the car. "Tell me."

"He had you help me get over my father's death," Heather said.

"And look what you did . . . what He did for us," Judi said.

Andy pulled his hair back and exposed his scar. "I have this scar, my dog is dead, my uncle is dead . . . What did God do for me?"

Welsh looked at Judi in a way that seemed to suggest they should take a break. "Andy, I think you need a little time to take all this in."

"C'mon, Pastor Welsh," Andy said. "Uncle Rip says—said— you were a straight shooter and weren't afraid to pull punches. Tell me . . . how did God help me? I don't have real faith. I was given an *advantage*. Uncle Rip always told me that faith is something that needs to be developed. Mine wasn't. It was *given* to me. I had the ability to hear and feel God, and I'm pretty sure I even saw Him in my dreams and in the garden. But now I *don't*."

"Well, poor you," Welsh said. "And you asked what God has ever done for you. Did you, even for a second, ever think about thanking Him for that advantage?"

Andy turned around again and gave Chelsea a funny look. "No, I didn't. But it doesn't matter now because the iPod is busted, I don't get the dreams anymore, and I don't feel anything when I look at the garden now."

Welsh tapped Andy on the leg. "Looks like you are out of luck then, pal. Because God didn't have anything to do with those things."

"Yes, He did."

"Sorry," Welsh said. "But I don't think so."

"What are you talking about?" Andy said. "*I know* it was Him."

"Hold out your hands," Welsh said. Andy did and Welsh took off his glasses like he was studying them. "I don't see your iPod, you aren't dreaming, and you aren't looking at the garden, yet you just told me you know it was God behind those things. So are you saying that you *do* believe in God?"

Andy glanced back at Heather and Chelsea and then at Judi. His blue eyes seemed to light up when he looked back at Welsh.

"Yes, Pastor Welsh," Andy said. "I guess I do believe in Him. The way you put it, I guess I really don't need those things to believe."

"Why don't you tell God that?" Welsh asked.

Andy looked at the sky and said robotically, "I believe."

"You don't sound too convincing for the only guy I ever knew who heard God through an electronic device. I still haven't heard you thank Him either. Watch how you feel when you do that."

Andy glanced back at the sky and then over at the garden for a long moment. "Thank You, God," he said quietly, without sarcasm.

"Who you talking to over there?" Welsh asked, studying him. "You feel Him again, don't you? But that was still a pretty feeble show of gratitude for the only guy I know who God talks to in his dreams. Let me hear you say you believe and thank God like your Uncle Rip would have."

Andy glanced quickly at Welsh and then stood up like a man on a mission. He threw his arms up in the air, looked at the sky, and then at the garden, almost as if something had called him from over there. Then he shouted at the top of his lungs, "I believe! I believe! Thank You!" He stared at the flowers and Judi could hear him trying to catch his breath. He looked back at Welsh. "What else do you want from me?"

"Nothing," Welsh said with a fatherly smile. "God loves you, Andrew . . . and He loves your Uncle Rip even more than you do."

Andy's lip quivered and he dropped to his knees on top of the ramp. He covered his face in his hands and then began to sob. Chelsea ran up the ramp and kneeled at his side. Judi walked around and went up the ramp as well while Pastor Welsh joined Heather at the car.

"It's okay, Andrew," Judi said. "It's okay, baby."

Judi could hear the heavy footsteps behind her on the front of the ramp. It was Pastor Welsh.

"Oh my heavens," he said.

Heather ran up the ramp as well and stopped at the very end.

"What's wrong?" Judi asked.

Heather just pointed across the canal and Judi stood.

The last section of the flowers was gone and all that stood in its place was a bald patch of cracked mud with a few shoots of grass coming out of it.

"How did that just happen?" Chelsea asked, blinking slowly as if she couldn't believe her eyes.

Judi squinted at the mud and noticed a deep divot in the front portion of the patch, followed by a straight line that ran all the way to the back.

"What is that line?" she asked.

"It's one of those," Heather answered, pointing behind them at the dried dirt and mud that surrounded the car. There were hundreds of tracks that had been made by Rip's and Andy's motorcycles. And then she pointed back across the canal. "It's a tire track. A motorcycle drove through the flowers."

Andy stood and craned his neck toward the garden. And then he jumped off the side of the ramp and ran down to the edge of the canal. He dived into the water and swam across with his good shirt, pants, and shoes on. But even Judi didn't say a word.

The only one to speak was Chelsea. "What's he doing? What's going on here?"

Andy dragged himself up the other bank, stood, and then ran to where the last section of the garden had been. Slowly he followed the straight line that ran through the center of the dried mud. Then he turned toward them, and even from across the canal, they could see his joy.

"He made it! Uncle Rip made it!" He kneeled down and studied the divot where the motorcycle must have landed, and then stood and walked the length of the straight line. "This track is from his bike!"

"What's he talking about?" Chelsea asked.

Andy walked around in the bald patch for close to five minutes, and they all watched as he dropped to his knees and touched the motorcycle track. And then his hand pointed around the rest of the dried mud and they heard him laugh before he stood and held his hands in the air. "There's paw prints too!"

"I still don't know what he's talking about," Chelsea said.

Welsh put his hand on Chelsea's shoulder. "He's just trying to figure things out, sweetie."

"That section was for Andy," Judi whispered, wiping tears from her cheeks with her palms. "The third one was Rip's, not Kevin's."

She looked at Heather, who had her hand over her mouth and a pair of tears weaving down her left cheek.

"But I thought . . . Why wasn't he healed?" Heather asked.

Judi didn't answer and waited for Pastor Welsh to say something. He didn't. Welsh was watching Andy, who had just walked out of the bald patch and into the high grass back toward the canal. He jumped back in The Frank and Poet to swim toward them.

He came up the bank, and right when he reached the ramp, Judi saw it happen. She looked quickly at the others. They had seen it too. The bald patch was gone. What was just there a few seconds earlier, the only remnants of the garden, was now the same wavy knee-high grass that ran the length of the canal and back to the gates of McLouth Steel. She'd seen it sprout and grow, right before her very eyes.

Andy turned around and when he saw the far bank of the canal, he smiled.

Judi stepped up next to him and put her arm around him. "I love you, Andy."

"I love you too, Mom," he said, pulling her close. "I want to celebrate. But there is something from my dream I forgot about that I have to do."

"Now you're talking," Welsh said, placing his hand on Andy's shoulder.

Andy nodded and then went back to the ramp. He walked up to the very top and stopped, his left foot hanging over the edge. He held his right fist up and smiled. Not at where the garden once was, but at the sky.

"Pound it, bro!" he yelled, fist bumping the air.

Gooseflesh covered Judi's back and arms as her eyes welled again with tears. Heather took her by the arm and they held each other as Andy opened his hand.

In it was the iPod.

"This is for you, Uncle Rip!" he yelled, wrapping his fingers around the iPod and cocking his hand behind his head. He thrust his arm forward, sending the iPod and earbuds straight over their heads. Judi turned around just in time to see it splash, disappearing right into the center of The Frank and Poet.

Andy came down the ramp and they all huddled, hugging and holding each other before piling into Judi's Tempo.

"Why wasn't he healed?" Heather asked again. "I heard it said twenty times. If Rip could make it into the garden, he would be healed."

"You want to answer that?" Welsh said to Andy.

"He was," Andy said simply, reaching in the backseat and dabbing at Heather's tears with the pad of his thumb. "Don't you see?"

"No," she whispered.

"He was healed," Andy said with a smile. "In heaven."

EPILOGUE

SEVENTEEN MONTHS LATER

And I'm thankful that my daddy came home safe," Sarah Chapman said from the center of Heather's fourth-grade class at Parson's Elementary School. "I don't like when he goes over the seas for a long time."

"Very good, Sarah," Heather said. "That's a good thing to be thankful for and thanks for sharing."

Sarah gave Heather a beautiful smile, and when she hunched her little shoulders together, the way her ponytail hugged against her neck made Heather smile too. "You're welcome, Ms. Gerisch."

"Who wants to go next?" Heather asked.

Billy Allen raised his hand. He was a cute little redhead and was as thankful as they come, but he was notorious in class for taking his allotted two minutes of thankfulness sharing time and turning it into ten. She called on him, and when he started, she couldn't count the number of eyes that rolled on the other little faces around the room, including Marjo Cochran's, Heather's best student.

While Billy began to talk about how thankful he was for his big brother and sisters, Heather looked over in the last row, two seats from the back, at Jason Coleman.

Heather had noticed a suspicious string of bruises earlier in the school year on Jason's left arm, and when she asked him about it, he said he hurt it getting tackled during Little League football practice for the Huron River Yellow Jackets.

Jason was relatively new to the area and was a big kid for his age, easily five inches taller and thirty pounds heavier than anyone in class, and Heather figured he had to be an amazing football player. So in a show of support for one of her students, she swung by the football field the Saturday after seeing the bruises to watch Jason play.

Jason didn't play football for the Huron River Yellow Jackets.

She didn't say anything to anyone for a couple more weeks, until Jason missed a couple days of school and then showed up with a bruise on his neck and another on his left arm.

Heather had called two different protection agencies and even asked Duke Ruthenberg with the Benning Police to snoop around and see what he could find out.

Both of Jason's bruises disappeared after about ten days, as did any serious inquiry as to what had caused them.

Two weeks later Jason came to school with a black eye and a splint over the pinky and ring fingers on his left hand. Heather pressed for an investigation and, at the risk of losing her job as a teacher, went to Jason's home. Nobody answered the door.

And then a week went by, and then another, without bruises. Jason started talking more in class, his grades improved, and he made friends.

Heather asked the department if any arrests had been made and none had. She left messages with both protective agencies, and neither of them returned the calls.

It was impossible for Heather to look at him and not wonder

what had happened to make the abuse stop. But she was thankful anyhow, because it had.

"And that's what I'm thankful for," Billy Allen said, concluding his thankfulness dissertation.

"Thank you for sharing, Billy," Heather said. "Those are good things to be thankful for."

A little sliver of guilt tapped at Heather's side. She hadn't listened to a word of what Billy had said.

"Anyone else?" she asked.

Jason Coleman's hand went up and Heather smiled.

"What are you thankful for, Jason?"

The entire class turned around and Jason smiled bashfully.

"I'm glad my mom's boyfriend moved away."

An awkward silence hung in the room and Marjo was on the spot to break it.

"Why did he move away?" Marjo asked.

"Because I told him to," Jason said confidently.

"You told a grown-up to leave?" Billy Allen asked. "What did you say to him?"

Jason shrugged, then reached in his pocket and pulled something out. "I really don't remember. This told me what to tell him."

He opened his hand.

In it was an iPod.

AUTHOR'S NOTE

*G*od *must be in prison, because that's where so many people seem to meet Him . . .*

I heard that line well over ten years ago, and as funny as it seemed at the time, it's interesting how its meaning has changed for me since then. With that said, I wouldn't have forgiven myself had Gerald Ripley not encountered that phrase—or some variation of it—in the story. I owed it to him, because truth be told, he reminds me quite a bit of someone I know very well.

I love being an author, and writing *The Sinners' Garden* was a lot of fun. It also presented quite a few challenges for me from the first couple of drafts to what ultimately became the book you are holding now. Andy's character has undergone significant changes, including going from a twenty-four-year-old who rode a moped to a fourteen-year-old who rode a motorcycle. Kevin Hart's fate changed dramatically, not by the stroke of a pen, but by my accidental deletion of the original ending along with around nineteen thousand other words, which was roughly the last twenty percent of the book. As miffed as I was when it happened, I'm now looking back and am kind of glad it happened, because everything really does happen for a *reason* and rewriting it gave me an opportunity to take the story in a much different direction, including having Kevin Hart in the Cochran house at the end. Sorry about that, Kev-O.

I think most authors want to entertain readers, but as a Christian author with a checkered past, I thought it was extremely important to try to share some of the lessons I've learned, and I hope that readers walk away from *The Sinners' Garden* feeling closer to God from the experience.

Lots of people helped me hone and craft my story, so please bear with me . . .

First of all, I would like to thank the readers. I hope you enjoyed the story as much as I did writing it and that it somehow makes a difference in your life.

Thanks to my good friend with the English accent, Alan Bower from Author Solutions. Alan has been a proverbial godsend to my writing career. He has an amazing passion for publishing, and the interest he takes in the authors he works with is second to none. Thanks also to his better half, Erica Dooley-Dorocke. Together, you have gone out of your way to help me and I recognize the difference you made.

Chris Cancilliari is the first one to see anything I write and has been the recipient of countless last-second phone calls and e-mails, where I'm usually asking her to proofread something I'm about to send off to the wonderful editors I work with. Thanks, Chris. I usually ended our calls by calling you my hero or the greatest of all time. I meant it.

Natalie Hanemann and Lisa Bergren are my wonderful editors. Both of these ladies epitomize what many refer to as "the patience of Job." I am truly blessed to be able to work with them, and I know I've said it before, but there is no one in the world I'd rather have help me tell my stories. Thanks for putting up with me and for guiding me through the rough spots in the book. You have taught me so much, and I'm truly appreciative. Thank you.

I'd like to thank everyone who either offered advice or read an earlier version of the book, particularly: Brett Kays, Hyacinth Palmer, Cousin Sharon Coventry, Bob Deragisch, Angel Mason, Kim Falkowski-Lewis, Cherilyn Barber, Melissa West Morris, Donna O'Brien, Susan Tant, JoEllen Hurst, Belinda Cornett, Rhonda Raft, Elizabeth Sloan, Duke Malnyok, Tommy Arsenault, Fred Bisaro, Lynn "LJ" Bisaro, Carol Bodenhorn, Jil Burks Cooper, Cindy Benedict Barclay, Pat Pittsnogle, Joe Milosic, Kay Campbell, Gail Welborn, Karla Dorman, Liz Zeller, Judi McNair, Tom Ayers, Aunt Paulette Pedigo, Cousin Susan Shelton, and my sister, Karen. Sometimes an author can get so close to a story that he can't see it and all of your input and suggestions made my life a lot easier. Thank you so much.

Thanks to Daisy Hutton and her team at Thomas Nelson, including Ruthie Dean, Katie Bond, Ami McConnell, Amanda Bostic, Becky Monds, Jodi Hughes, and Kristen Vasgaard. What a year of changes we've all had. I appreciate everything you do.

Marjo Myers. Thanks again for your friendship and for getting the ball rolling by reading the original galley of *The Reason*. I'm guessing that you may have recognized a special little girl's name in *The Sinners' Garden* . . .

Thanks to all of you who have read *The Reason* and helped make it a bestseller. I've enjoyed meeting many of you, and your phone calls, e-mails, and letters have meant so much to me and have changed the reason why I will continue to write.

Speaking of *The Reason*, this may sound like a bit of a roll call of the book's characters, but I want to thank my family. Thanks to Jim, Shirley, Kim, Karen, Kathy, Kaitlyn, and Macey. A special thanks to Ken and Alison for their support and belief in my writing. I love you all and thank you again for being you.

Finally, I want to thank God. You have been way too good to me. I'm so glad that You never step aside or quit doing Your thing. I am living proof of Your miracles and grace and will do my best to do the only thing You ask of me.

And that is to *only believe.*

William Sirls
Gibraltar, Michigan
June 5, 2013

READING GROUP GUIDE

1. What did the garden symbolize for you?
2. Do you think Rip actually made the jump over The Frank and Poet? Why or why not?
3. Why do you think we don't see as many miracles today as they did in Bible times?
4. Rip had a sign above his front door that said "SERVANTS' ENTRANCE." How do you apply this in your life?
5. Is there a voice inside of you that tells you what to do? What are some examples?
6. At Bible study, Rip talks about how people get into daily routines that don't include time for God. Is this a challenge for you? If not, what are some strategies you use to make sure you have time?
7. Judi spent a great deal of time living in the past. What did she need to do to move forward with her life? Have you or someone you loved ever struggled with the same thing? How did they/you get past it?

8. Have you ever pondered the spiritual whereabouts of a deceased loved one? How did you deal with that?

9. Rip believed that the Bible tells us to confront someone when we see them going astray. Do you agree or disagree?

10. What did Andy learn from little Marjo? Have you ever needed to hear something similar? Discuss.

11. Rip mentioned that being one person on Sunday and somebody else the rest of the week wasn't uncommon in the world. What did he mean by that? Do you agree or disagree? Why?

12. Andy wanted to celebrate at the end. Why don't Christians celebrate more at funerals?

13. Andy told Judi, "It's your time to show others God's strength in you . . . His ability to heal." Have you experienced an opportunity to do this? Describe.

14. Pastor Welsh told Rip that being a Christian comes with a great deal of responsibility. What do you think he meant by that?